KILL MY DARLING

Recent Titles by Cynthia Harrod-Eagles from Severn House

THE COLONEL'S DAUGHTER
A CORNISH AFFAIR
DANGEROUS LOVE
DIVIDED LOVE
EVEN CHANCE
HARTE'S DESIRE
THE HORSEMASTERS
JULIA
LAST RUN
THE LONGEST DANCE
NOBODY'S FOOL
ON WINGS OF LOVE
PLAY FOR LOVE
A RAINBOW SUMMER
REAL LIFE (*Short Stories*)

The Bill Slider Mysteries

GAME OVER
FELL PURPOSE
BODY LINE
KILL MY DARLING

KILL MY DARLING

A Bill Slider Mystery

Cynthia Harrod-Eagles

This first world edition published 2011
in Great Britain and in the USA by
SEVERN HOUSE PUBLISHERS LTD of
9–15 High Street, Sutton, Surrey, England, SM1 1DF.
Trade paperback edition first published
in Great Britain and the USA 2012 by
SEVERN HOUSE PUBLISHERS LTD .

British Library Cataloguing in Publication Data

Harrod-Eagles, Cynthia.
  Kill my darling. – (A Bill Slider mystery)
  1. Slider, Bill (Fictitious character)–Fiction.
  2. Police–England–London–Fiction. 3. Missing
  persons–Investigation–Fiction. 4. Family secrets–
  Fiction. 5. Detective and mystery stories.
  I. Title II. Series
  823.9'2-dc22

ISBN-13: 978-0-7278-8137-3 (cased)
ISBN-13: 978-1-84751-398-4 (trade paper)

All Severn House titles are printed on acid-free paper.

Severn House Publishers support The Forest Stewardship Council [FSC],
the leading international forest certification organisation. All our titles that
are printed on Greenpeace-approved FSC-certified paper carry the FSC logo.

MIX
Paper from
responsible sources
FSC
www.fsc.org   FSC® C018575

Typeset by Palimpsest Book Production Ltd.,
Falkirk, Stirlingshire, Scotland.
Printed and bound in Great Britain by
MPG Books Ltd., Bodmin, Cornwall.

ONE
Failure to Lunch

At first Connolly thought he was crying; but after a few minutes she realized he just had a left eye that watered. The gesture of taking out a handkerchief and drying it was too automatic not to be habitual.

He was spare, rangy – one of those old men who are all bones and sinews, with blue-veined, knuckly hands and the deeply-lined face of a smoker. She supposed his age to be about seventy but she was aware she was not much good at judging ages and he could have been fifty-five for all she knew. She was also wary of old people in general: they were unpredictable, and frequently had no boundaries. Back home in Dublin you were always being seized by the arm by some owl one you barely knew, and subjected to an embarrassing catechism. It was one of the reasons she had come to London in the first place. Your man here had a very sharp and knowing eye. He looked as if he might say anything.

She was also wary of basements: she had entered his flat gingerly, but although it was gloomy and bare, it was tidy and, thank you Baby Jesus and the orphans, clean, with no worse smell than a faint whiff of stale tobacco. Actually, it wasn't entirely a basement. Because the big old house on Cathnor Road was built into a slope, it was a basement at the back and the ground floor at the front; for the same reason, the flat upstairs was ground floor at the back and first floor at the front, with steps up to an imposing door with a portico over it. Above that the house had been divided into two more flats, one to each level, which had their entrance at the side.

Outside, despite being April, it was bitterly cold – the country still in the iron grip of a north wind coming directly down from the Arctic, so sharp you could have filleted sole with it. It wasn't any too warm inside here, either. Your man was obviously the

Spartan type. She kept her coat on, but she unbuttoned it and loosened her scarf – otherwise, as her mammy said, she wouldn't feel the benefit when she went out again.

'So, it's about your neighbour upstairs, is it?' she asked, having refused an offer of tea that sounded too perfunctory to be accepted. She took out her notebook and rested it on her knee. The flat was one long room, lit by a window at each end, the rear one subterranean, looking out on to a well. Both were barred – did Victorian servants have to be kept from escaping? A small kitchen at the rear end was divided off by a kitchen counter, at which a solitary stool indicated where the eating was done. On the counter was a twelve-inch TV, so ancient the instruction manual was probably in Latin.

The front end of the room contained a bed against the wall under the window, a single armchair in front of the gas fire, a Utility sideboard and a tall, narrow wardrobe. Through a partly-open door she could see the small, windowless bathroom. And that was it.

There seemed to be no possessions, papers, photos – nothing on display. Whatever – she checked her note – Mr Fitton owned, it was tidily stowed away. The bed, on which he sat, for want of anywhere else, was neatly made with a grey blanket and a single pillow, and he himself was clean and shaved, his hair neatly cut. There was something about this almost monastic spareness and order that was familiar. The solitary man, the ingrained tidiness – had he been a soldier? She had family back in Ireland who'd been in the army. Or, wait, a sailor – neatness enforced by the confined space on shipboard? Whatever. She recognized it from somewhere. It'd come to her, eventually.

'What's her name?' Connolly asked, pencil poised.

'Melanie. Melanie Hunter.' He watched her write it down.

'And when did you last see her?'

'To speak to, not for a few days. But I heard her go out last night. She parks her car just outside my window. She went out about half seven. And I heard her come home later.'

'What time would that be?'

'Round about ha'pass ten. I was watching the ten o'clock news and they'd got on to the weather forecast.'

'Did you see her?'

'No, but I heard the car. And there it is,' he concluded, with a jerk of his head. Through the bars you could see the green Polo parked on the paving where the front garden had once been.

'Did you hear her go out again?'

'No, but I might not hear her if she went out on foot. Probably would if she took the car.'

'So what makes you think she's missing? She could have gone out again this morning.'

He shrugged. 'I wouldn't have thought anything about it if I hadn't heard Marty up there.'

'Marty? Is that her boyfriend?'

'The dog,' he said shortly, as if she should have known. She had noticed it, of course, when she came in – she liked dogs. It was a big mongrel, black with ginger linings, the colour of a Dobermann, but more like an Alsatian in its square-ness and sturdiness and the density of its coat and tail. It had stood up politely when she entered but had not approached her, and now was lying on the floor at the end of the bed, chin on paws, looking rather depressed. Its ginger eyebrows twitched as the brown eyes moved from face to face, following the conversation, and when Mr Fitton spoke its name, the tail beat the ground twice, but it did not otherwise move.

'Oh. I thought it was yours,' she said. 'Marty.' She wrote it down.

'First I heard him bark. That was unusual enough. Normally he's quiet as a mouse. A good dog, that.' He looked down, and the tail beat again. 'But he gave a sort of wuff or two about eightish this morning. Then for the next couple of hours he was barking on and off. Then this afternoon he starts howling as well.' Fitton shook his head. 'I knew something must be wrong. I started wondering if she'd had an accident. Slipped in the shower or something, and he was trying to call for help. So I went up and knocked. There was no answer, but Marty started barking like mad, so I let myself in.'

'You have a key?' Connolly asked, trying not to sound interested.

But he gave her a canny look that said *wanna make some-thing of it*? 'Yeah, I got a key. *She* gave it me, years ago. I've waited in for workmen for her, taken in parcels, that sort of thing. Why not? She's at work all day and I'm – not.'

There was the faintest hesitation before the last word, and Connolly wondered if he had been going to say 'retired' – which was what she expected – and why he had changed it.

'Fine. So you went in?'

'I called out, but there was no answer. Poor old Marty was frantic. He led me straight to the kitchen. Both his bowls were empty, and he'd done a pee on the floor. That was what was upsetting him most, I reckon. It worried me, because she was devoted to that dog. I looked into the other rooms, but I guessed she wasn't there, or Marty would've led me straight to her. So I cleaned up the pee, took his bowls and his bag of biscuit and brought him down here with me. I couldn't leave him alone. I took him out for a quick walk, just round the block. But she's still not turned up. So I rang you lot.' He met her eyes with a steady look she couldn't quite interpret. 'I didn't want to get involved,' he said. 'But I knew something must've happened to her.'

Connolly found the look unsettling. She lapsed into automatic. 'I understand you're concerned about her, sir, but I think it's a bit early to be talking about her being missing. I mean, it's only Saturday afternoon, and you don't know when she went out – it could be just a few hours, and she could be anywhere.'

That was as far as she got. 'You're not listening to me,' he said. 'A dog will hold its bladder all day rather than foul the house, so he must have been left alone longer than he could hold on. I reckon she must have gone straight back out last night. Meant to come back but was prevented. She'd never put Marty through that deliberately. If she was held up somewhere she'd've rung me. She knows I've got the key and I never mind seeing to him.'

'Do you often look after him?'

'No, not often, but now and then. If she was just going to be away just the one night she might ask me to take him out and feed him. If she was going away a long time – like, on holiday – she'd take him round her mum's. They live out Ealing way.'

'Have you spoken to them? They might know where she is.'

'I haven't got the number. But if I had, I wouldn't go blurting it out to them that something's wrong. I keep telling you, she wouldn't've left the dog like that. Something's happened to her.'

'It's nice that she has you to worry about her,' Connolly said placatingly.

'She's a nice girl,' he said. 'Smart, too. She's a palaeontologist. Works down the Nat His Mu.'

'The what now?'

'Natural History Museum. Down Kensington. Always called it the Nat His Mu when I was a kid. Yeah, she's smart, Mel. Got a degree. Not that that always means anything, but she's smart all right. But she never looks down on you. Always polite and friendly. Not like her boyfriend.'

'You don't like him?'

'It's not me has to like him, is it?' He paused a beat, then added, as if it were justification, 'He's an estate agent.'

Connolly almost smiled, but realized he meant it. 'That's bad, is it?'

'I reckon there's something shady about him.' He made the 'money' gesture with his forefinger and thumb. 'On the make. He came down here once, trying to persuade me to sell this flat. Said he had a buyer interested. I know what his game was. Wanted to buy it himself, knock it back through with Mel's, turn it into a maisonette.'

He gestured towards the oddest feature of the room, the staircase that went up behind the kitchen wall and ended at the ceiling. When the house was a house, it would have been the servants' access to 'upstairs'. Now it was being used to store the only personal items in view – a small collection of books. It hadn't occurred to her before, but stairs made a good bookcase. She could see some of the titles from here. Dickens, Shakespeare, Graham Greene, Hemingway. Hold me back! And what was that big fat one, looked like a textbook? Con-something. Constitutional history? Ah, yes, *Your 100 Best Acts of Parliament.* Janey Mack! That lot was so dry you could use 'em to mop up oil spills.

'Be worth a fortune, a maisonette,' he went on, 'price of houses round here. But *he* tries to make out that mine's not worth anything. "Needs too much doing to it," he says, like he'd be doing me a favour, taking it off my hands.' He made a sardonic sound. 'I know what it's worth, thank you very much, Mister Smarmy. The parking spaces alone are worth a mint.' He jerked a thumb towards the front window. 'I bought all three when I had the chance, years ago. And that was *before* residents' parking. I rent 'em out. Seventy quid a week, each.'

Connolly wasn't sure this was getting them anywhere. She tapped her pad with her pencil. 'This boyfriend – have you got his name and address?'

'Name's Scott. Scott Hibbert.'

'Address?'

'He lives upstairs. They live together.'

'Oh, I didn't realize.'

'Been here two years. Don't know what she sees in him. He's not *that* good-looking. I suppose he's got money in his pocket. Maybe she just likes to have someone to take her out, buy her meals. Women are funny: go for real creeps rather'n be on their own. What's wrong with your own company?'

He seemed actually to be asking her, and she reflected that it was the opposite to what she was usually asked – which was, from the aunties and neighbours back home, when are you getting married, why haven't you got a boyfriend? But the first rule of interviewing was don't get sidetracked into responding. *Ve vill ask ze qvestions.*

'Where was the boyfriend last night, so?'

'I don't know. Mel told me he was going away for the weekend, when I saw her Thursday morning. I was outside having a smoke when she was leaving for work. I said, "Never mind, nearly the weekend," and she said, "Yeah, I'm looking forward to it. Scott's going away and I've got it all to myself." Something like that. Said she was going to lie on the sofa and watch soppy films all weekend.'

'She didn't say where he was going?'

'No.'

'Only, she might have gone to join him,' Connolly said, thinking aloud.

He drew an audible breath. 'I've told you,' he said with suppressed energy, 'she would *never have left the dog.*'

'Right,' said Connolly. She was finding being with him in this confined space unsettling. She wanted to be out of here. 'I don't suppose you have his mobile number? No. Well,' she concluded, standing up, 'I'll make a report about it, but unless it's a minor, there's not much we can do at this early stage.'

She didn't add that it also needed a more involved person than the downstairs neighbour to report someone missing. Mr Fitton plainly felt himself to be Melanie's gateway guardian, but that was not how the law saw it; but she didn't want to rile him any more with the suggestion. There was a sort of gleam deep in his eyes that made her nervous. Old geezer or not, he had a sort of wiry strength about him that required cautious handling.

Nobody liked missing persons cases. Most of them were just a waste of time: the subject turned up in due course with a perfectly reasonable excuse, or a perfectly excusable reason – or, on the odd and more entertaining occasion, with the guilty look of a dog with feathers round its mouth. Then they cursed the reporting party for making them 'look a fool'. Such was human nature, the police often got it in the neck for 'interfering', and came in for a helping of bile. There's always so much to go around.

The exceptions, when the missing person really was missing, were even less likeable: time-consuming hard work, often unresolved; and when there *was* a resolution, it was hardly ever a pleasant one.

It was the quiet time of a non-match Saturday afternoon when she got back to the station, and she found her boss, Detective Inspector Slider, propping up the doorway of the charge room talking to *his* boss, Detective Superintendent Fred 'The Syrup' Porson. Connolly, a latecomer to Shepherd's Bush nick, had assumed that the sobriquet was ironic, since Porson was noticeably, almost startlingly, bald. It had had to be explained to her that when his dear wife had died, he had abandoned the rug: a hairpiece so unconvincing – so said

Slider's bagman and friend, Detective Sergeant Atherton – it was not so much an imitation as an elaborate postiche. Connolly had had to have that one explained to her as well. She had not been impressed. Atherton, she opined, might be a bit of a ride, but he'd want to ease up on the gags. He was so smart you'd want to slap him.

It was not Porson's weekend on, but as he was not a golfer, he didn't have much to do outside the Job since his wife died. His only daughter was married and lived in Swindon so he didn't see much of her, and he often found himself turning up, faintly surprised, at the shop when he should be elsewhere, like a cat returning to its former home. Slider was leaning comfortably, arms crossed, but Porson, who never stood still, was fidgeting about in front of him like a partnerless man dancing the schottische.

They both looked relieved at the interruption of Connolly's arrival.

'Hullo,' Slider said cordially. 'How was it?'

'What's this? Been out on a case?' Porson enquired eagerly.

Connolly explained and Porson deflated gently like a balloon on the day after the party. 'Nothing in that. Ten to one she turns up before long.'

'Yes, sir. But he was very insistent she wouldn't have left the dog. Said she was pure dotey about it.'

'Not much of a dog lover if she keeps a big dog in an upstairs flat,' Porson complained.

'It's actually the garden flat, sir,' Connolly said, uncertain if she should be correcting the Big Cheese.

'Still leaves it alone all day when she's at work,' Porson pointed out triumphantly.

'Maybe she'd asked someone to take care of it, and they forgot,' said Slider, making peace. But Connolly could see he had taken the point. There was a slight thoughtful frown between his brows.

Porson's had drawn together like sheep huddling from the rain. 'Waste of bloody time. The dog that barked in the night? Or didn't bark, or whatever it was.'

But Connolly, encouraged by the fact that Slider evidently trusted her instincts, made bold to say, 'I just got the feeling there was something in it, sir. This Mr Fitton – there was something about him. I'm not sure what it was, but . . .'

'Wait a minute,' Porson said, suddenly interested. 'Fitton, you say? Not *Ronnie* Fitton?'

Connolly glanced at her pad. 'Fitton, Ronald. That's right, sir.'

'Come with me,' said Porson.

When the record was brought up on the computer screen, Connolly recognized the face of her interviewee, despite the accretion of years. In fact, he'd had all the same lines when the mugshot was taken, they'd just got deeper; and his hair, though longer and bushier then, had been grey already. The intense eyes were the same. He'd been quite a looker, in the lean, craggy, Harrison Ford sort of mould.

'Fitton, Ronald Dean,' Porson said. 'Recognize him now?'

'I think it's the same man, sir,' said Connolly.

But Porson was talking to Slider.

'I don't know that I do,' he said.

'Maybe it was before your time. He was quite a cause celeb at the time. Got sacks o' love letters from daft women.' Porson shook his head in wonder. 'One bit o' fame and they're all over you like a certifiable disease, never mind what you've done.'

'What *did* he do, sir?' Connolly asked.

'Murdered his wife,' Porson said. He looked at her, as if to judge her reaction. Connolly got the idea he was enjoying himself, and remained sturdily unmoved. 'Caught her in bed doing the horizontal tango with the bloke next door and whacked her on the head. She died in hospital a couple of hours later. Funny thing, he never touched the bloke. Just threw his clothes out the window and told him to hop it. Bloke ran out in the road starkers and nearly got run over; white van swerved to avoid him and went into a lamp post.'

'I remember the case now,' Slider said. 'It was before my time, but I remember reading about it.'

'Couldn't miss it, with details like that.' He rubbed his hands with relish. 'White van man turned out to have a load of stolen plant in the back, so they got him at the same time. Then

Fitton's ripped the leg off a chair to hit her with. You wouldn't've thought it to look at him – stringy sort of bloke. The tabloids were burbling about madmen having the strength of ten.'

'But he went down, didn't he?'

'Oh yes. Funny, though, he could've got off with a lighter sentence – he was respectable, got no previous, never been in trouble, he only hit her the once, and there was provocation. And like I said he never touched the bloke. Only, he wouldn't express any remorse. Said she had it coming and he'd do it again in the same circs. Said adulterous women deserved to die. That didn't go down well with the women jurors. And prosecuting counsel was Georgie Higgins – remember him?'

'Wrath of God Higgins? Yes, he was quite a character.'

'Anyway, he thundered on about taking justice into your own hands and judgement is mine sez the lord and let him who is without doo-dah stow the first throne and so on. That all went down a treat with the beak, who happened to be old Freeling, who was so High Church God called him sir. Freeling gives Fitton one last chance to say he's sorry, and Fitton not only refuses but comes out with he's an atheist, so Freeling goes purple and jugs him as hard as he can. You could see he was itching to slip on the black cap, if only they hadn't gone and abolished hanging.'

'So he got life?'

'Yes, and then he buggered up his parole by getting into a fight with another prisoner and putting him in the san.' He stroked his nose reflectively.

Now Connolly had placed that monk-like spareness and tidiness: not a soldier or sailor but a long-sentence con. 'Nice class of a character you had me visiting,' she muttered.

'Well, apart from that he was a model prisoner. And there was provocation,' Porson said. 'The other con had it in for him, apparently, and he had form for starting barneys. So,' he reflected, 'Fitton's back on our ground, is he? And a young lady he's interested in's gone missing.'

Oh, right, Connolly thought. *Now* she's a missing person. That's what happened when bosses came in on their days off.

What Mr Porson needed was a hobby. She glanced at Slider and saw the same thought in his face.

'Too early to say that, sir,' Slider said mildly.

'It's the early bird that gathers the moss,' Porson retorted. 'If it goes bad, the press'll be all over us for not jumping to it right away. You know what they're like. They love a damson in distress.'

Slider barely blinked. He was used to Porson's hit-or-miss use of language, and the old boy was sharp as a tack and a good boss. A bit of Bush in the boss was worth bearing for the sake of the strand in hand.

'But we've got no reason to think she *is* missing,' he said. He anticipated Porson's next words: 'And Ronnie Fitton would hardly call us in and draw attention to himself if he *had* done something to her.'

'Hmph,' Porson said.

'It's not even twenty-four hours yet. And nobody close to her has reported her missing.'

'As you say,' Porson said, and took himself off as if tiring of the subject; but he turned at the end of the corridor to say, 'I just hope it doesn't come back and bite you in the arse.'

Connolly caught Slider's momentary stricken look, and when Porson had gone said indignantly, 'The meaner! That was below the belt, guv.'

But Slider did not let his firm criticize senior officers – not in front of him, anyway. 'Haven't you got a report to write up? And if you're short of something to do, I've got some photocopying.'

Slider was not on the following day. He was celebrating a Sunday off by sitting on the sofa, nominally reading the papers and watching little George while Joanna practised in the kitchen, but in reality conducting frequent essential checks on the inside of his eyelids, when the telephone rang.

It was Atherton, obscenely breezy. 'Your supposed missing person just got missinger.'

'That's not even a word,' Slider rebuked him with dignity. 'And what are you telling me for?'

'I thought you'd like to know. The boyfriend just reported she's gone walkabout. We haven't told him Fitton already reported it, just in case.'

'In case what?'

'Well, Mr Porson thinks Fitton did it.'

'That doesn't mean he didn't.'

'What a *volte face*! Yesterday you wouldn't admit there was an it for him to have done. Connolly said you had to bite your cheeks at the suggestion.'

'In any case, the boyfriend must know by now that Fitton spoke to us, because Fitton has the dog and he'd have had to go to him to get it back.'

'That's a point. He didn't mention the dog. All right, you go back to sleep. I'll handle everything. And if I need help, I can always pop upstairs and ask Mr Porson.'

Slider sat up. 'Bloody Nora, what's he doing there?'

'There's no way to answer that without laying myself open to disciplinary action.'

'And what do you mean, he didn't mention the dog?'

'Do you want me to read you the interview transcript?' Atherton enquired sweetly.

'No, no. You win. I'll come in,' Slider said, sighing like a whale with relationship problems. 'Connolly felt there was something to it. That girl's developing good instincts.'

'But you did the right thing,' said Atherton. 'Couldn't go on Fitton's say-so. And we still don't know she's missing, for the matter of that – only that she's not at home. She may just have done a runner, and from the look of the boyfriend, who would blame her?'

'If you're trying to comfort me you must think things are bad.'

'Not *yet*, they're not,' Atherton said significantly.

Joanna was used to such interruptions but she was human. She only said, 'It's a pity I've already put the beef in,' but combined with the scent of it on the air, it was enough to break a man's heart.

'You and Dad will enjoy it, anyway,' he said. His father shared the house with them, a very nice arrangement for babysitting, and for relieving him of anxiety about the old man living alone. 'I probably won't be gone very long.'

'Why have you got to go in, anyway? Just for a missing person?'

'There's an ex-murderer involved.'

'Ex, or axe?'

'Ex as in former.'

'Can you *be* a former murderer? Surely what's done is done.'

'You quibble like Atherton. Anyway, Mr Porson's gone all unnecessary over it, so I want to make sure everything's in place, just in case it turns out to be anything.'

'You'd sooner do it yourself than inherit someone else's mess,' she summarized.

'Wouldn't you?'

She kissed him. 'Go, with my blessing. Cold roast beef's almost better than hot, anyway.'

He kissed her back. 'You're a very wonderful woman,' he said.

'I said "almost",' she reminded him.

Slider was not a tall man, and Scott Hibbert was, and since he didn't like being loomed over, he freely admitted that he started off with a prejudice against the man. Hibbert was both tall and big, but going a little bit to softness around the jaw and middle. He was not bad looking, in an obvious, fleshy sort of way, except that his mouth was too small, which Slider thought made him look weak and a bit petulant. He was wearing jeans and an expensive leather jacket, and shoes, not trainers (one plus point), which were well polished (two plus points); but the jeans had been ironed with a crease (minus a point). His carefully-cut hair was dressed with a little fan of spikes at the front like Keanu Reeves, and his chin was designer-stubbled (minus too many points to count).

Having privately indulged his prejudices for a satisfying few seconds, Slider dismissed them firmly, and prepared to interview Hibbert with a completely receptive mind.

'So, Mr Hibbert, tell me when you last saw Miss Hunter.'

'I already told the other guy everything,' he complained.

Guy. Another minus – no, no, no. Concentrate. 'I'm sorry, but I really would like you to tell me again, in your own words,' said Slider.

Hibbert looked uneasy, and kept crossing and recrossing his legs, and though he was not sweating, his skin looked damp. He licked his lips. 'Look, shouldn't you be *doing* something?' he asked querulously. 'Like, I mean, *looking* for her or something?'

'I assure you the other officer will already have put things in train for a general alert. I need to hear your story so that we can refine the search. You last saw her when?'

'Like I said, Friday morning, before we went off to work,' he said, frowning. 'We usually walk to the tube together, but I was taking my car in because I was going down to the West Country later, so I offered to drop her off at the station. But she said no, she'd rather walk.' His left leg was jiggling all on its own, and he sniffed and wiped the end of his nose on the back of his hand. Slider found these unstudied gestures reassuring. Stillness and composure in witnesses were what worried him. 'She was a bit pissed off with me, if you want the truth,' Hibbert added in a blurty sort of way. 'I was going away for the weekend and she was narked about it.'

'Because?'

'I was going to this wedding in the West Country – my mate Dave – we were at school together – and she didn't want me to go.'

'Why not? Wasn't she invited?'

'Oh, she was invited and everything. Of course she was. Except there was this stag thing on the Friday night that was men only. She didn't want to go to the hen night because she didn't really know Julie, that Dave's marrying, and anyway she'd already got this thing arranged for Friday night with some of her girl friends. I said, so come down on Saturday, then, but she wouldn't. She said she hates weddings anyway, and she never really liked Dave. Well, she can't stand him if you want to know the truth. I mean, they've only met a couple of times and it ended in a stand-up row both times, and she said she never wanted to see him again. I suppose he's a bit blokeish for her, but he's a laugh, and he's my best mate.

There's some of her friends I don't like. Well, that's all right – she has her friends and I have mine, why not? We don't have to do everything together. And I couldn't let old Dave down, not on his wedding day, could I?'

Slider guessed he was hearing the essence of the row that had been. Hibbert was justifying himself to him. He nodded neutrally.

'When I first told her about it, she said it was all right, I should go on my own and she didn't mind,' he went on. 'But Friday morning she was really narky about it, kept saying things about me and Dave getting drunk together. Well, what's a stag night for? And everybody gets drunk at weddings. I said *you* won't have to see us, so what's the problem? And she said wild horses wouldn't drag her there. We had a bit of a barney and she storms off to the bathroom. So then I cool down a bit and when she comes out I say d'you wanna lift to the station, babes, and she gives me a look and says no, she'll walk. And she did.'

'She works at the Natural History Museum? And where do you work?'

'Hatter and Ruck – you know, the estate agents? – in Knightsbridge.'

Posh, Slider thought. 'So you could have dropped her off at work, instead of just offering a lift to the station? You'd go right past it.'

He looked uneasy, and shifted to another buttock. 'I wasn't going in to the office first thing, I was going to look at a house in Hendon. I don't normally take the car in when I'm just in the office because parking's a nightmare up there.'

'And that was the last time you saw her?'

He nodded, looked stricken at the reminder, and found yet another buttock to shift to. How many did he have in there?

'Or spoke to her?'

'No, I rang her Friday evening, while she was out with her mates. I rang her up to make peace, if you want to know, but she was all right again by then. She'd got over and it and just said have a good time and everything and I'll see you Sunday. She's like that – she never stays mad for long.'

'And that was the last time you spoke to her?'

He nodded.

'Did you go home after work on Friday?'

'No, I went straight down to the West Country.'

He kept saying the West Country. Slider thought that odd. 'Where, exactly?'

'Salisbury,' he said. 'Dave lives in Salisbury.'

'And what time did you eventually get home?'

'I was supposed to come back Sunday night – there was a lot of us from the same school and we were going to get together Sunday lunchtime – but I was missing Mel, so I called it off. Well, we'd been talking and drinking all Saturday afternoon and evening, so I reckoned we'd said everything anyway. I didn't sleep very well Saturday night so I got up really early Sunday morning and left. I was back home, what, about ten? She wasn't there, and I knew right away something was up.'

'How?' Slider asked.

Hibbert stared in perplexity at the question.

'How did you know something was wrong?'

'I don't know,' he said. Now he was still, thinking about it: buttocks at rest at last; even the lone break-dancing knee had stopped and held its breath. He scowled with the effort of analysis, and Slider got the impression he was not very bright; and yet, of course, it is easy enough to fake being dumber than you are. It's the opposite that's impossible.

'I dunno,' he said at last. 'It just felt wrong, as if no one had been there.' He thought some more. 'Oh, for one thing, the answer-machine wasn't on. If she'd gone out, she'd have put it on. And she'd have left me a note to say where she was going. She always leaves a note.'

'Even if she was still mad at you?'

'But she wasn't any more. When I spoke to her Friday night she was all right again.'

'Anything else?' Slider prompted. Hibbert looked puzzled by the question, having apparently gone off on another train of thought. 'Anything else you noticed that made you think something was wrong?' He was going after the dog, absence of, but what he got was quite unexpected.

Hibbert's face cleared. He looked as though he'd just

got the last answer in the jackpot pub quiz. 'Her handbag was there.'

'Her handbag?' Slider said, trying not to sound like Edith Evans.

'Yeah, her handbag,' he said excitedly. 'With her purse and phone and everything in it. But not her door keys.'

'Excuse me,' Slider said. 'I have to make a phone call.'

TWO
Deep-Pan, Crisp and Even

Joanna was resigned. 'I'm not surprised,' she said. 'I know once they get hold of you, they won't let you go. That place is a black hole.'

Even over the phone, he thought he could smell the roast beef and Yorkshire. 'It's not that,' he said. 'The case just turned into a case. The girl's handbag is in the flat.'

'Her *handbag*, singular? Tell me any woman of that age who only has one.'

'The handbag she was using, I mean. With her gubbins in it. So it's looking more like foul play, I'm afraid.'

'Oh dear. Well, keep the chin up. There may be an explanation you haven't thought of, and she'll come wandering in looking surprised.'

'I'll settle for that. See you later.'

Atherton drew up just short of the house and craned his head to look. 'No press. Thank God. Amazing no one's spilled the beans yet. Now, where's that key?' He felt in his pocket for the key ring Slider had received from Scott Hibbert.

He was hampered by the seat belt and Connolly only watched him struggle for a millisecond before saying, 'Undo the belt, you looper. And don't bother, because I have me own.' She dangled it before his eyes. 'I got it off Mr Fitton before I left.'

'How did you manage that?'

'He volunteered. Gave it me and said, "I won't be needing this any more."'

'Did he, indeed?'

'Ah, cool the head, it doesn't mean anything. Sure, he'd know we'd check on him as soon as I got back, and find his record, and then we'd want the key offa him anyhow.'

'Yes, but saying he wouldn't need the key any more suggests he knows she's dead.'

'Well *I* know it, so why not?'

'You don't know any such thing. It's still odds-on she'll walk back in any minute. They usually do. And don't forget she took her keys with her. Why would she do that if she wasn't coming back?'

'Don't *you* forget she left her mobile. She'd grab that before her keys, every time.'

Atherton yawned ostentatiously. 'Well, if there is anything in it, we've got the prime suspect under wraps back at the factory, so relax.'

'Scott Hibbert? He didn't do it. He's just a big gom.'

'I take it "gom" is not an expression of approval.'

'Why do you *talk* like that?' Connolly cried in frustration.

Atherton smiled, satisfied now he had goaded her. 'Why don't you like him?'

'What's to like? He's like a big transport-caff fry-up. Everything right there on the plate, and none of it very appetizing. I like a bit of subtlety.'

Atherton slapped his chest. 'Right there,' he addressed the invisible audience. 'She stepped right into my heart, folks. Subtlety, *c'est moi.*'

Connolly gave him a look so cold it could have hosted the Ice Capades. 'What are we looking for up there?'

He became sensible. 'Firstly, anything that suggests she was doing a runner – empty spaces in the wardrobe and so on. Secondly, signs of a struggle, anything that might have been used as a weapon, signs of blood. Also signs of hasty cleaning up. Someone who's just killed someone is usually in too much of a panic to clean properly, which is lucky for us. And always, of course, anything that strikes you as anomalous.'

'As a what now?'

'Odd. Out of place. Wrong. Peculiar.'

'Why didn't you say so in the first place?'

Atherton, having done this so often in Slider's company, used his nose first, as Slider would have, and noticed that the flat had a cold smell about it, as if no one had been there for a while. It occupied a big area in square-footage, but the conversion was an old one, and clumsily done, so the space was not well used. On either side of a large, wasted entrance hall there was a sitting room and a bedroom, both with bay windows on to the front, with a slice cut off at the back to make a bathroom and kitchen, side by side. It all needed modernizing; and a cleverer architect (or indeed, given when it was done, any architect at all) could have made a much nicer flat out of it. If recombined with the basement (as Fitton had said Hibbert had been plotting) it would make a very glamorous maisonette, with a big kitchen/breakfast-room downstairs, and living room, two beds and modern bathroom upstairs. With the big rooms, high ceilings, mouldings and so on, it would fetch a stone fortune in up-and-coming Shepherd's Bush; so it wouldn't be wonderful if Hibbert, who was in the business after all, had spotted the potential.

Leaving aside the property-developing crying-shame it represented, Atherton noted that the furniture was modern but cheap, and that the place was ordinarily tidy. In the bedroom, the bed had been made, in that the duvet had been pulled up, but it hadn't been straightened or smoothed. There was a built-in wardrobe with sliding doors and a free-standing one so stuffed with clothes the doors wouldn't close at all. An exercise bike in the corner had clothes heaped over its saddle, and there were more clothes dumped on a wicker armchair – it would be fun trying to work out what she had been wearing, should the need arise. But there were no used plates or mugs or dirty clothes strewn around, and the floor was clear and the carpet clean. The sitting room was tidier, with only a newspaper, a novel (Laurie Graham, *At Sea*, face down and opened at page 64) and an emery board lying around to show occupation. And the handbag, large and tan leather, which was on the sofa, at the end nearest the door.

Connolly gestured to the remote, lying on the coffee table next to the emery board. 'She coulda been sitting here, doing her nails and watching the TV. See, the TV's not been turned off at the switch – it's on standby.'

'Ninety per cent of people habitually turn off the TV with the remote,' he said. 'Doesn't mean she was interrupted.'

In the bathroom he observed that the inside of the shower and the bath were dry, as were both bath towels, stretched out on a double towel-rail, and the bath mat, hanging over the side of the bath. But there were drops of water still in the basin, and the hand towel was crumpled and damp inside the creases.

'Which accords with no one having showered in here since Friday,' he said. 'Sonny Boy says he came home at ten this morning. So he didn't shower, but did at least wash his hands. Probably after he went to the loo. There are droplets round the loo bowl as well.'

'To much information,' Connolly said, making a face.

'Water droplets, from the flush. Don't be sensitive. Got that torch?' he asked.

The bathroom was fully tiled, and there was tile-patterned acrylic flooring, but both were old, chipped here and there, the grouting discoloured and breaking. Atherton went over everything with the torch, looking sidelong to catch any smearing or marks, shone the torch down the plug holes and under the rim of the toilet ('Rather you than me,' Connolly said) and then did the same in the kitchen – equally old and shabby, but clean and tidy, with the last lot of washing-up (cereal bowls and mugs and a small plate – Friday's breakfast?) clean and very dry in the dish rack.

'A big fat nothing,' Connolly concluded, sounding slightly disappointed.

'If she was abducted, she went without a struggle,' Atherton said, 'and if she was killed here, it was very quick and clean. Or Hibbert's a better housekeeper than he looks. Or –' he gave Connolly a look – 'she walked out of her own accord and will shortly come prancing back through the door demanding to know what we're doing here.'

Connolly studied him. 'You don't think that any more. You're starting to think there's something in it.'

'Not really. Except for the mobile. You've got me worried about the mobile.'

'Hah!'

'Only a bit,' he equivocated. 'If she was just popping down the offy for a packet of fags she might not grab it along with her keys.'

'But then she'd have taken her purse.'

'Not if she took a tenner out of it.'

'But then she'd have come back.'

He shrugged. 'I just think, on balance, given her age and sex, she'd have been more likely to have taken her mobile, and that that constitutes an anomaly. Unfortunately, the only one. If we'd found signs of a struggle or clean-up we could have got a forensic team in, but as it stands there's no evidence to justify it. But we'd better take the handbag back with us. Might be all sorts of goodies in it, besides the phone. Run and get an evidence bag, will you?'

On her way back from the car, when she got to the foot of the steps, Fitton appeared suddenly round the side of the house, where his own front door was, and stood looking at her.

'You came back, then,' he said. 'Decided there was something in it after all.'

'Well,' she said, wondering what it was right to say to him.

He examined her expression in a way that made her shiver. He was too noticing. 'You know about me,' he said flatly, his mouth making a downturn that was more sad than sour.

'How—?'

'I can tell from the way you're looking at me. Like I'm a mad dog that might bite.'

'No,' she protested. 'It's not like—'

'Didn't take long,' he said. 'Knew it wouldn't.' He poked his forehead with a finger and thumb. 'Branded for life.'

'It's just standard procedure,' she said helplessly, not understanding why she wanted to protect his feelings. 'Our Super recognized your name. But it doesn't mean—'

'Just remember I called it in,' he said. 'Benefit of the doubt. All right?'

'It's all in writing,' she said. The dog, Marty, padded round from the side of the house – Fitton must have left the door open – and came up behind him, shoving its head up peremptorily under his hand. He caressed it automatically, and the tail swung.

'You've still got her dog, so,' Connolly said, and cursed herself for the stupid remark.

He jerked his head towards the upstairs flat. '*He* never asked about him. Dipstick probably doesn't even remember he exists. I'll keep him till somebody takes him away.' He started to turn away, the dog sticking close to his side, then looked back to say, 'Benefit of the doubt. Remember.'

'I'll remember the dog likes you,' she said to his retreating back. What an eejitty thing to say. God, she was a thick! She scurried up the steps before she did anything else to embarrass herself.

Swilley was going to see the parents. She had often drawn the short straw in these cases because (a) she was a woman and (b) she was regarded as unflappable. It was better for bad news to be delivered by someone with an air of calm. But since having a child of her own she had liked this task less and less.

Joining the Job at a time when women had to prove themselves not just as good as men, but the same as men, she had early grown a shell against taunts, insults, slights, come-ons and filthy jokes. She had been helped by being tall, blonde, athletic, and beautiful in a sort of wide-mouthed, small-nosed, *Baywatch* way, which rendered most of her tormentors tongue-tied if she actually faced them one-to-one. She was also blessed with an iron head and concrete stomach, which meant she could match them pint for pint and curry for curry; and she was deceptively strong, was a blue-belt in judo, had twenty-twenty vision, and was a crack shot.

Joining Slider's firm had been wonderful for her, because he thought she was a good detective and treated her as one, and at least had the decency to *appear* not to notice her gender. After one early, disastrous mistake she had made it an iron rule not to go out or get involved with any of her colleagues. After a time they had stopped trying and written her off as frigid and probably a lesbian, which she had borne patiently; and eventually had accepted her as one of them, an honorary bloke. Her nickname, Norma, was a tribute to her machismo, and she had worn it with pride. It had been hard won.

So for years she had maintained an icy virginity at work and a wonderfully patient, amazingly understanding secret boyfriend at home; but eventually Tony had grown restless. He disapproved of her refusal to go for promotion. Well, the money would have been nice, but she did not want to have to go through that whole process of training a new lot of resentful males to accept her for herself. The very prospect exhausted her. Also, patient though he was, Tony was still all man, and he didn't like the fact that she kept him secret, as if she was ashamed of him. Not ashamed of him, she told him, but of *them*. But in the end she had to give him *something*, and the price of being allowed to go on being her was first marriage, and then the baby.

She was very happy being married, and Tony had reverted to being patient, adaptable, and helpful to a saintly degree when her job prevented her doing wifely and motherly things; and she adored little Ashley and wondered how they had ever lived without her. But she paid with whole new layers of sensitivity towards lovers, married people, parents, the bereaved; and new layers of fear that the things she saw happening daily to the anonymous victims of crime might happen to her own small family. She had become vulnerable; she had lost her ice. She hoped she had not also lost her edge.

But she approached the present task with resignation. There were lots of things in the Job you didn't necessarily relish – smelly houses, vomiting drunks, decomposing corpses, road accidents – but you did them just the same.

Melanie Hunter's parents weren't called Hunter – she had them down as Wiseman, Ian and Rachel, so either the mum had remarried, or Melanie had changed her name for some reason. They lived in a nice part of Ealing, typical suburbia, Edwardian semis on a street edged with those trees that went into pink blossom like screwed up tissue paper in spring. Of course, they were bare now, the freezing weather having held everything back. Most of the houses had turned their gardens into hardstanding for cars, but where they still had front gardens, they were neatly kept, with clipped privet hedges, and hard-pruned sticks that would be roses later, and oblongs and squares of bare, weeded earth that would be flower beds, showing only the blunt green noses of bulbs.

The faint, watery sun had broken through, and even though it did nothing to mitigate the biting cold, it gave an air of festivity to the street. As it was Sunday, there were cars parked before most of the houses, kids were trundling about on bikes and scooters, and one brave or barmy man was washing his motor with a hose with a foaming sponge attachment. All very Mrs Norman Normal – as were all lives until the meteor of chance hit them, the hurtling rock from the sky crashed at random through their roof.

In the front garden of the Wisemans' house, there was a girl of about eleven or twelve, in a cropped top and skinny jeans that exposed her belly button (why the hell wasn't she freezing? Kids these days! Swilley thought), picking the sugar-pink varnish from her nails with all the destructive boredom of Sunday afternoon. She eyed Swilley with intense interest, scanning her from her pull-on woolly hat down through her camel wool wrap-around coat to her long boots.

'Hello,' Swilley said. 'Are your mum and dad Mr and Mrs Wiseman?'

She nodded.

'Are they in?'

'Mum is,' the girl said, and then, in a burst of confidence: 'She won't buy anything. She never buys anything at the door.'

'That's all right, cos I'm not selling. Can I have a word with her? It's important.'

The girl twisted her head over her shoulder without removing her eyes from Swilley's face and yelled through the half-open front door, '*Mu-u-um*! There's a lady wants you.'

Oh, ever so much a lady, Swilley thought.

'Are you a social worker?' the girl asked abruptly. 'She's not my real mum, she's my stepmum. I like your colour lipstick. What's it called? Do you like vodka?'

A woman appeared behind her, saving Swilley from answering. She was middle aged and ordinary, dressed in slacks, a cotton jumper and an unattractive big, thick, chunky cardigan. She had her glasses in one hand and a biro in the other, and a look between wariness and embryo annoyance on a face that held the remains of prettiness behind the soft plumpness of middle-aged marriage. 'Yes?' she said.

'Mrs Wiseman? I wonder if I could come in and have a word with you,' Swilley said, and showed her warrant card. The woman looked immediately put out and flustered, but the child's eyes opened so wide Swilley was afraid she'd see her brain.

'You're the cops,' she breathed. 'Are you going to arrest Mum?'

'Bethany!' the woman rebuked automatically, but her worried eyes were searching Swilley's face. 'Is it Ian? Is it an accident?'

'No, nothing like that. It may be nothing at all. Can I come in?' Swilley said. The man two doors down had ceased wiping his car's roof and was staring with his mouth ajar and the hose soaking his feet, ha ha.

'Oh, yes. Yes, come on through.'

Bethany slipped in before Mrs Wiseman shut the door firmly behind Swilley. 'Come in the lounge,' she said. Swilley followed her, and as she turned with a question in her face, made a quick sideways gesture of the eyes towards the child, which fortunately the woman was *compos mentis* enough to catch and interpret. 'Bethany, go out in the back garden and play,' she said, sharply enough to be obeyed.

'Play?' the girl complained. 'What am I, a kid? I don't *play.*'

'And shut the back door after you. Don't let all the heat out.'

The girl extracted herself by unwilling inches, leaving Swilley alone with her mother in a knocked-through lounge decorated and furnished in exactly the sort of middle-income, suburban taste Swilley would have expected.

'Would you like to sit down?' Mrs Wiseman said automatically.

Swilley saw she had been doing some sort of paperwork on the coffee table in front of the sofa, and took an armchair.

Mrs Wiseman sat in the chair opposite, looked enquiringly at Swilley, and then suddenly something seemed to come over her. She swayed, gripped the arm of the chair, and said almost in a whisper, 'Oh my God, it's Melanie, isn't it? Something's happened to Melanie!'

She stared at Swilley, white with some awful foreknowledge, and Swilley thought perhaps it was there, latent, in every mother's mind, an instinct born at the moment of conception: the fear that one day some stranger would come and tell you your child had been taken from you. She felt horribly impressed, and a little queasy.

'It's probably nothing to worry about,' Swilley said, though Mrs Wiseman's certainty had communicated itself to her, now. 'It's just that Melanie's not at home, and her boyfriend doesn't know where she is. Have you heard from her lately?'

'I spoke to her – Friday,' Mrs Wiseman said. 'She rang me from work. She rings me two or three times a week, just for a chat.'

'You're close, then?' said Swilley.

'Always have been,' she said, but with some reservation in her voice Swilley didn't understand.

'Did she tell you anything about her plans for the weekend?'

'She said she was going out for a drink with friends on Friday evening. It was her best friend Kiera's birthday, and they were meeting some others at the Princess Vic.'

'And what about the rest of the weekend?'

'She said she hadn't any plans. Scott – her boyfriend?' Swilley nodded.

'He was going away for the weekend, so she said she was just going to relax. I asked her to come for Sunday lunch but she said she had some work to catch up on. She's a palaeontologist, you know,' she added with a huge pride that carried the touch of bewilderment of any parent whose child surpasses them by such a length. 'She works at the Natural History Museum. They think the world of her there. I don't know where she gets her brains from,' she added with a little affected laugh. 'It can't be me. I was never even in the sixth form.'

'From her father, perhaps?' Swilley suggested, wanting to keep her talking.

A shadow passed over Mrs Wiseman's face: it looked to Swilley almost like wariness. 'Her father's dead,' she said abruptly.

'Oh, I'm sorry.'

'He was killed in the Greenford rail crash,' she said, as though that ended the topic for good and all. That had been – Swilley counted – eleven years ago: it had been in all the papers, of course. Rail crashes were so thankfully rare, they were all remembered, catalogued in the public mind for ever by their location: Potters Bar, Hatfield, Southall . . . Greenford had had an unusually high number of fatalities. 'Ian's my second husband,' Mrs Wiseman concluded.

'Of course,' Swilley said. 'That accounts for why Melanie has a different surname. And Bethany is . . .?'

'She's Ian's, from his first wife. He was a widower too.'

'So has Melanie any brothers or sisters?'

'No, I just had the one. Why do you ask?'

'I'm wondering if there was anyone she might have gone to visit, that's all. Any aunts, cousins?'

'Not that she'd go and visit. I've got a sister, but we're not close, and Melanie never cared that much for her cousins.'

'What about your husband's family?'

'You mean Ian's? Oh, she would never go to *them*,' she said firmly.

'Does she not get on with her stepfather?'

'They're all right, they get on OK, but they're not what I'd call close. She doesn't think of him as her stepfather, anyway, just my husband. No reason why she should. She was practically grown up by the time I married, and I told her from the beginning, I'm not marrying him for you, I'm marrying him for me.'

Some history there, Swilley thought, making a mental note. Smoothly she went on, 'What about her boyfriend, Scott? Is everything all right between them?'

'Oh yes,' she said with enthusiasm. 'He's a lovely boy – just the sort of man I always wanted for her. Steady, nice manners, a good job. Very polite to me and Ian. And they're mad about each other, no doubt about that.'

'But he went away for the weekend without her,' Swilley suggested. 'Did she mind that?'

'Oh no,' she said quickly. 'You mustn't think that. You see, Scott's got this friend from school, they go way back, but he's not Melanie's sort at all. Loud, and – well, what I'd call vulgar. Tells dirty jokes; and the way he is with women . . .! Always leering, and making coarse remarks, *you* know. Melanie can't stand him, but of course Scott's fond of him, knowing him all his life – in and out of each other's houses when they were kids. Well, Dave, this friend, was getting married so of course Scott had to go, but there was no need for Melanie to put herself through that. Scott understands. It was all quite amicable. She told me on Friday she was quite happy to stay home, and Scott would enjoy himself more if he went on his own. But . . .' She faltered, remembering what she had happily forgotten for a few moments. 'You're saying he doesn't know where she is?'

'She wasn't there when he got home this morning, and she hadn't left him a note, so he was worried.' She didn't mention the dog or the handbag: no point in upsetting the woman yet. 'I just thought, if they'd had a row, she might have walked out on him – to teach him a lesson, sort of thing . . .'

'Well, she was all right with him when I spoke to her on Friday,' Mrs Wiseman said, frowning, 'but of course they might have quarrelled since then. I wouldn't know. But if they'd quarrelled that bad, why wouldn't she ring me, and come over here?'

'Could be many reasons,' Swilley said inventively. 'If she knows how much you like him, she might not want to admit to you they'd had a row. So, can you think of anyone else she'd go to? This friend Kiera, for instance – can you give me a contact number or address for her?'

'Yes, I've got that somewhere. She might go to Kiera – they're very close. And she's got lots of other friends. I don't know who they are, really, but Kiera could tell you. There's one she works with, Simone, at the museum – she talks about her sometimes. She gets things from me for her – for Simone. Cosmetics and perfume. I sell cosmetics from home,' she added, casting a glance at the paperwork. 'I've always been in Product Demonstration, you see, ever since I left school. Started off at the Ideal Home. I've done all the big shows. I used to sell Tupperware, when I was married the first time, but cosmetics and fashion jewellery pay better – and you meet

a nicer class of person.' She looked at Swilley with professional interest. 'I see you take care of your skin. I could let
you have some nice things, if you're interested. It's a good
discount. And they're all quality products, top names.'

It was odd, Swilley thought, given the dread she had exhib-
ited at first, how difficult she seemed to find it to keep that at
the front of her mind. Perhaps it was a defence mechanism
– think about anything except that something might have
happened to Melanie. Or perhaps there was something even
worse she was trying to keep at bay – something she didn't
want Swilley to discover.

She let her yatter on about her products for a bit while she
thought about it, and then went about taking her leave. She
got the address and phone number of Kiera, and of Scott's
parents in Salisbury because she really seemed to want to give
them; and she asked for and received a very good photograph
of Melanie, taken the year before, which she had been looking
at, sandwiched between heavy glass with a silver foot on a
chiffonier across the room. It was quite a formal picture, of a
very pretty young woman sitting on a stool with her hands in
her lap, smiling at the camera. She had thick tawny-blonde
hair, artfully highlighted, hanging in a bob to her shoulders,
regular features and very nice teeth. Swilley could see the
resemblance to her mother, but she had better cheekbones and
a more interesting nose.

'It was a studio portrait,' Mrs Wiseman said proudly. 'She
had a whole session last year – Scott paid. It was her birthday
present. He's got a friend who's a photographer so he got a
discount. He says when they get married they'll get a really
good deal.'

'Are they going to get married?' Swilley asked.

'Well, eventually, of course, but they haven't any plans just
at present. But I hope it will be soon. She doesn't want to
leave it too long to have children. And Scott will make a lovely
father. It was him insisted she give this picture to me – he
knew I'd like it. Always so thoughtful – such a nice boy. I
think *he*'d get married tomorrow but Melanie's hesitating – you
know what girls are like these days. Don't want to give up
their freedom. But Scott was hinting about next year the last

time I saw him. He doesn't want them to have kids without being married, which is just the way it should be.'

She was smiling now, and Swilley mentally shook her head at this degree of self-hypnosis. Far be it from her to shatter the protective bubble. Maybe Melanie would turn up before she need look her fears in the face.

At the door she asked, 'By the way, what does your husband do?'

'Ian? He's a teacher at Elthorne Manor – PE and sports. He's out at the moment – Sunday League down the Rec.'

But the new subject had done it. The smileyness drained from her face and the dread was back in the eyes.

'You'll find her, won't you?' she asked in a husk of a voice. 'She'll be all right? Only, it's not like her just to go out like that, and not say anything.'

'I'm sure there's a logical explanation,' Swilley said heart-eningly, and made her escape. She was sure there was a logical explanation, but that didn't necessarily mean it would be good news.

As she was getting into her car, a silver Ford Galaxy pulled up on to the Wiseman hardstanding and a man in a tracksuit got out, pulling a sports bag after him. He was of medium height, well built about the shoulders, with very dark hair and a tanned, hard face that missed being handsome by some small, inexplicable degree. He stood for a moment staring at Swilley, scowling, his head up as if ready to take affront. She wondered if he had seen her coming out of his house as he drove up. She hastened to get into her car, not wanting to talk to him, especially as he did not seem in a good mood. Let Mrs W explain all – she had had enough for one day.

When a young woman is murdered, there is always one photo-graph the press latches on to. It is splashed over every paper and news bulletin all through the investigation, at the arrest, during the trial, and on sentencing. It defines the case, and sometimes even the age, so that forever after that person, who would have lived out her life in obscurity, is as instantly, iconically recognized by millions as Marilyn Monroe with her skirt blowing up, or Princess Di looking up from under her fringe. It was as if, Slider thought, their fate had been decided at the instant the photographer's finger had pressed the button. From that moment, they moved as inevitably towards their doom as a package on a conveyor belt.

Slider had always found old photographs unsettling, and he'd had a bad feeling from the moment Swilley returned with the studio portrait of Melanie Hunter. He knew they would use it, because it was clearer than the snapshot Hibbert had given them from his wallet; and he knew the media would love it, because she looked pretty and smiley and good, a nice girl with a good school record and a fine career ahead of her. How much more saleable of newspapers than a grim-looking, shaven-headed kid with a string of ASBOs.

He was afraid that from now on that studio portrait, taken with pleasure in mind, would go together with the words 'The Melanie Hunter Murder' like gammon and spinach – or, nowadays, like hamburger and fries. He felt horribly, guiltily, as though they had sealed her fate by taking over that photograph. He had no hope now that she would wander back home or they would find her alive, and he felt ashamed of his defeatism.

An urgent phone call to Swilley from Atherton had diverted her on her way back from Ealing and she had arrived with a stack of pizza boxes, so they had all had lunch after all – rather belated but better than nothing. Connolly had made Slider a proper cup of tea to go with his, but he had eaten absently, looking at Melanie Hunter's picture in-between reading the reports from Connolly, Atherton and Swilley and trying not to fear the worst.

They had done all they could by way of circulating the picture and description to police and hospitals and the usual agencies, and ringing anyone she might have visited or telephoned, while outside the thin sun had dipped out of contention through a red sky, and the icy cold had returned like a marauder, as if it had been hanging around in the shadows all day just waiting for its chance.

There was no news of Melanie Hunter, either good or bad, by the time Slider called it a day and went home to a cold beef supper, which he could not taste through the dust and ashes of his certainty that she was a goner. And too many people now knew she was missing for it not to get to the press, and there would be all the parade and palaver that the media so loved, the questions and appeals and endlessly repeated factlets about her last known movements, all presided over by the photo – the photo – the photo; until eventually the sad, crumpled, discarded body would be found, and they'd have a murder investigation on their hands. Sometimes he hated his job.

THREE

Babe in the Woods

Probably it was the pizza, but he had a restless night, not falling asleep properly until half past five; and then the telephone roused him at seven from such a depth it was almost an agony to open his eyes. But his brain clicked back into position an instant later, and he knew as he reached for the bedside phone what it would be.

It was Atherton. 'Found her.'

'Where?'

'By Ruislip Lido. In the woods.'

'Oh God.'

'My sentiments exactly.'

'I'll see you there.'

Slider had lived a large part of his first marriage, to Irene, in Ruislip, so he knew it well. He had taken the kids to the Lido on sunny Sundays. It was the poor man's seaside – in his case, time-poor as much as anything. The north part of Ruislip ran up into the foothills of the Chilterns, so it was both hilly and much wooded – surprisingly country-like, considering it was still part of London. The Lido itself had started life as a man-made reservoir intended as a feeder for the Grand Union Canal, before becoming a swimming-and-boating day resort in the thirties. It had declined since its heyday, but still had a sandy beach, children's playground, pub/restaurant and mini-ature railway. The woods came down to it for three quarters of its circumference. They were popular with ramblers, dog walkers and horse riders, so they were not exactly unfre-quented, but they covered several hundred acres, so could still be reckoned a good place to abandon a body if you got off the main paths. Slider anticipated a long trek from the car park. Still, it had been freezing cold for so long – he'd lost count now how long, but weeks, anyway – the ground at least would not be muddy.

There had been a frost in the night, such a stiff one it was lying along the branches like snow, half an inch deep; roofs were white with it, and in the fields every stem of grass was outlined and rigid like the blade of a Zulu spear. The woods looked beautiful as the sun reluctantly rose for its low-slung hibernal trajectory across the sky, sparkling and tinged with pink.

The hard winter had taken its toll on the road surfaces, and in Reservoir Road, the approach to the Lido, there were potholes you could find lost tribes in. Slider bumped and manoeuvred his way carefully down to the car park. Despite the early hour, there was quite a crowd there already. Some, all, or more of the people they had spoken to yesterday must have contacted the press, because they were out in force; and the residents of surrounding streets had followed the flashing blue lights for a good morning gawp. It was only lucky it was Monday and a school day, or there'd have been no getting through them.

Barriers were in place and the car park was being kept clear for the police and associated vehicles. Two local bobbies were manning the access, and Slider had to tell them who he was. Ruislip fell within Hillingdon, a different part of the Met altogether.

But Porson was there – good grief, did the man never sleep? – gaunt as the first Duke of Lancaster, swathed in his Douglas Hurd-style greenish greatcoat, the folds of which were so voluminous a Bedouin could have kept his entire family in there, and several of his favourite horses as well. He was talking to his Hillingdon counterpart, Det Sup Fox, known down the ranks as Duggie. Slider had thought for a long time his name must be Douglas, but in fact it was Clifford. But Fox was a very large man in all respects and had, apparently, noteworthy man-breasts.

He also had the coldest eyes Slider had ever encountered. Slider could feel the frost creeping across his skin as the chilly grey orbs took him in, analysed him and filed him, probably under No Action Required. The Syrup swung round to see who was being freeze-dried, and his eyebrows went up in a greeting that was effusive by comparison.

'Ah, there you are. I've just been telling Mr Fox that you know this area like the back of your onions.'

Fox looked pained. Not everyone could cope with Porson on an empty stomach.

'He's very kindly going to hand the case over to us.'

'Very kind, sir,' Slider said with an irony so deep Beebe couldn't have reached it.

'We've got more than enough on our hands as it is,' Fox said – though, given that Heathrow Airport was in his ground, that was probably no more than the truth. And then, perhaps feeling he had been ungracious, he said, 'After all, you've done the preliminary work, and the investigation will mostly fall in your ground – tracing the last movements and so on. Makes sense for you to handle it. We'll hand over as soon as you've got enough men here. Of course, Fred,' he added to Porson, 'we'll give you any help we can. Can't promise you any warm bodies, I'm sorry to say.' He looked about as sorry as a lottery winner. 'But smoothing the path, local knowledge and suchlike. Just ask. But as you say, your man here knows the ground . . .'

'We'll manage. Thanks, Cliff. Appreciate your corroporation,' Porson said with dignity.

Slider left the mighty to confer at their exalted level, and went to find someone lowly to talk to. He spotted one of his own, DC McLaren, on the far side, nearest the woods, conferring with a Hillingdon detective, Pete Remington. He headed that way. There was something odd about McLaren that he couldn't put his finger on. Also he would have wondered how McLaren had got here first, given that he didn't live out this way, but he had other things on his mind.

In response to his terse question, McLaren filled him in. 'She's in there, guv.' He nodded towards the woods behind him. 'Not far in, but off the path. Fully dressed, shoes and all.' Shoes often went missing when a body was moved. 'Looks like she was whacked on the head and strangled.'

'Who found her?'

'Local man, sir,' Remington answered. 'Name of William

McGuire. Walking his dog early this morning – dog led him to her.' It was funny – or perhaps not – how often this was the case. Without dog walkers, Slider wondered, how many bodies would remain undiscovered? 'He lives in Lakeside Close,' Remington went on. This was one of the little cul-de-sacs off Reservoir Road. 'He was very shaken up. As it was close by, we sent him home with one of our uniforms – Patsy Raymond. No sense keeping him standing here in the cold.'

'Quite right,' Slider said. 'I'll talk to him later. I'd like to see the body first.'

'We had the photo you sent out,' Remington said, 'and there's no doubt it is her. That's why we got right on to you.' He cleared his throat. 'Sorry it turned out this way,' he offered. 'It's always a bugger when a young woman goes missing, but you always hope . . . Well, anyway.'

Slider nodded to the unexpected sympathy, saw Remington look at something over his shoulder, and turned to see the firm's wheels, Freddie Cameron's Jaguar, and Atherton's car bumping into the car park in careful convoy. And a short way behind them, even more welcomely, the tea waggon. Someone early on the site must have sent out the 'teapot one' call sign as a first priority. Slider had left breakfastless, and last night's supper had not had much staying power: the sight gave him the first comfort of that cold morning. And it made him realize what it was that had been odd about the look of McLaren: for perhaps the first time in his life, he wasn't engaged in eating anything.

She was lying on her back in the litter of dead leaves and other natural debris, half under a bush a short distance from the path. It looked as if some attempt had been made to hide the body, but not much of one. As soon as anyone strayed this way – as they well might if their dog suddenly dashed off excitedly – they would have seen it: it wasn't covered in any way. Was the murderer scared off, or had he sickened of the whole business by then? He could have gone a lot further from the car park and done a lot more concealing. For the matter of that, there were other woods in the general area that were more dense and less frequented – though on the other hand, they didn't all have easily accessed car-parks. If you were shifting a body by car, that was a consideration. Of course, she may have walked into the woods on her own two feet and been killed here. Probably that was more likely. If you were intending to hide a body, you would surely go a bit further from civilization.

She was dressed in a black skirt-suit over a sapphire blue jumper, and a thick grey wool reefer jacket; flat black shoes and opaque black tights. Because her clothes were all present and correct, it was unlikely she had been sexually assaulted: as the forensic pathologist, Freddie Cameron said, it would be a particularly obsessive and bonkers killer who would put his victim's clothes carefully back on after death. It was difficult, too – as with trying to get your tights back on in a swimming pool changing room. 'So I'm told,' he added hastily as Slider's eyebrow went up.

The strangling had been done with a silk scarf, presumably her own – it was Indian-patterned in shades of blue, purple and bottle-green – and the scarf was still in place round the neck, but there was no sign of the swelling or reddening that usually accompanied strangulation.

'A pretty half-hearted effort,' Freddie said, easing the silk away from the neck to look underneath. 'In fact, I'd say it was for show only. It's hardly marked the skin. It was the whack on the head that did for her, pound to a penny.'

Slider was grateful for any small mercies. When you've seen enough of them you can be objective about dead bodies, but you never stop *minding*. He was glad of a seemly corpse, quietly composed: her eyes were closed, her mouth just a little open, her head naturally over to one side; no signs of struggle or convulsion. One hand was resting on her chest, the other was down by her side; there were dead leaves in her hair, which was thick and heavy, and fell back from her face on to the moss beneath her head. He recognized the face from the photograph Swilley had brought back, but of course this was not Melanie Hunter, just the fleshly envelope that had once housed her. She had departed, permanently; how, was what he had to find out.

Freddie was demonstrating to him now the wound to the

skull, slipping his hand under the neck to turn the head with professional skill but still, somehow, a gentleness. 'See, here – the parietal bone is completely fractured, just above the junction with the occipital. I'd say just one blow, but a pretty hard one. Death would have been almost instantaneous.'

'So there wouldn't necessarily be much blood?' Slider said.

'Maybe, maybe not. Scalp wounds can bleed a lot in a short time. But there's nothing here, under the head, just a smear or two. Of course, the body must have been moved – she wouldn't have fallen on her back like this from a blow to the back of the skull – so there may well be some more blood somewhere else, either in the immediate area, if she was killed here, or wherever she was killed.'

'Or in the car that was used to move her,' Slider finished.

'Well, quite.'

'Time of death?'

Freddie pursed his lips. 'It's hard to say, in this cold weather. The cold tends to slow down the processes. There's still some rigor in the limbs, so perhaps less than three days. Between two and three days. You've got her disappearing when?'

'So far, the last she was seen was on Friday night.'

'Well, that would work. Friday night or early Saturday morning. But you know, old dear, that anything over eight hours and it's just guesswork.'

Slider nodded, and stared away through the trees, getting the lie of the place, the impression of light and shade, the undergrowth and open spaces. The forensic boys would do a fingertip search of the immediate area, in case something had been dropped or there were footmarks or fabric threads or anything that might identify the murderer. Why here? he was wondering. Why not further in? Perhaps she was too heavy to carry. She was not a tall girl, and was lightly built, but the dead weigh more than the living. Hard to tell in this sort of woodland if she was dragged. The ground was too hard to take impressions. It was horribly cold here, out of the little warmth the sun could give; numbingly cold. Slider could see his breath rising before him, and his fingers and the tip of his nose were aching.

Breaking his reverie, Atherton, beside him, said, 'It looks as if there's been some digging – just there.'

'Probably the finder's dog,' said Bob Bailey, the Crime Scene Manager.

'It's an animal, all right,' Freddie said. 'But I think it's more likely a fox. There's some damage to the fingers of this hand.' He raised the hand that was lying among the leaves by her side. 'A bit of gnawing's gone on. I suppose it was too cold and hard actually to remove them. And the left ear's been bitten, too, the one that was nearer the ground – though those teeth are smaller. Too small for a dog or fox. Stoat, maybe.'

Slider heard their voices as if at a distance, echoing a little in the empty woodland air. Further off he could hear a murmur of talk from the people gathered in and around the car park; far away, in the country quiet, a crow was yarking monotonously. And the dogs shall eat her in the portion of Jezreel, he thought. An undeserved fate – but wasn't it always? Otherwise it wouldn't be murder.

'Well?' said Atherton as they made their way back over the safe-route boards. 'What do you make of it?'

'Nothing, yet,' Slider said. 'Just the usual questions. Why her? Why here?'

'There is one thing that leaps to mind.'

Slider frowned at him. 'You couldn't make it leap a bit higher, I suppose?'

'One blow to the head – the same way Ronnie Fitton killed his wife.'

Slider sighed. 'Well, I suppose he's got to look like a tasty suspect. Certainly the press will see it that way as soon as they find out who he is. But what reason would he have to kill her? The only person he's ever killed is his wife.'

'Sexual jealousy,' Atherton said. 'The strongest motive of all. He could have been brooding about her for years, while she's been going out with Hibbert, who is not worthy of her.'

Slider shook his head. 'Then he'd kill Hibbert, surely.'

'No, no. He'd make sure of his Precious – put her beyond the greasy Hibbertian fingers for ever.'

'You're not serious.'

'On sheer propinquity alone,' Atherton said.

'Hibbert propinks just as well.'

'If not more so,' Atherton admitted. 'What now?'

'We go and talk to the bod who found her. By the way,' he added, as they crossed the car park and the tea van reminded him, 'what's wrong with McLaren? When I got here this morning, he wasn't eating anything.'

'I noticed that,' Atherton said. 'He has been off his nosebag, lately. And there are no food stains down his front – in fact, I think that's a new tie.'

'It's unsettling,' Slider said.

'You're right. I'll do a bit of detective work when I've got a minute.'

'We've more important things to do. Don't waste any time on it,' Slider cautioned.

'No, no,' Atherton reassured him. 'I'll take the short cut. I'll ask him.'

William McGuire lived in Lakeside Close, the fancifully-named cul-de-sac that led off Reservoir Road on the side further from the Lido, and was therefore not on the lake-side, even had the Lido been a lake. The house was a tiny little Victorian railway worker's terraced cottage, a typical two-up, two-down yellow-brick, slate-roofed doll's house that only a greedy developer could have thought worth splitting, and then only in a serious housing shortage. McGuire had the downstairs remnant, for which 'maisonette' was an over-generous description. It was a bed-sitting room opening straight off the street, with a kitchen at the back and a bath-room crammed between the two. The only advantage it boasted was the garden, twelve feet wide and fifteen feet long, but as McGuire was plainly no gardener, and it ended in a British Leyland hedge that had been allowed to grow to twelve feet high, it had nothing but underprivileged grass in it, and had no view but the tops of the trees in the woods behind.

It was the policewoman, Raymond, who opened the door to them, with a look of hope that quickly faded to disappointment. 'I hoped you were my replacement,' she said. 'I think they've forgotten all about me, sir.'

Slider thought it likely. Most of the Hillingdon contingent had gone by now. 'I'll get one of my own people in as soon as I've done here,' Slider reassured her.

'Thanks,' she said. 'He's in the kitchen. He hasn't been talking at all. I think he's really upset about it.'

The tiny cramped rooms were depressingly decorated in woodchip paper covered in historical layers of beige paint so they resembled congealed porridge, or a skin disease. There was cheap beige carpet on the floor, with stains that would have been of interest to an archaeologist, and the cheapest, nastiest furniture, the sort that shows the chipboard underneath when the veneer gets knocked off. The curtain over the front window was hanging by the last few hooks from a broken curtain rail, and the place smelled of dog, alcohol and feet in about equal proportions. It was, however, tidy, and the bathroom, as they passed it, looked clean, though shabby.

Slider had heard the dog barking ever since Raymond opened the door, and when he reached the kitchen door, it came bustling importantly towards him, stood its ground a foot away and barked officiously, woofing so hard it lifted its small body slightly off the ground at each explosion. It was a stout, short-legged Jack Russell type, mostly white, but with a few black patches, including one over one eye that gave it an unreliably jolly look.

The kitchen had cheap units painted yellow, a melamine table with two plastic chairs, lino on the floor, and a half-glazed door on to the garden. There were two empty mugs on the table, and McGuire was sitting in front of one of them, his elbow on the table and his head propped in his hand in an attitude almost of despair. The smell of booze was stronger still in here, easily beating feet and dog into second and third places: it was coming from McGuire, reeking from his pores so you could almost see it. He had evidently tied one on last night.

'Mr McGuire?' Slider said politely, when he was sure the dog was not going to do more than mouth off. 'I'm Detective Inspector Slider and this is Detective Sergeant Atherton.'

The man finally looked up, tilting red and doleful eyes that wouldn't have been out of place on a basset hound in his direction. His nose and cheeks were rife with the broken veins of the boozer, and he looked haggard with emotion at the moment, but otherwise it was not an unhealthy face. He was brown with the settled tan of someone who works out of doors; his hair was thick and light brown, going grey; his body was sturdy and his hands looked strong, though seamed with manual work. The most surprising thing about him was the beard. There were not so many men these days who wore beards; and this was not one of those little dabs here and there such as young men sometimes affected, but the full Captain Haddock, thick and bushy and a darker shade of brown than his hair. While trying not to be pognophobic, Slider instinctively distrusted beards, on the basis that a man could change his appearance so completely by growing one or shaving it off, he might become unrecognizable. In his business, you needed to know who you were dealing with.

'I'd just like to ask you a few questions, if that's all right,' he went on, when it seemed that McGuire was not going to volunteer anything. 'About what happened this morning.'

At once, large tears formed in the basset brown eyes and rolled over, but McGuire roused himself enough to wipe at them almost angrily with the back of his hand, and to say sharply, 'Toby, *shut up!*'

An astonishing silence fell. The little dog looked at him, and then almost with a shrug turned and pottered away, hopping through the dog door into the garden with a familiar flip-flap sound.

McGuire got out a large handkerchief, blew his nose and wiped his eyes. There was something about the weariness of the action that suggested he had been blowing and wiping for some time. 'Would you like another cup of tea?' Slider suggested in sympathy.

'Yeah – thanks,' he said. He made no move to get up, though, and Slider looked at Raymond and jerked his head towards the kettle.

'I'll make it,' she said obediently. 'What about you, sir?'

'Yes, thanks, No sugar.'

Atherton declined. Slider took the other seat at the table, so Atherton lounged gracefully in the doorway, trying not to look threatening – there simply wasn't any other place he could be. As it was, Raymond had to ooze past him to get to the kettle. The dog came flip-flapping back in, stared at them all a moment in case there was any more barking that needed doing, then went to his basket in the corner, turned round three times and flopped down, chin on paws.

When Raymond put the mugs on the table, McGuire roused himself to say, 'Thanks,' and felt in his jacket pocket and brought out a pill bottle. 'Aspirin,' he said, seeing Slider's look. 'Got a rotten headache.' He unscrewed the bottle one-handed and slid two into his palm, tossed them into his mouth, re-lidded the bottle and holstered it like a fancy gunslinger displaying his dexterity. Again, seeing Slider watching, he said, 'Had a bit to drink last night.' He shrugged. 'I suppose you guessed that.' Slider nodded, and it seemed to touch some pride in him. He straightened a little in the chair and said, 'I only drink at the weekends. That's my prerogative, right? I don't let it interfere with work.' And almost immediately the expression of despair returned to his face and he slumped again by the inches he had pulled back.

'What job do you do?' Slider asked him.

'I work for the council. Parks and Gardens department. Mowing, cutting, pruning, planting – you name it. You can ask them – I've got a good employment record. Two years with never a day off.'

'I'm sure you have,' Slider said. 'You look well on it.' He could imagine the lonely-man regime, working off by physical exertion through the week the booze taken on board at week-ends. Though if he didn't let it interfere with work, how come he was boozing on a Sunday night? Friday and Saturday ought to be his drinking nights.

'I keep all right,' McGuire admitted.

'And I expect Toby gives you plenty of exercise,' Slider suggested pleasantly, edging him back closer to the point. 'I expect you try to give him a walk every morning before work?'

'He comes to work with me,' McGuire said. 'That's one of

the good things about the job. But it isn't the same as a walk. A dog needs a couple of good walks a day, never mind what else he's doing.'

'Well, you're living in the right place for it,' Slider said. 'Lots of good walks round here. Tell me about this morning. Was it your usual routine?'

The brown eyes moved away and he frowned, remembering. 'Yeah. I was up at six, same as usual. Got ready for work.' He was dressed in a battered tweed jacket, tough-looking cords and work boots scarred and stained with ancient mud – his work clothes, presumably. 'Took Toby out. Went through the car park into the woods.'

'Do you always go the same way?'

'Nah, different every day. Just as the fancy takes us.'

'And that would be – what time?'

'About half past, give or take. Time I'd washed and had a cup of tea and a bit of toast.'

'Go on.'

He shrugged. 'Not much to tell. Just walking through the woods when suddenly Toby goes stiff all over, like he's seen something. I thought it was a squirrel – he likes to chase 'em. Then he goes off to one side, growling, his whiskers sticking out and his hair all on end. It wasn't like him, usually, so I followed. And there—' He swallowed. 'There she was.' The tears welled up again effortlessly. 'That poor girl,' he said in broken tones. 'Who would do such a thing? That poor—' His face was quivering. He dragged out the handkerchief, blew and wiped and regained control. 'Have you found out who she is?' he asked from behind it.

'Yes, we know who she is,' Slider said.

'Her parents – they must be going mad, wondering. If she was my kid . . . Have you told them?'

'Someone will be with them now,' Slider said. It was usual to send a uniform round with the news – more official and reassuring than plain clothes, so was the thinking.

McGuire shook his head. 'I'll never get over seeing her there like that. I'm just – I can't get my head round it.'

'I know,' Slider said. 'Just tell me what you did. Did you touch her or move her in any way?'

'No, of course not,' he said quite sharply. 'I know better than that.'

'Not even to check if she was dead?'

'Didn't need to. I could see she was. I just grabbed Toby and came back here to phone the police.'

'Did Toby touch the body?'

'No, he wouldn't go near it, just stood growling and whining. He was upset. See him now, sleeping – that's not like him, this time of day. Normally he'd be raring to go. I suppose dogs can feel shock, same as us.'

'So you didn't recognize the girl?' Slider pursued.

'Course not. Why should I?' he said sharply.

'No reason. I just thought you might have seen her walking round here before. A lot of people come here for walks, don't they?'

He seemed disconcerted by the question. 'She wasn't dressed for walking,' he said in the end.

'So you've never seen her before?'

'I said so, didn't I?'

'And have you seen or heard anything suspicious, the last two or three nights? Cars coming down here late at night, for instance, or anyone acting strangely.'

'There's people coming down here all the time,' he said. 'I wouldn't notice anyone, particularly.'

'But movement or noises in the middle of the night?'

He shook his head.

'Were you at home Friday and Saturday nights, and last night?'

'I was out Friday night,' he said. 'I went down the pub.'

'Which pub?'

'The Bells.'

That was the Six Bells on Duck's Hill Road, the nearest – in fact, only just round the corner.

'And Saturday night and last night?'

'I stayed in,' he said, and added, as if as an afterthought: 'It's cheaper.'

Atherton made a restless movement behind him, and Slider agreed – there was nothing for them here. Most people didn't notice cars going past, whatever the hour, and would probably only notice someone shifting a dead body if they attempted to bring it into their own front room. He drank off his tea, and stood up. 'Well, thank you, Mr McGuire. If you do remember anything that might help us, anything at all, please give us a ring.'

McGuire stood up too, looking at Slider with a desperate sort of appeal in his eyes, as if begging not to be left alone with his memories. 'She – that girl—?' Slider paused receptively, but all he said was, 'Do you think she suffered?'

Of course she suffered – she was murdered, Slider's brain shouted impatiently. *What do you think?* But outwardly he showed nothing, and seeing the man's haunted eyes, he did the best he could for him. 'We believe death was almost instantaneous,' he said. Between the 'almost' and the 'instantaneous' lay the cavern full of horror, but there was nothing he could do about that. And perhaps McGuire, hung-over as he was, wouldn't notice.

At the street door, Atherton said, 'Well, that was fun.'

'You have to go through the motions. But the chances of him knowing anything, given that she'd probably been there two days, were slim.'

'It amazes me that no one found her before. Unless she was hidden somewhere else and then moved last night.'

'Thanks, we don't need any more intriguing possibilities.'

'So – what now?'

'Back to the factory, start tracing her last movements,' Slider said. 'Until and unless Freddie comes up with anything different, we'll assume she was killed on Friday night and taken straight to the woods. You have to start somewhere.'

Raymond had followed them to the door and, blinking in the sunlight, said, 'What about me, sir?'

'As far as I'm concerned, you can leave him now. I don't think he has anything more to tell us. Why don't you radio in and ask your skipper?'

'Right, sir, thanks.' She glanced over her shoulder. 'Maybe I should check if he's got someone he can call to come over. He's really upset.'

'That's a kind thought,' Slider said, and left her to it with a faint and guilty feeling of relief that it was someone else's problem. McGuire didn't strike him as the sort of person who had either friends or relations. 'But he's got Toby,' he said aloud as they headed back towards the car park. 'Man's best friend.'

FOUR

I Only Have Pies For You

Kiera Williams, the Best Friend – these days the title tended to come with capitals – was a tall, eager-looking young woman with thick, curly brown hair and a wide mouth made for smiles. She reminded Slider – and he meant nothing insulting by it – of a nice, big dog. She was at the moment, however, more bewildered than smiling. He had noticed before that in the early period after learning about a death, people often did not know what they ought to be feeling, and were puzzled by their apparent failure to conform to any predigested norm.

'I just can't take it in,' she confessed. 'It doesn't seem real.'

Slider nodded. 'The realization comes later.'

'Does it? I suppose you'd know. You must have gone through this so many times. But I've never known anyone who got murdered before. And Melanie, of all people! I mean, who would want to hurt her?'

'That's what we hope to find out,' he said.

She frowned and recrossed her legs. She was wearing a very smart dark-green calf-length skirt over long boots, and a chunky dark-brown crew-neck sweater. Her creamy, lightly-freckled face was carefully made up, but she still did not manage to look entirely like a grown-up. It was the wideness of her eyes and the unstudied expressions of her face, he decided, that made her seem younger than her years. She had not adopted that unlovely cynicism and world-weariness that was currently fashionable.

She had come direct from work, having set off that morning before the news broke generally: now it was on the rolling TV news and all over the Internet. Who needed newspapers any more? He had had her brought up to his office – no need to subject her to the horrors of the interview rooms – and provided her with good coffee from Atherton's filter machine next door. Despite the situation, she had been looking around with noticing interest ever since she arrived, and he liked her for it. Improving the shining hour was something he was always urging on his children.

'So, tell me about Melanie,' he said. 'You've known her a long time?'

'We grew up together, in Northwood – practically next-door neighbours. We lived in Chester Road and they lived round the corner in Hallowell Road, so we were in and out of each other's houses. And we went to the same school,' she said. 'St Helen's. We were scholarship girls.' She made an equivocal face – an automatic apology for being bright. 'We both did maths and sciences, so we were outcasts anyway – I suppose that's what kept us close. We were the Geeks, and that was before there was any Geek Chic, like now – when it was still an insult.' He smiled, and she responded with a glimmer of her own that hinted at what she could do if she really gave it everything. 'Then we both went to London University, though not to the same college. She went to Imperial and I went to UCL. But we shared a flat, with some other girls at first and then just the two of us, until we graduated. Then she went to the Natural History Museum and I started working for Shell – I'm in data analysis. They're on the South Bank, so it wasn't really convenient any more to share. But we've always stayed friends. We talk to each other every week on the phone, and meet up whenever we can, and—' She stopped, thrown off balance by the present tense.

'It takes time to come to terms with it,' he said, answering the appeal in her eyes.

'I'll never see her again,' she said. 'I can't believe it.'

'Don't try. It'll come in its own time. Did you have any brothers or sisters of your own?'

She took the question like medicine, knowing it was good for her. Talking stopped her thinking. 'No, I was an only child as well. I suppose that was another reason we were close.'

'You must have been a great comfort to her, when her father died.'

'Oh, God, that was terrible. We were just fourteen, fifteen,

when the train crash happened. That's a hard time anyway,
for a girl. And then, you couldn't get away from it. It was
everywhere, the same pictures over and over again, in the
papers, on the television, as if they were *trying* to make it
worse, as if they were gloating. I hated them then – the media.
But Mel was wonderful. I'd have been totally trashed, but
somehow she held it together. I think she, like, pushed a lot
of it down inside, bottled it up. You see, her mum was no use
to her – she just went to pieces, and Mel had to comfort *her*,
instead of the other way round. And she'd always loved her
dad so much, in spite of everything.' She paused, looking
carefully at Slider.

'Go on,' he said.

'Well, the thing is – I don't want to speak ill of the dead
– but her dad was never a very satisfactory person. He never
had a steady job, and he was always having these mad ideas
that were going to make a fortune, but they never did, they
just left them broke again. Like the time he went in for
ostriches: ostrich meat was going to be the next big thing, but
of course it all fell through – after he'd put all their savings
into it. And then another time he invested everything in this
camel farm. This man convinced him there was going to be
a market for camel's milk and yoghurt and stuff. They were
going to call it the Dromedairy.'

Slider saw it was all right to smile, and she smiled too,
ruefully, and shook her head.

'He was always looking for the easy way out, the money
for nothing, and of course what they always ended up with
was the nothing. Mel never had any nice clothes – everything
was second-hand. Mrs Hunter had to work, and they lived
most of the time on what she could earn, which wasn't much.
She used to do those Tupperware parties for extra cash. Mel
always felt ashamed about that. I told her it was silly, that
there was nothing wrong with it, but she couldn't help it. But
through all that, she still loved him. He was one of those
charming losers, you know?'

Slider nodded.

'I was mad about him too, when I was a kid. He used to
take Mel and me out for these Saturday outings – our Adventure

Days, he used to call them. The Round Pond, the Kensington Museums, art galleries, Trafalgar Square, the Lido in summer, or the Serpentine – anything that didn't cost anything. Sometimes it was just a ride on the top of a bus – we'd sit in the front seat and pretend to be the driver, and he'd tell us stories and we'd sing songs together. Whatever it was, it was always fun. He was always smiling and jolly, and telling jokes, and he could do conjuring tricks – you know, finding a coin behind your ear, that sort of thing? – so he didn't really seem like a grown-up at all, not like my dad, who was really boring. But then when I got older I could see the difference between my dad, who went to work every day without complaining and kept us properly, and Mr Hunter, who was lovely but always letting people down. Mel saw it too, but she couldn't help loving him. Well, he was her dad,' she concluded simply.

'So it must have been devastating when he died,' Slider said, to keep her going.

'Yes. He was on his way down to Devon or Somerset or somewhere to "see a man" about some new scheme that was going to make him rich. No surprises there. He was always going to "see a man" and it was always going make a fortune. But then the train crashed and all those people were killed, and one of them was Melanie's dad. It was awful.' She looked down at her hands, frowning at the memory. 'Then a year later, her mum married Ian. I suppose she just couldn't cope on her own. He was a widower – his wife had died suddenly, and he had a baby daughter, so it made sense for him. He was very different, though – a teacher. You couldn't get any more respectable and steady than that, could you?'

'You didn't like him?' Slider hazarded.

'Oh, he was all right, just a bit strict and churchy and – you know, by the book. Not like Mel's dad. Not that I had much to do with him – just about then, for some reason or other, I didn't see so much of Mel. I don't know if he was stopping her going out or something, but I never seemed to see her outside of school, and in school she was sort of quiet and – moody maybe. I suppose it was a bit of an adjustment for her, a new stepdad and everything. But she settled down in the end. After a few months she was back to normal – not like before her dad died, exactly, but normal for like she's been ever since. Well, we were just about to go to university, so that made it easy. We got into a flat share and Mel left home, and Ian and Mel's mum moved to Ealing, to be nearer his school. So he and Mel never had to live together after that, which probably made it easier. Mel's mum always said he wasn't meant to be a father to Mel, just her husband. She told Mel no one expected her to call him "Dad", and she never did.'

'And then there was Scott,' Slider suggested.

She made a face, and then put her hand over her mouth apologetically. 'Oh, I shouldn't say anything. He's all right, really. And Melanie's mad about him.'

'Is he mad about her?'

'Well, they're all over each other. Very lovey-dovey. They're living together now, and he's talking about marriage and everything.'

'What don't you like about him?'

She seemed alarmed. 'I didn't say I didn't like him. He's perfectly all right. My goodness, some of my friends go out with real horrors! I just don't think he's good enough for her – but she's my Best Friend since forever, so I don't expect I'd think anyone was good enough for her.' She smiled disarmingly. 'I think he's a bit dull, that's all. But if it's what she wants – after all, she had a bellyful of a lovely, fun man who was no good as a husband when she was a kid. I expect she wants reliability now, above anything.' She stopped herself again, and looked dismayed. 'I forgot again. How could I forget?' She looked at him appealingly. 'How long does this go on? It's not *real*!'

'Give yourself a chance,' he said kindly. 'It's all very new to you. Tell me about Friday.'

She pulled herself together visibly. 'It was my birthday drinks. We always do that on each other's birthdays. I was twenty-seven on Friday.' She shook her head in wonder at the thought. 'Melanie's six months younger than me, she's still only twenty-six. She always rags me about that, calls me old lady and gran and so on. Anyway, she arranged for half a dozen of us to meet at the Princess Victoria for drinks and a meal.'

'Isn't that a bit far from home for you? I'd have thought you'd meet half way.'

'Sometimes we did, but my mum's not been well so I said I'd go and spend the weekend with her afterwards. She still lives in Northwood. And two of the other girls come from out that way, and one of them, Rebecca, doesn't drink, so she said she'd drive us back straight from the pub. It was a bit of a waste, really, with Scott being away – Melanie and I could have had a nice long time together – but we've got some other things planned so it didn't matter too much. I mean, we *had*,' she finished dolefully.

'How was she that evening? Was she in normal spirits?'

'Oh, yes, she was in great form. We had a laugh.'

'She didn't have anything on her mind at all? Wasn't worried about anything?'

'Not that she mentioned.'

'Everything all right with Scott?'

Her eyebrows went up. 'Oh, I see what you're after. She said she was feeling a bit guilty because she'd been crabby with him earlier. Did you know about that?'

'Yes, I heard it from Scott. About the wedding.'

'Right. He's got these very thick friends he likes to hang out with. But it was nothing. She'd sort of snapped at him, and then she was sorry. It happens.' She shrugged. 'Anyway, he called her during the evening, and they were all lovey-dovey again, so that was all right. She and Scott were fine, really. You weren't thinking . . .?' She looked alarmed.

'I'm not thinking anything yet. Just trying to assemble a picture for myself. So were you all together at the pub the whole evening?'

'Yes. We met up between half past seven and eight, had some food and some bottles of wine, and we stayed until about ten.'

'That seems early. It wasn't as if it was a work night.' Slider put a question mark at the end, and she nodded.

'I suppose it was, but Mel – well.' She looked awkward, and lowered her voice. 'She'd got the curse and she wasn't feeling all that brilliant. That's probably why she snapped at Scott earlier. Anyway, about ten-ish she said she was all in and apologized and said she wanted to go, so that broke up the party really.'

'You wouldn't go on without her?'

She smiled faintly. 'That's the sort of person she is. If she leaves, it all goes flat. She's just – I don't know. If I say "the heart and soul of the party" it makes it sound as if she's loud, but she isn't a bit. She's just nice, and kind, and good, and everybody loves her, and everybody wants to be with her, and – well, if you were having a party, you'd find out what date she could make first, before you asked anyone else.'

'I understand. So she didn't talk about anything in particular that evening? Any concerns she had, or plans? Anything different in her life, any changes ahead?'

'Nothing at all. It was just the usual chat.'

'Did she say what she was doing the rest of the weekend?'

'She was going to veg out on Saturday – you know, get up late, do the laundry, get a takeaway and watch a movie. That was all she felt like. And Sunday she said she had some work she had to catch up on. Stuff for the museum. She wanted to get it done before Scott got back Sunday evening, while it was quiet.'

'And did anyone else ring her during the evening?'

She frowned. 'I don't know. Everybody's on the phone all the time these days, I probably wouldn't notice. I only know about Scott because I was sitting next to her and talking to her when he rang, so he interrupted me. And of course I heard her side of it, so I knew they'd made up and everything.'

'Weren't you sitting next to her the whole time?'

'No, we moved about and changed seats a bit. So she might have had other calls, I just wouldn't notice.' She looked at him. 'So you've no idea who did this? None at all?'

The usual thing was to say 'we're following up various lines of investigation', but meeting the clear gaze in the young, freckled face, he couldn't prevaricate. 'Not yet.'

'But she wasn't attacked on the way home? Didn't it say on the news she went home from the Vic all right, and then disappeared?'

'So it seems.'

'But I don't understand – why didn't Scott know she was

missing? They were always talking to each other on the phone. They were like two little lovebirds. If she didn't answer the phone, he'd surely think something was wrong.'

It was a good question, Slider thought when she was gone. There was definitely something about Mr Hibbert that invited investigation; but everything in its time.

Fred 'The Syrup' Porson might have had the looks and charm of a bunion, but he had still managed to beguile Duggie Fox into lending him enough uniforms to do the immediate house-to-house canvass. Of course, this only involved the lightly-housed Reservoir Road and the three small culs-de-sac that led off it, so it wasn't in the order of a lifetime commitment; but Slider gave his boss all credit for extracting anything at all from a man whose attitude towards beneficence resembled that of the proverbial duck's rectum to pond water.

It meant that most of Slider's firm had drifted home by the time he held the first meeting: Mackay and Fathom were still at the house. McLaren and Connolly had done a forage stop on the way back, at the stall on the corner of the market, where they not only did sausage sandwiches and bacon sandwiches, but also a home-made meat pie specifically designed to be eaten on the move without spilling anything down the front – a masterpiece of pastry engineering, very popular with lorry drivers. Connolly had brought a sandwich for Slider – 'Sausage, guv. Wasn't it rashers last time? And I remembered the tomato sauce!' – and he scoffed it in huge bites before going out into the squad room. It was all very well for him to wave a benevolent hand and say, 'Carry on eating,' to the troops, but he had his dignity to maintain.

At the last minute, Porson oozed in, carrying a cup of tea with the saucer on top as a lid, on which reposed two custard creams. He raised an eyebrow at the general noshing that was going on – and his eyebrows were so large and bushy, it was not a negligible gesture, something akin to the raising of Tower Bridge – but he only said, 'Late lunch? Keep it off the papers, that's all!'

Slider gave him a distracted look, having to tear his attention from the fact that McLaren – the man who *knew* the answer to the question 'who ate all the pies?' – had empty hands and an empty mouth, and was gazing off into space with a sappy look of contentment on his face.

Porson perched on a desk off to the side, gently eased his cup on to its saucer, nudging the biscuits along to make room, and barked, 'Right!'

Slider snapped back to attention as DS Hollis, the beanpole Mancunian who was always office manager in these cases, began. 'The murder of Melanie Hunter, age twenty-six. She was found around six thirty this morning in the woods by Ruislip Lido. We are assuming, for lack of any evidence to the contrary, that she was killed some time on Friday night, after ten thirty when she's last known to have come home from a night out.'

'But it's possible, isn't it, that she was abducted first, and held somewhere, and killed later – say on Saturday night?' said Atherton.

'Possible,' Slider said, 'though there were no visible marks of violence or restraint on the body. It's hard to hold someone against their will without marking them.'

'Doesn't that suggest she left the flat of her own free will – whatever time it was?' Swilley asked.

'You can be abducted,' Atherton returned, 'by wiles and beguilement. I was only meaning to point out that we don't know she was killed on Friday night.'

'And I was only meaning it was likely someone she knew,' said Swilley. 'It usually is.'

There was always a bit of tension between those two, but sometimes it could be productive, so usually Slider left them to get on with it. He nodded to Hollis to carry on.

'Death was apparently caused by a blow to the back of the head, but there wasn't a lot o' blood at the site, so she may have been killed elsewhere and the body taken to the woods to hide it.' He looked up. 'Might've been killed at the flat, maybe?'

'There was no sign of disturbance when we went in,' Atherton said. 'So unless the murderer was very thorough at cleaning up . . .?'

'We've got a forensic team in there now,' Slider said. 'If

there's any blood, they'll find it. It's not easy to carry a body downstairs and get it into a car without making a noise, and without anyone seeing anything. But that's the next thing on the list – canvass the other residents of the house, and the immediate neighbours.'

'If she was killed at the flat, you're thinking it was the boyfriend that did it?' Swilley said.

'He wasn't even in London,' Atherton objected.

'So he *says*.'

'He was at a wedding. Hundreds of witnesses. You can't fake that.'

'That is something we'll have to check on,' Slider said.

Hollis made a note. 'Hibbert alibi.'

'Add "Hibbert motive" while you're at it,' said Atherton.

'It's not just him,' Connolly put in. 'So far everybody loved her. She was so nice she'd get on your nerves.'

'It needn't be Hibbert, even if she was killed at the flat,' Atherton said. 'Could be someone she invited in. Or someone who followed her home.'

'McLaren's been looking into her route home,' Slider said.

Connolly jabbed an elbow into McLaren, who returned to earth with a bump. 'Yeah,' he said, 'there's a street camera right opposite the Princess Vic that's got her coming out eight minutes past ten. You can see it's her clear enough. Then she turns down Becklow Road, where she's parked the car. You can see her get in and drive off, towards Askew Road, the way she was facing.'

'But if she didn't get home until nearly half ten,' Connolly said, 'that's too much time. Sure, it's only five minutes – ten at most – in the car.'

'She must have stopped somewhere,' Swilley said.

McLaren was nodding. 'I was gonna say, there's a camera at the Seven Stars, and that's the way she'd come, if she was going straight home. She'd go down Becklow, left into Askew, left at the Seven Stars on to Goldhawk, left into Cathnor, bosh. But she never appears out of Askew Road. I went all the way up to midnight.'

'So either she went all through the back streets to get home, which is daft,' said Hollis.

'Or she doubled back and went home the Uxbridge Road way,' said Swilley.

'But why would she?' said McLaren.

'Maybe she thought of something she wanted on the way home from the shops on Uxbridge Road,' Swilley said. 'There's a couple of late-nighters along there.'

'Like what?' McLaren demanded.

'Tampax,' Swilley suggested, to embarrass him, but it was Hollis who blushed.

'Or maybe she went somewhere else completely,' said McLaren.

'She couldn't have gone anywhere much if she was back home by half past.'

'She could have picked someone up and taken them home with her,' said Atherton. 'Fitton didn't see her go in, only heard the car, so she could have had someone with her.'

'And then later she could have offered to drive them home,' McLaren said excitedly, seeing a possibility.

'She left her handbag behind, you plank,' said Connolly.

'If it wasn't far, she might just've grabbed her keys,' he defended himself. 'If she wasn't gonna be long.'

'And the murderer returned her car afterwards and put the car keys back in her handbag?' Atherton said witheringly.

But Swilley repeated his words in an entirely different voice. 'And the murderer returned her *car*, and put the *keys* back in her *handbag*! That solves all the problems!'

'Except that the dog didn't bark when the murderer let himself in at some unearthly hour, with her blood on his hands?' Atherton countered.

'I'm about sick of that dog not barking,' Porson said, making them all jump, because they'd forgotten he was there. 'This is not a bloody Shylock Holmes story. You're all forgetting one thing: we've only got Ronnie Fitton's word for it that she got home by ten thirty. Or at all.'

It gave them pause. Slider had had that possibility in the back of his mind all along, but he had been hoping not to have to look at it, because if Fitton had no alibi, there was no reason he should have, which was the worst of cases to prove. He knew the victim and had the key to her house, and he knew the dog. But he'd had two days to cover his tracks, if tracks there were, so how would they ever catch him out?

'If the victim's car was used, that meant it left the space in front of Fitton's window and returned there without him hearing anything,' he said.

'Or he's lying about not hearing anything,' Porson concluded.

Slider caught Connolly's eye, and a sympathy flashed between them. He could see she didn't want it to be Fitton either, though presumably for different reasons. 'Why would Fitton kill her?' she said. 'He liked her.'

'Maybe he liked her too much,' said Atherton.

'Well, there's got to be a car in it somewhere,' said Slider. 'She didn't walk to Ruislip. We'll take hers in, check it for traces. We'll have to canvass the immediate area, Cathnor Road and Goldhawk to either side of the turning, see if anyone saw anything. Interview the people upstairs – they may know something, or have heard something. Any cars in the area behaving suspiciously – check any possible route from Cathnor Road to the Lido for that. And McLaren, you carry on checking her route home – all the cameras there are, bus cameras, shops, private houses, the lot. And we'll have to get after the motive. We'll have to talk to her friends and family, find out who else was in her life recently, what she's been up to, who she knew.'

'There's one other thing no one's mentioned,' Porson said. They all looked at him. 'Stamford House.'

'What's that?' Connolly asked. She was fairly new to the area.

'It's a secure home for violent young offenders,' Slider said. 'Right next door to Cathnor Road.'

'Just over the wall from their back gardens, in fact,' Atherton expanded. 'They had a lot of trouble there a couple of years ago. Drugs, fights, breakouts. I thought they'd got it all under control again, though. I haven't heard of anyone getting out recently.'

'Doesn't mean somebody didn't get over the wall and back in before anyone noticed,' Hollis said.

Slider said, 'I'm reluctant to jump immediately into suspecting the obvious suspect—'

'Obvious is as obvious does,' Porson said obscurely.

'—but in any case, it doesn't fit in with the whole body-in-the-woods scenario. A violent random attacker would just leave the body where it was. And none of those kids would have a car.'

'Always steal one,' McLaren said with a shrug.

'Better look into it,' Porson said. 'Find out if any motors went missing from the area that night. And whether any of the YOs went AWOL. Best to leave no stone unthrown. You never know.'

Slider sighed. A tea urn had nothing on him. That was the trouble, he thought. Sometimes you never did.

By the next day the press had got hold of Ronnie Fitton's past history, and it was splashed all over everywhere, all the details of the murder of his wife, the court case and the sentence, with photographs from the time. By the time Slider got in to work, there had been telephone calls of complaint from the upstairs neighbours that the house was besieged by press and they couldn't get out. Uniforms had been dispatched to clear the access, but there was no way in law to stop reporters shouting questions at the residents as they hurried to their cars, or taking photos of them through the car windows as they backed out.

When Slider reached his room, the phone was ringing. It was Freddie Cameron. 'You'll get the full report in writing, of course, but I thought you'd like to know—'

'You've done the post-mortem?' Slider interrupted. He wasn't at his best until the first cup of tea hit his bloodstream.

'No, I've been using my magical powers to peer into the past,' Freddie said with patient irony.

'Sorry,' said Slider.

'Granted. I thought you'd like to know that death *was* caused by the blow to the head. A single blow of considerable force with a rigid object, probably metal, at least eight inches long, probably with squared edges.'

'Something like a large spanner?'

'That's possible. Unconsciousness would have been immediate and death probably followed within a very short time, a minute or two at the most. So there will be blood somewhere, but possibly not much of it.'

'And you've nothing more to say about the time of death?'

'Sorry, can't help you. But the hypostasis suggests that she was probably placed where you found her straight away. As you know, the livor mortis starts much sooner after death than the rigor – in as little as twenty minutes – and the staining is permanent. So we'd know if she'd been moved into a different position.'

'Right,' said Slider. 'But she could have been abducted first, and killed later than Friday night?'

'Except that there were no signs of her having been restrained or tied up, no marks of rough handling, and, as we guessed from the fact she was fully dressed, no sexual violence.'

'What about consensual sex?'

'Not recent,' Cameron said, and became extra dry. 'The subject was menstruating, old bean. That vacancy had been filled.'

That fitted with what Kiera had said. 'What about the ligature?' he asked.

'Ah yes, there was some bruising of the neck, but manually inflicted, and very superficial. I had to look hard for it. Someone might have gripped her and shaken her in a fit of pique, but without any intention to cause serious harm, or even as a joke, perhaps. The ligature was placed post-mortem.'

'Why on earth—?'

'That's your job, old thing, not mine,' said Cameron. 'Human nature's a mystery to me. It's the reason I became a pathologist – nice, quiet dead patients, no lawsuits.'

Slider was thinking. 'Perhaps the stomach contents can give us an idea of when she died?'

'I've secured them and sent them for analysis. And I've sent the blood for a tox screen, but there's no pathology to suggest drugs of any sort. And I've sent off the clothes. Apropos of which, they were pretty neat and tidy – again, no sign that she had been held anywhere, tied up in a dusty attic or crammed in a car boot. And she must have been carried, not dragged, after death.'

'Well, that all adds up to a mystery,' Slider said.

'It's the way you like 'em,' Cameron said cheerfully.

'I don't like 'em at all,' he said, 'but I still get 'em.'

His tea arrived, with Connolly on the other end of it.

'I've had Mr Fitton on the phone, guv, complaining that we ratted him out to the press,' she said. 'He says they're all round the house. I told him it wasn't us – it wasn't, was it?'

'Not officially. And I'm very down on leaks. But there must be a hundred people here and in Hillingdon who know about him being her neighbour. Any one of them could have spilled the beans, and there's no way to find out who.' He eyed her curiously. 'Are you feeling sorry for him?'

'Not him,' she denied hastily. 'The dog. He says to me, how can he take the dog out for its walks with them surrounding him every step, and he daren't shove 'em aside for fear they'll put a charge on him.'

'So he still has the dog?'

'Yeah, boss – he says your man Hibbert's never asked about it. Too heartbroken, maybe.' She hesitated.

'Yes? Out with it?'

'Well, guv, apparently the parents used to look after the dog when she went on holiday. So I thought, maybe if one of us was to go over to fetch it and take it to them . . .?'

'You're not a dog warden.'

'But it'd be a chance to have another go at Mr Fitton.'

'If I want to talk to Fitton I can have him brought in.'

'At least that'd give him a bit of peace and quiet,' Connolly grumbled. 'But, guv, if I did the dog thing first, it'd look friendly, not so official, and he might tell me things he wouldn't say in an interview room.'

Slider considered. 'I think you may be underestimating Fitton. Someone who's done fifteen years inside knows how to guard his tongue.'

'Then you'd never scare anything out of him, either,' she said reasonably. 'Might as well let me try charming it out, guv. What harm?'

Slider considered. 'D'you want to take someone with you?'

'Sure God, he'd never open up to me if I'd a minder with

me. And he'd have to be a mentaller to take a crack at me with all them peelers and the world's press outside.'

'Well, you can have a go,' Slider said, 'but don't get your hopes up too much.'

'OK, guv. At least it'll be a kindness for Marty.'

'Marty?'

'The dog.'

'Oh, yes.' Probably not for Fitton, though. As things stood, the dog was likely the only friend he had in the world. 'It'll be a good opportunity for talking to the parents, as well,' he said. 'I'd like to see them for myself. Pick me up when you've got the dog and we can go together.'

'Yes, guv,' she said, leaving Slider to wonder why she looked so pleased about it.

FIVE

All Mad Cons

When Ronnie Fitton let her into his flat, Connolly appreciated what Slider meant about him giving nothing away: there was no sign in his face or manner that the murder of the girl upstairs or his hounding by the pack outside had affected him at all. He did not look haggard or sleep deprived or worried or indignant. The only thing about him that was not blankness was that same glint of fire in his eyes that had made her nervous before. But he had let her in readily, and she did not believe he meant her harm.

She had telephoned ahead and explained the plan, and he had agreed, and he opened the door just enough for her to sidle in as soon as she knocked, while behind her the shutters shut and the questions snapped like mosquitoes, trying to get in before the door closed.

'Sorry about all that,' she said, gesturing over her shoulder. 'Mad bunch a gougers! It wasn't us, I swear.'

He shrugged. 'Bound to happen. Cup o' tea?'

It wasn't offered with any more enthusiasm than before, but this time she accepted, the better to get chatting to him. 'Ah, thanks. Me mouth's rough as a badger's arse.'

He went to put the kettle on. 'You're right about Marty though. It's no life for him here.'

The dog was lying on the floor between the bed and the bathroom door, where she had seen him last time, though now he had a folded blanket under him for comfort. 'He looks down in the mouth,' she said. He was chin-on-paws again, but this time did not look at her. He was staring at nothing, and when she crouched beside him and stroked his head, he did not even move his tail in token acknowledgement. 'Poor owl feller. Aren't you the heart-scald?'

'I think he knows she's gone,' Fitton said – surprising her, because it was a bit of a girl thing to say, really, for a man who'd survived fifteen years in the Scrubs. 'It'll be better for him out of here, at her mum's.'

'You'll miss him, though.'

He shrugged. 'Never had him more than a night at a time. He's not my dog.'

'I wonder you don't get one of your own, you like 'em so much,' Connolly said.

'Haven't got the time for one.' The kettle clicked and he poured water into mugs. 'Milk? Sugar?'

'Milk, no sugar. Thanks.'

He brought her the cup and sat down on the bed, looking at her. She had a feeling he knew exactly why she was here.

'Thanks,' she said again, gesturing with the cup.

'All mod cons,' he said. 'Don't know how long they'll last, if I can't get out to the shops. Another reason old Marty ought to go.'

'What about your job? Are they all right with you not coming in?'

He shrugged.

'What was it you did, again?'

'I don't have a job,' he said. Again he made the finger-and-thumb gesture, like a beak pecking at his forehead. The vulture of retribution. 'I'm branded, remember? Criminal record. Nobody would take me on.'

'That's terrible,' she said.

He gave a cynical smile. 'Well, would you? Mad wife-murderer, me – or didn't they tell you?'

She refused to be baited. 'Have you never had a job, so, since you came out?'

'Not what you'd call a job.'

'And that's – what? – ten years? How'd you pass the time? Doesn't it have you driven mad with boredom?'

He shook his head a little, wonderingly, as if asking himself what she would say next. 'I know all about boredom,' he said. 'Expert on it.'

'Sorry. What was I thinking? Pay no mind to me – me tongue runs like a roller towel, so me mammy says.'

He sipped his tea and said, 'Why don't you ask me what you want to ask me? You've come here full of questions, and you're not going to sucker me by pretending to be a thick Mick, which I know you're not, or pretending to be interested in my welfare, which I know you're not either. I knew you lot'd come after me sooner or later. I'm just glad they sent you instead of some sweaty plod with big feet.'

'They didn't send me. It was me own idea to come.'

'And they let you? Visit a woman-murderer alone in his flat? Don't they like you?'

He was playing a game with her, and she wasn't going to blink first. 'Ah, sure God, you wouldn't harm me, with all them people outside. They'd break the door down the minute I screamed.'

'Maybe. But it'd be too late for you by then, wouldn't it? You'd be dead. And prison doesn't scare me any more.'

'But you wouldn't want to go back,' she said shrewdly.

Something changed in his eyes. He wasn't baiting her now. 'Ask your questions,' he said, and she had to stop herself shivering.

She searched around for the best way in. She was sure she wouldn't get to ask many questions, so she needed to ask the right ones. 'What did you think of Melanie and Scott Hibbert?'

She had surprised him – it wasn't the question he expected. That was good.

'She was mad about him. But she knew he wasn't good enough for her. She was talking herself into it.'

'Why would she do that?'

'There's a lot you don't know about her. She wasn't a happy person. She had things in her past.'

'D'you mean her father getting killed?' she asked when it was clear he wasn't going to say any more.

He neither assented nor dissented.

'Wasn't that a long time ago, though? I mean, what, ten years or more? Surely she'd got over it?'

Still nothing.

'You must have known her well to know how she felt about her dad's death.'

'We talked sometimes,' he said.

'Here? Or in her flat?'

'Just in passing. Tuesday mornings, putting out the bins. She told me more than she thought she did. She hadn't got anyone to talk to, that was her trouble.'

'I thought she had loads of friends. And her mum, and Scott . . .'

'You ever see someone, always the life and soul of the party, and everybody's feeding off 'em? It's like they've got to perform, put on the show, and everybody goes away satisfied except them. They have to act. Nobody cares what they want, what they really feel. And everyone says what a great person they are, but inside they're just—'

He stopped, as if hearing that he had said too much. But Connolly thought, this is a controlled man, who knows just what he's saying. He *wants* me to think he's just blurted something out. But what?

'Boy, you really did know her well,' she said in an awed murmur. 'I'd no idea.'

'I know people, that's all,' he said. 'Plenty of time to observe 'em.'

'So, d'you know who killed her?' She hadn't known she was going to ask that, but she was glad she had, though for a moment she went cold and thought, *what if he says he did? What in the name a God do I do then?*

But he said, 'No. But your bosses will think I did, and I don't blame them. I'd probably think it was me if I was you. I'm on the spot. And I've got no alibi.'

Connolly thought of the secure home over the back. 'Were you here all the time on Friday?'

'Why?'

'I was wondering if you saw anyone hanging around.'

'I was out all afternoon.'

'Where?'

'My business.'

'Was someone with you?'

'My business. I was here to see Mel come home at half past ten. That's all you need to know.'

'You didn't hear anything else that night? Anyone else arriving? Melanie going out?'

'I slept soundly. Always do. I got a clear conscience.'

She knew that wasn't an answer. 'But you'd have heard if she – or anyone else – drove her car away later that night?'

'Maybe. But I didn't.'

'Or if there was any kind of a row upstairs? A fight, furniture turned over, a body hitting the floor?'

'I didn't hear anything.'

She shook her head in frustration. 'Where d'you keep your car?' she tried. 'I mean, you rent out these spaces—'

'Haven't got one,' he said. 'I can't drive.' His eyes gleamed as though he was enjoying watching her flounder.

'Really? That surprises me. I mean, most men—'

'Never saw the need. Lived in London all my life.' He put his mug down and leaned forward, resting his elbows on his knees, to look at her more closely. 'You're just a kid,' he said. 'Look, I didn't kill her, and you'll never prove I did, but you'll waste a lot of time trying because I am who I am. Tell your boss that.'

'Mr Slider?'

'Yeah. I know a bit about him. Tell him to leave me alone.'

'Is that a threat?' she said doubtfully.

His expression changed. He stood up, and she got quickly to her feet, not liking having him tower over her. 'And that's enough questions,' he said coldly. 'You take Marty to her mum and dad's. I hope they're not too out of it to look after him. But anywhere's better than here.'

He went to the kitchen, found two plastic carriers and put the dog's bowls into one and the opened pack of dog biscuit into the other. Then he got the lead and went over, knelt down by the dog and stroked it for a long time, and the dog looked up at him and wagged its tail, and after a bit rolled over on its side like a good dog. Finally Fitton snapped on the lead and, without turning, held it out behind him to Connolly. 'Go on, then,' he said. He wiped his eyes with his handkerchief, and she wondered whether he was crying, or if it was just the old leakiness.

When he turned, his face was set again. 'I hope you can get out all right.' He urged the dog to its feet and Connolly led it over to the door. Fitton put his hand to the latch. 'Ready? You'll have to be quick.'

'I'm ready,' she said, though, loaded with bags and the reluctant dog, she didn't think she'd be able to manoeuvre too nimbly.

Fitton looked at her as though he wanted to say something, and she paused, raising her eyebrows receptively. But all he said was, 'There's things you don't know about Mel. Things no one knew.'

'Not even you?' she asked.

'Me least of all,' he said, and opened the door.

In the top floor flat lived Andy and Sharon Bolton. Mr Bolton was at work, and Mrs Bolton was heavily pregnant, bored, and ready to take full advantage of any thrill that was going to wile away the time.

'It's my first,' she told Swilley, making instant coffee in the tiny slope-roofed kitchen. 'Of course, it's not suitable, having a baby up here – all those stairs for one thing, and only one bedroom – but rents round here are terrible and we can't afford anything bigger. We've been on the list for a council flat for years and I thought we'd get moved up with the baby coming, but my mum says all the flats go to unmarried mothers and asylum seekers. My dad says Andy and me shouldn't ought to've got married, then we'd be set up, but he's only kidding. They both love Andy – well, everybody does. He's a gas fitter – it's a really good job, he's got City and Guilds and he's Corgi registered and everything – but in the evening he's an Elvis impersonator. You should see him – he's wonderful! He really looks like Elvis. He's got the hair and he can do that thing with his mouth going up one side. And he's got a lovely singing voice. He does weddings and parties and bar mitzvahs and everything – ever so much in demand. Makes a lot of money at it.' The glow faded a little and she sighed. 'But it's still not enough, with the baby coming and me giving up work.' She brought the coffee over to the table and sat down. 'And now with this awful stuff happening downstairs, we've *got* to move. We're going to have to go further out, but all Andy's work's round here and it'll mean driving a lot more. But my mum says if we go out somewhere like Greenford or Hayes we can get a bigger place for the same money, only it'll mean coming off the council flat list. But Andy says they're never going to give us a flat anyway. We're better off going private. I forgot, do you want sugar?'

'Yes, please,' said Swilley.

She heaved herself to her feet again and went for the tin and a spoon. 'I've stopped having it,' she said. 'I was putting on too much weight. It's surprising how you don't miss it, after a bit. I tried to get Andy off it, but he burns it off, he's on the go so much. We're saving for a place of our own with his Elvis money, but you've got to have such a big deposit these days. But we've *got* to move now. It gives me the willies, thinking about that poor Melanie – such a nice girl she was. Of course, I only knew her just to say hello to, but she was always friendly and nice – not like that lot underneath, the Beales, always complaining if we so much as scrape a chair, and making a fuss about Andy practising. And is that right, him in the basement turns out to be a murderer? I read in the paper he killed his wife. Why haven't you arrested him?'

'There's no evidence to suggest he had anything to do with it,' Swilley said, trying to be patient.

'Well, it must have been him. Stands to reason. If he's killed once, he's bound to kill again. None of us are safe as long as he's around. There was this woman on a phone-in this morning when I was getting Andy his breakfast, who said it was a disgrace he was on the loose, any of us could be killed in our beds for all anyone cared. I always thought he had funny eyes – not that I've ever spoken to him, he keeps himself to himself, but they always do, don't they? My mum says—'

'So you didn't know Melanie very well?' Swilley broke in before the flood could carry her away again.

'No, like I said, just to say hello to. But Andy's friends with Scott. They go drinking together sometimes, when Melanie works late or she's out with her friends. I don't go, I don't like pubs. But Andy brings him back here for coffee and a chat. And Scott goes to Andy's gigs sometimes, helps out with the sound equipment, that sort of thing. He wants to be an impersonator himself, Scott does, but he hasn't got the voice. I mean, you can't just wiggle about for half an hour – people expect the songs as well. Andy does "Heartbreak Hotel" so's you couldn't tell it *wasn't* Elvis, he's that good,' she said proudly.

'Do you like Scott?' Swilley got in while she took a breath.

'Oh yes, he's lovely. Oh –' her face changed to tragedy-mode – 'he must be heartbroken about Melanie. He was mad about her. They were such a lovely couple. Besotted. He must be kicking himself that he went away for the weekend. If he'd been here, it wouldn't have happened.'

'Do you know where he was?'

'Oh yes, he told Andy. It was a friend's wedding, and he was doing his Elvis thing at the stag night.' She made a face. 'He doesn't even have the right hair – he has to wear a wig. He isn't a patch on my Andy. But Andy watched him rehearse and gave him some tips. He wasn't going to get paid for doing the stag night, so I suppose it didn't matter so much, and I expect they'd all be too drunk to notice anyway. You know what stag nights are like.'

'So were you and Andy home on Friday night?'

'Yes, and it makes me feel faint to think about it. To think we were up here watching Graham Norton while that horrible man was killing poor Melanie, and we never heard a thing.'

'You didn't hear any sounds of disturbance from downstairs? Anyone come in or go out? Any cars arriving or leaving, during the evening or night?'

'No, Andy came home, oh, about half past seven, quarter to eight, and we had our meal, and then we settled in to watch the telly. We went to bed about eleven, just after, and that was that. Andy sleeps really heavily, he's that tired at the end of the day. And even if I'm awake, I can't hear anything for him snoring. Mind you, we wouldn't hear anything from up here anyway. We never do. The Beales, *they're* the ones who are always complaining about noise,' she concluded bitterly. 'You can't *move* up here without them moaning. You should ask them.'

'I will,' said Swilley.

But the Beales – whom she had to track down at work – could not help. They were extremely indignant that their lives had been disrupted by the press, and asked, like Sharon Bolton, why Fitton had not been arrested, and how a convicted murderer could be allowed to roam around unsupervised, putting everyone's lives at risk. But they had been out at a friend's for dinner on Friday evening, going straight from work, and had not arrived home until after midnight. They had not seen anyone else around, nor heard any sounds during the night. They had gone out at about half past ten the following morning, to shop and then to lunch, and had not heard or seen anything untoward before leaving. They had not heard the dog barking, though they had heard that creature upstairs moving furniture about, and playing the radio far too loudly. You'd think she was roller-skating on the bare boards, sometimes, the noise she managed to make.

They had known Melanie Hunter only to say hello to, and had thought her nice, friendly, pleasant. They had spoken to Scott Hibbert once or twice. He seemed a very nice man, too. He worked for an estate agent, but it was an upmarket one – was it Jackson Stops? No, Hatter and Ruck, that was it – which of course made a difference. He had a plan for turning the house into two maisonettes by getting rid of the undesirable top floor and basement people. The Beales could have a really nice maisonette if they could incorporate the top floor into their flat. Hibbert had thought the freeholder would be willing, and the top floor were only renting, and he said there were always ways of getting renters out, but that man Fitton actually owned his flat, so he had to be persuaded to sell. Scott Hibbert had raised the matter with him but so far without success. Mr Beale wanted to know what the position would be when Fitton went to prison for murdering Melanie Hunter. Would his flat be seized, and would it go on the open market? He wondered whether the notoriety would raise the price or suppress it. He seemed hopeful it would be the latter. Mrs Beale had doubts about remaining there at all, now this had happened, but Mr Beale thought property was hard enough to come by in this area, and one shouldn't be foolishly squeamish, especially when turning the flats into two maisonettes would considerably more than double the value of each. When would they be arresting Fitton?

The Beales, she told Slider when she reported back, were a charming couple, but cold and ruthless.

'A sort of Steve and Eydie Amin?' Slider offered.

'But it does at least tighten up Scott Hibbert's alibi, boss,' Swilley said, not knowing who Steve and Eydie were. 'If he was actually doing an entertainment at the stag night on Friday, there was no way he wouldn't be missed. And though he might have a motive for getting rid of Ronnie Fitton and the Boltons, he had none for getting rid of Melanie.'

'Except,' Slider said, 'if he had any reason to expect to inherit the flat on her death, so he could double its value and keep all the profit himself. But that's a meagre sort of motive, and not one I'd like to have to convince a jury of.'

'He couldn't double its value without getting Fitton to sell,' said Swilley. 'But if Fitton went down for the murder, that would get him out of the way.' She was joking, he could see, but there was some serious thought behind it.

'Go on,' he invited.

She smiled. 'And then the other people leave because they don't want to live in a murder house, the price falls because of the notoriety, he snaps up the other flats cheap, and then he redevelops the whole house and makes a killing. Pardon the pun.'

'Ingenious,' Slider said.

'Yeah,' said Swilley apologetically. 'It'd make a good movie. And nobody likes estate agents. But anyway, he loved her – everyone says so.'

'All the same, we need to check up on his movements. Since we don't know exactly what time Melanie was killed, there's still the possibility that he drove home from Salisbury during the night and went back afterwards. And –' he forestalled her objection – 'we can work on the motive afterwards, if necessary.'

Connolly was glad to see the dog perk up as she pulled up in front of the house. There were neighbours and pressmen gathered along the pavement, keeping a respectful but agog distance from the front door where a uniform – Dave Bright – was keeping guard. He came down to the car as she stopped, but recognized Slider and nodded. He was an old-fashioned copper, large, authoritative and serene, and such was his presence that no one moved when he opened the car door for her. When she encouraged the dog out after her, there was a murmur among the neighbours and a stirring, like a wheat field in a summer breeze, among the pressmen, but Bright looked left and right and raised a massive hand, and everyone came to rest again, though there was a frenzied zip-zip of photo-shutters, like a caucus of cicadas. Slider's exit was met with a barrage of questions from the fourth estate, cancelling each other out since he could not hear them over each other – though they seemed to be mostly about Ronnie Fitton. He ignored them sturdily, following Bright, Connolly and the dog up the path, past the family car, to the front door.

In the house of mourning, tea was brewing, as it always was, and a large, spongey woman was ministering to Mrs Wiseman in the sitting room, and was introduced as 'my friend' by Mrs Wiseman and 'Margie Sutton from number forty-eight' by herself. Bethany was in the kitchen with a school friend – 'we couldn't make her go in today, not with all this going on, and reporters everywhere' – and Mr Wiseman was also home, hovering angrily between sitting room and kitchen, his clenched fists shoved into his pockets and his face twitching with tension. He seemed irritated not only by the crowds outside but by the presence of 'Margie' inside.

'My wife felt she needed support,' was all he said, but it was the way he said it.

Slider could see that Margie might come across as irritating, obviously relishing the tragedy and the opportunities it opened up for being sentimental and gushingly supportive.

'Ooh, I *know*,' she crooned to anything Mrs Wiseman said, while urging her to 'put her feet up', 'be kind to herself', and not 'hold it back'. She had soft, moist eyes like over-boiled gooseberries, and such a cascade of chins her fat white face looked like a cat on a pile of cushions.

But there was no doubt Marty the dog was pleased to see them. He strained forward on the leash, wagging his entire back end with gladness, and when Connolly released him, shoved his nose into the crutch of each person in turn, swinging his body round for patting, and panting with happiness. Mrs Wiseman seemed distracted and inclined to weep at him, but

Mr Wiseman was hugely glad of the distraction and petted the
dog extensively, saying, 'Good old boy. Good old dog,' over
and over. Bethany and her friend came to the door to see what
was happening, and were easily persuaded to take Marty out
into the garden and play with him; which, when a little sema-
phore between Slider and Connolly had taken place, left the
kitchen free for Slider to interview Mr Wiseman, while Connolly
worked her magic on the distaff side in the sitting room.

Wiseman seemed relieved to be in the presence of just
another man, and his tension seemed to drop back a notch –
though he was still wound so tight it didn't make him the king
of cool by several nuclear reactors' worth. 'Would you like a
cup of tea?' he offered, with a slight awkwardness that
suggested he thought this was a woman's opening, and that
he only felt constrained to make it because of the unusual
circumstances. Slider calculated that Wiseman would not sit
down so was better off with something to do, and accepted.
It got his fists out of his pockets, at any rate – Slider was
worried for his stitching.

He studied the man as he moved about the kitchen, making
a fresh pot. Ian Wiseman was not exceptionally tall – about
five ten, Slider thought – but there was no doubt he was in
shape. His face was lean and tanned, his hair thick and curly
and with very little grey in the brown, his shoulders and arms
powerful, his body neat and his legs muscled. He was wearing
cord trousers and a V-necked sweater over a check shirt, open
at the neck – just the clothes Slider would have expected of
a teacher off duty. His hands shook slightly as he made the
tea, the tendons stood out in his neck and his expression was
grim with, Slider presumed, maintaining control in such difficult circumstances. Otherwise, he thought, he would have
been quite good-looking, in a dark-haired, blue-eyed, Irish
sort of way.

'This must be difficult for you,' Slider said in sympathetic
tones, by way of opening the conversation.

'It certainly is,' he snapped back immediately. 'Crowds out
there so we can't get out of our own front door. Our life not
our own. We've had to unplug the phone. I had to keep Bethany
home from school, and God knows she can't afford to lose

any more days. She's already had time off this term with a cold, and with her grades she needs to keep her nose to the grindstone. And then to cap it all my head sent a message to tell me not to come in this week!' He crashed the lid on to the teapot with a kind of suppressed fury. 'Not that I would have been able to go today, the way things are, but to have him write me off, and for the whole week! I've got a hockey team to coach for the play-offs, I've got soccer teams, I've got basketball inter-schools coming up, I've got kids lined up for private coaching – and I'm stuck indoors here. I can't afford to take a week off.'

Interesting approach to bereavement, Slider thought, not without pity. It took different people different ways, and he could see that, for an active man, being cooped up with two dripping females and nothing to do would be trying. Still it was not his job to sympathize.

'And you must be upset about Melanie,' he said.

Wiseman's back was to him, pouring the tea. He seemed to pause for a beat, and then said, rather stiffly, 'Of course I'm upset.' He finished pouring and brought Slider's cup and saucer to the table. 'Do you take sugar?'

'No, thanks,' said Slider. 'Are you not having one?'

'I'm up to here with tea,' Wiseman said savagely, and then went and stood by the window with his fists in his pockets again. He seemed to have been working on control, because he said in a quiet tone, 'Look, she wasn't my own child – you know that?'

'Yes,' said Slider. He wished the man would turn round. He liked faces to his words.

'But I did my best by her. Rachel was widowed – you know about that?'

'Yes, her husband died in the Greenford rail crash.'

'That's right. And my wife died suddenly, leaving me with Bethany, who was only eighteen months old. So we were both – we needed each other. I don't say there wasn't a bit of – well, I suppose you don't call it rebound when it's a case of bereavement, but it was something like that. We married very quickly. Graham – Rachel's husband – had only been dead just over a year, my wife a bit less than that. Some people

were shocked we married so soon. Well, it was none of their
business,' he added in a sort of growl.

'No one else can know what you were feeling,' Slider said,
as if agreeing.

Wiseman turned and stared at him intently, perhaps judging
his sincerity. Apparently he passed muster. 'You're right,' he
said. 'I got sick to death of being judged. We dropped all our
old friends – friends, they called themselves. There was Rachel
with a teenager at the worst possible age for a thing like that,
trying to manage all on her own, and I've got a baby, going
on a toddler, and trying to hold down a very demanding job.
You may think it's a cushy number being a PE teacher, but I
can tell you it's not.'

'I'm sure it's not,' Slider said sincerely. 'It must take a great
deal out of you.'

He seemed mollified. 'Well, it's not nine to five,' he said
forcefully. 'There's all the out-of-hours coaching, and travelling with teams to competitions, and these days there's all
the paperwork that goes with it, too. And one has to keep
oneself fit, and that takes time. It was impossible to give
Bethany any kind of decent home life. So Rachel and I joined
forces, and—' He didn't quite shrug, but Slider got the impression that if he wasn't such a gentleman he would have hinted
that the bargain hadn't been evenly balanced. 'I always tried
to do the right thing by Melanie. I did my best.'

'Did you and she not get along?' Slider asked neutrally.

Wiseman gave an exasperated sort of sigh. 'Oh, it wasn't
that. Not the way *you* mean. But she was sixteen, her father
was dead – and she and him were always close. She was
bound to be upset and mixed up and so on. She had all the
usual teenage problems, only more so – and I wasn't the
answer to them, as far as she was concerned. All I could do
was give her a stable home and the right influence. I dare say
she'd have liked me better if I'd been permissive and let her
do whatever the hell she wanted, but that's not how you bring
up children. I wouldn't have been doing my duty by her if I
hadn't come down hard on certain things. And she thanked
me for it in the long run. I mean, she knew I was right, once
she got herself sorted out. But for a couple of years it was

hard going. And Rachel was no help. Well, she was devastated by Graham's death. I didn't realize until later how much it affected her.' His face darkened, and Slider read between the lines that he wouldn't have married her if he had. 'She would never take any kind of line with Melanie, it was always left up to me. And she wasn't even my child.'

'I can see how difficult it must have been. But your relationship did get better in the end?'

'Oh, we were all right with each other. The last few years – once she'd got herself sorted out. She pulled herself together – got a degree, worked hard and got a good job – and that made all the difference. Once she'd got some self-respect, she knew I'd been right to take a tough line with her. I wouldn't say we were ever really close, not warm, but we respected each other, and that was enough.'

'Did you see much of her?'

'Not really. She had her own life, you know what kids are. She rang her mother often, and she came over for Sunday lunch once in a while. You wouldn't expect more at her time of life.'

'When did you last see her?'

'About a fortnight ago, it was; she and Scott came over for Sunday lunch. That would be the last time I spoke to her. Though she rang her mother, I think, on the Friday – on the day.' He stopped abruptly, his face dark, his eyebrows pulled together like storm clouds.

'What did you think of Scott?' Slider said.

'*He*'s all right,' Wiseman said, and Slider thought the emphasis revealing. 'Steady lad, good job, nice manners. He wanted to marry her, you know,' he burst out as though it was impossible to bear, 'but she was the one holding back. I didn't approve of them living together like that. It's not respectable. But Scott was working on her, bringing her round. *He* had the right ideas. It was—' He stopped again, brooding. 'If she'd married, this would never have happened. If she'd listened to me . . .'

'Do you know if Melanie was worried about anything, the last few weeks?' Slider tried. 'Was there anything you and her mother were concerned about?'

'Apart from her not marrying Scott? No, not that I know of.'

'She wasn't in money trouble?'

'She never said she was. And Scott earned plenty.'

'Or mixing with any unsavoury types?'

'Scott would never have allowed that. No, she was all right, as far as I knew.'

Slider drank off his tea. 'Well, thank you, Mr Wiseman. You've been very helpful. Just one last thing – were you at home on Friday evening?'

Something happened. Slider had been going to ask about phone calls during the evening, but Wiseman stiffened like a fox smelling the hounds. 'What d'you want to know that for?' he asked, suppressed anger all present and correct again.

'Purely routine,' Slider said soothingly. 'We like to know where everyone was at the time.'

'If you're thinking I had anything to do with Melanie's death, just because I'm her stepfather—'

'Not at all. It's just a routine question, nothing to worry about. Where were you, in fact?'

Wiseman scowled horribly. 'I was coaching a school soccer team in the early part of the evening, if you must know, and after I got home I watched television with my wife until bedtime. As she'll tell you, if you can't take my word for it.'

Slider made a placating movement with his hands. 'There's no need for that. I assure you, the question was not meant disrespectfully. We ask everyone, just to clear the field.'

Wiseman evidently liked the word 'disrespectfully' and his hackles slowly went down. Through the kitchen window Slider could see the school friend playing with the dog, but Bethany was nowhere to be seen. He wondered what Wiseman would think of her absenting herself without permission – but there had not seemed anything particularly cowed about Bethany in the brief time he had observed her. More pertinently, he wondered how Connolly had got on; and that, at least, he could do something about.

SIX
Thirst Among Equals

Margie was hanging around in the hall as he passed through.

'Rachel's gone upstairs to have a lay down. I think that little talk with your lady upset her. I left them to it – private, you know – but I think I'd better stay on a bit in case I'm wanted,' she concluded wistfully.

'Has my colleague left?'

'Oh yes, a few minutes ago. Was – is Ian OK? Such a lovely man. P'raps I'd better go and make him a cup of tea? It can't be easy talking about something like this.'

There isn't something like this, Slider thought. But some malicious sprite prompted him to say, 'Good idea. I expect he needs a cup.' She scuttled off with a new mission in life and Slider escaped through the front door. The first thing he saw was Connolly, down the side of the house, deep in conversation with Bethany, so he turned his back on them and talked to Dave Bright for a bit, to give her space. He'd have gone and sat in the car, but that would have left him vulnerable to the crowd.

Connolly had been surprised when Mrs Sutton had offered to leave her alone with Mrs Wiseman, levered herself up on tiptoe and crept out: an elephant of tact. She had thought missing the interview would be the last thing Mrs Sutton would want to do, and gave her points for having more depths than was at first apparent.

Mrs Wiseman had been only too eager to talk. Grief had made her loquacious, though rambling. She kept weeping, like a slow bleed, but it did not interfere with her speech.

'I knew, when that other police-lady came, I knew she was gone. I had this premonition, somehow, that she was dead.

My Melanie. I can't seem to make it real in my head, d'you know what I mean? I keep thinking she'll ring me any minute. And yet I just knew the moment she said she was missing that she wasn't coming back.'

She wiped at her nose hopelessly with a soggy tissue that was in danger of disintegrating. Connolly passed her another and murmured something about a 'mother's instinct'. Mrs Wiseman jumped on that eagerly.

'That's what it was! That's what it must have been. A mother's instinct. Because Ian's been saying he always knew it would end up like this, but that's not right. It's not right to say something like that, just because she had that bit of trouble. That was years ago, and she's turned her life right round since then. It's not right to keep harping on about it. She was just a girl, and her dad had been killed, and it's no wonder she went off the rails a bit. I said at the time he ought to be more sympathetic, but he's so hard, Ian, he never makes allowances. He thinks everybody ought to be as together as he is. Oh, I know he thought he was doing right by her, being strict and everything, and I expect it did help her, in the long run, but to be saying a thing like that now, all these years later, when she's such a lovely girl, and she's really made something of herself. She's got a lovely job and a lovely boyfriend and there's no reason *at all* to say "I told you so" about something like this. I mean, nobody deserves to have that happen to them, and she was a good girl, a really good girl.'

'What was the bit of trouble she got in?' Connolly asked. 'When her Dad died?'

'Well, it wasn't right away, that's the funny thing. She was wonderful at first, a tower of strength to me – because I just went to *pieces*, I can tell you. It was the most terrible, terrible time; but Melanie was so wonderful, and she really adored her dad, you know, they were so close, but she supported me and did all the things that needed doing, and she was so calm and everything. I suppose in the end it was bound to come out, like a sort of – of . . .'

'Belated reaction?' Connolly offered.

'That's right,' said Mrs Wiseman. 'Anyway, it all seemed to come over her suddenly, after Ian and I got married.' She frowned. 'She didn't really approve of that, she thought it was too soon, and anyway you know what children are, they think you should never look at a man again, but I was only twenty when I had her so I was much too young to throw myself in the grave with him, so to speak. And Graham – Melanie's dad – well, he was a charmer all right, but he wasn't a good husband. Melanie had no idea, of course – well, that's not the sort of thing you tell your daughter, is it? Especially when she adores her dad like she did. But he was always in and out of different jobs and running up debts, and spending what we didn't have. It was hand to mouth the whole time with him. You never knew where the next meal was coming from. He was the sort of man who'd leave the gas bill unpaid but take us away for a weekend in a hotel. Always bringing home presents and useless things for the house – he was gadget mad, that man. But Melanie had holes in her shoes and no winter coat.' She shook her head at the memory and wiped her eyes again. 'So when Ian proposed to me, I wasn't thinking about it being too soon, I can tell you. A good man – a churchgoer and everything! And with a steady job – *and* ready to take on a stepdaughter just at the difficult age? I'd have been mad not to snap him up. But then Melanie sort of went to pieces. She sulked, and she was rude to me, and she'd barely talk to Ian, and Ian – well, I don't think he had the knack of handling her, not that anything would have helped much, the way she was then. But they were like two cats glaring at each other, and if one said white the other said black and off they'd go. Well, anyway, the upshot was my poor Melanie got into bad company. She started smoking, she was always out late and not saying where she was – you know the sort of thing.'

Connolly nodded helpfully.

'And all the time it was like she was defying Ian to stop her. Oh, he tried, and the rows were terrible, but it just seemed to make her worse. And then she—' She stopped, biting her lip.

'She got into trouble?' Connolly said, to help her along.

Mrs Wiseman nodded her head, lowering her eyes in shame. 'She got pregnant. We didn't know she'd been going with boys. You know – having sex, I mean. Because she was always

a pretty girl and naturally boys liked her and we knew she
had boyfriends, but not that she was – doing that. Well, it was
like the world came to an end. I mean, Ian – he's really strict
about anything like that. The rows before were nothing to what
happened then. And she wouldn't say who the father was. Ian
was raging, he wanted to go round and make the boy face up
to it, but she wouldn't say who it was. And then in the middle
of one row – I don't know if it was just to wind Ian up, or if
it was true – I can't believe it was true – she said she *didn't
know who the father was*.' She put a weak hand to her face.
'Ian just went mad.'

Connolly handed over more tissues in silent sympathy. She
could imagine the cataclysm. And she could imagine the young
Melanie facing her stepfather down, sixteen or seventeen,
confused, miserable, pregnant and frightened, having it made
clear to her she had nowhere to turn. *I hope he dies roaring
for a priest*, she thought with unexpected savagery.

'So what happened?' she asked after a moment, when the
mopping was finished. 'With the baby, and all?'

Mrs Wiseman hauled up a sigh from so deep it could have
turned her tights inside out. 'She had an abortion. Ian arranged
it. I was a bit surprised, him being a churchgoer and all, but
he said having the baby would blight her whole life. And ours.
I suppose he was right. Well, I know he was, because when
it was all over, Melanie sorted herself out, buckled down at
school, went to university and everything, and she couldn't
have done that with a baby in tow. But I always wondered.'
Another sigh. 'Well, you can't help thinking, can you, what
if? And it would have been my grandchild. I'll never have one
now.'

'But Melanie agreed that it was the right thing to do?'
Connolly asked. It was hard not to get sucked into this kind
of sorrow.

'Oh yes – she knew it was the only way. And we managed
to hush it all up, so that no one ever knew. Luckily it was the
beginning of the school summer holidays, so Ian arranged for
us all to go away, and it was done at a private clinic. By the
time school started again it was all over and done with, and
she was fit and well again, so there was no need for her friends

or the teachers or the neighbours to know about it. It was like a clean start for her, and to do her credit, she took full advantage. She cut herself off from the bad gang and became, well, a model student. And daughter. And she thanked Ian, in her heart, for putting her right, I know she did. I mean, it wasn't something we ever talked about, not directly, but once or twice when I've said how well she was doing, she's said something like, yes, it was the right decision.'

'And she got on with Ian all right in the end?'

'Oh yes. Like I said to the other lady, I wouldn't say they're all over each other, but underneath I think there's a real respect and affection. She *knew* he saved her from a terrible mistake. Everything she had, really, was down to him.'

Connolly relayed this story to Slider as they walked down to her car, settled in and drove away. 'It accounts for why the best friend Kiera didn't know anything about it – Melanie got whisked away, and came back with her sins scrubbed clean. Everything tidied away under the carpet. After that she put a shape on her life, and ended up on the pig's back, but you can't help wondering if there wasn't some bit of her thought it could have been different . . . What was your man like?'

'Mean, moody and magnificent,' Slider said. 'Well, mean and moody, anyway. It's obvious he likes to control. He'd be a strict father.'

'Yeah, I got that. Must a been cat for him, married to that blancmange of a woman.'

'What did you get from the child – Bethany?'

'That one! Eleven going on thirty-five. She waylaid me as I came out the door, couldn't wait to wear the ear offa me.'

Connolly had heard her hiss as she stepped past Dave Bright, and looking back had seen the child standing down the side access, beckoning.

'My dad's mad as fire about all this,' she confided as soon as Connolly was close enough. 'Mel getting killed and everything.'

'Why would he be mad?' Connolly queried.

''Cause he thinks it's getting us talked about. He's always

going on about what the neighbours think. Who cares what
the poxy neighbours think, that's what I say. But he worries
about that sort of crap. It's being a teacher. Got to be ultra-
respectable if you're a teacher, or it's all over the tabloids.
That's why he's a sidesman at church. Thinks it gives him
Brownie points.' She snorted in derision. 'Dad thinks I'm
gonna be a teacher when I grow up. Catch me! I'm not doing
anything where some poxy boss can tell me what I can do
and can't do. Dad's mad because Mr Bellerby – he's the head
at Dad's school – told him not to come in. Dad thinks he
thinks he's letting the school down, or some crap like that.'

'I don't suppose your dad likes you using words like crap,'
Connolly said.

Bethany looked surprised, and then narrowed her eyes.
'You're not cool like that other one that came, the tall one.'

'Oh, I'm way cooler than her,' Connolly said. 'What did
you think of Melanie?'

Bethany shrugged. 'She was all right. She let me try her
make-up and things, when she was a student. But she turned
into this boring grown-up with a boring job, just like everybody
else. I'm not going to be like that.'

'Did you see a lot of her?'

'She come over every now and then. For Sunday lunch.'
She rolled her eyes. 'The burnt offerings, Dad calls it.'

'Isn't your mum a good cook?'

'You kidding? She thinks the smoke alarm's a timer. That's
what Dad says. She's not my real mother, but I call her Mum
and everything. I don't remember my real mum – she died
when I was a baby. Of gusto enteritis. I'm gonna be a
doctor when I grow up, but not a poxy GP – a big posh
consultant, me, so nobody can tell me what to do. Dad married
Mum when I was a baby so he'd have someone to look after
me and cook and clean and everything. Good luck with that!
He says she's as much use as a sick headache.'

'He doesn't say those things to you?' Connolly said,
privately shocked.

'No, course not. I hear them rowing, and he says it to her.'

'Do they row a lot?'

'Yeah. She gets on his nerves. And she snores, so they don't sleep in the same room any more. She wakes *me* up, sometimes. It's like the house is falling down.' She looked troubled for a moment, and said, 'She's all right, really, my mum. I mean, I love her and everything. She's just not very good at "mum" things.'

'Different people are good at different things,' Connolly said, and the child looked relieved.

'Yeah, that's right. She sings nice, my mum. She used to sing to me at night when she tucked me in. Course, I'm too old for that now, but I like it when she sings round the house, when she's on her own and she thinks no one's listening. And when Mel came, sometimes they'd sing together, soppy old songs from the dark ages, but it sounded nice.'

'When did Melanie last come over?'

'Two weeks ago, on the Sunday, but they weren't singing then. Her and my dad had a right old ding-dong. They were in the kitchen making the tea after lunch and I was in the lounge with Mum and Scott, but we could hear 'em all right.'

'What were they rowing about?'

'Oh, the usual – her not being married and living with Scott. Living in sin, Dad calls it – honestly!' She snorted in eye-rolling derision. 'Dad kept saying Scott wanted to marry her and she should be grateful, and she said she didn't have to be grateful to any man, and Dad said she ought to be grateful to *him* for saving her neck, and she said that didn't give him the right to run her life, and he said she was just throwing everything away when he'd worked so hard to make us respectable, and she said *you* can talk and then he slapped her.'

'He hit her?'

'Oh, not hard. Just slapped her face for being cheeky. They didn't talk any more after that and when they came back in with the tea they pretended nothing had happened, but I could see her cheek was a bit red.'

'Does he hit you?'

'He used to, sometimes, but he doesn't now. He got scared of the social lady coming round. He was mad as fire about the government saying you couldn't hit your kids any more. He said the country was going to the dogs. But like I said he's got to be dead careful because of being a teacher, so he couldn't afford to get mixed up with that social lot. They'd send you to prison soon as look at you. That's who I thought the other one was, the other lady policeman who came before. I thought she was from the social at first. But they don't have such nice clothes. It says in the papers a man killed Mel – that man in the basement.'

'I'm sure it doesn't say he killed her, because nobody knows who killed her.'

'Well, it says he was a murderer, he killed his wife, so it's gotta be him, hasn't it? Are you going to arrest him?'

'Not up to me. Anyway, we haven't got any evidence yet. You can't arrest anyone without evidence.'

'You don't know anything, do you? My friend Georgina says her dad said the police are a load of tossers,' Bethany confided pleasantly. 'He says you couldn't find your own arse with both hands and a torch.'

'That's not a nice thing to say,' Connolly said sternly.

'No, but it's funny.' She grinned, and ran off into the back garden.

'So wouldn't you say that was interesting, guv?' Connolly said, heading up the Uxbridge Road. 'Your man's starting to look a bit tasty for it. He's narky as hell, he clatters his kids, he was giving out to Melanie as recently as a fortnight ago. And he was out Friday evening.'

'Yes, he told me. He was coaching a school soccer team.'

Connolly took her eyes off the road to give him a level look. 'Mrs Wiseman says he didn't come home until late. She went to bed at eleven and it was after that. Sure, school soccer practice doesn't go on that long.'

'Ah,' said Slider. 'He gave me the impression he was home fairly early – he said he watched television with his wife.'

'He coulda gone for a jar after, I suppose,' Connolly said, to be scrupulously fair.

'But then why wouldn't he have said so?'

'Because he thinks himself fierce posh altogether, and hanging around in boozers is not respectable,' she suggested. 'Or . . .'

Slider considered, watching the shops lining the street glide

away behind them. 'There's certainly a lot of anger in him,'
he said. And suppressing it in the name of respectability, when
his anger was righteous in origin and ought to be applauded,
must be an extra strain, he thought.

'Guv, suppose after praccer he went over to Melanie's to
give her another earful about not marrying your man Hibbert?
She tells him to mind his business and he goes mental and
lamps her.'

'Possible, but there's not enough time for him to get her to
Ruislip and be back home by eleven.'

'But he could go home right after killing her, wait'll everyone's in bed and go back and do the rest.'

'Surely his wife would notice if he got up in the middle of
the night?'

'No, the kid told me they don't sleep together. Your woman
snores something fierce. So that'd cover any sound he made
leaving the house.'

'Ingenious,' Slider said.

'And possible,' Connolly urged.

'You've forgotten one thing, though. The dog.'

'Oh, saints and holy sinners, that dog!' Connolly cried,
thinking Mr Porson wasn't so wrong in thinking it was the fly
in the woodpile. 'Wait, though. It knows him, the dog. Say it
was in another room when he killed her, maybe it wouldn't bark.'

'But he couldn't leave it with the body in the flat while he
went home. It'd cut up Cain,' Slider pointed out. They'd
reached the station now and she was turning into Tunis Road
– going too fast and winding the wheel like a mad mangler.
'You couldn't—'

'No, no, wait'll I think it!' she interrupted urgently, winding
again, turning into Stanlake. The gates to the yard slid open
and she kept winding. 'I've got it! He could take the dog home
with him, leave it in the car while he establishes his alibi, then
take it back.' She looked at him triumphantly as she backed
into her space. 'We could test his car for dog hair.'

Slider let her have a moment before saying, 'Had we not
just taken the dog over there. And even if we hadn't, he could
always say the dog had been in his car on another occasion.
Why not?'

'Yeah,' said Connolly, deflating.

'All the same,' Slider said, 'he's definitely become interesting. There was obviously a history between him and Melanie, and he's – not exactly lied to me, but he's misled me about his whereabouts on Friday. There's something he doesn't want us to know. I think we must look into him in a bit more detail.'

'Righty-oh,' she said happily.

'But carefully,' Slider warned. 'We don't want to ruin his life if he's innocent. Teachers have to be above reproach, you know.'

'That's what the wean said.' She rolled her eyes as she remembered. 'You'd want to hear the mouth on that kid, guv! Sure, the carry-on of her's so bad, she could end up on the news.'

It was Hollis's birthday, and he had invited the firm for a quiet drink – followed by several noisy ones – at the British Queen, which had become one of their after-work boozers as the poncification of local pubs drove them further and further down the road. Slider said thanks but no thanks – he had a long-standing dinner date with Atherton and Emily – but chipped in to the drinks pot anyway, as guv'nors were expected to; and watched in amazement as McLaren slipped away without saying anything to anybody.

'McLaren not going?' he asked Hollis.

'He said he might join us later,' Hollis said, evidently equally baffled. McLaren never missed a drink, having legendarily no life outside the Job. He lowered his voice. 'Guv, I was taking a leak just now and he was in there, *shaving*.'

'But he was clean-shaven this morning,' Slider remembered. In fact, he had not had to exhort McLaren to stand closer to the razor for weeks.

'Aye, and I know them leccy shavers don't do the job like the old cold steel, but still . . .'

'Yes,' Slider said thoughtfully. Twice in one day? McLaren? The man who'd need the full-time attentions of a valet just to achieve the level of *mal-soigné*?

'Guv, I'm wondering if he's poorly,' Hollis said awkwardly.

No man likes to talk about his colleagues behind their backs. Especially on sensitive subjects. 'He's lost a bit o' ground lately. Been off his oats.'

Slider nodded. McLaren had never been fat, but there had been the fleshiness of the chip-eater and beer-drinker about him. Now his lines were less blurred. 'Maybe I should have a word with him.'

'Discreet, like,' Hollis added hastily. 'You won't let on—?'

'Of course not.'

Which meant that at Atherton's bijou terraced house in West Hampstead – which he called an artesian cottage because it was so damp – the conversation was, surprisingly, on McLaren rather than the case for the first half hour. Joanna had met them there, having left Slider's father to babysit. Emily was doing the cooking for once, which meant that Atherton was rather distracted in any case, listening – and smelling – for crises in the kitchen. Not that Emily couldn't cook, but she had her ways and he had his; and besides, he had been so famed for his dinner parties before they met, it was hard to give up the tiller to the cabin boy. He occupied himself giving each of them a gin and tonic large enough to have stood in as a water feature in a medium-sized courtyard garden, and fiddled about rearranging the cutlery on the table.

Outside the slicing wind had not let up, and as the glazing was Victorian, the crimson velvet curtains over the windows heaved and struggled like an opera singer getting dressed – much to the delight of the cats, who pretended they thought there was something hiding behind them that needed killing. The sealpoint Siameses, Sredni Vashtar and Tiglath Pileser – usually known as Vash and Tig – were relics of a previous relationship (divorce is so hard on the children, Atherton was wont to say) and had at least two cats' worth too much energy for a house this size. Which was why he and Emily were talking about trying to get a bigger place, with a garden. Slider tried not to let his feelings show when this topic was discussed, because Atherton had never before had a relationship that got that far. For him, commitment had been remembering her name in the morning. But now with Emily . . . Slider was so happily married, he wanted the same thing for his friend – like the tailless fox, Atherton said cynically.

Slider had relayed his conversation with Hollis as Atherton went round with nibbles (olives, not crisps – oh, there's posh!)

'There's something up with him,' Slider concluded. 'Hollis thinks he's ill. But why would someone who is ill start to dress smartly and shave twice a day? I can see the losing weight bit makes sense . . .'

Atherton considered. 'Maybe he was going to see a specialist, and that's why he was poshing up.'

'Oh, really!' Emily exclaimed from the kitchen, immediately followed by a crash and an: 'Oh damn!'

Atherton froze. 'Everything all right?' he called.

'Fine!' came the breezy reply. 'Just dropped a saucepan lid. No, seriously, why would someone dress up to see a consultant?'

'People used to tidy up when the doctor was coming,' Slider defended his lieutenant.

Joanna smirked. 'In the fifties, maybe. When Janet and John roamed the earth. You really are a couple of clots. Aren't they, Em?' she called.

'S'obvious!' she called back. 'Plain as the nose on your face.' There were some more noises off, with muffled curses, and then she appeared in the kitchen doorway, holding an empty tumbler. 'What about another of these?'

'Are you sure?' Atherton said. 'I mean, while you're cooking? Kitchens are dangerous places – naked flames, hot superconductive surfaces . . .'

She stuffed the glass into his hand and kissed the end of his nose. 'Has anyone ever told you you have a cute face?'

'No, but I have acute anxiety,' he responded. But he did another round of drinks. 'So what *is* this bleedin' obvious answer we're all missing,' he asked, tipping gin into glasses with abandon.

'Not all,' Joanna said. 'Just you poor old hairy chaps. He's in love.'

'*McLaren*?' Atherton stopped in the act of uncapping the tonic. The cats had come mincing over, looking for mischief. Tig was trying to get his head up Atherton's trouser leg, while

Vash appeared to be calculating whether he could jump straight from the floor to the top of Atherton's head. He'd done it before. It wasn't the process that hurt but the arrival. Heads were slippery and required landing gear to be down.

Emily counted on her fingers. 'Sudden interest in his appearance, stopped stuffing his face, distracted expression, disappearing on his own instead of going for drinks.'

'Yes, but – *McLaren*,' Atherton said again.

'Why not? It happens,' Joanna said. 'To golden girls and lads and chimney sweepers.'

'Love makes the world go round,' said Emily.

'So do large amounts of alcohol,' Atherton retorted, handing her the first glass. She grinned and disappeared into the kitchen.

'It makes sense, I suppose,' Slider said, staring at nothing. 'He turned up at the murder shout before everyone else. I wonder if she lives out that way?'

'Has he never been married?' Joanna asked.

'Oh yes – years ago, before I knew him. I don't think it lasted very long. She left him. Usual copper reasons, I suppose – the unsocial hours, the drinking, blah blah blah. Since then – well, he's not really a ladies' man, our Maurice.'

'More a pie, pasty and bacon sarnie man,' Atherton said, handing Slider his drink.

'Thanks.' He was staring distractedly at an ornate Victorian pot on a tall stand in the corner. 'Didn't you use to have an aspidistra in that?' he asked. It was empty now.

'Aspidistra? You dear old-fashioned thing,' Joanna said. 'It was a fern, wasn't it, Jim? What happened to it?'

'The kits ate it. FYI, ferns go through cats like the proverbial dose of salts. It took me a while to work out what was causing it, but the results were definitely antisocial. As the saying goes, with fronds like those, who needs enemas?'

'I wonder how serious it is,' Joanna said. 'Not the diarrhoea – McLaren's fancy.'

'I wonder if we'll ever meet her,' Slider said. 'If that *is* what it is, and he's being this secretive . . . Is he ashamed of her?'

'More likely doesn't want to be joshed to death by you dinosaurs,' Emily called from the kitchen. 'Dishing up now. A little help?'

Emily's cooking was not as elegantly finished as Atherton's, but it tasted good, and they tucked in happily to a chicken-and-rice dish raised above the everyday by fat black olives and slices of preserved lemon.

Slider recounted the day's advances and Connolly's theory.

'She's an ingenious girl,' Atherton said. 'But you can't get over the dog.'

'That's the same whoever it was,' Slider said.

'He could have put the body in his car boot, driven home to establish his alibi, then gone out again in the middle of the night to dump it. That gets over the dog,' Emily suggested.

'But that would surely have left some sign on her clothes,' Slider said. 'Creases, oil stains. It seems to me most likely she wasn't killed at the flat.'

'You've only got this Ronnie Fitton's word for it that the dog didn't bark,' Joanna said. 'Didn't you say the upstairs people were out all evening? And the top floor ones never heard anything anyway?'

Slider nodded. 'But why would Fitton lie about that?'

'Maybe he didn't lie. Maybe he really didn't hear anything. Which means it could have happened at the flat. Or, if he was the murderer, maybe he wanted to distract attention from himself.'

'But if he was going to lie, wouldn't he lie the other way?' Emily asked. 'Make out that there was a rumpus up there, make you think someone else was there.'

'No,' said Slider. 'Safer not to give false clues that can rebound on you. He wouldn't know what other witnesses might say. Not hearing anything is the default setting – no one can prove you're lying about that. But if you claim to have heard something that never happened, or at a different time from everyone else, questions get asked.'

'So – you think he might have done it, then?' Joanna said, working out his negatives.

'He's the obvious suspect,' Slider said. 'He had a key, he knew the dog, he was on the spot.'

'And he's got a record,' Atherton said.

'Yes, the press have had a field day with that,' Emily mused. She was a freelance journalist. 'Nice people, aren't we?'

SEVEN
Deliver Us From Elvis

By the next morning, they had had to close off half of Cathnor Road, to the annoyance of local residents. The crowds were three deep, the press had got themselves all settled in with fleece-lined jackets and telephoto lenses on tripods, and the television news channels all had someone there, wearing a smart knitted scarf with the two ends pushed through the loop, talking to shoulder-cams and trying to make much of little. Add the police cars and forensic vans, and you had a three ring circus. The only happy people were the upstairs residents across the road who had rented out their windows to paparazzi, and the ingenious downstairs couple who were selling tea and sandwiches to the bored journos.

Because there really wasn't anything to see. The Beales had moved out and gone to stay in their second home, a cottage near Marlow, from which, Mr Beale had told Commander Wetherspoon at some length (it turned out they had met once at a fund-raiser, which was enough of an 'in' to allow him to bend his ear), it was both costly and time-consuming to commute to work. The inconvenience and expense was intolerable considering that the police had the obvious suspect in plain view and could have arrested him right at the beginning and saved everyone a lot of trouble, which was surely what they paid their taxes for.

Slider had been happy for them to go – their alibi had checked out, not that there was any reason to suspect them in the first place, and the fewer people cluttering up the place the better. It was just a pity that out of sight was not out of earshot.

The Boltons had also moved out, to stay with Mrs Bolton's parents in Hayes, because the strain was thought to be too much for Mrs Bolton's condition. And Scott Hibbert had had to give up the flat to the forensic team as soon as the misper

'On the other hand, if the deed wasn't done at the flat – what then?' Joanna asked. 'Doesn't that bust it right open?'

'Yup,' said Atherton, not happily.

'Well, it's early days yet,' Slider said, though he knew it wasn't, not really. After the first forty-eight hours, it got more and more difficult. And thanks to the 'missing persons' element, the forty-eight had been a diminishing dot in the distance before they were even called to the scene. 'There's got to be evidence out there. All we have to do is find it.'

'And on the basis that it's always the person closest to the victim, it will probably turn out to be either the boyfriend or the stepfather.'

'In fiction,' said Emily, 'it often turns out to be the first person you suspected.'

'Which brings us back to Ronnie Fitton,' said Atherton.

'We're going to have to do something about him,' Slider sighed.

'Ah, but what?' Atherton finished lightly. 'Shall I open another bottle?'

case had turned into a murder, and had been provided with a room in an hotel in Hammersmith, where the proprietor was used to such things and was primed to raise the alarm if there were any suggestion of flitting. So there was nothing for the media to observe at the house but the forensic comings and goings, and nothing to hope for. but a sight of Ronnie Fitton, who was lying low behind drawn curtains. The old case of his murder of his wife was all over every paper and on every news broadcast, despite anything the Commander and other high-ups could do. It was in the public domain, and the suggestion that if there ever were a court case, it would be jeopardized by the impossibility of finding anyone for the jury who didn't already think of Fitton as guilty, cut no ice with the media barons.

Porson, having been summoned to an early meeting at Hammersmith, returned to Shepherd's Bush in a fouler. Commander Wetherspoon had that effect on people. He was tall, pompous, blame-allergic, and so ingratiating of those above him, generally all you could see of him was his boots.

'All they care about is it's a good story now,' said Porson of the press. 'And if there's a trial and it goes wrong that'll be an even better story, so why should they care? There's nothing they like better than having a poke at the police – but who do they come screaming to if some punter shoves 'em out the way and they fall down and hurt their little selves?' He rubbed at his jaw, pushing his head sideways to stretch his neck, and then used his other hand to knead his shoulder. 'And to cap it all,' he snarled, 'I got this nostalgia all down one side. It's bloody killing me.'

'Ah yes,' Slider murmured. 'I used to have that.'

Porson straightened up and gave Slider a sharp look. 'There's a lot of pressure on me to arrest Fitton.'

'We haven't got any evidence against him,' Slider said.

'There's more things to consider than evidence. Like it or not, we're engaged in a public relations exercise every time we stick our noses out of doors. Nothing and nobody's sacrospect these days. You got to be seen to be doing something, and if that something is Ronnie Fitton – well, you can't bake bricks without eggs. If we can't keep the press busy they'll be muddying the waters so we can't see the wood for the pile anyway. I got more people on my back than a donkey at the beach, and a bird in the hand's as good as a wink to a blind horse any day.'

When Porson was agitated, his grasp on language became even more random than usual. You could tell how riled he was by the degree of dislocation. Slider put his current rage at around seven-point-five on the sphincter scale.

He had sympathy for the old man – he was always grateful to Porson for standing between him and the PR aspects of the job – but right was right; and he knew Porson believed that too. He maintained a steady gaze and said, 'If we arrest Fitton too soon, it could jeopardize the case against him if we later find we have one to make.'

Porson stared, and then translated his restlessness into pacing back and forth behind his desk. 'I know, I know,' he said more evenly. 'And I said all that to Mr Wetherspoon. But they've got different priorities from us up there in the stratosphere, God help us. And the Police Service isn't a democracy.'

Slider was reminded of a joke of Atherton's: in a democracy, it's your vote that counts; in feudalism it's your count that votes. Definitely feudal, the Job. 'I know, sir. But if we do Fitton we've got to do it right.'

'I know, laddie, I know.' Porson paced a couple of times more, and said, 'I'll hold 'em off you as long as I can. But if it comes to it, we may have to sacrifice the sheep for the goats. Fitton's a big boy. He won't call for his mum if we do give him a tug. But we'll leave him where he is for now. Only for God's sake get yourself in gear and get me something. I can't keep Mr Wetherspoon happy by showing him my legs.'

On this horrifying thought, Slider left.

When he was crossing the squad room on his way back to his own, Swilley called him, waving a couple of forensic reports. Slider eyed the pile of papers on his desk, visible through his open door – frankly, it would have been visible from space – and said, 'Precis them for me.'

'This one's the stomach contents,' she obliged. 'Food was still present in the stomach, suggesting the victim died less than three hours after her last meal. Recognizable elements in

the partially digested contents were some kind of fish, vegetables and sponge pudding.' She looked up. 'That accords with
the meal she had at the Vic, according to her mates – pan-fried
sea-bass with roasted vegetables and sticky-toffee pudding.'
She rolled her eyes slightly. 'And if they were eating between,
say, eight o'clock and nine, allowing for having drinks first
and waiting for service, that means she was probably killed
about half ten, eleven o'clock time.'

'So that rules out imprisonment and a later murder,' Slider
said. 'Well, it's a relief to get that out of the way. She went
home and was killed soon afterwards.'

'Which makes it more likely she was killed at the flat,
doesn't it?' Swilley said. 'And that brings us back to Fitton.'

'Or anyone who had a key or she might let in. What's the
other one?' he asked, of the paper in her hand.

'Examination of the clothes. Nothing much there: on the
back of her coat and her skirt, some traces of earth and partially
composted vegetable matter – I think they mean leaves, boss.
They match the earth and leaves of the site – big surprise.
And some hairs that turned out to be dog hair – no surprises
there either.'

Slider nodded. 'Shove 'em on my desk, then. I'll look at
them later.'

Before either of them could move, Atherton came in, waving
a large paper bag. 'Another day, another doughnut,' he said. 'I
stopped on the way. Thought I'd do my bit for the common
weal.'

It was amazing. Instantly he disappeared in a passionate
press of bodies that had been quietly at their desks the instant
before. From inside, his voice emerged. 'What can I say? It's
something I've always had.'

When the scrum evaporated, he brushed himself smooth
and said, 'So, what's up?'

'The pound, and Mr Porson's blood pressure,' Slider said.
'But not our tails.'

Hollis drifted over. 'What are we on today, guv?' he asked.
'We've still got canvassing to complete – Mackay was supervising that yesterday?' He made it a question and Slider nodded
agreement. 'Fathom's on cars – local stolen, parked, and

ANPR'd in the area. And McLaren's still trying to trace her route home.'

'Forensic's in the flat and the public areas of the house,' Atherton added. 'And the garden, such as it is. What else?'

'There's Hibbert's alibi to check. That means going down to Salisbury.'

'I'll do that,' Swilley offered.

'No, I want you and Connolly to keep interviewing her girl friends. And go over her papers. I want to know more about her life. You've read Connolly's report?'

'About her little bit of trouble?' Swilley said. 'Yeah, boss. You think she wasn't as white as she was painted?'

'I'm not making any judgements,' Slider said. 'But she had a secret in her past, and that makes her interesting. Did anyone else know it? And did she have any others?'

Atherton shook his head. 'Three perfectly good suspects and you want more?'

'Three?'

'What about Wiseman? I like him even better than Hibbert.'

'That's because you're an iconoclast. I suppose we'll have to check his alibi, just to be on the safe side. Soccer practice is as good as they get, but he was rather late home.'

'I'll do it,' Atherton said.

'No, I think I'll put Connolly on to it when she's done with the girl friends. It might involve talking to teenagers, and she's got the most street cred amongst us.'

Atherton and Swilley exchanged a rare look of sympathy. 'He's just comprehensively trashed the two of us, you understand?' he said.

'You're always telling me I'm really mumsy now,' said Swilley, who looked like Barbie made flesh, and was mumsy in the same way that the middle of the Atlantic was really dry.

'But what does that make me?' Atherton enquired querulously.

'It makes you on your way to Salisbury,' Slider said.

'Me?'

'Yes, you. Why not?'

'He was at a stag do with an entire football team's worth

of witnesses. What's to find out? Can't I just do it on the phone?'

'There may be things that people will tell you face to face. Hibbert may have the most solid alibi outside tea with the governor in Pentonville, but he might have said something to his friends in a drink-induced open moment that will give us a lead.'

'A lead where?'

'If I knew that I wouldn't need to send you. I need someone with subtlety, perseverance and an enquiring mind.'

Atherton was not beguiled by the compliments. Too little, too late. 'You need me at your side,' he said. 'I don't want to leave you high and dry.'

'I've never been lower or wetter,' Slider assured him. 'Go!'

So when Andy Bolton came in, Slider went down to talk to him himself. He was a short young man, very muscular and fit, good-looking in an obvious sort of way and sporting a tan which, given the time of year, might well have been sprayed on. He had no obvious resemblance to The King other than blue eyes and a thick head of black hair styled in the manner, with quiff, duck's arse and sideburns all present and correct. Perhaps the tan was part of the act, Slider thought. It certainly made his teeth look very white.

'The wife said you wanted to talk to me,' he said amiably, 'but I haven't had a minute to spare before now to get over here. It's a busy time of year, especially with this extra-cold weather. I'm a gas-fitter, you know? And I wouldn't've had a minute now, only I had to take the morning off to move our stuff out to Hayes, to the wife's mum and dad's. Well, she's got it into her head Mr Fitton downstairs is a murderer and there's no talking to women when they get like that. But I'm glad to have her out the way, anyway. It's like a madhouse back there, in Cathnor Road, with all the media and everything, and in her condition it's not good to put a strain like that on her. We're a bit cramped at her mum and dad's, and it's going to take me longer every day getting in and back, but it eases my mind to know someone's keeping an eye on her while I'm out. So what did you want to see me about? Only, I don't know as I can tell you anything more than Sharon – the wife.'

He obviously liked to talk as much as his other half did,
but his voice was light and easy on the ear – Slider could tell
he was a singer – so it was no great hardship. The rather round
blue eyes regarded Slider with friendly openness, and that in
itself was a pleasant change from the usual hostility and suspi-
cion. 'It's always good to get another perspective on things,'
Slider said.

It was enough to set him off again. 'Oh, I know, you people
have got your way of doing things. I'm just the same. When
I do a job I have to have my tools set out a certain way, I do
things in a certain order, I'm very methodical. Some people
make fun of me for it, but that's the way I am. I can't abide
messiness or carelessness – well, you can't take chances with
gas. Other people's lives depend on it. So, poor old Ronnie
Fitton down in the basement – he's having a rough old time
of it, isn't he? Is that right, he murdered his wife?'

'Haven't you read the papers?' Slider asked.

'Not to say *read*. I've seen the headlines. It gave me a shock,
seeing my own house right there on the front page. Some of
the others were talking about it, though, at this job I was on
yesterday – fitting out a new block of flats. The chippies and
plasterers were joshing me rotten about living in "the murder
house". But I haven't got time for reading that sort of rubbish.
Sharon – the wife – was glued to the telly all evening waiting
for the news but I made her turn it off. I said it wasn't fair on
the baby to dwell on that sort of thing. I took her down the
pub in the end, just to get her out – not that she's a drinker,
especially not with the baby coming. She just had a lemon and
lime. But it was a change of scene for her. She kept going on
about Mr Fitton – he's not really a murderer, is he? He seems
like such a nice old boy. Reminds me of my dad, a bit.'

'It's true he killed his wife, a long time ago,' Slider said.
'Nothing is known against him since then.'

'Well, I can't believe he'd kill Mel. Just 'cause he killed
his wife? Why would he? They were really friendly.'

'Were they?'

'Oh, yes. Always standing nattering – every time I went in
or out of the house, it seemed like. And they used to go down
the pub together.'

'*Did* they?' This was interesting news to Slider.

'Yeah, every once in a while. They used to go down the Wellington, down Paddenswick Road. Well, that's the nearest. Me, I like the Anglesea Arms – down Wingate Road?' Slider nodded. 'It's quieter, a bit classier. But maybe that's why Mr Fitton liked the Wellington – you wouldn't stand out in there, being's it's so noisy and crowded.'

'More anonymous?' Slider offered.

'That's it.' He shook his head sadly. 'I don't suppose he'll be going for a drink anywhere now, after having his face plastered all over the paper like that. It doesn't seem fair. I feel sorry for him – everyone's got it in for him now.' He thought a moment. 'Unless he *did* kill Mel. Do you think he did?'

'We don't know yet,' Slider said. 'How do you know he and Melanie went for drinks together?'

'Oh, she told me, when I saw her come in with him once. And I've seen them going into the Wellington when I've been passing on me way home. *She* liked him, so he must have been all right, mustn't he?'

'What did her boyfriend think about her going to the pub with him?'

'Scott? Well, I don't know if he knew,' Bolton said. 'It was of a Thursday evening, usually, and that was the night Scott always worked late. So she may have told him or she may not have. I mean, there was no reason he shouldn't know. No reason he should object. It wasn't like she was seeing another man or anything. I mean, Ronnie Fitton – well, he's old. He's not – you know, someone she'd have an affair with. And none of us knew about him being – about him killing his wife and that. But he's never said anything to me about Mel and Ronnie Fitton being friends, Scott hasn't, so I've never said anything to him. You don't go stirring things up, do you?'

'Why do you think it would stir things up? You think Scott *would* object if he knew?'

Andy frowned with puzzlement. 'No, like I say – well, not like that. But he's a funny old geezer, and I know if my wife struck up a friendship with him, to actually going to the pub with him, I'd think it was a bit funny.'

'Did Melanie ever tell you *why* she was friends with Mr Fitton? What the connection between them was?'

'No. I never asked,' Bolton said easily, with his frank, blue look. 'Not my business. D'you think I *should've* said something, then? To Scott?'

Do I look like an agony aunt? Slider retorted silently. 'Tell me about Scott Hibbert,' he said. 'Your wife said you and he were friends.'

'Oh, he's all right,' Bolton said, but without great enthusiasm. 'I dunno about friends. We pass the time of day, that sort of thing. And we've gone for drinks now and then. To the Anglesea mostly. He likes the Conningham and I've been there once or twice with him, but it's a Hoops pub and I'm Shed.'

The Hoops were Queens Park Rangers football team; the Shed was Chelsea. No further explanation was necessary.

'Do you like him?' Slider asked.

Andy Bolton seemed to struggle with this idea. 'He's all right,' he said again. 'He can be good company. But I mean – well, he strikes me as a bit . . .' He stared blankly as he thought. 'I can't say I know anything against him for a fact, but sometimes the way he talks, I get the impression he's a bit of a wide boy. A bit of a wheeler-dealer, you know?'

'You think he's not honest?'

He looked alarmed. 'Oh, like I said, I don't know anything against him. But if someone was to tell me he was up to something a bit shady, I wouldn't be surprised. He's a bit mouthy, you know? Always going on about the important people he knows and the big money he's gonna make. If you've been anywhere or done anything, he's always got to go one better ¬ like if you've had a trip on a hot-air balloon, he's gone skydiving with the Pope.'

'He's a fantasist?' Slider suggested.

'Yeah, like that,' Bolton agreed. 'Not that there's any harm in that. I mean, it's quite entertaining to listen to him sometimes. But I tell you one thing.' It seemed to burst through his natural unwillingness to speak ill. 'I don't like the way he is around women. He's always looking at them, and making remarks. I don't like that sort of thing. You may think it's funny, but I think women should be treated with respect. And while he was living with Mel, he shouldn't have flirted with other women, and talked dirty to them. Any chance he got,' he went on, thoroughly roused now, 'he'd have his arm round their waist and be whispering and sniggering. One time we went to the Conningham, there was this female, he'd been chatting her up, like I say, and she went off to the loo, and he went straight after, and he was away a long time. When he came back he sort of gave me a wink and smacked his lips. I reckon they'd gone out the back and . . .' He let the sentence die, and sat for a moment frowning down at his hands.

Well, well, Slider thought. So friend Hibbert is a bit of a Lothario? Somehow he wasn't surprised. Fantasist, Lothario and wide boy. Suspect-wise, what was not to like? 'I understand you were helping him with his Elvis impersonations,' he said, to prime the pump again.

Bolton looked up, startled out of his thoughts, and gave a reluctant smile. 'Sharon told you about that, did she? Well, it's something I've done for years. I know it sounds funny, but I make a bit of money at it. You can, if you work hard, but it's a crowded field, so you've got to be good. Well, Scott was always asking me about it. Just to take the piss, to start with. But when he realizes there's actual money in it, he starts to take it serious, and says he wants to get into it.' He shook his head. 'I always tried to put him off. I mean, I can't see he had any talent for it. And I was worried that what he was really interested in was the girls – you know, you always get some hanging around when you do a stage act, even if it's only in a pub or a community hall. Groupies, he called 'em. He kept talking about them being easy – like fruit falling off a tree, he said. I didn't like that. But he went on and on until in the end, more to shut him up, really, I said I'd help him.'

'He actually had a date – a booking?'

'I don't know if you'd call it that. It was a mate's stag night. They weren't paying him or anything, as far as I could gather. Good thing, too – I know he's a mate and everything, but it has to be said, he's a crap Elvis. Can't sing, can't dance – all he had was the dark glasses, and the white rhinestone suit he was gonna hire.'

'And that was on Friday – last Friday, wasn't it?'

'That's right.' He looked suddenly stricken. 'God, the poor bastard. He must be kicking himself that he went. If he'd stayed home, none of this would've happened. He must be heartbroken.'

'So he did love Melanie?'

'Oh yes. They were besotted – all over each other. I know maybe I've given the wrong impression – he was a bit of a pain in the neck sometimes, but he was all right really, and he did love her. I think he got annoyed with her sometimes because she wouldn't marry him.'

'Why do you think that was?'

He made a comical face. 'I know, women are all supposed to be mad to get married, aren't they? But this time I know for a fact *he* asked *her* and she said no – or not yet, anyway – because they both told me. All she said to me was she wasn't ready yet. She said they'd only been going out two years and it wasn't long enough, and she said she'd got enough on her plate as it was. But Scott wanted kids, and the sooner the better. They were already living together, the way he saw it, and he had plans for them to get a house – well, he *is* in the trade – and the next step in his mind was to get married, have kids. But every time he asked her, she said she wasn't ready.'

Slider nodded. 'It's a big step,' he said profoundly. Then, 'Do you know if there was anything in her past that might have made her reluctant to get married?' he tried. He wondered how far the information about Melanie's 'bit of trouble' had gone.

But Bolton shook his head. 'I wasn't that chummy with her, really. We'd have a chat, and she was very nice and easy to get on with, but she never gave anything away. It was just time of day, sort of thing. I never felt – well, I reckon there was another Mel inside the one I knew. Must've been, when you think about it – I was just the neighbour, after all. Scott's the one you need to talk to about that,' he concluded; but with a faintly puzzled air, as if he wasn't sure Hibbert *was* the person to apply to, actually.

Which was interesting for all sorts of reasons.

EIGHT
Attitude Sickness

S imone Ridware, Melanie's work colleague and friend at the Natural History Museum, was a different prospect from Kiera Williams: older, to start with – late thirties by the look of her – well spoken and obviously educated. What Swilley always classified to herself as a National Trust sort of person – posh and well off – but in this case clever too. She was apparently in the Micropalaeontology Section, and how that differed from the Palaeontology Section Swilley no more cared than she could spell it.

Simone Ridware had offered to take her to the canteen for their talk, but Swilley arranged to meet her in a café nearby, by South Kensington Station. Just going into a museum gave her vertigo.

Despite being called Simone she was not French, even a bit. 'It was a name my mother picked. She just had a liking for it,' she said apologetically. 'I have a brother called Hubert, so I suppose I got off lightly.' She came from Maidstone originally, where her father was a solicitor, had gone to Benenden, then Cambridge, had worked for BP for a short time and then found her home-from-home within the dreaming spires and glazed Victorian tiles of the Nat His Mu. She had married a subsurface geologist she had met at BP (bet *their* conversations at home are exciting, Swilley thought) and had two children, Poppy and Oliver, aged five and seven, and lived in a large Victorian house in the nice bit of Muswell Hill. No surprises there.

She was, however, wearing a very elegant suit on her enviable figure, and Swilley would really have liked a better view of her shoes. Who'd have thought palaeontology was a hotbed of fashion?

They ordered coffee and Danish pastries, and Mrs Ridware

opened the batting with, 'You want to talk to me about Melanie, of course. What can I tell you?'

She had short, dark hair, fine and curly, like soft black feathers all over her head, and an averagely good-looking face subtly enhanced by skilful make-up. A geek, but *hardly dull at all*, Swilley paraphrased to herself. To the penetrating eye, she looked a little pale and worn under the make-up, and Swilley wondered if it was on Melanie's behalf, and hoped so. She put aside her chippy prejudices and prepared to listen.

'What was she like?' she asked. 'Did you like her?'

'We were friends,' said Mrs Ridware, as if that said it all. And then, 'I had tremendous admiration for her. She came from quite a difficult background, but she never let it hold her back. What she achieved, she achieved on her own merits. She was very good at her job, and she had a brilliant career ahead of her.' She paused and, as if realizing that this sounded too much like a press release, added in a different tone, 'Yes, I liked her. We were very close, and I shall miss her very much.'

'When you say she had a difficult background—?' Swilley tried.

'She came from a poor home,' Mrs Ridware said. 'Her father was feckless and her mother was ineffectual, so she was thrown on her own resources. He was often out of work, and I believe he gambled, too, so money was always tight. And her mother was a poor housekeeper. All too often Melanie as a child came home to have to cook supper herself and wash and iron her own clothes for school. She never had the material things other girls had, and I know you may think that's character-building –' she smiled at Swilley, who hadn't thought anything of the sort – 'but girls can be cruel and it's hard always to be an outsider. But despite his inadequacies, she adored her father. I gather he was a charming wastrel.'

Swilley nodded.

'That sort can be the hardest to resist, and do the most damage.'

'Melanie told you all this herself, did she?' Swilley asked.

'Yes, over time. It was hard for her to confide at first – I think she'd held herself back for so many years it had become a habit. But we liked each other from the first moment she joined the museum, and bit by bit the barriers came down – with me, at least. She was always guarded with other people.' She hesitated, and Swilley gave an encouraging nod. 'She developed a technique of getting everyone she met to talk about themselves, so that she wouldn't have to talk about *her*self. To be the listener is always safer – and it makes people like you. Everyone loved her. She had a large number of friends. But I think fundamentally she was a very lonely person.'

'Why was that?'

'Partly her background – her parents, I mean – and partly her father being killed. You know about that?'

'In the train crash – yes.'

'It was a terrible blow to her, and she had to do all the coping because her mother couldn't. She had to suppress her feelings and get on with things. And then her mother remarried a basically unsympathetic man, so the protective shell just got thicker, until it became such a habit she couldn't break it. When she first came to the museum I think she was desperate to talk to someone, but simply didn't know how. Fortunately we struck up a friendship and—' She shrugged, elegantly. 'I was glad to be her confidante.'

'So she didn't get on with her stepfather?'

'She wouldn't have liked anyone who took her father's place. But I gather – I never met him, you understand – that he was somewhat *limited*. No imagination. Everything by the book because he couldn't think further than that. And she might have accepted that – her mother, after all, was no Einstein – except that he gave himself airs and claimed a superiority he didn't have, and used it as the basis for imposing discipline on her.'

Atherton should be having this conversation, Swilley thought resentfully. Or the boss. I'm a solid facts girl. *She didn't like her stepdad, and he tried to make her toe the line.* Why dress it up in all this airy-fairy psychobabble? 'Did he hit her?'

'I didn't mean discipline in that sense,' Mrs Ridware said, kindly enough to get up Swilley's nose.

'But did he hit her?' she repeated stolidly.

She hesitated. 'I think he did, on occasion – but not violently. I don't want you to think he was beating her, or anything like that. Not that Nigel and I believe in corporal punishment – we would *never* hit Poppy or Oliver – it sends all the wrong signals and teaches the wrong values. But many people believe that the occasional slap is justified, and I suppose Melanie's stepfather was one of them. Of course, she was too old by then to do other than resent it, especially as he wasn't her real father. They used to have tremendous arguments, she told me. I think it was a relief all round when she left home.'

'Did she tell you about the trouble she got into?'

'You mean—?'

'Getting pregnant,' Swilley said brutally. The girl was dead, for heaven's sake. The time to be holding stuff back was well gone.

'Yes, she told me about that. How did you know?'

'Her mum told us.'

'Oh. Of course. But I don't think she told another soul about it. Certainly nobody here knew except me. It was a desperately painful incident, and coming so soon after her father dying . . .'

'Did she resent her stepdad for making her have the abortion?'

'No, not exactly. She knew it was the only thing to be done, and she knew she wouldn't have had the same career if she *had* kept it. I don't think he forced her – of course, there was pressure put on her, but if she'd really insisted . . .'

Yeah, thought Swilley. That's all right from someone with nice supportive parents who always discussed things rationally with their kids. And where money had never been an issue. She knew what 'pressure' would have meant in Melanie's case, and how there would have been no alternative for a girl with no money and nowhere else to go.

'But she regretted it deeply, all the same,' Mrs Ridware went on. 'She brooded about the child she didn't have. She felt guilty because she hadn't protected it. And she doubted her fitness to be a mother, because she had failed so spectacularly at the first hurdle.' She sighed. 'It was something we talked about often, when we went out alone together, after work. She envied me my children, said how lucky I was to have had a normal life, with everything happening as it should, naturally and in the right order.' She looked at Swilley, her eyes suddenly vulnerable and troubled. 'I know I'm lucky, I really do. I have everything, and Melanie—' She bit her lip. 'Now she's had even her life taken away from her. Whoever did that—' She stopped abruptly and looked away.

She really had cared about Melanie, then. Swilley liked her better.

'What about Scott Hibbert? Did you ever meet him?'

'Once or twice, when he came to meet Melanie after work, and at the Christmas party. They'd only been going out for just over two years. I can't say I knew him well, except for what Melanie told me.'

'And what was that?'

'She was madly in love with him,' said Mrs Ridware, with a sorrowful look, 'but in my view he wasn't right for her. She had real depths and real intellect, but he was just a – a flashy, self-centred nothing. He was so shallow—' She paused, and Swilley finished for her without thinking:

'—it was a wonder he didn't evaporate?'

But she didn't take offence. She gave a small, controlled smile. 'Yes. I must remember that – it's good.'

'But they were living together and he wanted to marry her.'

'Yes, she said he'd proposed more than once. I think he thought she'd be a good corporate wife – an asset to his career. It was all about him. He was an awful snob, you know – still is, I suppose. I don't know why I'm talking about him in the past tense. At the Christmas parties he was always name-dropping, buttonholing the most important people, trying to ingratiate himself with anyone with a title. I think he thought Melanie would give him a leg up the social scale.'

'So he didn't love her?'

'Oh, goodness, I didn't mean that. I'm sure he did. He was certainly all over her, embarrassingly so sometimes. But I don't think he ever really – what do they say nowadays? – *got* her. He loved her for the wrong reasons, because he didn't really know her.'

'If he was so unsatisfactory, why did she love him?'

'He was handsome, well dressed, attentive, he loved her. That most of all, I think – she was desperate to be loved. But I think deep down she knew it was no good. Almost the whole time she's been with him she's been unhappy. They moved in together about three months after they met – almost exactly two years ago – and I noticed a change in her at once. Something's been troubling her, something she won't talk to me about, and I don't know what it could be if it's not Scott. And it gets worse the longer it goes on. Just lately she's been really worried, withdrawn and preoccupied. I know he's been pressing her to marry him, because he wants to start a family, and as I said, she has doubts about her fitness to be a mother. But I wonder if underneath she hasn't realized that Scott simply won't do?'

Swilley noticed she had slipped into the present tense. A good sign that they really had been close, and that her testimony was therefore worth something. 'Did she say that to you?' she asked.

'No, never. She's very loyal to him. As I said, these last two years there's been a part of her closed off even from me. But you know . . .' She hesitated, and went on with an appeal to Swilley, woman to woman. 'You know that women are always supposed to end up marrying their fathers? I think perhaps she'd realized she'd picked a man who, on the surface looked right – steady job, money in his pockets and so on – but underneath was like her father after all – an unreliable charmer.'

Or maybe she hadn't, Swilley thought, resisting the appeal. Maybe it was something else entirely. *All women marry their fathers, eh?* She considered her own Tony. Actually, ghastly thought, he *was* a bit like how she remembered her dad – not to look at so much as in personality – the kindness and patience, the way he'd look at her with that sort of what-are-you-going to-get-up-to-next wry smile, all up one side . . . She jerked herself back from the edge of the abyss.

'What can you tell me about last Friday?' she said, extra sternly to make up for having weakened.

Simone Ridware blinked, but stood up to the question bravely. 'It was just an ordinary Friday, as far as I remember. Let me see. Melanie had a bit of a tiff with Scott that morning, but that wasn't unusual.'

A tiff, eh? How posh, thought Swilley. 'What about?'

'Oh, it wasn't serious. Just one of the niggling little did-didn't arguments people have. He was going away for the weekend to see some of his old friends from home, whom Melanie didn't like: they were rather noisy and vulgar. Words were had; but she was over it by mid-morning. She said it was her fault – nobody likes to think their partner despises their friends. And she was going out herself that evening to meet some of her old friends from home, and Scott probably didn't like any of them any better. She was a very balanced person in that way – always able to see the other side.'

'So when she left work, she was in a normal mood, going out for a drink with the girls? Not unhappy or worried or anxious or anything?'

She frowned. 'I'm – not sure. She did seem very quiet that afternoon. Preoccupied. When I spoke to her just before she left, she was smiling and cheerful, but then she was always a good actor. I did feel there was something on her mind, something hanging over her. But it could just have been Scott's weekend away. Or I could have been imagining it.'

'You don't know of anything specific she might have been worried about?'

'Beyond her relationship with Scott – no.'

'She didn't have money worries?'

'Not as far as I know.'

'Health problems?'

'She never mentioned any. She seemed well.'

'Did she have a drug habit?'

'Good heavens, no!'

'And was that the last time you spoke to her? Friday going-home time?'

'Yes. Sometimes she would ring me at home in the evening for a chat, but as she was out with friends I wouldn't have expected that, on that Friday. And she didn't ring. So the last words I spoke to her were, "See you on Monday."'

She relapsed into a very despondent pose, looking as if she might cry. But Benenden girls don't cry in public. They breed a gritty sort of chap down there.

In fairness, Swilley suspended her automatic hostility to privilege for long enough to acknowledge that she really had cared for Melanie, and to be glad that *someone* had.

Atherton's idea of a trip to Salisbury would probably have featured a stroll through the cobbled streets looking in the antique shops, a glance round the Cathedral, and possibly tea in Ye Olde Precinct Tea Rooms if the time was right. It wouldn't by any stretch of the imagination have involved his standing in some very chilly rain on the edge of an arterial road (along which the traffic, suspiciously, was all heading *out* of the city at great speed, buffeting him in passing and dashing dirty spray at his back in the process) looking enquiringly into the Stygian shadows of an independent garage workshop. His nostrils flared at the smell of oil. There were oil patches on the floor and oily pictures of large-busted women on the walls. A red Ford Focus was up on the lift and dripping oil into the lube pit. Oil, he fancied he could say with some assurance, was the motif *du jour*.

A man emerged from the depths of the cavern, wearing oily overalls and wiping his hands on an oily rag. He had a puggily good-looking face, liberally streaked with yes-you've-guessed-it; his gingery fair hair was cut into a halo of spikes and – Atherton would have thought it unnecessary given the prevalence of freely-available dressing, but there you go – waxed to keep them in position. He said, 'Can I help you?' but without notable friendliness.

'I'm looking for Paul Heaton,' Atherton said.

'That's me,' said the man, with a slight increase in latent hostility as his eyes raked Atherton, in his well-fitting coat and expensive shoes, trying to guess who he was.

Fortunately, Atherton had spotted, lurking in the shadows, something a bit more interesting than a Focus. '*Like* the Aston,' he said. 'DB6, isn't it? Not as pretty as the five, but it handles so much better. Is it yours?'

'Yeah,' said Heaton, all resistance seeping away like water down the plug hole. 'I'm rebuilding it.'

He led the way over and a satisfactory conversation followed as they examined the car together in every aspect and Heaton described the condition he had bought it in, the processes he was going through to restore it and what he planned to do with it when it was finished. At the end of which Atherton was no longer a snotty-looking stranger and possible trouble but a fellow DB-lover, and was offered a cuppa. The tea came in a mug decorated with oily fingermarks (Atherton noted them professionally – you'd get beautiful lifts off those) and had a faint fragrance of Castrol about it, but he sipped it bravely and brought the conversation round to the wedding and Scott Hibbert.

Paul Heaton had been the best man – in the absence of the groom on honeymoon, the closest Atherton could get to the horse's mouth. And subtlety and perseverance turned out not to be needed. To a fellow DB fan, Heaton was happy to spill everything, and at once, no questions asked.

'Oh, he was at the wedding all right, but he never turned up to the stag do. Dave was pissed off about it, but what can you do? Scott's like that – unreliable bugger.' It was said without heat – blokes who'd been at school with each other accepted each other's little peccadilloes.

'Called off, did he?' Atherton asked, trying not to sound as if that was very, *very* interesting.

'I don't know about called off. He just never showed. Typical, when he was the one who'd made all the fuss – there *had* to be a stag night, and *had* to be done a certain way. He was the one who made all the arrangements, booked the place and phoned everybody up, and then *he's* the one who doesn't turn up.'

'But wasn't he supposed to be doing the entertainment?'

'Eh?'

'He was going to do his Elvis impersonation act, wasn't he?'

The pale-blue eyes under the raised sandy eyebrows were genuinely puzzled. 'Elvis act? What are you talking about?

Scott doesn't do anything like that. He organized a strip-pergram – she came dressed as a postman, because Dave's with the Royal Mail. She was good, too,' he added with reminiscent relish. Then came back to the present. 'What you on about?'

'He told a friend back home he was doing an Elvis imper-sonation at the stag on Friday,' Atherton said.

Heaton shrugged. 'That's Scott all over. He's a bit – you know.' He made the 'mouthy' gesture with the hand that wasn't holding the mug. 'You don't want to take any notice of half he says. He was always like that – at school he was always on about stuff he'd done, and you knew it was all bullshit. Like, he's driven his dad's car when he was ten, and gone all the way with a girl when he was twelve, and he'd done this, that and the other. Showing off, you know. But that's just his way. He's all right, really. Elvis impersonations!' He shook his head in amused wonder. 'What'll he come up with next? He's a joker!'

'So,' Atherton said, getting down to business, 'he didn't come to the stag, but he did come to the wedding?'

'Yeah, he turned up at the church, but he was like a cat on hot bricks. He was on the end of the pew behind me, and I could see him fidgeting about all the way through. Then as soon as the photographs were finished, he comes up to me and says he's not going to the reception – asks me to apolo-gize to Dave. Says he's got a really important piece of business for his firm he's got to see to. Says it's a massive deal and worth a big bonus and a promotion if he pulls it off. Then off he goes.' He shrugged. 'I didn't say anything to Dave right then – no point in upsetting anyone. But later on Dave comes up to me and says, where's Scott, I haven't seen him, so I tell him then. Well, he shrugs and says, same old Scott, but I could see he was a bit pissed off, when he'd missed the stag as well.'

'Did he say why he'd missed it?'

'I never got the chance to ask. He arrived at the last minute, and you can't chat in church, can you? Then there were the photographs, and time that was all over, he'd gone again. I suppose he wanted to get back to his bird. All that about a big deal going down – that's just the sort of thing he says. He's only an estate agent, for crying out loud. You'd think he was doing oil deals with Arab sheikhs.'

He swilled down some tea, and then a frown came over his well-lubricated face. 'Why are you asking me all this, anyway?' Awareness dawned. 'Oh Christ, I forgot about his bird – his girlfriend getting killed. Poor old Scotty – but you don't think he had anything to do with it? That's not why you're asking, is it?'

'It's just routine,' Atherton said soothingly. 'We have to establish where everyone was, whether we suspect them or not. It's like a pattern, you see – only if you know where everyone was, can you see who's missing.'

Heaton looked baffled, as well he might, by this piece of hoo-ha. 'I see,' he said doubtfully.

'So, have you any idea where he might have been on Friday night and Saturday morning?'

'No,' Heaton said, as though that were obvious. 'Why don't you ask him?'

Atherton dodged that one. 'Was there anywhere you know that he went when he was down this way? Where he might go? Other friends? Hobbies, sports, clubs?'

'No. I mean I don't know. He's lived here all his life, till he went to London, so it could be anywhere, couldn't it? Anyway,' he concluded with an air of relief, 'wherever he was, he couldn't have had anything to do with – with the murder.' Like many people, he found the word odd on his lips when it was real life and not fiction or the telly. 'He was dead keen on her. Always talking about her – how smart she was, how posh she was, what a good job she had, how she was nuts about him. They were going to get married in September.'

'Is that what he said?'

'Yeah, September. I remember because I usually have me holiday in September and he said I'd have to change it this year because of his wedding. He was going to fly everybody out to St Lucia for a week. Well –' he shrugged again – 'I took *that* with a pinch of salt. But it sounded good when he said it. This resort with all tropical flowers and a pool with a free swim-up bar, and they were going to get married on the beach at sunset, and Mel was going to arrive on a white horse, riding through the surf.'

'Romantic.'

He smiled unwillingly. 'Oh yeah, he can spin a tale, old Scott. You'd go to him every time for romantic. But whatever, he was dead keen on Mel.'

'Did you like her? You'd met her?'

'I can't say I *knew* her. He'd brought her down a couple of times, weekends, to see his mum and dad, and they'd come to the pub Saturday night, where a bunch of us get together. She was nice, but quiet, you know? You couldn't get much of an idea what she was like. She was very nice, though,' he said again, helpless to offer more insight. He fidgeted, some thought obviously bothering him, like a raspberry pip between the teeth. Atherton looked receptive, and finally he said, 'The second time I saw her, in the pub: that night Scott was a bit, well, bumptious. Going on about how much money he was going to make and the big house him and Mel were going to have and all that kind of stuff. Showing off, you know? And I think she felt a bit embarrassed. Well, *I* was embarrassed, and I know him! And it has to be said a lot of pints went down that night, and we probably all got a bit noisy. Anyway after that, she didn't come out with him again, down here, with our lot. I think that's why she didn't come to the wedding. He said it was because she was working, but maybe . . .' He stared a moment at nothing, ordering his thoughts. 'Course,' he concluded in fairness, 'it's not really a women's night out. There's eight or ten of us, all went to school together. We don't usually bring our birds, and if one or two of 'em does come, they sit off on their own and talk to each other. But o' course, she didn't know anyone, Mel. And then Scott going on about how much money he's making and the big car he's getting and all that. It was probably uncomfortable for her.'

He sniffed, finished his tea in one gulp, wiped his nose on the cuff of his overall, decorating it with another hydrocarbon smear, and said, 'That your Astra? VXR, innit? What is it, two litre? What's it drive like?'

Thus the two chaps were able to wade safely back before the incoming tide of psychoanalysis and – *aargh*! – 'relationships'

to the safe, dry shore of car ownership, and parted in good
humour with each other. Atherton even shook his hand, and
nobly waited until he was out of sight before getting out a
handkerchief to wipe it.

Bob Bailey, the SOC manager, tracked Slider down in the
canteen where he was having a very late lunch – so late he
had had to have a leftover portion of macaroni cheese heated
up for him in the microwave, and he only got that because
the canteen staff liked him, and it was a crusty bit from the
corner of the dish that no one else fancied. He had quar-
antined himself in a far corner with a heap of reports to
reread. On the other side of the room, nearer the windows
and a watery bit of sunshine that was attempting to creep
in through the soot of ages on the panes, various uniforms
were having their afternoon tea break, with a buzz of chatter
and the occasional burst of laughter.

Bailey eyed the congealing remains on the plate – Slider
wasn't getting on with it very well – and thought the bad news
he was delivering might usefully serve as a counter-irritant.

'I was passing,' he said, 'so I thought I'd come and report
to you in person.'

Slider pushed his plate away with every appearance of relief,
and said, 'Judging by your face, it isn't good news.'

'Depends on your point of view. I should think Scott
Hibbert's dear old white-haired mother would be very pleased.'
He sat down. 'We've gone over every inch of the flat, the stairs
and the common parts, and there's nothing to suggest Melanie
Hunter was killed there. We've also looked at her car, and
though she was obviously in there alive, there's no reason to
think she was restrained there or transported dead. In fact, the
back seats are so pristine I wouldn't think anyone's ever ridden
in them. I think you can take it as read that she left her own
premises alive.'

'I don't know that I'm surprised,' Slider said. 'It was always
a possibility that she was killed elsewhere, and there were
always problems about her being killed in the flat – the dog
being the main one.'

'Yes, most dogs would go nuts in a scenario like that.'

'But if she left the flat alive, why would she leave her handbag and take the door keys? Leaving the handbag looks like coercion, but taking the keys looks like a voluntary action.' None of the evidence made a lot of sense. 'Never mind.' He pulled himself together, and managed a polite smile. 'Not your problem.'

'Thank God for that,' said Bailey.

NINE

Lynch, Anyone?

'So,' Atherton said to his assembled colleagues, 'wherever Hibbert was on Friday night and Saturday morning, it wasn't where he said he was. And I checked the hotel he was supposed to have been staying in, and guess what, folks?'

'Why wasn't he staying with his parents?' Connolly asked.

'So as not to disturb them when arriving home drunk in the small hours from the stag do,' Atherton said.

'It doesn't follow that he didn't change his mind,' Norma said.

'I know,' said Atherton, 'and we'll have to check that.'

'Or he could have gone to a different hotel,' said Hollis.

'Rather than check them all,' Atherton said with irony, 'why don't we ask him? But it's my bet that, if he wasn't at the stag, and hardly at the wedding, he probably wasn't in the area at all. He was off doing something nefarious, and the wedding was just his alibi.'

'Not much of an alibi,' Connolly said derisively, 'when ya could bust it that easy.'

'He probably thought no one would check,' Atherton said. 'Swaggering overconfidence doesn't usually go with pain-staking analysis.'

'But he'd told her well before the date that he was going to this wedding. Told Andy Bolton, too,' said Mackay.

'The wedding was fact, not fiction,' Atherton said. 'What's your point?'

'Well, are you saying he planned to kill her as soon as he got the invitation?' Mackay asked. 'Or was it just lucky chance, he killed her spurathemoment and happened to have this alibi set up?'

'Lucky?' Connolly protested.

'For him, not for her.'

'There must have been a degree of planning,' Atherton said, 'because we know she was killed that evening, so he must have come back from wherever he was to do it. I can't see him plotting far ahead, but maybe it gradually grew on him he could make use of the occasion, if he was getting fed up with her for some reason.'

'Yeah, but what reason?' Mackay said.

'Never mind that for the moment. From our point of view, he's good because he's got all the time in the world to take the body out to Ruislip, do any cleaning up that's needed in the flat, and get back to Salisbury for an eleven o'clock wedding. He wouldn't be likely to interfere with her sexually. And he knows the dog, and it knows him. Did you notice how he didn't seem to want anything to do with it afterwards?' he added, looking round them.

'What does that prove?' Swilley asked.

'Well, I'm just thinking, if he had a bit of trouble with it at the time – and why wouldn't he? – he might have been very glad someone had taken it away when he got back. He might well be scared of seeing it again, in case it attacked him.'

Connolly said, 'But if it was him – and fair play to ya, he's a big enough thick to think no one would check the stagger alibi – why would he leave the wedding early? Why not stay on for the rest of the day?'

'Maybe he didn't want to be around his mates answering questions about why he'd missed the stag,' Atherton said. 'Maybe he was too shaken up by the murder to be around people at all. It takes a cool head to behave as if nothing's happened when you've just killed someone.'

Connolly nodded. 'And didn't we think it was queer he didn't know she was missing – that he hadn't rung her all Saturday? Well, why would he, if he knew she was dead?'

'But why,' said Norma, 'if it was Hibbert who killed her, would he take her door keys? He had keys of his own.'

Atherton declined to be dampened. 'To make it look as if she'd gone out on her own two feet.'

'But then wouldn't he have taken her whole handbag?' Norma said.

'That would just make more things to get rid of. Keys are easy to drop down a drain, but a handbag the size of Belgium, like you women all carry these days . . .'

It was at this point that Slider came in, just in time to save Atherton from being lynched for the 'you women'. Atherton told him about the busted alibi; Slider told them about the clean flat. 'So whoever killed her, it wasn't at home.'

Atherton was not downcast. 'Never mind, it still makes it Hibbert for my money. Who else could so easily lure her into his car and drive off without her putting up a fight? He only has to pretend it's something romantic – let's look at the lido by moonlight, something like that.'

'At that time of night?' Swilley objected.

'Best time for romance. Get Tony to explain it to you. Anyway, we know for a fact that he's lied about his alibi, and there must be a reason for that.'

'I agree that Hibbert's got some explaining to do about where he spent the night,' Slider began.

'If he was killing her and dumping the body,' Hollis said, 'he'd have been too late to drive to Salisbury and check into an hotel. More likely he just got changed at the flat and went to the wedding from there.'

'He'd have had to leave early, anyway, not to be seen,' Mackay said. 'Maybe slept in his car in a lay-by or something.'

'At least it gives us something to check,' Slider said. 'Whatever he was doing, there must have been some car movements. Fathom, put his reg number into the ANPR and see if you can find out where he was at any point between Friday morning and Sunday morning. I'd sooner have something concrete to face him with than just asking him blind where he was and having a whole lot of new lies to disprove.'

'You'll get them anyway,' Atherton said.

'At least we can narrow the field if we know whether he was in Maidstone, Maidenhead or Middlesborough.'

'I've got something else, boss,' Swilley said. 'This Hibbert talk's all very well.' She gave Atherton a look so cool you could have kept a side of beef on it for a week. 'But everybody agrees he's a prime plonker and about as subtle as a hand grenade. Plotting cunning murders and carrying them out—'

'Not that cunning,' Atherton protested.

'Not that obvious, either, or we'd know all about it.'

'A person can pretend to be more gormless than they are.'

'Oh, is that your excuse?'

'What's your point, Norma?' Slider intervened hastily.

She turned to him. 'I've been going through Melanie's papers, and I started off with her bank statements and so on. Well, she was doing all right, just about breaking even, like most of us with a mortgage. She and Scott bought the flat between them and they were paying half each, and I suppose the same went for the bills – I haven't got that far yet, but it's fair to assume. But the thing is, a couple of years ago she had a decent amount in savings, but it's been going down steadily. She's been drawing out sums of money in cash – five hundred, a thousand, two hundred – at irregular intervals for the last two years. Ever since she moved into that house. And Simone Ridware said that for about the same length of time she's felt Melanie had something on her mind, was worried and anxious about something. She thought it was to do with Scott, because she reckoned Melanie knew subconsciously that he wasn't good enough for her.'

'Makes sense to me,' said Atherton. 'The man's a tool.'

Swilley shook her head. 'That's crap. She'd only just met him – they'd only been going out for three months when they got the flat together, so they must have decided to live together almost from day one. Which means she was head over heels in love with him. That doesn't wear off in an instant. Two years ago she'd have been happy as Larry setting up home with her new bloke. But from the time she moves into *that house*, she's anxious, and lumps of cash start disappearing from her savings.' She looked at Slider. 'What does that add up to, boss?'

'I don't know that it adds up to anything more than her salary not quite being enough, but you're thinking blackmail?' he obliged.

'Right. And who in the house made mysterious hints about her having secrets no one knew? And went out to the pub with her but never saw fit to tell us? And has a criminal record?'

'Not for blackmail,' Atherton objected.

'No, for murder,' Norma said triumphantly.

'Why would he blackmail her?' Hollis asked, after a short silence paid tribute to the idea.

'For money, of course,' Swilley said, witheringly. 'He can't get a job, he's living on benefits – why not?'

'He owns that flat,' Connolly added, with a shade of reluctance. 'He doesn't rent it. How'd he afford it, on the broo?'

'No, I mean, what'd he blackmail her *with*,' Hollis said.

'I dunno. Maybe that abortion thing – maybe she didn't want Scott to know about it. Or maybe she'd done something else. We don't know – her mum said she got into bad company at one time, so she may have been hiding some other secret.'

'But then why would he kill her?' Hollis persisted. 'You don't kill the person you're blackmailing – that cuts off the supply. It's the other way round. The victim kills the blackmailer out o' desperation.'

'Well,' Swilley said, thinking, 'maybe she did get desperate – she was near the end of her savings. Maybe she finally stood up to him and threatened to go to the police. Fitton couldn't allow that. He'd be finished – he's out on licence, he'd have gone straight back inside so fast his head would swim. No, in the end he had more to lose than she did, and maybe she finally realized it. So then he realized she'd have a hold on him for the rest of his life, and decided to get rid of her.'

'*If* she knew about his past,' Atherton said. 'No one else seems to have.'

'Well, we don't know, do we?' she snapped. 'We can't ask her.' She appealed to Slider. 'It's just that it looks like a coincidence, boss, the timing. As soon as she comes into contact with Fitton, she starts shelling out cash, and goes round being anxious.'

Slider nodded reluctantly. 'There may be something in it. And I know Mr Porson would like to get Fitton in and sweat him a bit. There are unanswered questions.'

'And he has the mark o' Cain on his brow,' Connolly concluded disgustedly. 'Sure, give a dog a bad name . . .'

Slider looked at her kindly. 'We're just going to ask him some questions. He might even find it a relief – it can't be nice for him cooped up in that flat with the media howling for his blood. He might like a nice, quiet cell for a change. Get a good night's sleep.' Connolly looked at him reproachfully, but he wasn't joking. 'And a square meal,' he added. 'He probably hasn't eaten in days – can't get out to the shops, can he?'

'But guv,' Atherton said, 'what about Hibbert? Alibi blown, lies all round, absent without leave for the very time we're interested in?'

'Fathom can look for his car on the ANPR, and then we'll see. Don't look at me like that. We can always do him later. He's not going anywhere.'

As Slider predicted, Porson was thrilled with the new evidence, if that's what it was, against Fitton. '*That's* more like it. A nice juicy blackmail to get our teeth into.'

'It's only a suggestion, sir. We haven't got anything concrete to go on.'

'Except that he never told us about going out for drinkies with the girl, did he? That's enough concrete for a dam. Besides,' he added, his brows converging like animals round a waterhole, 'it's getting a bit ugly out there. Bloody lunch mob it's turning into. We don't want some bright spark chucking a rock through his window or pouring petrol through his letterbox. Better get him in. Poor bastard might even be grateful,' he added, echoing Slider. 'Get it over with. He must know we're going to have to tug him sooner or later.'

'It will give us a chance to go over his flat,' Slider said.

'Right. If he did kill her, it'd make more sense to do it in his flat, out of the way of the dog. Ask her to come down for a minute, boom. Then straight into her car and away.'

'Her car was clean.'

'He could have wrapped her in something.'

'And apparently, he can't drive,' Slider mentioned. 'He's certainly never had a licence.'

'Easy to pretend you can't drive when you can,' Porson dismissed the quibble. 'If it was the other way round . . . Anyway, bring him in. But not right now. Don't want to start a riot. Make it a dawn raid – snatch him in the early hours when there's nobody about. Try and get him out without any photos. Did you see this morning's effort? Photo of Melanie Hunter right next to that old one of Fitton's wife they used at the time. Talk about conflagatory! Might as well put "He Done It" in big letters right across the headline.'

Inflammatory and confrontational enough to create a conflagration, Slider thought as he went away to set things in train. There was economy in Porson's madness.

McLaren appeared in Slider's doorway. Slider was on the phone, and held up his hand while he finished the call, which gave him a moment and an excuse to study his detective constable's amazingly changed appearance. McLaren had had his hair cut, which was unusual enough – it was habitually on the shaggy and collar-brushing side – but it looked as if it had also been *styled*, which was weird in the extreme. As against that, he had definitely lost weight – his cheeks looked quite sunken – and today there was none of that sappy air of dreamy satisfaction. He was leaning against the door frame with a disconsolate look about him.

'Right,' Slider said into the phone. 'Thank you.' And put it down.

McLaren eased himself upright. 'Guv, I got something.'

Slider almost said, I hope it's not catching. But baiting this new McLaren wasn't so much fun. 'Let's have it, then.'

'I found out where she was, that missing ten minutes on her way home. I been doing all the shops up and down Uxbridge Road. First of all she parks up and goes to the ATM, takes some money out. I checked – it was two hundred quid. I got her on the ATM camera. And then, a couple of doors down, there's this Chinese place, the Golden Dragon Pavilion. It's a takeaway.'

'I know it.' It used to be called the Hung Fat. Perhaps they finally realized the name was not working for the English clientele.

'It's a family business – well, they always are, aren't they? Mum and Dad, couple o' young cousins in the back, and the eldest son on the till. Well, I shows 'em the photo, and they all say no, no, never seen, the way they always do. But I see the young lad clock her, so I hang about outside till mum and dad goes in the back, then I goes back in for a crafty word with him.'

'Does he speak English?'

'Oh yeah. He was born here. His mum and dad was, too. It's just the cousins that are over from the old country. But they all pretend not to speak English. Stops 'em being bothered.'

Slider knew this was a perennial problem with the Chinese community – the linguistic equivalent of the Great Wall. He had come across it in his Central days, when investigating anything in the Chinatown section of Soho had been a specialist job with its own unit. Mostly they just gave you the Look that said no understand, but if pressed they would burst into floods of hysterical-sounding Chinese, with hand gestures and deep scowls, to drive you away. But out here, away from the centre, they lived a quietly separate life and caused no trouble, so leaving them alone worked well both ways.

'So, did you get anything out of him?'

'Yeah, once I got him on his own he said he'd seen her face in the papers and recognized her. Course, he wouldn't come forward, but now I was asking – she come in that night, Friday, and bought a takeaway.'

'Did she, indeed!'

'Yeah, and they cook everything fresh, so it took eight, ten minutes – they had telephone orders to do before hers. She sat down in the corner to wait, and he said she stared at the telly for a bit, then she got out a pen and paper. He said she seemed to be working out sums, something like that – said it looked like numbers, not words. Anyway, then her order comes out. Sweet an' sour pork balls, spicy chicken with bean sprouts, and crispy fried noodles. She pays, and then goes off. That's between twenty and twenty-five past ten, he says. Which makes it right for her getting home around half past.'

'Which means she didn't go anywhere else or meet anyone else,' Slider concluded. Well, that was one thing cleared up. 'Did anyone come in while she was there?'

'Yeah, a couple of people come in for their telephone orders, but Lee says they never spoke to her. Didn't even look at her. Just come up to the counter, took their orders and left. But we can check that for ourselves, guv, because they got a CCTV camera. When he said she'd been in I said we've have to have the tape, and he said his mum and dad would never allow it. So I had to lean on him a bit. He went in the back and I could hear this almighty row going on – all scribble-talk, y'know? – but in the end he comes back with the tape.'

'Good,' said Slider. 'Even if she didn't speak to anyone, it's possible someone noticed her and followed her home.' Though that had always been a possibility, with or without a Chinese takeaway. But that scenario presented its own problems, because either she would have had to invite them into her flat to get murdered there, or have got into a car with them – theirs or hers – to be driven away and murdered somewhere else. And why would she do that? Being snatched between her car and the flat didn't work because she parked right outside Fitton's window and he would have heard the struggle; and there were no signs on the body of her having been restrained.

'Well, let's go and look at it,' he said. He followed McLaren to the tape room and watched over his shoulder as he ploughed through fast-forward until the right time cue came up and he pressed play. There was nothing much to it. The camera was above the television, so it showed anyone coming in the door three-quarter view, anyone at the counter side-on, and anyone on the chairs full face. But since everyone at some point had to look at the screen – the human who could be in the same room as a television and not look at it once had not been bred yet – there was at least one full-face of everyone.

Slider saw Melanie Hunter walk into the otherwise empty shop and up to the counter. She gave Lee the order – she didn't seem, interestingly, to study the menu on the wall behind him, but gave the order at once as if she had decided before she came in. She smiled at him, and he smiled back and said something – presumably something on the lines of 'it'll be ten minutes'. Then she went and sat on the plastic chair in the corner, at the end of the row of four, and gazed idly into the camera for some time.

It was a chance for Slider to study her face. People don't look at their best staring blankly at the idiot box, but he could see that she was pretty, and she looked tired. It was poignant for him, because unlike the people she had known, whom they had been interviewing, this was the first time he had seen her alive, so from now on it would be his only living memory of her. He looked at her, knowing that the sand was running rapidly out of her glass, that she was living the last minutes of her life without knowing it. To her it was just the end of another day. He saw her rub an itch on the end of her nose, push her hair back from her forehead: unconscious, natural movements that would always be part of his knowledge of her now. His life was so intimately bound with hers, for this intense period, he felt anguished and guilty that he could not tell the girl in the grainy greyscale picture what he knew, and save her. *Don't go home tonight!* But if it didn't get her tonight, would death come for her anyway, tomorrow, or next week? How determined was her murderer that she should die? And *why?* That above all.

She seemed to think of something. She pulled her handbag over on to her lap and rummaged in it, came up with a pen and a piece of paper – it looked like a till receipt – and began writing on the back. That Lee was a smart fellow, he thought: it *did* look like numbers rather than words. But it was not possible to read it. She jotted, totted, and thought; and meanwhile other customers came in, walked across to the counter, looked at the television, received their orders and went out. None seemed to notice the girl in the corner – certainly no one looked at her directly or addressed her.

Finally Lee came out with a stiff paper carrier bag and said something and she looked up. She balled the paper she had been writing on in her hand. Slider became tense. *What happened to that paper?* He watched it, rather than her, as she put away the pen and got out her purse, went to the counter, paid, received change, put away her purse and took up the handles of the carrier. At that point she seemed to become aware of the paper in her hand, and dropped it with the utmost casualness into the carrier. Slider let his breath out.

'Wonder what was on that bit of paper,' McLaren said, breaking the silence, and proving himself more of a detective than was often apparent.

'Whatever it was, it's with the rest of the rubbish now,' Slider said. 'Wherever that is.'

Melanie said goodnight, with a smile, to Lee, walked to the shop door, opened it and turned right, disappearing out of camera range.

'Can't see her motor,' McLaren said, 'but she parked outside the ATM, which is that way.' And a moment later, 'There. That's her.' He ran the tape back and watched again, slowing it as a small car, which could have been a Polo, and could have been green, went past in the road outside, just visible to the camera. 'You can't see the driver, but I bet that's her.'

'It doesn't really matter,' Slider said. 'We know she went home and she must have gone straight there because of the time.' The time cue in the corner was showing 22.25. She had driven away to her appointment with death, and there was nothing he could do to change it.

As they walked back to the main office, McLaren said, 'Guv, I been thinking.'

'I tried that once,' Slider said. 'Didn't take to it.'

'About that takeaway,' McLaren went on. His only defence against Slider's more inexplicable remarks was to ignore them. 'That's a meal for one. Not enough there for two.'

'I take your word for it,' Slider said, and meant it. McLaren was the oracle when it came to junk food. He had never met a ready meal he didn't like. Or, at least, that had bccn the case up until whatever epiphany had recently struck him.

'Well, then, what happened to it?' McLaren asked.

'You're right. We know she didn't eat it,' Slider said, 'because we have the forensic report on her stomach contents. If she'd eaten it so soon before she was killed, it would still have been in the stomach and recognizable.'

'Anyway, she'd just had a big dinner,' McLaren said.

'And she couldn't have bought it in a fit of absent-mindedness, since she had ten minutes to sit and think while it was being cooked. So, we have to conclude . . .?'

'That she bought it for someone else,' McLaren said. 'But who?'

'And then there's the money. I can't remember offhand but I'm pretty sure there wasn't two hundred pounds in her purse.'

'No, guv,' McLaren said. 'Forty pounds and some change. And she didn't spend a hundred and sixty on a takeaway.'

In the office, Hollis was still at work and Atherton and Swilley were back. They gathered round and Slider explained about the tape and Melanie's takeaway purchase.

'Not for herself, obviously. But who do you buy a takeaway for?' Atherton said. 'Someone you know. Someone you live with.'

'Hibbert was away,' said Hollis.

'Or was he?' Atherton countered. 'With Melanie dead, we've only his word for it. We certainly know where he wasn't. Suppose when he rang her at the pub that night he told her he'd seen the error of his ways and was on his way home?'

'And asked her to get him a takeaway?' Norma said scornfully. 'When he was on his way to murder her?'

'You don't know what the habit was between them,' he reasoned. 'She didn't know she was for the chop. Maybe it was customary after his nights at the pub. Maybe she asked him, "Shall I get you a Chinese as usual?" and he said yes rather than arouse her suspicions.'

'The person she lived with is the most likely person she'd buy a takeaway for,' Hollis allowed. 'But what happened to the containers?'

'Yeah,' said McLaren. 'Connolly was in there Saturday, and she looked round and in the bin in the kitchen, and there was nothing like that there. And they weren't in the dustbins, either.'

The contents of the household dustbins were secured on Monday – that was SOP – and since collection day was Tuesday, anything thrown in there over the weekend would still have been there.

'He could have taken them out and disposed of them,' Atherton said. 'He had plenty of time. They could be in any bin between here and Salisbury.'

'That's true,' Slider said. 'But why would he bother?'

'To hide the fact that he was there,' said Atherton. 'If we'd found the debris, we'd have got DNA out of the saliva traces and identified him as being at home when he was supposed to be at the wedding.'

'But would he think of that? This is the man whose alibi was cracked at the first question,' Slider said.

'You just don't know what he might think of. Or maybe he killed her first, then took it with him and ate it in the car,' Atherton said impatiently.

'It'd have been well cold,' McLaren said scornfully. 'He had to get rid of the body first.'

'You know who else she could have bought it for,' Swilley said. 'That she was friendly with. Who had time to get rid of the rubbish. And I bet he eats a lot of takeaways. And there's the money, too. If it wasn't in her purse, where was it?'

'Most likely Hibbert took it,' said Atherton.

'No,' said Slider. 'She means Ronnie Fitton.'

TEN
The Son Also Rises

Slider was holding down the fort at home that evening, as Joanna had a recording session, and for a wonder Dad had a date as well. Since selling up his home and coming to live with them, he had been available night and day, and Slider had often told him that he ought to go out more, get some interests of his own. It was said as a sop to Slider's conscience, not for his father's benefit, since he knew, deep down, that what his father liked best was being at home and looking after George; but it seemed that at last Mr Slider had heeded him and gone and joined a club. A Scrabble club, of all things.

'I didn't even know you played Scrabble,' Slider had said.

'Everybody plays Scrabble,' Dad had said. 'T'isn't difficult. Anyway, it's company. Gets me out o' the house.'

Slider had started worrying on a whole new level. 'Those dedicated Scrabble players can be peculiar people. Fiercely competitive. They know words all made up of Qs and Ks, and they're scornful of anyone who doesn't.'

Mr Slider had been untroubled 'It's not like that in this club. All amateurs – just nice people wanting a quiet game. You wanted me to go out,' he pointed out.

'I want you to be happy, though.'

'Your trouble is you never have enough to worry about. You're an addict. Even when you got plenty, you keep looking for more. Anyway, if I don't like it I can always leave, can't I? I got to go once, because I told someone I'd give it a try.'

'Oh? You've made a new friend?' Slider didn't know why he was surprised. It's just he never visualized his father outside the home, talking to anybody.

There was a gleam in Mr Slider's eye, as if he read this thought quite plainly. 'Not deaf and dumb, am I? I see people in the street, talk to them in the supermarket. Quite a friendly old place, this. Anyway, you needn't worry about me. I had half an hour with the dictionary while my boy was taking his nap, and I'm all primed up.' He patted his forehead, as if it were a willing horse. 'Quassia, quern, quincunx. Kukri, kowtow, kumis. Want to test me on the Js and Zs?'

It was odd, though, to see his father off and close the door, leaving himself in a silent house, empty except for George, asleep upstairs. He went up and had a look at him, just for the pleasure, then came down, feeling at a loss, and realizing how comfortable his life had been of recent months – always a fire lit and a meal ready when he came home, and sympathetic company to tell his day's experiences to. Ah well. He drifted into the kitchen, where his father had left him half a shepherd's pie in the oven, warming on a low light. There were vegetables, cut and ready to cook, but even as he looked at them he knew they were doomed to lie there undisturbed, and that when the moment came he would eat the shepherd's pie straight from the dish with a spoon. He was not a man who had been designed ever to live alone.

He thought he'd have a small malt whisky before eating, took time over choosing, and carried his Scapa into the sitting room. He intended to spend the evening doing some heavy reading and some even heavier thinking. He had the uneasy feeling he had missed something, or forgotten something – that someone had told him something important that he had put aside in his head and now couldn't lay his hand on. It was not unusual when he was involved in a complex case – probably just part of the way his mind worked – but it was uncomfortable all the same.

He decided to look at the paper first, while he drank his whisky, to see if leaving it alone would make the missing thing pop up of its own accord. That sometimes happened. He took a sip, put down his glass, took up the paper, read the first paragraph of the first story, and passed out, sandbagged by sheer exhaustion.

He woke an unknown time later with a stiff neck and a thumping heart as George's cry pierced the fog. He was on his feet and moving before he'd even opened his eyes, so he knew, as he hurried upstairs towards the sobbing, that it was the first cry he had heard. George was on his feet, clutching the side of his cot, his face contorted with grief and swimming with those great, fat, somehow extra glistening tears babies could produce as though their tear ducts were primed with glycerine. His hands went out with the familiar snatching gesture as soon as Slider appeared, and he swooped the boy up to his shoulder, felt the wet cheek against his neck, and the hands gripping his clothes with the ferocity of the bad dream that had wakened him. He was going through a phase of being woken by nightmares that he hadn't the vocabulary to explain, which was distressing to everyone.

'Was it a bad dream?' he asked, holding the tight little body close.

Nod.

'Never mind, it's all gone now.'

The hands clutched harder.

'What was it about, do you remember?'

Shake.

'Do you want to come downstairs with me for a bit?'

Nod.

So he carried him downstairs to the lighted room, where the fire had sunk, but was still giving warmth. He sat on the sofa and held George in his lap, and George stuck his thumb in his mouth and stared at the fire glow.

After a bit he unplugged and said, 'Story, Daddy.'

Slider embarked on the story of the ugly duckling from memory, adding in extra characters and action to pad it out, to give George time to get sleepy again. When the boy finally dozed off, Slider stayed put, to make sure he was really down before moving him again. He sat with the lovely weight in his lap, staring at the fire and not thinking of anything in particular.

And that was how Mr Slider found them, both asleep, when he got back from his Scrabble evening. The smell of the forgotten shepherd's pie was strong on the air. Good job I put it on low, he thought, with a fond and exasperated shake of the head.

*　　*　　*

Despite not having done any industrial-strength thinking, it was probably a good thing he'd had that extra sleep, Slider reasoned the next morning, when he went in to work feeling rested and firing on all cylinders. He stopped off to talk to Paxman, the duty sergeant downstairs, who told him that the operation had gone off smoothly, and Ronnie Fitton was safely banged up in the cells awaiting his fate.

'Did he give any trouble?'

'No trouble at all,' said Paxman, a large, heavy-built man, with stationary eyes and tightly curly hair that gave him a faint resemblance to a Hereford bull. 'Fact he seemed to be expecting it. Resigned. He got a couple of hours' kip once we'd processed him, and he's had a good breakfast, so he's ready for you any time.'

'Any trouble with the press?'

'Nah. Too cold for 'em to hang about all night on the off-chance. The one in the house across the road's the only one still around, and he missed his chance. Musta been cooping. The story's in the paper, but there's no picture, only of the forensics going in.'

'Oh, they're in already, are they? Good.'

Slider was about to pass on, when Paxman retained him with a large, beefy hand on his arm. 'Bill, are you sure about this one?'

'Sure? I'm not even close. Why, what's up?'

Paxman shook his head slowly, as if goaded by flies. 'I dunno. I've got a feeling about this geezer. There's something about him.' He waited for thought to develop. 'He's too quiet,' he concluded, as if that was not really what he meant, but was the closest he could get.

'He's the best suspect we've got,' Slider said. 'And we had to do something.'

Paxman nodded. He understood that. 'Just be careful. He could be trouble.'

'What sort of trouble?' Slider asked.

'I dunno,' Paxman said. 'Wish I did. Just – be careful.'

'I will. Thanks, Arthur.' Paxman was long on the job and old in the ways of men. Slider always took him seriously.

*   *   *

Slider had studied Ronnie Fitton's file, and there was much
about him that did not fit the usual criminal profile, and some
features that did. He was born to an ordinary working-class
family in West Acton. His father worked for British Rail as a
ticket collector and station attendant; his mother worked part-
time on a supermarket checkout. They lived in a small terraced
house, privately rented.

There had been another son, Keith, two years older than
Ronnie. He had been killed by a train when he was fourteen:
he and some friends had been trespassing on railway property
and Keith and another boy were playing 'chicken'. The other
boy survived; Keith was killed instantly, tossed up on to the
low embankment between the lines and the back gardens like
a stringless marionette.

That must have had the hell of an effect on Ronnie, aged
twelve, Slider thought. It was the sort of thing that could turn
a boy to the bad, but it seemed to have had the opposite effect.
Defence counsel at his trial had made much of the fact that
after his brother's death he had never been in trouble, had
worked hard at school and got three GCSEs, and had gone to
a vocational college and got himself a trade qualification in
graphic design. After working for various printing firms, he
had ended up as manager of a sign-making company, earning
a good salary. He had married a girl he had been dating for
a couple of years, and bought a house in Northfields not too
far from the business. Then, two years into the marriage, he
had come home unexpectedly early and found his wife in bed
with another man, and killed her.

It was the first break in the pattern of exemplary behaviour,
and on the surface it was inexplicable. He had no history of
violence: friends and neighbours agreed the couple had been
on good terms and there was no suggestion he had ever raised
a hand to her. But it was possible to imagine that he had been
affected by the shock and horror of the brother's death – they
had apparently been close – which had been brought upon
him by his own wrongdoing. Had young Ronnie buckled down
and behaved all those years, done the right things in the right
order, and at least subconsciously expected his reward to be
that his life would be blessed? – only to be betrayed by the

person closest to him. Slider thought there could well have
been deeply suppressed emotions – grief and rage – from the
time of his brother's death which broke through in that moment
of betrayal and caused him to lash out. The trouble was that
he did not say of himself that he had snapped, lost his temper
and lashed out. He had refused to say anything other than that
she had deserved it, thus portraying it as a calculated act and
not subject to mitigation.

What Slider came away with was a sense of a frightening
degree of control, which in turn suggested a frightening amount
of something underneath to need controlling. It would make
him a dangerous man, as Paxman hinted. You would never
know what he might do, or when he might do it. It was over
twenty years since he had killed his wife; the safety valve on
the pressure cooker might have reached its limits. And if it
was Fitton who killed Melanie, it would make sense of the
no-sexual-assault aspect. It was love and betrayal that had
sparked him to kill his wife. Had he loved Melanie? And had
she betrayed him in some way? Not sexually: Fitton's would
have been a secret and suppressed love, perhaps an idolization.
She would only need to do something he regarded as betraying
his image of her, something he thought beneath her.

Or, of course (he had to admit to himself) that fierce control
could have been simply covering up a series of criminal deeds.
He could have been a 'right wrong'un' all along, but with the
mental acuity not to get himself caught, and it was blackmail
after all. One thing you could be sure of – good man or bad,
he would not have wanted to go back inside.

Fitton seemed very calm. He sat in a relaxed attitude on the
chair in the interview room, his lean legs in the paper overalls
crossed, smoking a cigarette. His face showed nothing, not
fear or apprehension or even interest in what was happening
to him, but Slider felt that there was a point of carbon steel
somewhere in the middle of him, like the tip of a whipping
top. He might appear to be motionless, but that was only
because he was spinning so hard.

Slider took his place on the opposite side of the table.
Atherton came in behind him and sat by the tape machine.

Fitton did not look at either of them. He took a drag on his cigarette and blew upwards, watching the smoke and the ceiling.

'Cup of tea?' Slider offered.

Fitton shook his head.

'Are they treating you all right?'

'No complaints,' Fitton said.

'You've had breakfast?'

'Full house. You do a good one here.'

'Thank you. I'll mention it to the Michelin inspector.'

Fitton gave no reaction to the pleasantry.

'Have you had your phone call?'

'I've got no one to ring.' He said it as a plain statement of fact, not an appeal for sympathy.

'Solicitor?'

'Don't want one.'

That was usually a bad sign – the guilty man calleth his brief when no man pursueth, as the proverb had it. But in Fitton's case you couldn't read anything into it. He hadn't wanted anything to do with his legal team the first time round, either. He seemed to have a robust contempt for the profession.

'You're sure?' Slider said.

Now Fitton looked at him – and the level eyes were not calm, like the rest of him, but hard, with a spark in them like a glimpse of fire deep down in a fissure in the earth. There was a volcanic eruption somewhere being suppressed; molten magma was flowing along secret channels far below the surface. He said, 'I don't need one because I'm not answering your questions.'

'Why is that?' Slider asked.

'Don't try and make friends with me,' Fitton said. 'I didn't kill her and you can't prove I did. You're wasting your time.'

'If you didn't kill her, you must want to help us find out who did.'

'I don't care if you do or you don't. It won't bring her back. Time to help her was when she was alive.'

'Did you try to help her?'

'Not my business,' he said briskly. Then he paused, seeming, curiously, not to like the sound of that answer when he heard it out loud. He added, 'She knew where I was.'

Not the same, Slider thought. Not the same at all. He said, 'Well, then, you must at least want to see justice done?'

The spark flickered brighter for an instant. 'Justice? You talk about justice? You're all in hock to the press, the lot of you. You only arrested me because the newspapers kept demanding why you didn't, and your PR department told your bosses they had to do something about it. Bad press is the only thing that matters to you bloody lot these days. The press could get the Home Secretary and the Commissioner the sack if they put up a campaign against 'em, so the shove goes in, all the way down the line until it ends up with you. And you just have to do as you're told, whether you like it or not. So you pull me in because I've got a record. You call that justice?'

'You've obviously thought about it a lot,' Slider said evenly.

'Had a lot of time for thinking, didn't I?' He turned his head away again, drawing on his cigarette.

'Do you think justice was not done in your own case? Do you feel aggrieved about that?'

'Not much good at this psychological bollocks, are you?' he enquired of the air. 'I killed my wife. I never denied it. I was punished. I never complained about that. But justice had nothing to do with it. It was retribution.' He finished the cigarette and stubbed it out in the tinfoil ashtray on the table.

'In what way was justice not done, then?'

He looked at Slider with a sad shake of the head like a teacher dealing with a very thick pupil. 'It's *called* the Justice System. That's just its *name*. Don't get sucked in by fancy language. Crime and punishment, that's all it is. I killed my wife. That's against the law. I was punished. End of.'

'Very well, then, don't you want the person who killed Melanie to be punished?'

'Not interested. I'll have that cup of tea, now. Two sugars.'

Slider sighed inwardly, and nodded to Atherton. Depriving him of tea or cigarettes was not going to make any difference to a tough nut like this. But he had proved he liked to talk. The only chance was to build an atmosphere where he would sound off on his pet themes and perhaps let something slip.

While Atherton was at the door, talking to the constable outside, Fitton looked at Slider with a marked drop in attitude and asked, 'How's Marty?'

'We took him to Melanie's parents.'

'Who took him? That girl you sent round? The Irish one?'

'Yes. She said he seemed happy to be there.'

'I hope they treat him right.'

'Why wouldn't they?'

He looked at Slider thoughtfully for a moment, and then said, 'You know as much as I do. You work it out.'

Slider tried, 'You're fond of him? Marty?'

'I like all dogs. They don't mess you around. They can't lie to you. I'm glad that pillock Scott didn't take him back. He doesn't deserve a nice dog like Marty.'

'Did you have a dog when you were a kid?'

Fitton eyed him sidelong. 'I said, don't try to make friends with me. I don't like lies, and pretending is lying. You're not interested in me. You just want to get enough on me to charge me so you can get your pat on the back from the bosses. It's all political with you coppers nowadays.'

'I'm not like that,' Slider said, mildly but with truth. 'I saw her body. You say you hate lies – well, I hate waste. And no one had the right to take her life away from her.'

'People take other people's lives away all the time – not by killing 'em, but by crushing their spirit, brutalizing 'em, denying 'em education, chances, bottling 'em up in a ghetto of ignorance and hopelessness. They're as good as dead. A life like that is worse than death.'

Slider couldn't decide whether this was a deeply felt sociopolitical view or simply smoke being blown in his eyes to keep him from asking any more pertinent questions. Long winded discourse was a funny way of not answering, he thought, and he was glad other arrestees didn't resort to it. Policing was exhausting enough as it was without being lectured into the bargain.

The tea came. Fitton blew on it, sipped it, put it down, asked for another cigarette. He was the king of the custody suite, his attitude said. *I've done time for murder – this is kiddy league stuff in comparison.*

Slider decided to go for specifics. 'You gave us the impression that you knew Melanie only casually. But in fact you knew her quite well. You went out for drinks with her quite often. Why didn't you tell us about that?'

'That's my business.'

'No, it's ours now. Everything about everyone who knew her is our business.'

'That's your bad luck, then. I'm not answering your questions.'

'If you're innocent, why not?'

'Because I don't have to tell my business to anyone.'

Crap, Slider thought. 'You know, don't you, that murder always leaves forensic traces, which we will find. Sooner or later, the truth will come out. Why don't you make it easier on yourself? You chose the hard line the first time round, and where did that get you? There may be mitigating circumstances that can be taken into account. There may —'

'Don't make me laugh,' Fitton interrupted, with no laughter anywhere in sight. 'Mitigating circumstances! If you charge me I'm back inside for the rest of my kip. They'll throw away the key. I don't fancy that, thank you very much. My flat's not much, but it's mine, and I don't have to share it with some farting, snoring, nose-picking Neanderthal with stinking feet.'

'Then help us.'

'Help yourselves. I had a reasonable life, until you lot sold me out to the papers. All I wanted was to be left alone. Fat chance of that, now.'

There was a knock, and Atherton went to the door, conducted a whispered conversation, then said to Slider, 'Mr Porson wants you.'

Slider got up. 'I'll be back,' he told Fitton.

'Take your time,' Fitton replied.

Porson was looking worried, which was so unusual it gave Slider a qualm. Fierce or impatient were Porson's normal expressions, along with any degree of either in-between. The old man didn't do worried. He flung himself headlong at problems, sword in hand, slashing away – less in Zorro than in anger, Slider always said.

'Getting anywhere?' was Porson's first question.

'Like Bank Holiday Monday on the A303.'

Porson grunted. 'Being abstrapalous, is he?'

'Refusing to answer questions. He's too calm and a lot too cocky for my liking – but there's a lot of anger there, underneath. I can see him doing it. On the other hand, I don't get the feeling he's a bad man, basically.'

'You can be a good man right up to the moment you're not,' Porson said. 'But I had a phone call this morning that complicates matters.'

Oh joy, Slider thought. My life was too simple. There was just no challenge.

'In fact, it's chucked a bit of a spaniel in the works,' Porson went on. 'It was from the director of Stamford House.'

Stamford House, the secure home for violent young offenders. They had forgotten about that, Slider thought. Or had put it to one side, rather. 'Don't tell me they had someone over the wall on Friday?' Slider asked. 'We didn't think this looked like something one of them would have done – hiding the body and so on. They'd have had to have a car to—'

'No, no, it's nothing like that,' Porson interrupted. 'No, it was about Fitton.' He picked up a rubber band from his desk and stretched it round his fingers. 'He knows him, you see.'

'Personally? Or in a professional capacity?' Slider asked.

Porson began stretching and easing the rubber band. Slider took a surreptitious half step backwards. He could see it flying off Porson's fingers.

'Both. You see, it turns out he's been helping over there, with the kids.'

'*Fitton* has?'

Porson nodded unhappily. 'Started off with coming in to give 'em a talk about what it was really like in prison – explode the myth, show there was nothing glamorous about it, put 'em off it for life.'

'How did that come about? How did the director know about him?'

'He didn't. It was the other way round. Fitton volunteered. Said he wanted to help. Couldn't stand seeing those young kids going to the bad, like the ones he met inside. If he could save a single one, his suffering wouldn't be in vain, sort of effort.' Porson's eyebrows went up like a pair of herons taking off from a pond. 'Apparently he was very eloquent. Anyway, the director bought it. They've got a hell of a tough ask in there; anything and anyone that might help is welcome. After all due checks and percautions, they let him come in and do his talk, and a Q and A afterwards. The kids were well impressed. The staff even more so. He handled their questions with tact, didn't let them get purulent about the murder or make him some kind of hero, and they obviously related to him, gathered round when it was over, started talking about themselves, asking his advice.'

The rubber band flew across the room, just missing Slider's ear. Porson didn't even notice it was gone. 'Thing is, it's hard to reach these kids. Most of 'em view all grown-ups as the enemy. They desperately need guidance but won't let 'emselves take it. So someone who could talk to 'em, who they'd talk to, is worth his weight.' He shrugged. 'He's been going in a couple of times a week, taking groups sometimes, talking to individuals other times. Advice, information, sometimes just a shoulder to cry on. Doing good work, apparently – good results. Some real little nut jobs have calmed down a lot. So when it said in the papers we'd arrested him – well, the director was agog, the staff were up in arms. As far as they're concerned he was from the planet Krypton. Couldn't do wrong.' Porson raised sorrowful eyes to Slider's. 'He was in there Friday. All afternoon.'

'Ah,' said Slider. 'He told us he was out, but wouldn't say where. Said it was his business.'

So,' said Porson. It wasn't much, but his expression was eloquent. They were silent a moment.

'It doesn't necessarily follow—' Slider began.

'No, but it's a hell of a good indicator,' said Porson. 'It'd look good in court. Stand up on its own like a pair of soldier's socks.'

'He had good character the last time,' Slider pointed out.

'Last time he never denied it. Put his hand up right off. I think we got to tread careful. Don't want the press saying we're hounding a man who's doing his best to pay his debt to society.'

'They're the ones doing the hounding. They've been shouting his guilt ever since they discovered his record.'

'Well, you don't expect them to be rational. No, it's our nuts on the block here. We'll keep him until the forensic comes back on his flat, and then if there's nothing there, let him go. I still think he's tasty, but without evidence . . . He won't be able to go anywhere. Everyone in the country knows his face now.'

And Slider experienced a pang of sympathy for Fitton, which really, really annoyed him. He went back to the interview room feeling distinctly narked.

'Why didn't you tell us about your work at Stamford House?' he asked trying not to show it.

Fitton gave him that same darkly calm look. 'How many times do I have to say it? It's my business.' Slider took a breath to reply and he went on in a different tone, more conciliatory. 'Anyway, I don't want you bothering those kids. They've got enough on their plates, without the Vogons clumping all over 'em, asking 'em questions. You leave 'em alone. You could knock 'em back months, just when they're making some progress.'

'I'm not going to ask them anything. There's no need. The director told us about your involvement with them.'

'Oh, did he?' Fitton commented, and did a bit of a brood.

Slider tried to capitalize on the new mood. 'So what was the nature of your interest in Melanie Hunter?'

'Who said I had any interest in her?'

'Was it because she'd been in trouble at one time?'

He looked up at that. 'Criminal trouble?'

'No, not that. But she'd been a bad girl, and pulled herself round. That must have taken courage. Was that why you admired her?'

'I didn't know she had,' he said slowly, staring at some inner landscape. 'But I guessed there was something. There's a sort of look about girls who've been through the mill . . . She never said anything to me,' he added sharply. 'And I wouldn't ask. But I told your girl – the Irish one – there was more to Mel than met the eye. She was in some kind of trouble, but she never told me.'

'So why did you go for drinks with her? To try to help her? Did she see you as some kind of father figure?' He was seeing the edge of a scenario he really didn't want to contemplate, in which Fitton, driven to megalomania by his success with disturbed children, felt obliged to put the girl out of her misery – another crime which was no crime in his eyes, like the justice delivered to his erring wife. No one came out of prison after fifteen years entirely sane.

Fitton was silent a long moment, and Slider didn't think he was going to answer. Then he said quite abruptly, 'She wanted to help me.'

'Help you do what?'

'With the kids. She wanted me to get her into Stamford House. I told her it was way too dangerous. Those kids may be under sixteen but they're violent criminals. She thought she could help some of the girls. I see now, if you say she'd been there herself, why she thought that. But she had no idea. It wasn't on. Still, she kept asking, and even when she stopped asking, she liked to ask me about what I'd been doing and how they were getting on, the ones I was mentoring. And I—' A long pause, and then, almost sub voce, 'I enjoyed telling her.'

Yes, Slider could see that. A man so cut off from all normal discourse; the interest – the admiring interest – of a pretty young woman in the most important thing in his life. Very understandable; but also, given the nature of the pressure cooker, a potentially combustible situation. If something had threatened to take her away from him . . . Or she had said the wrong thing, lost interest in his mission, dissed his protégés, or appeared to . . .

A thought occurred to him. 'Did she ever give you money to give to them – to help them through a difficult patch, for instance?'

Fitton looked surprised, and then angry. 'I didn't take money from her. And I didn't give money to the kids. D'you think I'm some kind of amateur? If you want to know anything about them, go to the director. I'm done talking to you.'

Slider ended the interview; Atherton turned off the tape and called in the constable to return Fitton to his cell. As he passed him, Slider asked casually, 'Do you like Chinese food?'

But there was no reaction from Fitton's set face or grim voice. 'I can take it or leave it,' he said.

Slider and Atherton trod upstairs. 'It could still be him,' Atherton said. 'He obviously had feelings for her. And he's more than a little nutty.'

Slider nodded. 'In fact, I'm feeling bad, now, about sending Connolly round there. But this helping with the disturbed kids is a powerful thing on his side. Unless we get some real evidence from the flat, or an eye witness, we can't even hold him. But he's still got the best opportunity to get rid of the body and the takeaway cartons.'

'Unless he really can't drive.'

'And in any case, *what* would he drive? So far we haven't got her car logged anywhere on Friday night after she left the pub, and we don't know about any other car he has access to.'

'Right,' said Atherton cheerfully, 'so we'd better leave him to one side and concentrate on the person who had equally good opportunity, even better access, who could have been spending her money hand over fist for two years for all we know, and who's lied to us about his whereabouts and has a busted alibi. Do you like Chinese food, indeed! Let's ask Scott Hibbert the same question.'

'I suppose you're right,' Slider said. 'As soon as Fathom gets his report in, we'll reel him in for a chat.'

They reached the door of the office, and Hollis came towards them, looking like a worried peperami stick, with Mackay eager at his elbow.

'I was just going to ring down to you, guv,' Hollis began.

Mackay couldn't wait. 'Hibbert's had it away!'

'What?'

'On his toes.'

'Done a runner,' Hollis amplified.

'See?' Atherton said in triumph. 'I told you so.'

ELEVEN
That Bourne to Which No Traveller Returns

athom was looking worried. He wasn't one of the very brightest: if brains were air miles, he couldn't have got further than Birmingham. But stick him in front of a computer with a well-defined task and you couldn't go wrong. So as he loomed in Slider's doorway with his forehead resembling the winning entry in a drunken ploughing contest, Slider was alarmed.

'Guv, I've tracked Hibbert's motor last weekend. He's got a silver Ford Mondeo – well,' he sidetracked himself, 'it's reckoned an OK car now, since James Bond's drove one in that film. I mean, it used to be really boring, but now all the reps want one, even the ones that used to drive BMWs—'

'Hibbert's movements?' Slider prompted him gently.

It was like watching an oil tanker doing a U-turn. The turbines thrashed painfully for a moment before he righted himself. 'Oh, yeah. Well, I've picked him up on the Watford Way, the A41, at Fiveways Corner.'

'He said he was going to Hendon on Friday morning,' Slider said, 'so that fits.'

'Yeah, guv. That ping's Friday lunchtime, ha'pass twelve time. Then he's took the M1, M25, round to the M3, and I've got him filling up at the Fleet Services, westbound.'

'So it looks as though he was heading down to Salisbury,' Slider said. 'But leaving early in the day – I wonder if his employers knew he was taking the afternoon off?'

'Dunno,' Fathom said. 'He didn't go to Salisbury, though – not right away. He's stopped on the M3. I've picked him up Winchester, Eastleigh, then he's took the M27, A31, I've caught him at Ringwood, then he's on the A338 towards Bournemouth. I've lost him after that. There's not so many cameras down that way as there are in the London area. But I reckon he must have stopped somewhere in the Bournemouth area, because the next time he's pinged is at Ringwood again, going north this time on the A338, which takes him to Salisbury. That's half ten-ish Saturday morning.'

'Which looks like heading for the eleven o'clock wedding,' Slider said.

'Yeah, guv,' Fathom said, with an anxious look. 'So how did he get from Bournemouth to Shepherd's Bush to murder Hunter without getting pinged?'

Slider glanced at the paper in his hand. 'What are the rest of his movements?'

'Back to Bournemouth straight after the wedding. Then Sunday morning I've got him on the A303, M3 back to London. He stops on the motorway all the way to Sunbury, then I've got him Richmond, Barnes, and Hammersmith Bridge at ten to ten. Which is right for him getting home at around ten, like he said. So if that's the way he went home Sunday, how'd he do it Friday?'

Slider shook his head. 'There are ways, I suppose. Not every road has a camera on it by a long chalk. He could have gone a roundabout route, by the back roads—'

'Yeah, guv, but how would *he* know where the cameras were?'

'Or even that there are cameras,' Slider completed. Few people did, and even if they knew, or suspected, driving habits were so ingrained it was hard for them to keep the idea in mind when going from A to B. A man with no criminal background would be unlikely to govern his movements by fear of being caught by the ANPR. 'However,' he said in a comforting tone, for Fathom was looking as bereft as if his puppy had been taken away from him, 'there is another possibility – that he did the journey in a different car.'

Fathom's face cleared. 'Oh, yeah!' That was altogether more explicable. A man might not know about the cameras, but he might just grasp that if his car was spotted in the wrong place at the wrong time it could spell trouble.

'What's exercising me more is what he was doing in Bournemouth.'

'The Bournemouth area,' Fathom corrected. 'There's a lot of places he could have gone from there, if he didn't go on the main roads.'

'Let's say that when I say "Bournemouth", I mean the Bournemouth area,' Slider said.

'Maybe it was something for his firm after all,' Fathom said. 'He went straight there from London. And didn't that bloke, the best man, say he was talking about doing a big deal?'

'True. And I suppose even a liar and fantasist might tell the truth sometimes, by mistake. Well, you've done some good work here, Fathom.'

'Thanks, guv.'

'And given me lots of questions to ask Mr Hibbert – as soon as we find him.'

'Yeah,' Fathom said, his momentary pleasure at being praised flagging. An all-cars, all-areas general shout had gone out for Hibbert. He had achieved fugitive status, and other eyes than Fathom's would be scanning the ANPR for the silver Mondeo now.

Slider gave him a consolation prize. 'I'd like you to get on to his employers – Hatter and Ruck – and find out if he was doing anything for them in Bournemouth, and whether they've had any contact with him since Friday. And if he wasn't on company business in Bournemouth, whether he's ever mentioned the place or has any connection with it.'

Porson had been talking to headquarters at Hammersmith, as was apparent from the redness of his right ear and his air of restrained frenzy. 'Mr Wetherspoon first, and then the PR girl – woman – person.'

'Lily Saddler,' Slider offered her name, to get Porson out of the PC mire. It was no wonder he had difficulty remembering it. She was the third in two years – it was a job no one stayed in very long, largely, Slider thought, because of Mr Wetherspoon, whose tact, sensitivity and sweetness of nature made him about as popular as Hitler at a bar mitzvah.

'Saddler, that's her,' Porson said. He gave a sigh that would have registered on seismographs all round the world. 'Bloody PR again! I don't know why we don't just get Saatchi and

Saatchi in to run the police and have done with it. Anyway, the upshoot is they've decided there's no harm in letting the press have Hibbert doing a runner. They'll get on to it sooner or later, and Mr Wetherspoon thinks it'll be good to have something else already on the go for if and when we have to let Ronnie Fitton out, so they can't say we've been wasting our time chasing our own tails while the real villain gets away.'

'It's a point,' Slider conceded.

Porson eyed him. 'I can see through you like a book,' he said. 'You think Fitton's a washout, don't you?'

'I wouldn't go that far, sir. I certainly think he's capable of it. I'd even say it looks like his kind of murder – done in a moment of rage, the hands round the throat and the single blow to the head. But I also think, who better than him would know how to cover his tracks? If he did do it, we may never be able to put together a case against him. Unless they find some blood in his flat. Just evidence of her being there won't do, because they were friends, there's no reason she shouldn't go in there.'

'You're full of bloody sunshine, you are,' Porson said disconsolately. 'When are you expecting the forensic report?'

'Some time today. They finished the site examination yesterday – the flat's so empty it was relatively easy – so we're just waiting for the swab analysis. Unofficially, Bob Bailey isn't hopeful. But that doesn't mean he didn't kill her elsewhere, of course.'

Porson grunted. 'Trouble is, elsewhere's a big place. I'm going to have to get on to Mr Fox, see if we can widen the search area, look around those woods for some blood, or some bloody clothes. I'd be grateful,' he said with an air of pathos, 'for a nice pair of discarded surgical gloves.' He pulled himself together. 'Meanwhile, we'll have to pin our hopes on Hibbert. One thing, getting the press involved will find him quicker. If he's gone to ground, once his picture's in the papers, someone will recognize their new next-door neighbour.'

Connolly was waiting for him when he got back to his room. 'Boss, I know we're all off our heads about your man Hibbert doing a legger—'

'It doesn't mean we can't keep our eyes open in other directions,' Slider said.

'That's what I was thinking.' She was wearing smart grey slacks and an enormous reddish-coloured shaggy sweater with one of those roll-necks that didn't fit closely, so her neck and head rose from it like something growing in a flowerpot. She had recently had her hair cut shorter so it was a flower with the petals furled, he thought.

'There's something here,' she said, waving the papers she was holding. 'I was going over the interviews with the friends Hunter went for a jar with on Friday. You know one of the questions we asked them was if she had any phone calls? Well, this one, Leanne Buckley, said she had a phone call from her dad.'

'But when I spoke to Ian Wiseman, he said he hadn't spoken to her for two weeks,' Slider remembered. 'He said she'd spoken to her mother on the Friday.'

'Yeah, boss. Her mammy said she'd phoned her in the afternoon, from work. So he wouldn't have been around. He couldn't have just taken the phone from her for a quick hello, and then forgotten it.'

'So what's your point?'

'I went back to this Buckley female, just to check, and she's quite sure about it. She said she was sitting next to Hunter when the call came in, and she seemed upset by it. Didn't say much, just yes and no and I see, that class o' caper. But whatever was being said was annoying her, and finally she said, "Yes, all *right*, Dad," really narky like. And here's the best bit, boss –' she forestalled his comment – 'this was around ten o'clock, and soon afterwards Hunter says she's feeling like shite and wants to go home, and she breaks the party up.'

'I always felt it was a bit early,' Slider said.

'Yeah, me too, boss. When you get together with your mates for a crack, especially on someone's birthday, you don't hang up your boots while the trains are still running. So I'm thinking, what if Wiseman asked her to meet him somewhere?'

'Given that they had a row last time they met, why would she go?' Slider objected.

'Well, he is her dad. Even if she didn't like him, you kind of do what the owl ones ask, don't you? And say he said he wanted to make up with her? He was sorry for giving out to her, and wanted them to be friends. So she thinks better get it over with, and says OK.'

'She might perhaps want to do that for her mother's sake.'

'Yeah, boss. It'd be uncomfortable for her mammy with the bad blood in the house, so she could think, I'll do it for her, sure the owl man's making the effort, have to give him the benefit of the doubt.'

Slider thought about it. 'And the Chinese takeaway?'

Connolly frowned. 'Well, to be honest with you, that has me a bit confounded. But I suppose he might have said, I'm just coming from praccer and I've not eaten, could y'ever get me a takeaway on your way home?'

'But he could have got his own takeaway, if he was going over there by car.'

'I know. I haven't quite worked that one out. But the fact is –' she stared at him earnestly, like someone trying to persuade through Pelmanism – 'he said he didn't speak to her and he did, and she got upset and left early. That's got to be worth something, hasn't it?'

'Yes,' said Slider. Besides which, Wiseman was good for villain. Quite apart from his being her stepfather – most murders were done by someone close to the victim – there was his disposition, his disapproval of Melanie; the fact that he had rowed with her in the recent past, *and* hit her; his daughter Bethany's evidence that he spoke contemptuously of Melanie's mother (though of course what children said always had to be taken with a pinch of salt).

And his conflicting testimony about his alibi. 'He told me he got home in time to watch television with his wife before going to bed, but Mrs Wiseman told you he got home late, after she was in bed,' he said.

'But if he went to see Melanie after footer, and ended up killing her . . .'

'That would account for it,' Slider finished for her. He thought for a moment. 'All right, this is how we'll do it. You find out what you can, discreetly, about the football practice – where, how long, when it finished. See if you can get hold of some of the kids to ask. I'd sooner not go to the school authorities yet – they'd be bound to refer it to him and I don't want to spook him if he is guilty, or have a lawsuit brought down on us if he isn't. And try and find out if he was accustomed to go for a drink anywhere after school or after practice. You can find out a lot more about a person in a pub than anywhere else.'

'Right, boss,' Connolly said. 'Leave it to me.'

'If he does frequent a pub, let me know. I might send in Mackay – sometimes a man's better in that environment than a woman.'

'Depends on the boozer,' Connolly said, and she wasn't wrong.

The ANPR did not take long in picking up Hibbert's car on the same route down to Bournemouth that it had traced on the Friday. They remained on alert for any further movement, but as long as he was thought to be in the Bournemouth area, the actual searching for him on the ground had to be handed over to the local police, leaving Slider's hands tied.

Fathom meanwhile had interviewed the staff at Hatter and Ruck and learned that Hibbert had indeed been going to Hendon that morning, to look at a large house that was going on the market. He was then supposed to call in at the Hampstead branch on internal business, but had phoned them to say he had been delayed and was running late and would not be coming in after all. He was supposed to be working at home in the afternoon. They had not seen or heard from him since Friday, but of course they had not expected to once the murder became known. They had sent him a text of condolence, saying he should take leave of absence for as long as necessary. He hadn't responded to that. It had been quite awkward because he had some papers with him which they needed, and they'd had to do a lot of the work again, but you couldn't go bothering someone at a time like that, asking them for documents, could you?

As far as they knew he had no business down in Bournemouth, and had certainly not told anyone that he was going there. They had a branch in Dorchester that dealt with Bournemouth and all places west, in any case: it would not go through Knightsbridge, unless it were something very big, like a major

development, which would require the services of their specialist
commercial section. Scott Hibbert was not involved in commercial property. He was purely residential. They had no complaints
about his work. He had so far proved reliable. And he was
quite well thought of.

'They didn't rave about him, guv,' Fathom reported. 'They're
a right nobby lot in there – real Eton-and-Oxford types, with
posh accents – and I kind of got the impression they thought
he was all right for a chav, know what I mean? This bird
Belinda something said something about him I didn't catch,
and the others kind of smirked behind their hands.' He looked
indignant. 'And him just widowed and everything! Though I
s'pose,' he added, in fairness, 'that they probably don't reckon
he deserves so much sympathy, now he's scarpered.'

Connolly was reliving some of her worst nightmares. Though
she had been a moderately sporty child, and had enjoyed
gymnastics, tennis and some athletics, she had hated outdoor
team games, especially muddy ones. The agonies of school
hockey were burnt into her memory. The mist of a chilly winter
afternoon with the sky going pink behind the bare trees, the
pitch frozen harder than iron, the grass frosted to cutting
sharpness; the encroaching numbness of feet, the blue and
crimson knees and knuckles, the breath smoking, the way the
voices bounced on the winter-hard air, echoing like a swimming pool; the agonizing, bone-deep pain of a whack on the
shin, the way cuts wouldn't even bleed until you got back in
the pav and started to thaw out; the maddening, burning itch
of reviving skin . . .

This wasn't hockey, but soccer, but all the other elements
were there. Still, it was a job to be done. She hunched deep
into her coat, woolly hat on head, muffler wound round her
neck and chin, and watched the poor eejits running up and
down with blue noses, steaming like horses into the icy air.
There were two matches going on on two pitches, one big
guys and one medium. A lot of kids and a handful of adults
were scattered around the touchlines watching. She didn't feel
she stuck out too much. The referee in one match was a short,
bandy-legged older guy, scurrying about with a whistle in his

mouth. In the other, supervising the bigger guys' game, a young man, tall, hunky and fit, in shorts and a dark-blue rugby shirt, was a bit of a ride.

She idled along towards where a group of girls was sitting on a couple of benches watching the senior game. She strolled casually behind them and paused, listening to their chatter. Two of them on the farther bench had their heads together and were texting and giggling in tight, breathless bursts. The other three, on the nearer bench, their hands in their pockets, their jaws moving ruminatively like cows round their chewing gum, were having a 'she said, and then I said, so she said' kind of conversation. She took them to be about fourteen.

She moved slightly, coming forward at the end of the bench so that she was in their sight line. They all looked at her and then away without interest, which was good. One of the boys on the pitch went down to a tackle, to a combined groan from the onlookers, the whistle was blown, and the ridey feller ran over to adjudicate, disappearing into a small knot of vehemence as both teams protested.

'You're rubbish, Jackson!' one of the girls shouted, and they all giggled. 'Sanchez never even touched him.'

'God, I wouldn't be them,' Connolly commented. 'That ground's hard. And why do they make 'em wear shorts on a day like this?'

The one who had shouted, who had so many freckles it looked like a skin disease, said, 'Where there's no sense, there's no feeling,' and they exchanged sly grins.

'D'you go to this school?' Connolly asked.

'Yeah,' said Freckles, and rolled her eyes at the others. Read the uniform, dork, said the gesture.

'We wouldn't be sitting here if we didn't,' said the smaller, darker one with curls.

'Oh, I dunno,' said the third, podgy and fair, with the sort of pink face that always looks sticky, and shiny lips as if she'd been eating boiled sweets. She threw a glance at the boys playing, and they all giggled. 'The view's not bad.'

'Yeah, some of 'em are well fit,' said Curly.

'Except for Jackson,' said Freckles. 'Remember that time his shorts come off and he wasn't wearing any underpants?'

'I bet you all laughed like drains,' Connolly said. 'Poor guy.'

'What are you, his mother?' Freckles said, with routine rudeness. It was not a question.

They all watched for a moment, then Connolly asked, 'Did you see the game last Friday?'

'What game?' Podgy asked, blowing out and snapping her gum like a professional.

'Here, after school.'

'Oh, I thought you meant on telly,' she said, losing interest.

'Thursday, you mean,' said Curly. 'Thursday nights after school.'

'Oh, I thought it was Fridays.'

'Nah,' Freckles said scornfully. 'The teachers wouldn't stay late on a Friday night. They all bugger off home as fast as they can, soon as ha'pass three comes.'

'Don't blame 'em,' said Podgy. 'Get enough of this dump the rest of the time.'

'Oh, look, there's Freya,' said Curly, looking along the line at another group of girls.

'Lets go and see if she's got any fags,' said Freckles, and they all got up and hurried away, hunching together like a many-legged single entity, whispering and giggling. Apart from the fag remark, which Connolly guessed was a show-off for her benefit, they had shown her so little interest she was sure she and her questions would be forgotten within seconds. That was the beauty of that age. And grown-ups asked stupid questions all the time, so you got used to it.

Connolly moved to a different part of the touchline, watching the good-looking teacher so intently that at one point, when he ran near her, he glanced over and met her eyes. She smiled, and he gave a brief half smile in response, earning Connolly a bitter look from two sixth-form girls huddled together and presumably on the same mission.

When the games finished, the older man headed straight to the changing block with his team, while the younger teacher gathered his boys round him for a debriefing talk that went on until it seemed he suddenly noticed it was getting even colder (can't *believe* it's April!) and they were hopping on the spot and rubbing their own arms. He went off with them without a glance around, so Connolly had no chance to talk to him. Well, you just have to *make* a chance, she told herself. There was a small parking area beside the changing block which she assumed was for the teachers. Beyond that was a small flight of shops, and she went and bought a newspaper and then sat on a bench on the far side of the parking area and watched.

She was in luck. In ones and twos and groups the boys came out and hurried off; some adults retrieved their cars and left; the little bandy man got in a Fiesta rust bucket and disappeared; but the ridey teacher was still inside. She got up, stuck her paper under her arm, and began to wander towards the remaining cars, pretending to rummage in her handbag while watching the door under her eyebrows.

It took a degree of skill to extend the rummaging the required length of time and still make it look natural; it took skill and a certain gymnastic agility, when the man came out (alone, thank God, in a cosy-looking padded jacket with a large Adidas bag on his shoulder) to wander into his path at just the right moment and allow him to knock her over.

'Oh, God, I'm so sorry!' he cried, swinging his bag to the ground to offer both hands for her assistance.

'My fault, I wasn't looking,' she said. She had managed to spill a few things from her handbag, and when he had pulled her to her feet he crouched and gathered them up, while she brushed down the back of her coat. 'Thanks,' she said, as he restored the items to her cupped hands.

'Are you all right?' he asked. 'Not hurt?'

'No, no, I'm fine. Only me dignity's smarting.'

'I'm so sorry. Clumsy of me.'

'T'wasn't your fault. I wasn't looking where I was going.' She looked up and directly into his eyes. Good, he was interested. 'I saw you taking the game with the boys. You wouldn't be Mr Wiseman, would you?'

'No, I'm afraid he's not here.'

'But he'll be here later, will he? For the late practice. Don't you have practice after school on Fridays?'

'No, Thursdays,' he said. 'Never on Fridays.'

'Oh – I thought there was something last Friday, after school.'

'No, we've never had after school games on a Friday.' He gave a rueful smile. 'Too many of the parents want to get away for long weekends.'

'Oh, so I've missed Mr Wiseman, then.'

'Is it anything I can help you with? My name's Rofant. Simon Rofant. I'm the other games teacher at the school. Um . . .' He hesitated. 'I'm afraid Mr Wiseman probably won't be in for a while. Something rather awful happened. His daughter got killed.'

'That's terrible! The poor guy. What happened?'

He hesitated again, and said, 'Look, it's too cold to stand here. Do you fancy a cup of tea? There's a café just along there.' He gestured along the line of shops.

'That'd be nice, but don't you have to be somewhere?'

He raised his hands, almost in a 'guilty' gesture. 'Nope. Footloose and fancy free. But what about you?'

'Same here,' she said, and smiled. He smiled back. Bingo, she thought.

In the café – very small and functional, six Formica tables with tubular chairs and counter service of tea and coffee, cakes, sandwiches, and an all-day vat of soup that smelled like unwashed bodies – there was a diminishing knot of schoolchildren, buying sweets and snacks with agonizing indecision. But they were gathered at the counter, and left with their purchases without sitting down, though not without giving Rofant and his companion a long, interested look followed by head-together sniggering. One table was occupied by schoolgirls, but they were all texting away, heads down, and nothing, Connolly thought, short of the Last Trump would draw their attention away from their little screens.

Rofant ignored them all magnificently, insisted on buying her a tea ('It's the least I can do after knocking you down'), and when they were seated, told her all about the Melanie Hunter murder – from the point of view of the general punter, which was interesting. Connolly explained her ignorance of the matter by saying she'd only just come over from Ireland

and had been so busy with the moving the last few days she hadn't had time to read the papers or watch the news.

'Poor guy,' she said. 'What a terrible thing to happen. He must be really cut up.'

'Yes. The head told him right away to take the week off. I must say our head's decent like that. But I don't suppose he'll be back next week either. I mean, apart from what he must be feeling, and his wife, you don't want to expose yourself to the kids at a time like that. Staring eyes and prying questions. Curiosity always overcomes tact.'

'Not just with kids, either,' Connolly said. 'It must be really hard to get away from it, even for a minute. I suppose he can't even go down to his usual pub for a bit of relief.'

'No, especially not in his case. He's famously teetotal,' Rofant said. 'Disapproves of pubs and the demon alcohol.' He said it lightly, seeming to think, even as he said it, that it was a bit disloyal. He looked uncomfortable for an instant and then said, 'What was it you wanted to see him for, anyway? Perhaps I can help.'

This was always going to be the danger moment. 'I heard he did private coaching – out of school hours, I mean.'

'I think he does. Who told you that?'

'A neighbour of mine knows someone who knows someone he's coaching. I think she's in the sixth form,' Connolly said vaguely. The coaching would have to be for herself – she didn't want to have to invent a child.

'Oh. That must be Stephanie, I suppose. Stephanie Bentham. Small, fair girl – lives in Boston Manor somewhere?'

'I've never seen her. But I think that was the name. Well, I suppose he won't be doing any coaching for a long time now – if ever, poor guy.' She finished her tea, and made leaving movements, eager to get away now. 'Well, thanks a heap for the tea. That's warmed me up. I can't believe it's so cold – you'd never think it was spring.'

'My pleasure,' he said, standing too, his eyes on her. 'It's been nice meeting you. Would you – I wonder, would you like to go for a drink sometime?'

She would, she definitely would, but that was the trouble with what she did. You couldn't start a relationship with a subterfuge; now she had fooled him, she could never get to know him. Besides, it was near impossible to go out with any man who wasn't in the Job. They just didn't understand. While men in the Job understood too well, and were all neurotic bastards anyway. She'd had two bad relationships with coppers that ended in heartbreak and that was enough for one lifetime. As long as she remained a copper, she would have to remain alone.

'I'd really like to,' she said, putting sincerity into her eyes, 'but I'm kind of half seeing someone else. I came over here to see if we can make a go of it. Well –' she shrugged – 'you know. But thanks for asking.'

'That's me all over, wrong place at the wrong time,' he said self-deprecatingly. 'Well, if it doesn't work out, you know where to find me.'

'You've got it,' she said with a smile, and they parted on a handshake.

Isn't that just like bloody life, she thought, heading for her car. You meet a total ride, who's interested in you, who's also available – and how often does that happen? – and you can't do anything about it. Not because you've already got someone, oh no, that'd be too easy, but because you've been forced to make up someone in order to get out of going out with a bloke you *want* to go out with. God was just a big, bloody tease, so he was, and it wasn't *fair*.

TWELVE
Crowd Cuckoo Land

'**B**ut if there was no soccer practice on Fridays, why wouldn't Mrs Wiseman know that?' Atherton asked. 'She's been married to him long enough.'

Connolly counted on her fingers. 'She's confused, she's not that interested, he's told her and she's forgotten, or he's just not told her. You don't get the feeling there's much communication in that marriage. "I'm off out, dear." "All right, dear." And she sees he's got his bag with him, so she thinks, oh, he's off to football. Sure, she's not going to say "Where the hell have you been?" when he comes in, not her, not to a man like him.'

'Yeah,' said McLaren, who had been just waiting for her to finish this, which, to him, was the uninteresting part of the problem. 'But then where was he Friday evening? Even if it was him phoned Hunter at ten o'clock and arranged a meet, he wasn't with her from after school till then.'

'He wasn't where he said he was,' Atherton replied, 'and that's enough for us. Maybe he was driving about, working himself up into a rage, or planning how he was going to do it.'

'Maybe he was doing private coaching,' Connolly felt obliged to offer.

'But then why would he lie to his wife about it?'

'We don't *know* he lied. She's not that bright or on the ball. She maybe just got the wrong end of the stick. Or like I said, he never told her and she just assumed.'

'Well,' said Slider, 'we'll have to ask.' He shook his head. 'Two suspects with stupid, easy-to-bust alibis.'

'They weren't stupid alibis as long as no one checked,' Atherton said. 'They were very good, solid as the Bank of England alibis. A stag night and a soccer match – dozens of witnesses to prove you were there. Much better than Fitton's "I was alone at home all evening".'

'Right up to the point when it wasn't. What's the world coming to, when villains can't even be bothered to construct a decently professional lie?' Slider complained.

'What about Fitton, guv?' Hollis asked. The forensic report had come back negative – no traces of blood or tissue in the flat, on any of the objects confiscated, or down the plugholes or in the drains. Nothing to say Melanie Hunter had been murdered on the premises. There had been no large sums of cash knocking about, and Fitton's bank account showed nothing but his benefits going in each month and coming out week by week, so nothing to suggest blackmail. That was not to say he could not have killed her outside the house, or indeed have hidden money elsewhere, but you could only go on what you had evidence for.

'We let him go,' Slider said. 'And keep an eye on him. Release him later tonight, when it's quieter around the house.'

'Ironic, isn't it?' Atherton said. 'Fortunately we've got another suspect to take attention away from him. Unfortunately, they both live in the same house.'

'There'll be plenty in the papers tomorrow about Hibbert. They'll have had time to do their homework. Let's hope all the attention will flush him out,' Slider said. 'Meanwhile, we keep our eye on Fitton. And there's going to be a fingertip search of the woods as soon as it gets light tomorrow, in the hope that, if she wasn't killed at home, she was killed there, and there's something to find.'

'And what about Wiseman, boss?' Connolly asked.

'We bring him in and ask him some questions. I'll talk to Mr Porson about it now. I think it would be nice to take him late tonight, give him a night in the cells to unsettle him, and have a go at him in the morning when he's had time to think about the error of his ways. And while he's in here, one of you can go and offer his wife a shoulder to cry on, see what comes out.'

'And the kid,' Connolly added. 'Bethany. That one'd have you mortified, the language on her, but she has a useful habit of eavesdropping. You never know what she's found out about her dad.'

*　　*　　*

It turned out to be an exciting night, not only with the arrest of Ian Wiseman, who was not pleased about it and made his feelings known as vocally as a cat on the way to the vet's, but because late that evening the Bournemouth police found Scott Hibbert.

'What was it, a tip-off?' Slider asked. He had not been home yet. He was downstairs talking to Paxman about the treatment of Wiseman when the news came in, and hurried upstairs to find Mr Porson in the office, along with Atherton, and Hollis, who was night duty officer and the only one of them who was actually supposed to be there.

'Better than that,' Porson said. 'The woman he was lying low with gave him up. She sneaked in the kitchen while he was watching telly and told 'em to come and get him. They went straight round there. Found him in his underpants.'

'I wonder why they didn't think of looking there first?' Slider murmured. Atherton shot him a look. He shouldn't, he really shouldn't.

Fortunately Porson didn't catch it. He was too full of the wonder of Hibbert. 'He was watching himself on telly, the dipstick. On the twenty-four-hour news. No wonder she wanted rid of him. He burst into tears, apparently, when the Bournemouth plod came in. Anyway, they're wrapping him up and sending him over to us right away. They've got the woman in, giving her statement, pending our decision whether we want her banged up for obstruction or not.'

'We'll want to question her, won't we?' Slider said.

'Got to think of the practicosities,' Porson said. 'We can't clutter up our cells with all these bodies at the same time. You've already got Wiseman, Hibbert's coming, Fitton's going – it's getting like a murderers' convention in there. Anyway, I want you to have a crack at Hibbert tonight, while he's off balance.'

'Yes, sir, but I'd still like to get the woman's side of it while it's fresh.' He turned to Atherton. 'You'd better get down there and interview her first thing tomorrow.'

'I'll have to have a word with Bournemouth, then, grease the whales,' Porson said, and stumped off to his own room.

'Why are you here, anyway?' Slider asked Atherton when they were alone. 'Haven't you got a home to go to?'

'Emily's in Ireland, covering the euro crisis,' he admitted. 'I didn't fancy going home to an empty house.'

Blimey, he did have it bad, Slider thought. Atherton had always been the cat who walked alone; now he was so much a part of the Jim-and-Emily combo, the house didn't feel right without her. 'I wouldn't have thought the house would feel empty with those hooligan cats of yours,' he said.

'Not the same,' Atherton replied. 'A cat doesn't keep you warm at night. Well, it does, but – you can't cuddle a cat. Well, you can, but—'

'I get the picture,' Slider said hastily. He didn't like to think where that litany was going. 'Hadn't you better go back for a bit of shut-eye before Bournemouth?'

'I'd sooner see how Hibbert turns out,' said Atherton.

But in the end, they didn't get to have a crack at Hibbert, because he was in too bad a state when he arrived. He had been in tears all the way up, according to the stone-faced Dorset coppers accompanying him; and as soon as he walked in from the dark to the brightly-lit station he started shaking, and rapidly got so bad they had to get the surgeon in to give him a tranquillizer. After that he got a lot happier but it was impossible to interview him properly – his responses had slowed down so much it was going to take them most of the night to process him – so Slider gave it up until the morning. 'Get the woman's end of it first, then we can tackle him tomorrow from a position of strength.'

'Tomorrow's getting to be quite a day,' Atherton said as they trod out into the darkness.

'Today, now,' Slider said.

'So between Hibbert and Wiseman, which do you fancy more?' Atherton asked. 'Or is it still Fitton?'

'*I* don't know. There's something to be said for all of them.'

'All of them? You mean some kind of *Murder on the Orient Express* scenario?'

'Each of them, then, if you must be pedantic.'

'Why are people who are just trying to be accurate always called pedantic?'

'Beats me. God, I'm hungry.'

'Fancy going for a curry?' Atherton suggested. 'I know one that's still open.'

'At this time of night? You're so young.'

'All right for you,' Atherton grumbled. 'You've got a nice warm wife at home, who'll probably leap out of bed and cook you bacon and eggs. All I've got is the sound of my own broken sobbing.'

'Oh, go on then,' Slider said. As it happened, he felt wide awake and didn't want to go home yet. And it was ages since he'd had a curry. This marriage lark certainly put paid to a lot of the old social habits. 'We can talk some things through.'

'Good. There's a question that's really been bugging me,' Atherton said as they turned towards the Uxbridge Road.

'What?'

'Who on earth thought of putting an "s" in the word "lisp"?'

In the end, Atherton didn't go to bed: it probably wasn't a good idea to try to sleep on a substantial curry anyway, and he thought he might as well get the journey down to Bournemouth done in the early hours when the roads were quiet. So he had a shower, shave and change of clothes, played for half an hour with the cats, who were querulous about not having seen anyone All Day, and was down in Bournemouth well before breakfast time.

The first thing he learned at the station was that the woman, Valerie Proctor, was no longer there.

'She insisted on going home,' said the duty officer, one Kevin Bone. 'She'd come in voluntarily so we couldn't stop her unless we arrested her, and we didn't want to do that, because she'd have clammed up right away and asked for a brief. She's a bit of a stroppy cow, and I reckon you'll get more out of her if you don't rile her.'

'She's at home now?' Atherton asked. 'How do you know she won't do a runner?'

'In her mind she's got nothing to run from. She's turned him in, she's the good guy,' said Bone. 'Anyway, we've got a uniform on her door. To protect her from the press, we told her, but it cuts both ways, o' course.'

'Excellent,' said Atherton. 'Well, if she's safely confined, I've got time to read the reports and have breakfast before I go over.'

'We do a cracking bacon sarnie up in the canteen,' said Bone.

A female uniformed officer, Hewlitt, drove Atherton to the house and would sit in with him at the interview. 'You don't want to take chances with this one,' Bone had said.

'You think she'll jump me?' Atherton had asked. 'I know I'm generally considered irresistible, but . . .'

Bone, of course, did not know Atherton, and his way of talking was evidently unfamiliar down in Dorset. He had given him a very odd look, cleared his throat, and said carefully, 'She's the sort who might make an accusation against you, so you'd better have a woman PC with you, for safety's sake.'

'Thanks,' Atherton had said, chastened. No more jokes for you, my boy, he had ordered his overactive brain.

But in the car, Hewlitt, who was evidently a brighter spark, wafted her hand about in the air after driving for a few minutes and said, 'Phew! Are you planning to gas her and get her to confess while she's under the influence? Cos I have to tell you, that's against the rules.'

'Ripe, is it?' Atherton said with a grin.

'Eight hundred on a Geiger counter, at least,' she said. 'Evacuate the reactor building without delay.'

'Sorry.'

'I don't mind. I love curry. But she might claim it was cruel and unusual. There's some Trebors in the glove in front of you. Better suck a couple.'

Mrs Proctor lived in Winton, which Hewlitt explained was a bit of a mixed area, on the edge of the classier Talbot Woods, and with some nice houses, but some not so nice.

'And what's she like?'

Hewlitt flung him a sidelong look. 'I don't want to sound bitchy.'

'Oh go on – treat yourself.'

'You're funny, you are,' she said, almost in wonder. 'Well, she's not Talbot Woods, I'll say that. And if I hadn't sworn never to be mean about other women, I'd say she was mutton dressed as lamb.'

'Good job you did swear, then,' said Atherton. 'Nobody likes catty females.'

The house, when they came to it, was a meanly proportioned, yellow-brick modern one in a small estate of identical raw new buildings, each functionally square, with the sort of porch tacked on that was a flat concrete canopy supported at the front by two metal poles from which the paint was already peeling. Each house stood at the back of a small unfenced front garden which was half unsuccessful grass and half hard-standing for a car. Each house owed its upward-mobility credentials to having a garage, and a three-foot-wide strip of separation on either side between it and its neighbours. Atherton couldn't help thinking that an extra six feet of room inside would have been a better use of the space, but for reasons no one could explain the word 'detached' had mysterious magical powers over the asking price of a house.

There was a car on the hardstanding in front of the garage, a sporty-looking red Zetec S-Max.

'Menopause car,' said Hewlitt, who seemed to have forgotten her pledge.

Atherton made a note of the number and made a quick call to Hollis, to have it ANPR'd. Then they went in.

Atherton's first thought was that if Mrs Proctor hadn't turned Hibbert in, he probably would have surrendered himself in a short time. The inside of the house was decorated with so much exuberant bad taste he thought for a minute he had wandered into a traveller wedding. Mirrors, chandeliers, orna-ments, pelmets; gilt, onyx, Dralon; huge vases of artificial peonies and roses; reproductions of classic paintings in gaudy gold-coloured frames crammed together in the spaces between the tassel-shaded wall-lights; a life-size china greyhound sitting in the hearth of the modern gas fire which, on this chilly day, was alight behind its glass panel and showed realistic flames licking up, inexplicably, from a heap of pebbles. There was so much bling and so many conflicting patterns, within seconds he was getting an ice-cream headache.

Atherton's second thought, which arrived on seeing Valerie Proctor, was almost as unallowable as Hewlitt's. Though nowhere near menopausal, she was obviously quite a bit older than Hibbert, at least in her late-thirties, more likely early forties. She was trim and well corseted, and had evidently redone her make-up and hair as a priority when she got back from the station, for both were impeccable. She must have changed, too, for she was wearing a smart suit. Though more subdued than her decor, it was still bright yellow trimmed with black and rather shorter in the skirt than was strictly necessary; and she was wearing very high heels, and a great deal of costume jewellery. But despite the effort she must have put in, she looked worn underneath the maquillage and somehow – to Atherton almost touchingly – even mumsy.

His momentary softness passed as she tottered towards him like an infuriated giraffe. 'I want to make a complaint, a serious complaint, about the way I've been treated,' she snapped, skewering him with a look you could have barbecued king prawns on. 'I went to the police voluntarily, doing my civic duty, and I've been held at a police station all night answering questions and now I've got you bursting in to harass me all over again. It's no wonder everyone hates the police when you treat honest citizens the way you do. You ought to try getting out and catching a few criminals for a change, instead of persecuting people who are trying to help, hanging about motorways stopping people who just accidentally creep a couple of miles over the speed limit, when the road was practically empty, there was no one else about, it wasn't doing the slightest bit of harm to a soul. It's a disgrace the way you persecute motorists, just because you can, and particularly women because you know they won't cause trouble. It's all about the money, just like the cameras. You're not really inter-ested in road safety, you just want the fines.'

From the seamless segue from the general to the particular and back, Atherton surmised she had recently been stopped for speeding in her sporty red car and hadn't managed to talk her way out of it. He dialled the charm up to blatant, smiled at her admiringly, and said, 'I think it's wonderful the way you've come forward to help us, at considerable inconvenience to yourself, and I'm sorry I have to ask you to go through it all again for me, but from my own point of view I can only say it's a privilege to have the chance to visit you in your lovely home. If you wouldn't mind me just asking a *few* more questions, I can take myself out of your hair as soon as possible. Where *did* you get those beautiful flowers at this time of year?'

The needle was quivering on the edge of the red zone, and he could sense Hewlitt staring at him with her mental mouth hanging open like a door. For a breathless moment of silence he thought he had gone too far; but then Mrs Proctor almost visibly dismounted from her high horse and said with something close to a dimple, 'They're artificial. You can't get peonies like that in April, silly. But they're very good, aren't they?' A little laugh. 'I sometimes think they're real myself, for a moment, when I catch sight of them out of the corner of my eye.'

And so it was all right. Tea and 'something stronger' were offered and refused, and in short order Atherton found himself sitting on the sofa, with please-call-me-Valerie in the armchair almost knee to knee with him and ready to tell him whatever he wanted. He was glad of the presence of Hewlitt, who sensibly removed herself out of Valerie's line of sight, but remained on hand in case of trouble. He had a feeling he was in for the long haul, and was only glad, from the way Valerie leaned forward as she spoke, that either she had no sense of smell or was particularly fond of curry and peppermint.

Wiseman knew about his rights and insisted on them, refusing to answer any questions until he had seen his solicitor, and since the one he requested couldn't at first be contacted and then took some time to arrive, a good part of the morning had worn away before Slider actually faced him over the table in the tape-room.

The solicitor, Drobcek, a small and swarthy man with an amazing crop of black curly hair, turned out to be one who had advised some pupils at Wiseman's school who had got into trouble with the law. He had a substantial criminal practice in Hayes and Southall, but he specialized in juvenile, and seemed a little puzzled that Wiseman had called on him. But he was prepared to do his best and got the first punch in, complaining that there had been no call to drag Wiseman in in the middle of the night.

'My client had made no attempt to abscond, and he is a pillar of his local community. You could just as easily have *asked* him to come in voluntarily to answer questions, which he would have agreed to do. Or if you *had* to arrest him, you could have done it at a more reasonable time, not dragged him from his bed in that ridiculous, melodramatic way, upsetting his wife and child.'

'Your objection has been noted,' Slider said, studying Wiseman's face. He looked more drawn than he had on Tuesday, as if he had not had much sleep between then and now; but the suppressed rage in him seemed to have been turned down a notch, as though some of it had been replaced with some other emotion. Apprehension, perhaps? But he still had enough anger for two normal people, and his fists – which looked very hard, on the end of extremely whippy arms – kept clenching and unclenching, as though he'd really like to smack his way out of the trouble he had found himself in.

'But as you are here now,' he went on to Wiseman, 'perhaps we should get the questions over with as quickly as possible, for everyone's sake.'

'I've nothing to say to you,' he snapped. 'You came to my house, I talked to you then, openly and freely, and nothing has changed. Don't you realize the effect arresting me is going to have on my career? There are always people who say things like "there's no smoke without fire". Isn't it bad enough that we've lost our beloved daughter, without you ruining my livelihood as well?'

'She was your stepdaughter, not your daughter,' Slider said, the better to goad him.

He was goaded. 'Oh, is that what this is about? You've been reading too many fairy stories about wicked stepmothers. I always looked upon Melanie as being as much my own daughter as Bethany.'

'Even if that were true,' Slider said, 'she didn't look upon you as her father, did she? She resented your marrying her mother, and wouldn't accept your authority. You had a hard struggle with her from the very beginning.'

'All I ever tried to do was my best, to bring her up properly,' Wiseman said, his face tight with emotion. 'But it seems these days people who try to do the right thing are mocked and abused. There's no reward or admiration for virtue any more.'

'Did Melanie mock and abuse you?'

He was about to reply, but caught himself up. 'I don't have to answer your questions. I'm not saying anything to you.'

'I don't want you asking my client any leading questions,' said Drobcek.

'We're not in court,' Slider said. 'I can ask him what I want. You're right,' he addressed Wiseman, 'you *don't* have to answer my questions. But you must think of the impression it gives if you won't. It's true, isn't it, that Melanie refused from the beginning to accept your discipline? A young girl, who'd recently lost the father she adored – it wasn't surprising if you had difficulty in taking his place.'

'I never tried to take his place,' Wiseman said, provoked. 'He was a lazy, shiftless, work-shy, spendthrift waster and the world was better off without him.'

'Rachel Hunter in particular was better off without him. You were a much more satisfactory husband – one who knew his duty towards his wife and family.'

Wiseman looked put out, as if he couldn't be sure praise really was praise and suspected a trap. 'The facts speak for themselves,' he said stiffly. 'I've supported my wife and the girls properly through my own efforts right from the beginning.'

'So it must have been extra frustrating when you found you couldn't guide Melanie along the right paths for her own good.'

Wiseman glanced uncertainly at Drobcek, who gave a small shrug, indicating that there was nothing wrong with the question. 'I – did my best,' was all he said.

'And when she defied all your attempts to guide her, she got into trouble, and *you* were the one who had to bail her out of it.'

'I don't want to talk about that,' he said through rigid lips. 'It's all in the past.'

'Unfortunately, all of Melanie's life is now in the past,' Slider said, and saw the words give Wiseman a jolt. 'Isn't it true that you have something of a hasty temper?'

The fists clenched. 'I do *not*—' he began angrily, and then controlled himself with an effort. 'I won't answer any more questions.'

'And that you have hit both Bethany and Melanie on more than one occasion?'

'My client is not to be asked to incriminate himself,' said Drobcek.

Slider ignored him. 'And that in fact you hit Melanie on the last occasion you saw her before the night of her death? When she came to Sunday lunch a fortnight before, you had a blazing row with her and hit her across the face.'

Wiseman went white. 'Who told you that?' he asked furiously; and then: 'It's a lie! Who told you such a monstrous lie?'

'Your house doesn't have very thick walls. Several other people were in the next room,' Slider said, and added conversationally: 'It's curious how far the sound of a slap travels – I suppose it's the pitch.'

'I tell you it's a lie!' Wiseman said vehemently. He leaned forward, fists on the table. 'People are out to blacken me. You tell me who told such a lie about me, and I'll—'

'You'll kill them?' Slider finished for him unemphatically.

Wiseman blenched and fell back.

'Lies *have* been told,' Slider went on, 'but not about that. Not about you, but *by* you.'

'I think this has gone far enough,' Drobcek said, and Wiseman threw him a glance of relief. 'If you have evidence against my client, you had better produce it, and stop all the innuendo.'

'Very well,' Slider said. 'Where were you on Friday night, Mr Wiseman? From the end of the school day until you got home?'

'I've already told you, I was taking soccer practice,' he said.

'And there's the lie,' Slider said calmly. 'From your lips, before witnesses and on tape. There was no soccer practice on Friday. There never is soccer or any other game after school on Fridays. The teachers are always in a hurry to get home.'

He blinked. 'I—' he began. He looked at Drobcek.

Drobcek shrugged. 'Better clear it up,' he said. 'Otherwise it does look bad.'

'It wasn't an official, school practice,' Wiseman said, thinking hard. 'It's a scratch team – local kids – I help out. We meet every Friday after school. Keeps them out of trouble. It's – a sort of voluntary work I do, to help the community. A thing I do out of the kindness of my heart.'

'Give me the names of the boys involved.'

'I . . . I can't remember.'

'Give me one name.'

No answer.

'You can't remember the name of a single boy? Even though you see them every Friday?'

'I'm – under a lot of stress at the moment. I can't think clearly when I'm being attacked like this.'

'I'm not attacking you. I'm trying to get at the facts. How long did this football practice go on?' Slider asked.

He must have sensed the trap. 'I don't remember. We play until they've had enough. It goes on longer than a school practice would.'

'As much as two hours? Three?'

'Easily that. They're very keen.'

'And where did you go afterwards?'

'Home, of course.'

'So you'd have been home by – what – half past seven? At the latest. School comes out at half past three. It would hardly have gone on longer than four hours.'

Wiseman stared, his eyes desperately trying to strip meaning out of Slider's face.

'Half past seven? Would you say you got home by then?'

And Wiseman said, in a strangled voice, 'Yes.'

'And there's another lie,' Slider said. 'Your wife said you weren't home until late, until after she went to bed. Something like half past eleven.'

'She wouldn't know,' he cried. 'She's confused. She's thinking of another night. She never knows what day it is anyway. You can't take her word for it. Woolly-minded. Hopeless. You can't rely on her for anything.'

'Then *you* can't rely on her to give you an alibi for Friday night, can you?' Slider said, while Drobcek gave Wiseman an exasperated look, and Wiseman stared from one to the other, his lips moving as if there were words somewhere, but he wasn't managing to capture them.

Atherton was working his way patiently through Valerie Proctor's life story towards the part of it that interested him. He could see she was enjoying herself, and little as he wanted to afford her the satisfaction, he knew from the gleam of self-righteousness in her eye that she was the sort of person to whom umbrage was not something you took but something you were born with a right to. In the long run it would be quicker to let her do it her way than put her back up and have to deal with the consequences.

So he went through her childhood ('I was such a talented child. I could have gone on the stage but Daddy wouldn't have it. I sing, you know, and play the piano'), and her marriage to Proctor ('My maiden name, Critchfield, was a much better one – *and* a proper Dorset name – but Steve insisted I change, and once you have it's too much hassle to change back'), and the divorce ('I hope I'm a fair-minded person, but I'm sure I put more into this house than ever he did, so why should he have it, just to make a pigsty out of it, the way he did everything?').

She told him how she had gone into the estate agency business straight from school. 'It was always what I wanted to do – well, once I gave up wanting to go on the stage, which was never really a possibility once Daddy put his foot down. I mean, that's something you have to have support to do.' She had started as an office junior and worked her way up. 'I have a qualification, you know – NFPP.'

'NFPP?' Atherton enquired, and then wished he hadn't.

'The National Federation of Property Professionals,' she explained. 'The Technical Award in Residential Letting and Property Management is an important qualification. I mean, it's equivalent to an A-Level, you know.'

They did a brief résumé (though not brief enough) of her career through various estate agents, finishing with the Hatter and Ruck branch in Poole ('dealing with all the really expensive properties, five and six million, swimming pools, boat houses, you name it'), marrying and divorcing Steve Proctor on the way, and came at last to meeting Scott Hibbert.

'It was at an IREA – the International Real Estate Alliance – trade show. The London Property Exhibition at Earl's Court. Scott was on the Hatter and Ruck headquarters stand. I was divorced by then, of course, and – well, it was attraction at first sight. We had such a lot in common – you know, both being in the business and everything, and both being forceful, go-ahead, ambitious people. But I won't deny there was a definite animal attraction between us. A sort of mutual magnetism we simply couldn't resist. It was as if we were meant for each other. Of course,' she added, with a descent into bathos, 'I had a hotel room – it was a two-day show – which was a definite advantage.'

'I can see,' Atherton said patiently, 'that it would be.'

THIRTEEN
Discomfort Zone

After a break, requested by Drobcek to consult privately with his client, and the bringing of tea, which Drobcek drank and Wiseman didn't, Slider, with Mackay as his assistant, went back in and the taping was resumed.

Drobcek opened the batting. 'My client wishes to say that he was mistaken in his previous statement about taking soccer practice last Friday. His state of emotional turmoil and grief left him confused. I'm sure you will understand that.'

Slider understood, all right. 'So where were you on Friday evening, Mr Wiseman?' Drobcek opened his mouth and Slider forestalled him. 'I would like to hear it from Mr Wiseman himself.' Legally it was no less valid if Drobcek said it on instruction, but Wiseman was a self-proclaimed virtuous man and a churchgoer, and if another lie was coming Slider knew instinctively it would make a difference to *him*. He wanted to make him say the words and face the shame.

Wiseman gave him a look that could have charred a thousand-acre forest, but he seemed to have himself under control. His arms were folded so tightly across his chest it was a wonder he could breathe, and his face was rigid, but he said in a calm voice that sounded almost normal, 'I was doing individual coaching. I have several young protégés who I see privately for one-on-one coaching.'

'And which one, or ones, did you see on Friday night? Names and addresses, please.'

'I am not going to give you any names,' Wiseman said. 'It would be quite wrong to expose them to this unpleasantness.'

Ah, that was the way he was going, was it? That accounted for his air of serenity. He thought he'd found a winning formula. A glance at Drobcek showed him worried, but hopeful.

'I'm afraid I must insist,' Slider said.

'And I'm afraid I must refuse,' Wiseman said with an air of moral superiority that got right up Slider's nose. 'I am in loco parentis to these young people, and I could not betray their confidence, or do anything to expose them to unpleasantness. It would be quite wrong of me to sacrifice their privacy simply to convenience myself. I must hold to what I believe is right and face the consequences, even if they are unpleasant to me personally.'

Ooh, don't you just hate it when that happens? Slider enquired of himself ironically. Wiseman was looking at him now, satisfied he had got the upper hand, and the longing to wipe that smug look off his face was strong.

'Never mind,' said Porson. 'We'll see. He who last laughs, lasts longest.' He paused a fraction of a second, as if aware that hadn't come out right, shrugged, and went on. 'I'm not bothered about upsetting his sacred bloody young people. Flaming Nora, the stuff they watch on telly and see on the Internet these days, *I'm* more sensitive than they are! We'll find out who he coaches, if he does coach anyone. And appeal to their parents to let them come forward. It is a case of murder, after all. No sympathy to be had in that. And in the end, it's up to Wiseman to prove his alibi.'

'Yes, sir,' said Slider, comforted but not entirely cheered by Porson's confidence. 'But it's up to us to prove he killed her, even if he hasn't got an alibi.'

'Ah well. Can't make cakes without straw,' Porson said. 'We'll get him, laddie, one way or another.'

'Did you know he was involved with someone else?' Atherton asked. As it was turning into a long session, Hewlitt had gone to make tea, and Valerie kept casting nervous glances in that direction – not, Atherton surmised, because she was afraid he would jump her without supervision, but because she was afraid Hewlitt would mess up her kitchen. But the question brought her attention sharply back on him.

'Of course not. What do you take me for?'

'Did you ever get invited to his place in London?'

'No,' she admitted. 'But he told me he only had a little bed-sitter. It wasn't nice like my place. And he said it was a treat for him to get away from London, so we always met down here. If I'd known there was another woman on the scene, I'd have made him sort it out double quick, believe you me. I don't share. That's what I told Steve. I said you choose, right now, because I don't share with anyone. And when he dithered about it, that was that. He was out on his ear.' She gave him a nod, her lips tight closed, the meat of her face trembling a little with the emphasis.

'Quite right too,' Atherton said, still buttering her. 'So how often did you and Scott meet?'

'Oh, every couple of weeks, I suppose. We were both busy people, and the time just flies by, doesn't it?'

'And this has been going on for . . .?'

'A year. A bit over a year. The London Property Exhibition was February.'

'And I read in the transcript of your statement last night that you had a business relationship with Scott, as well as a personal one.'

Surprisingly, she went red, visible even under the several layers of make-up. 'We did – he did – there was . . .' She didn't seem to know how to phrase it. She looked at him appealingly, opening her eyes wide and leaning forward a fraction more. 'Look, I'm not going to get into trouble, am I?'

'It depends what you've done,' Atherton said, but with an easy, I'm-relaxed-about-minor-infractions smile.

'Only,' she said, 'I did come forward and turn him in. At considerable inconvenience, not to say danger, to myself, and if there was a bit of – let's say – irregularity about our business deal, well, no one was hurt by it. It goes on all the time, believe you me, but one's bosses can be a bit strict about it – well, they're bound to be, really, I suppose – but if everything was always done strictly by the book—'

'I'm only interested in the murder,' Atherton said. 'Anything else that went on is not my business.'

She looked relieved. 'So I don't need to tell you. Only, I wouldn't have said anything at the station, but I was flustered and it sort of slipped out.'

'I said it wasn't my business, but I do need to know the exact nature of your relationship with Scott, so I'm afraid you will have to tell me what you and he were doing. It could have a profound effect on the case.'

She was not fetched by the waffle. 'Does that mean I'll have to stand up in court about it?' she asked sharply.

'It probably won't come to that.'

'Will you give me your word?'

He gave a stern look. 'I'm afraid I can't do that. You will have to do your duty, whatever that turns out to be. But I know a woman of your strength of character will meet that challenge head on, with the same courage you've shown in your actions so far.' She didn't quite buy it, tilting her head a little to one side and eyeing him speculatively, so he went on in a quiet, firm tone. 'Tell me what you and Scott were doing – besides your private relationship.'

She made up her mind. 'Well, it was just a matter of bringing client and vendor together and adjusting the price between them. Which is what we do all the time anyway, estate agents. Only,' she sighed, 'when the circumstances were right, Scott would come in and convince the vendor to drop the price, and the purchaser would split the difference with us. It was a win-win situation – nobody was hurt.'

'Except the vendor,' Atherton suggested.

'Well, not really, because we'd do the sale privately so he wouldn't have to pay the agency its commission.'

'Ah,' said Atherton. Yes, he could see it all. The real victim was the agency, but as that was a company and not an individual, people like Valerie and Scott wouldn't regard harm to it as any harm at all. It came under the heading of making private calls from your company phone, stealing stationery from work or adding a new carpet to the insurance claim – a victimless crime.

'Anyway,' she went on, 'if the vendor looked likely to be difficult, I'd just stop them getting any other offers, so then I could tell them it was because the price was too high, and if they dropped it they'd be able to sell all right. And then, of course, when they dropped the price and the offer came in, I was proved right, so *they* were happy.'

'Wouldn't they wonder why other people's houses were selling for more?'

She looked dismissive. 'You can always find *something* about a house to bring the price down. The punters don't know any better.'

'And presumably you'd only be doing it on really top price houses,' Atherton said. 'So a small percentage worked out at a nice commission.'

She seemed to take this as a criticism. 'We didn't do it very often,' she protested. 'It would've been too risky to chance anything but the occasional property. And the circumstances had to be right – the purchaser had to be on board. But Poole being what it is . . .' She shrugged.

Yes, thought Atherton – the most expensive real estate in the country, hitched on to a top-whack marina.

She looked unhappy. 'But just lately I'd been feeling that the risk wasn't worth it. I was on at Scott to stop while we were ahead, and for him to make the break with London, move down here. I wanted us to set up as independent estate agents. We had all the skills between us, and the contacts, and I couldn't see why Hatter and Ruck should get all the benefit from our hard work and expertise. With the money we'd already made we could cover set-up costs, and there's plenty of scope for a new player in the field. Frankly, Hatter and Ruck are a bit stodgy and old-fashioned. I mean, they're OK for selling Georgian vicarages, but for the new sort of client that's coming into the market now, people with lots of cash money to spend, especially for the newer properties, places like Poole, and the luxury flats that are going up in Bournemouth . . .'

'And Scott wasn't willing to go along with your plans?' Atherton asked sympathetically.

'Oh, it wasn't that. But he wanted us to do one last job, a big one, make a big killing before we stopped. And I was a bit nervous about it. It was outside my comfort zone, if you want to know. But he said he'd be doing all the hard work and taking all the risk. Well, I didn't quite see it that way. But anyway, I said that if we were going to do something like that, he should make the break with London, he should move in to my house, we should get married.' She looked to see if he understood.

'You wanted some kind of assurance that you were in it together?' Atherton said.

She looked relieved. 'Yes, right. Well, even though we'd been going out for over a year, we didn't see all that much of each other, and I didn't feel I knew everything about him. Which proved to be true,' she added bitterly, 'because when I said that about getting married, he told me about being involved with someone. Actually living with her.'

'How did he explain that away?' Atherton asked.

'He said it was all over between them before he met me. He said he'd been going to leave her for a long time, but she was very neurotic, and he had to pick the right moment because she might self-harm. He said she was anorexic and she'd been having psychiatric treatment so he had to be careful. He promised he would sort it all out and we would get married, but he couldn't control the timing.' Now she lifted to his face eyes that were haunted. 'I never knew,' she said, 'I swear to you I never knew that he was going to kill her. That wasn't what I thought he meant. If I'd had any idea, I'd have gone straight to the police. That poor girl . . .' She shuddered.

'But you'd seen in the papers and on television that she'd been murdered?'

'I'd seen it, yes, but I wasn't that interested. I mean, there's always someone being murdered, isn't there? I don't read the gory stuff, I just skip over the headlines. And of course, I never knew her name, so I never connected it with Scott. Why would I?' she appealed for forgiveness.

'He hadn't contacted you, then, since the weekend? Not to tell you she was missing or anything like that?'

'No, I never heard from him – but that wasn't unusual. He wasn't a great one for talking on the phone. Usually I'd just get a call when he was planning to come down again. I never even knew when he turned up here Thursday night. I mean, he looked terrible – unshaven, dirty, smelling of drink. He'd just really let himself go to the dogs. Obviously something bad had happened.'

'Didn't you ask what?'

'I started to, but he said, "Leave me alone. I can't talk now," and I could see he was in a real state, so I thought I'd leave him alone till he was a bit more together. To be honest, I thought he'd finally broken up with this other woman and it had been a bit difficult, so I thought a bit of sympathy on my part would—'

'Point up the contrast,' Atherton supplied.

She looked a little reproachful, but didn't contradict him. 'But then he started watching the news all the time, and I saw the police were looking for him. I said, "What have you done?" and he said, "Nothing." But then he said, "They're after me for Mel's murder." *Then* I got the connection. Well, then I knew what I had to do. I gave him a lot of scotch, to try to make him fall asleep. But he just wouldn't go off. But he was so into the telly and looking at himself on the news, I thought he wouldn't notice anyway. So I told him his clothes needed washing – which they did – and took 'em away so he couldn't make a run for it. And I phoned the police. And they came round and took him away.' She looked distressed. 'You should have heard his language! And then he started crying. I didn't know where to look, I was that ashamed.' She shook her head, musing. 'I don't know how I could have been so wrong about him. I should've known from the beginning he was no good. When I first met him, at Earl's Court, and we went to my hotel, instead of his house.' And she added in a burst of angry frankness. 'Going up to my room, he farted in the lift.'

'That's wrong on so many levels,' Atherton murmured.

Mrs Wiseman was beyond being of any help to anyone. She seemed to have sunk and spread into the armchair she sat in, like a jelly on a plate beginning to melt. It was Bethany who answered the door, and hurried Connolly into the living room as if she hoped she could save them both; and she hung around the back of her mother's armchair looking by turns scared and defiant.

'D'you want to go and make your mammy a cup of tea?' Connolly urged, to get her out of the way.

'She's not my mammy,' Bethany objected, 'she's me mum. You don't half talk funny. And she's had cups of tea all morning.'

'I bet she could do with another,' Connolly said.

'You want me out of the way so you can talk about Dad killing Mel,' Bethany said. 'Well, he never. He wouldn't do that. My dad's the best, and when he gets out he's gonna sue the lot of you for false arrest, then you'll be sorry.'

Connolly looked at her kindly. 'I know you're upset, and no wonder, but we're not going to hurt him. We just want to ask him a few questions, that's all.'

'Then why d'you have to arrest him for? That's like saying you think he did it.'

'Not a bit. We arrest a lot o' people. It's a process we have to go through. We ask them questions then they're free to go. We only want to find out the truth about what happened to Melanie. You must want that too.'

'I don't care,' Bethany said, close to tears. 'She's dead. I just want my dad back.'

'Well, hop and make your mum a cuppa, and let me ask me questions, so. The sooner that's done, the sooner we can sort it all out. Ah, g'wan, that's a good girl.'

She extracted herself by unwilling inches, and all this time Mrs Wiseman had been sitting staring at nothing, only her fingers moving as they screwed and shredded a damp tissue between them. Connolly hunkered down by the chair so that she was at face level, and said, 'Mrs Wiseman, it's me, Detective Constable Connolly. Rita. We talked before, d'you remember?' There was no response, and no eye contact, but she thought the woman was listening. 'I just want you to cast your mind back to that Friday, the day Melanie disappeared.'

'The day she was killed,' Mrs Wiseman amended harshly. So she was listening.

'Your husband was out all evening, is that right? Until what time?'

'I don't know. I don't know anything any more. What does it matter anyway? Mel's dead. She's not coming back.'

'But you still have Bethany,' Connolly said. 'You've got to be a mother to her, poor wean. You've got to make the effort to hold on.'

The tortured eyes came round, red-rimmed and exhausted. 'You think Ian did it? You think he killed her?'

Connolly had to take the opportunity. 'Do you think he could?'

'I don't know.' She stared, her mind revolving like something trapped in a space too small. 'He was out that evening,' she said at last. 'But he was often out, after school. Only, he was later back that night. He didn't come in until after I was in bed. That couldn't have been school stuff, could it?'

'Where did he say he'd been?'

'He didn't say. He didn't speak to me. I was in bed. I heard him come in and go straight to his bedroom.' She shook her head wearily. 'We never talked about his work any more. In the beginning he'd sometimes tell me what he'd done at school that day, but not lately. Not for years.'

God, what a sterile life, Connolly thought. 'Could it have been private coaching he was doing that night? Did he do private coaching?'

'No. I don't know. Maybe,' she said. 'He never said he did.'

Connolly tried, 'Could he have gone out again after he'd gone to bed? Would you have heard him if he did?'

'I'm a sound sleeper. I wouldn't hear.' Still she stared into the mid-distance, but not in the dazed manner of before, but as if she were watching something unfolding, a movie of events being replayed for her private torture. Her eyes widened as if she saw a new scenario she had not yet contemplated. 'A father wouldn't kill his own child,' she said, almost in a whisper. 'It's not possible.' Suddenly she gripped Connolly's forearm with fingers that hurt. 'Did he do it? I have to know. Did he kill my Mel?'

Connolly tried gently to unlatch the fingers, but they were like steel bands. This poor tormented woman deserved the truth, but what was that? Connolly didn't know. 'I can't tell you. I don't know. We're trying to find out, that's all.' She put a bit more effort into prying the fingers loose as her arm was going dead under the pressure, and the next moment something flew at her and hit her round the back of the head, not hard, but heartfelt.

'Don't you hurt my mum!' Bethany cried as Connolly, her arm released, fell awkwardly on her behind on the carpet. 'I'll kill you! Don't you touch her.'

'I didn't hurt her,' Connolly said, wondering whether to rub her arm or her head. It was only the rolled-up *Radio Times*, she saw, in the child's hand. If she'd come from the kitchen, lucky it wasn't a knife. Did homicide run in families?

'You get out! I knew I shouldn't leave her alone. You get out now!' Bethany shouted, elevated above the childish by her furious defence of her stepmother. Connolly moved towards the door, with Bethany ushering her like a sheepdog. Connolly almost expected to have her heels nipped. At the front door she paused with her hand on the latch and said, 'Bethany, we have to find out where your dad was, so that we can cross him off. There has to be someone who can say where he was. Only, he wasn't at soccer practice, you see.'

'If you knew where he was, would you let him go?' she asked, suddenly sharp.

'Yes, if we can find someone who can swear to it. Did he have private pupils? You know, for sports coaching?'

Bethany suddenly looked very young, and frightened. 'I don't want to get into trouble.'

'You won't, I promise.'

'But you won't tell Dad I told?'

'No, pet, I won't.'

Bethany chewed her lip. 'Only, my friend Georgia's dad does some work in the evenings he doesn't want anyone to know about, 'cos of the taxman, and she says he'll go to prison if anyone finds out. You have to tell the taxman everything you do, and he doesn't.'

'So your dad is teaching private pupils in the evening, is he?'

'I dunno. I think so. Only, you won't tell him I told you? And you won't tell the taxman?'

'Neither one nor t'other,' Connolly swore solemnly. 'How d'you know about it?'

'I heard some sixth-form boys at our school talking about someone seeing one of the teachers after school, and then one of them said my dad's name, and one of them said, "He's working on her forehand grip," and then they laughed. I don't know why – it wasn't funny.'

'No, *alana*, it wasn't. Is her name Stephanie?'

'I don't know. I never heard. It was me dad's name that made me listen. He must be giving her tennis coaching.'

'Is that where your dad was on that Friday?'

'I don't know. But this time, Georgia was in her mum's car coming home from her gran's, and they passed our car on the A40, and there was a girl sitting beside me dad, like, older than me. He never looked round so he didn't see, but Georgia said it was definitely him but she didn't know the girl. And that was a Friday night.'

'Did Georgia's mum see him and the girl?'

'No. She was looking at the traffic lights, saying, "Don't change, you bastards, don't change." Dad doesn't let me say bastard. He says it's swearing. But Georgia says it isn't really, it just means someone you don't like.'

'Well, you'd better not say it if your dad doesn't like it,' Connolly said judiciously, glad the child had calmed down. She didn't like to leave her all alone with a whacked-out mum. 'Would your mum's friend not come in and mind yez both?' she asked. 'That Mrs Sutton? She seemed nice.'

'She's all right,' Bethany said listlessly, and then thought of something. 'Would she cook us some dinner? We haven't had anything to eat today, except cornflakes, cos I can do those.'

'I bet she would,' Connolly said with utmost sincerity. 'Wait'll I ask her. Number forty-eight, isn't it?'

She was eager to get away and track down Stephanie Bentham, but she could not in conscience leave this waif to cope alone. But she felt sure that Margie would be only too willing to get back on stage, and negotiations would take only as long as it took her to grab her handbag.

Slider left Wiseman to stew for a bit, and went to see if Scott Hibbert was back from the land of the fairies. He looked terrible, and didn't smell any too good, either. Obviously his stay first at the hotel, and then at Valerie's, with no work to go to and nothing to take his mind off his sins, had sent him on a downward spiral, for he was sporting several days of beard and did not seem to have bathed for the same length of time. He was wearing a nasty pair of sweat pants and a zipped fleece top over a T-shirt, his hair was matted and his feet were shoved bare into a pair of battered-looking trainers that were adding something of the ripe Gorgonzola to the olfactory mix in the cell.

Slider looked at him through the wicket. His eyes were inflamed and rather crazed-looking, and he sniffed constantly and wiped his nose on his cuff. 'Is he all right for interviewing?' he asked O'Flaherty, the sergeant on duty.

'If y'ask me,' O'Flaherty said without sympathy, 'him and reality's never been on first name terms. But he's no worse than the average headbanger we get in here. Sure, you can talk to him if you think it'll help. The doc's signed off on him, and he's about as able for't as he'll ever be. Tape Room One?'

'Trot him along. I'll be there in five minutes,' Slider said, and went to collect Norma, so as to have fresh ears on the case.

Hibbert scrambled to his feet as soon as Slider entered, and was gently pushed back down by Gostyn, the uniform minding him. 'Are you the boss around here?' Hibbert asked, his eyes flitting nervously to Swilley and back. 'I want to talk to the boss.'

'I'm the investigating officer,' Slider said, and introduced himself and Swilley. 'Are they treating you all right?'

'Yes, yes, but I want to talk to you,' he said urgently.

'You can, son, just settle down. I'm going to ask you some questions and I have to ask you if you want a solicitor to be present.'

'They've already asked me that,' he said almost petulantly. 'I don't want a solicitor. I just want to talk to whoever's in charge.'

Slider managed to shut him up for long enough to get the tape rolling according to protocol, and then he was off.

'You've got to understand, it wasn't the way it looked. Valerie. It was just a business arrangement. Of course I had to keep it secret from Mel because she wouldn't have understood. Women never do. But Val was good, the best in the business, and she had the contacts, so I needed her for that end of it. And she was – well, you saw her. She's not a bad-looking woman but she's a lot older than me, and a bit desperate. Anyway, she made it clear enough I was going to have to give her a bit more than just money to get her on board with it. What was I to do? I had to keep her sweet or she could have blown the whole thing and landed us both in trouble. She wasn't that bad, actually,' he said, his mind wandering. He stared vacantly at Swilley, who stared back blankly, not to disturb him. 'I mean, she knew a thing or two – you know, in bed – and I'm not saying I'd have needed my arm twisted in normal circumstances. But I didn't set out to be unfaithful to Mel.'

'What was the nature of this business arrangement you had with Valerie?' Slider asked, to get him back on track.

Hibbert explained it pretty much as Valerie had to Atherton, but with a lot more detail. 'But the thing was,' he went on, 'she was obviously more interested in me than the job, and she'd started hinting about me moving down there with her. Then she started talking about marriage. So I knew I didn't have much longer before I was going to have to dump her. But we had this really big job coming up. It was a developer thing, the biggest job I'd ever had a hand in. This row of houses with big gardens. The developer wanted to pull 'em down and put up blocks of flats. He didn't mind saving a bit of money wherever he could. If we could get the owners to sell, and get the prices right, we were sitting on a million quid for our trouble – and all cash, tax free. You don't get chances like that every day of the week. So I had to keep her sweet, Valerie, until it was done. I had to pretend it was her that mattered to me. I even had to pretend I might marry her. But I never *wanted* to be unfaithful to Mel. It was just business.'

He looked to them for sympathy for his predicament.

'Tell me about that Friday, the weekend of your friend's wedding.'

'Well, I was down there, of course. Doing this deal. Val and me had to wine and dine the developer and get it all tied up. The wedding was a blessing, because it meant I could get away on Friday. There was a stag night thing going on, so I said I was going to that. Saturday I had to go to the wedding, but I got away as quick as I could, and Val and me pretty much worked through the night putting it all together. Then she started on about our marriage plans again, and saying we could have a lovely Sunday together, just her and me, so I thought it was a good idea to get out while I could. So I went back to London Sunday morning.'

'So it wasn't the case that Melanie was the one thing standing between you and your new life down in Bournemouth, making lots of lovely money in a hot housing market?' Slider said.

Hibbert looked stunned. He licked his lips. 'I know you think I killed her. I've seen it in the papers, and on telly. You think I did it. Well, maybe I did. She was a cracking girl, Melanie, but she was too good for me. All her friends thought so. She was smart and clever and educated and everything, and all I had was – well, I don't know what she saw in me. I'm good at what I do, that's all. I'd got this plan to turn the flats in the house where we live into two maisonettes. Would have made a lot of money. But I don't think she liked it, because it meant getting that old fool Ronnie out of the basement, and he didn't want to go. She liked him, God knows why. I think,' he said, with a hint of anger, 'she liked him more than me, sometimes. It was always waifs and strays with her. Anyone with a hard luck story. She didn't appreciate someone who got on and got ahead through their own efforts. She just didn't appreciate money, thought it didn't matter, though she didn't mind spending mine. It was a good job I made good bread because she never had a cent. Dunno what she spent it on. But I still think she'd have loved me more if I was an ex-con like Ronnie or a waster like her father.'

'It's hard not to be appreciated,' Slider said.

'Yeah,' said Hibbert. He flicked a look at the impassive Norma, then returned his congested eyes to Slider. 'Maybe that's why she had to go, so I could start a new life with Val. *She* appreciates me. She knows she's lucky to get me. I'm good-looking, I'm young, I've got a nice car, I've got what it takes to make money. What more does a women want? She made me mad sometimes, Mel, the way she was always so much better than me. I couldn't drop my socks on the floor, had to put them in the laundry basket. It's my bloody floor, just as much as hers! Bloody laundry basket – who has one

of those? And the way I held my fork – that didn't please her.
And she was always correcting my grammar. How d'you think
that makes me feel? She didn't like my ties. She didn't like
my signet ring – *her father* never wore jewellery, she said.
And everything in the house had to be done the way *she* liked
it. I brought her home this ornament once – kind of like a
fairy, with wings and everything, holding some flowers – china
you know. Well, Val's got one, and she likes it, and I saw one
like it in a shop, so I brought it home, a present for Mel, and
you should have heard her! Well, she didn't actually *say*
anything, I mean she said thanks and everything, but you could
see she didn't like it. Practically put gloves on to touch it.
And you know, that fairy never made it to the mantelpiece. I
never saw it again. I reckon she must have put it in the bin
when I was out of the way.'

'She didn't like your friends, either, did she?' Slider
suggested.

He glared at Swilley, who seemed to be becoming a substi-
tute for the absent. 'No, she bloody didn't. She thought she
was too good for them. She said they were boring. That's why
the wedding was such a good excuse, because I knew she'd
never want to come.'

'So it served her right, really, that it *was* just an excuse.'

'Yeah!' Hibbert cried. 'Stuck up, snotty cow! Served her
right! You're all the same, you bitches, think you're better than
us!' And he flung himself across the table at Norma, trying
to grab her by the throat.

Norma moved like lightning, catching his wrists and slam-
ming them down on to the table with a strength hard-won in
endless arm-wrestling bouts since she first joined the Job.
Slider and Gostyn were round the table and got a grip on his
elbows, but in truth Swilley could have held him on her own.
Motherhood had taken none of her edge, Slider thought with
satisfaction.

But Hibbert didn't struggle. He'd cried out in pain when
his wrists hit the table, and yielded as soon as Slider and
Gostyn grabbed him. When they let him go, he collapsed
slowly forwards on to the desk, cushioning his head in his
arms, and sobbing brokenly. 'I killed her,' he wept. 'I really,

really loved her. I don't care if Dave said she was a snotty cow. I loved her, and I killed her, and now I've got nothing. I wish I was dead!' He finished on a howl, and said nothing more coherent.

Slider watched him dispassionately, knowing there would have to be another visit by the doctor to make sure he was not hurt – his cry of pain was on the tape, and the sounds of scuffle – and that if another tranquillizer was administered they wouldn't get to interview him again for hours, by which time the impetus would be gone.

FOURTEEN
Virgin Athletic

When Connolly finally tracked down Stephanie Bentham, she was with a bunch of other youngsters in typical Saturday afternoon mode. There was a patch of green with a bench and a bus stop beside it, and they were hanging about there, some sitting on the bench, some standing, one sitting, arms crossed, on his bicycle, pushing himself an inch forward and backward monotonously with his foot. They were chatting, laughing, texting, two of the girls were smoking with faint defiance, and the atmosphere was so heavy with teenage hormones it could have triggered a Control Order under the Clean Air Act.

Stephanie was a little apart, sitting on the rail surrounding the green. Connolly thought she had never seen anyone look so unhappy. She was hunched, her hands between her knees, and when Connolly stood before her she raised wide desperate eyes like a cornered hind staring at the hunter.

'Are you Stephanie?' Connolly asked, showing her brief, but discreetly, shielded by her body from view of the others.

Stephanie nodded.

'I need to talk to you. D'you want to walk along with me? No need for them to know your business, is there?'

She seemed beyond being grateful for that, but she hitched herself off the rail and fell in beside Connolly, walking away from the group, some of whom, Connolly noted from her eye corners, looked their way, but not with great interest, God love 'em. Ah, the self-absorption of youth!

'I've me car round the corner,' she said to Stephanie when they were clear. 'We can sit in that for a chat if you like.'

Stephanie looked a moment of alarm. 'No. Not in the car,' she said quickly; then seemed to collect herself and said: 'Can't we just walk? There's the park down there.'

The car, Connolly surmised, was playing some leading part in the feature movie going on in the girl's head; or maybe she was afraid of being abducted.

'Walking's fine with me,' Connolly said cheerily. 'Sure I don't get out in the fresh air enough.'

She thought she would wait until they were in the park to begin, to build up some trust between them, or at least let her get used to her, but before they reached the gates Stephanie made the first move. 'It is right?' she asked, without looking at Connolly. 'Did – Mr Wiseman – did he really kill his step-daughter, like they're saying?'

'Who's saying that?' Connolly asked.

'The others.' She gestured backwards. 'Everyone at school. They say that's why he's not been in. They say the head's sacked him, and now you've arrested him.' Now she looked at Connolly, appalled. 'If he's a murderer . . .'

'We arrest a lot of people,' Connolly said for the second time that day. 'It's what we have to do sometimes to question people – it's a technical thing. I won't bother you with it, but it doesn't mean they've done anything, necessarily.' Stephanie was staring at the ground again, trudging miserably. 'You care about him, don't you?' Connolly said gently. A startled look. 'Ah, g'wan, I know all about it. You can tell me.'

The head went even further down. Her next words were so tiny they were almost indecipherable. 'Will my mum and dad have to know about it?'

'It may not come to that,' Connolly said. 'You're seventeen, right?'

'Last December,' she confirmed.

'I can talk to you without your parents, so. Look, pet, if I can keep it quiet I will, but it's not entirely in my hands. But you've got to do the right thing. You know that, don't you?'

Nod.

'Did you know Melanie Hunter?'

Shake. 'Only what's in the paper. My mum reads every word, she's obsessed with it. Knowing that – Mr Wiseman's one of our teachers makes her more interested. If she knew – you know – she'd go mad. My dad'd kill me. And the

others – they wouldn't understand. They think he's just a
boring grown-up, a teacher. They don't know . . .'

'The other side of him,' Connolly suggested. Pass the sick
bag, Nora.

Stephanie looked up, eager and hopeful of understanding.
'He's not like he seems in school. He's different. More –
gentle, and – he talks to me, like a real person. Not like
Mum and Dad. They just, like, issue orders, and when they
ask you questions they don't listen to the answers. But Ian –
Mr Wiseman—'

'You can call him Ian to me,' Connolly said.

Stephanie looked doubtful.

'You're quite close to him, aren't you?' Connolly went on.
Anyone who could think Ian Wiseman was a fluffy bunny-
rabbit must be pure dotey on him. It'd sicken you, she thought,
but she kept her face kindly and interested. Plenty of time to
throw up later. 'You're fond of him?'

'I love him!' Stephanie burst out. Evidently the pressure to
tell had overcome the dam of fearful restraint. 'And he loves
me! I know he's married, but he doesn't love his wife. How
could he? She's old and fat and dull and – and she doesn't
understand him! She's not interested in anything he does, just
sits at home watching TV all the time. He's a wonderful person,
and she just doesn't get it, how lucky she is. And now he's in
trouble, and he needs me, and I can't see him! *She* won't be
any use to him. He's all alone, and I can't help him!' Huge
tears formed in the doe eyes.

Connolly hastily thrust a tissue at her. Love a' God, she'd
want to listen to herself! 'Come on, Stephanie. Cool the head,
now. Sure, nothing's happened to him. He's just answering
some questions for us. And you *can* help him.' A blurry look
of hope. 'Stop the crying, now, blow your nose, and talk to
me like a sensible woman.'

They had come to a bench, fortuitously empty, and Connolly
thought it better to sit down while Stephanie got herself
together. She provided a couple more tissues, and mopping
up was soon achieved. Stephanie stopped crying as easily as
she had started, but she still looked miserable – and why not?
Connolly thought.

'So tell me about Ian,' she said. 'He's coaching you, is he? What is it, tennis?'

'No,' Stephanie said. 'That's just the excuse. Someone saw us together and one of the other teachers asked him, so he said he was coaching me. It kind of spread, a bit, and a few people at school think I'm getting coaching, which is a laugh really, because I'm no good at sports. If it got to my mum and dad they'd go mad, because they'd know it wasn't coaching, cos they'd have to pay for it, and they're not, so you won't tell, will you?'

'So what *do* you do together?' Connolly asked, leaving that one.

'Go out in his car, mostly. Go for drives. We stop somewhere and sit and talk, and—' Suddenly she blushed, richly, and Connolly felt a quickening of pulse. 'We go to the pictures sometimes,' Stephanie went on quickly, as if to avoid the subject. 'And for meals, or we get a takeaway and eat it in the car. When the weather was nicer we sat outside, like on Horsenden Hill or somewhere like that.'

'It's been going on for a while, so?'

'Since September. When we came back to school. I bumped into him the first day back and dropped my books and he helped me pick them up and kind of touched my hand accidentally and we sort of smiled at each other. And then he said, "Glad to be back?" and I said, "Yes," and he said, "Me too," but I knew he meant something different by it, from the way he was looking at me. And I started hanging about after school to see if I could catch him coming out, but he's got games a lot after school. So I started staying to watch and he saw me and one day after a match when he came out from the changing rooms he saw me and said I must be frozen and would I like a cup of tea.' Her eyes were misty with rapture. 'So we went to this café out Uxbridge way, where nobody'd know us, and we talked and talked. And that was the start of it.'

'So you've been meeting regularly since then?'

'Whenever he can. It was awful over Christmas because there was no school and he was with his family and I was with mine and all I could think of was that we ought to be

together. I couldn't wait to get back to school. And the minute
I saw him—'

'Great,' Connolly said, to forestall any more syrup. Gak!
That muscle-bound, narky little eejit? The girl was a looper.
'Did you have a regular day you met?'

'No, it was any time we could manage, but it was often a
Friday evening because there are no games after school on a
Friday. Weekends were harder, because of our families.'

'What about Friday week past? Did you see him then?'
Connolly asked, as casual as open-toed sandals.

Stephanie sighed like a high-speed train going into a tunnel.
'That was the last time I saw him.'

'Tell me about it.'

She seemed only too glad to – a chance to discuss her
beloved? Bring it on! 'We met straight after school. I walk up
to the main road and there's a place where I wait for him,
where there's never anyone around, and he comes along in
the car and picks me up.'

'And what did you do then?'

'We went to the pictures,' she said.

'Where?'

'The Royale Leisure park. You know, on the A40, by Park
Royal station. It's big enough so no one'd see us. We went to
the four fifteen show, then when we came out we got something to eat.'

'In a restaurant? Or a pub?'

'He doesn't go into pubs. He doesn't drink. He says it rots
your brain and ruins your body. We went to cafés sometimes,
but more often it was takeaways.'

'And that Friday?'

'He took me to Starvin' Marvin's – you know, that American
diner, sort of opposite the Hoover building?'

'I know it,' Connolly said. Your man's a prince, she thought.
It sat beside the A40 trunk road, a silver Airstream caravan-
type construction, decorated inside with chrome and neon and
boasting of real American diner food of the nachos, wings,
ribs and burgers type. Reviews Connolly had heard of it were
mixed, though the malted milkshakes were supposed to be
good. McLaren had been an occasional customer before his

recent epiphany, but as McLaren would famously eat a dead pony between two baps that didn't necessarily count as an endorsement. But romantic candlelit tryst it was not.

'Let me see,' she said. 'You went to the four fifteen show, so you'd be out o' there, what, half six?'

'Quarter to seven,' Stephanie said.

'And you'd be in Marvin's an hour, maybe?'

'I don't know. I wasn't watching the clock. About that, I s'pose.'

'So call it eight-ish. What did you do then?'

'Went for a drive. It was a lovely night – cold, but kind of icy-clear, you know? Ian said we should go somewhere out in the country where we could see the stars. You can't see them where there are street lights. So we did.'

'Where did you go?'

'I don't know. We drove for a while. Where we ended up, it was kind of hilly, and there were a lot of trees, and not many houses about. Something Woods, I think he said. Ash Woods, was it? I dunno. But we ended up in this car park on top of a hill, with, like, all trees round it, and in front it kind of dropped away down the hill. And you could see millions of stars up above. It was beautiful.'

'And you did what there?'

'Talked,' she said. She blushed again.

'And? Did he kiss you?'

She looked mortified.

'More than that?'

Hurt and angry eyes in the blazing face met Connolly's. 'We were lovers! He was my first ever. We'd been lovers all along, nearly since the first time! You think I'm just some stupid kid with a crush on my teacher, but you don't know! We loved each other! We were going to get married!'

'Did he tell you that?'

Amazingly, the blush intensified. She was so red you could have stuck her on a mast to keep aircraft away. 'We talked about it that night. He said how unhappy he was with his wife. He said he was going to leave her as soon as he could find the right time to tell her. Then we'd be together. We'd get married. He said he'd probably have to leave his job, but he'd

soon get another one. And we'd have to move away somewhere
people didn't know us. And he said he'd have to find a way
to tell his daughter, because she wasn't that much younger
than me and she'd find it hard to accept. But he said all problems were there to be solved, and we'd solve them.'

Connolly didn't know what to make of this. Was he flying
a kite, or shooting a line? Did he really want to cut loose with
a wee teeny-bopper, or was he just saying it to keep her sweet?
Or – the idea came to her with a sudden rush of blood to the
head – was he planning his post-murder escape, and thinking
he might as well have some company along for the ride? The
bit about having to leave his job . . . moving away . . . Another
thought occurred to her, unwelcome and shocking, but it would
explain some things, notably Stephanie's deep unhappiness.

'You're not pregnant, are you?'

She couldn't get any redder, but her eyes filled with tears. 'No,'
she said. 'Course not. We do all about that at school. But I wish
I was! Then I'd have something of his. I don't care what you
say, I don't believe he's a murderer. You don't know him like I
do. He could never do that. He'd never lift a finger to a soul.'

Connolly thought of telling her that he hit his daughters,
but didn't. Sure, the whole thing was blown now and she'd
probably never see him again, so what harm? 'So how long
did you stay there, makin' love and gazin' at the stars?'

Her eyes narrowed. 'Are you making fun of me?'

'Far from it. I see no fun in the whole caper. Did you not
think he was spinning you a line? You'd want to cop on to
yourself, a nice bright girl like you. Men like him don't leave
their wives.'

'They do! All the time!' she cried passionately, but in her
eyes was the bitter knowledge that Connolly was right.

'Listen, willya – men that are going to leave do it right
away. The ones that talk about waiting for the "right time"
never do it. Ah, c'mon, I'm not givin' out to ya. We've all
gone through it, fallen for the wrong geezer and made a holy
show of ourselves. You're not the first and you won't be the
last. But this time it's important, because other things hang
on it. So I need you to tell me how long you were up this hill,
wherever it was, and what time you came home.'

'I don't know how long we were there,' she said, half sulky, half passionate. *Sure if she tells me love knows no time I'll be forced to clatter her*, Connolly thought. 'It was hours, anyway. We didn't want to leave each other. But my dad goes mad if I'm out after midnight – honestly, he's such a dinosaur! – so we had to go. Ian drove me home and dropped me at the end of my road, like usual, and when I got in it was a quarter to twelve.'

Ah, thought Connolly. Another grand theory down the Swanee. 'You're sure about that?'

'Yeah. Course. I looked at the clock to make sure I was all right.'

'So you'd been with Ian the whole time, every minute, from around four o'clock until a quarter to midnight? Every moment?'

'Yeah,' said Stephanie, looking vaguely proud of her prowess as Ian-time-consumer; until something else occurred to her, her eyes widened and her jaw dropped like the temperature on a Bank Holiday. 'Is that – does that mean – is it his alibi? Am I his alibi? Does it mean he didn't kill her after all?'

'If you're telling me the truth,' Connolly said.

'I am! I am! I swear it! Oh, I knew he didn't do it! He couldn't!' For a moment euphoria reigned, and then drained slowly from her young little face. 'But – it'll all come out now, won't it? I'll have to go in court and swear it, and my parents'll know, and everyone at school. Will he get into trouble? I mean for – for me? I'm over age, but . . .' Her face had sunk to misery level again. 'But he's married, and he'll have to take care of his wife and kid. He'll go away and I'll never see him again. It's all over,' she concluded with absolute certainty.

'Yeah,' said Connolly. She could say no less; but she said it with sympathy. The poor kid had got it bad, and she wasn't one to dance on the body, even though this was one wake that should be welcomed by all. Stephanie'd had a lucky escape, though she was too dumb to see it. But she'd only want a run-in with Mr ClearBlue to put sense on her.

'So when someone was killing Melanie, Wiseman and Stephanie Bentham were in a car park somewhere wearing the head off each other,' Connolly told Slider on the phone. 'She says he left her home at a quarter to twelve.'

'That's too late for him to have got over there and murdered Melanie before the food left her stomach,' Slider said. 'Which means he's in the clear. Unless she's lying?' he added.

'She's knickers mad about him, and she'd tell a lie at the drop of a hat to save him, but I don't think she is. She told me all that before she realized she was givin' him an alibi. I think it's gospel, all right.'

So Slider went back to Wiseman, who was looking worn now, more than angry: worn and depressed. Probably the realization of the complete destruction of his life either way had arrived in his brain.

'Do you want to tell me where you really were on Friday night?' Slider asked.

'I've told you,' he said, with an effort at a snap. 'I have nothing more to say.'

'Even if I tell you I *know* where you were, and with whom?' Wiseman flinched.

'And it was nothing to do with coaching – or not coaching of any sport known to the Olympics board, anyway.'

'How *dare* you make jokes—' Wiseman began, mottling.

'I truly don't think it was very funny,' Slider said seriously. 'You're lucky the girl was of age, or you could be facing very serious charges.

'I never—' He swallowed. 'I don't know what you're talking about.'

'Oh, must I spell it out for you?' Slider said wearily. 'The girl has told us everything, voluntarily. You've been having an affair with one of your pupils, a seventeen year old called Stephanie Bentham, and at the time of Melanie's death you were with her, having sex in your car in a car park. A very shabby figure you will cut if that comes out.'

'She – I never taught her. She wasn't my student,' Wiseman said feebly.

'I don't think that is going to make any difference, do you? So here's the thing – this brave girl is willing to risk her reputation and face angry parents and the ruination of her hopes and future to give you an alibi. Unless, of course, you want to confess to murdering Melanie, and tell us where you really were and exactly what you did that night.'

'But I didn't! I didn't kill her! I *was* with Stephanie. Now you know I'm innocent, you'll *have* to let me go.'

'You're going to rely on Stephanie, are you? Let her sacrifice herself for you? Hasn't she sacrificed enough already?'

'What do you want me to say? I *was* with her. She's telling the truth. I was with her all evening. I can't tell a lie, can I?'

'It hasn't bothered you before,' Slider said.

Drobcek objected, but his heart was no longer in it. There was going to be no brilliant defence of a murder charge to make his name after all. He was back to juvenile shoplifters on Monday.

'But I couldn't contradict Stephanie and call her a liar when she's telling the truth,' Wiseman said. 'You have to let me go now, don't you? Doesn't he?' he appealed to Drobcek.

'Do you have any other evidence against my client?' Drobcek asked.

'Hold your horses,' Slider said, though it was mere endgame flourishing. 'We have to check the alibi first.'

'It sounds as though he's covered, then,' Porson said with disappointment. He had wanted Wiseman ever since he heard about him hitting Melanie. He didn't like hitters. And the nature of this new evidence made him unhappy. He doodled a series of ducks on his phone pad. He liked ducks. They always sounded as if they were laughing. They took your mind off things. When he retired, he was going to find a house with enough room for a pond and get some. 'What about this girl? Is she pukka?'

'Connolly believes so. We can check the early parts of the alibi, but the important part, covering the murder time, is down to her alone.'

'What do you think?' Porson asked sharply, looking up.

'My gut instinct is that she's telling the truth, and therefore that it wasn't him.'

'Hmm,' said Porson.

'And we don't have any other evidence against him. If we let him go, and it was him, it might put him off his guard.

Then if anything turned up, we could catch him unawares with it.'

'Suppose he scarpers?'

'I don't see him as the type, sir. He sets a lot of store by respectability. Once he's free, he'll want to re-establish his reputation.'

'And what about the girl? She'll be in a shedload of trouble.'

'Unless we charge him, her evidence need never become public. If she keeps her mouth shut, and Wiseman does, it may all blow over for her.'

It was the best they could hope for. Porson nodded. A big pond. With a little island in the middle, so they can sleep safe from foxes. 'He's ruined anyway. He wasn't wrong about that. The school won't want him back.'

'But he's been vindicated. They'll have to take him, or disparage the rule of law. And that will be good reason for him to keep his mouth shut about the girl, because he'd certainly lose his job over *that*.'

'Why should he get away with it?'

'He shouldn't. But if he doesn't, she doesn't.'

Maybe a duck house – just a plain one. A little wooden cabin. He sketched straight walls and a sloping roof. 'I suppose you're right,' he said. He thought of the girl infatuated, and Wiseman debauching her, and Melanie still dead, and sometimes he felt the whole weight of human nature on his neck, crushing him down. He *needed* ducks. The simplicity of them. And the quacking.

'Let him go,' he said. 'Warn him to keep his mouth shut about the girl. And get after Hibbert. Half a confession's better than no bread.'

'Yes, sir.'

Slider was at the door when Porson said, 'What's that poem? Learnt it in school. About bees, or beans, or something, and living on an island, and a cabin, or some such?'

Slider, who had long ago given up being surprised by anything Porson said, dug through his brain. 'Do you mean "The Lake Isle of Innisfree", sir?' He quoted, '"Nine bean rows will I have there, and a hive for the honey bee."'

'Sounds like it. Mention a cabin?'

'Yes, sir. "And a small cabin build there" – that's the second line.' He waited for enlightenment.

Porson grunted. 'Any ducks?'

'Ducks? I don't think so. But to be honest, I only know the first verse. I suppose there might be ducks later.'

'Have to be later,' Porson said. 'Retirement plan.' Slider was looking at him, just faintly puzzled. 'Well, what are you standing there for? Get on with it!' he barked.

Slider got.

As he reached the office on his way to his room, Norma was on the phone saying, 'He's in with Mr – oh, no, here he is, just walked in.' She held out the receiver to Slider. 'Atherton, boss.'

'I'll take it in my room,' he said.

Swilley looked at him with motherly affection as he trudged past thinking vaguely, though she knew it not, of ducks and beans and sex in cars. 'You look cream crackered, boss. Shall I get you a cuppa?'

'Would you? I need one before I go and tackle Hibbert again. He's all we've got now.'

'Bad news on Wiseman?'

'I'll tell you when I've taken this call. Maybe it'll cheer me up.'

But Atherton, always cheery, said, 'It's bad news. It looks as though Hibbert's a washout.'

Slider whimpered. 'But he's confessed.'

'Really?'

'Sort of.' Of course when a man was in the emotional state Hibbert was – and particularly if he's a self-obsessed, grandstanding sort of bloke with a taste for fantasizing – there was always the danger of false confessions. But hey, when you got nuthin you got nuthin to lose. A man can dream, can't he? 'And Wiseman's no good. We found his alibi.'

'You had to go looking! So – what? He was doing private coaching?'

'Of the carnal sort. Nice young sixth-former says he was with her all evening, and at the crucial time they were testing his car's suspension in a deserted car-park, somewhere, we guess, in the Chilterns.'

'No wonder he lied about it. And didn't tell his wife,' said Atherton. 'Instant dismissal for that. But it lets him out?'

'Unless she's lying, but we don't think she is. And now you're telling me Hibbert's no good?'

'I've been running the marathon with Valerie Proctor,' Atherton said wearily. 'It seems—'

'I've heard all about the scams and the doinking from Hibbert,' Slider forestalled him. 'He was only servicing her to keep her on side, according to him.'

'She didn't know about Melanie, according to her. What a prize pair!'

'We can compare notes later. But what's this about an alibi?'

'On Friday evening, when he wasn't at the stag, Valerie says they took a developer out to dinner at a posh restaurant in Christchurch, to discuss Hibbert's idea for a big scoop. There were delicate negotiations to be made, feelers to put out to see if the developer was crooked enough to go along with it, so oiling the wheels was considered a good idea.'

'You keep saying "the developer". Doesn't he have a name?'

'She didn't want to tell me that, and I didn't press, because she says they'll certainly remember them in the restaurant. Apparently merry was made and the festive board groaned. The bill came to over six hundred quid, and restaurant staff tend to remember that, especially in Bournemouth – on the subject of which—'

'Which?'

'Bournemouth – can I come home now? I promise to be good.'

'Don't you like it? Jewel of the south coast, I've always heard.'

'Valerie's interior decor's given me a migraine. And it's not good for me to mix with people who think dishonesty is just fine, as long as they're the ones doing it.'

'You're too delicate to be a policeman. Remind me again how you got into the Job.' It was a famous mystery, long disputed in the canteen, but Atherton had always liked to be enigmatic and had never told, not even Slider.

'Nice try, guv,' came the reply, 'but no banana.'

'So what time did the party leave the restaurant?' Slider

asked, going back to work. Not that there was any urgency about it, if Hibbert was blown and his confession just self-indulgent hysteria.

'Close to midnight, she says. A fine cognac was going round – and round – and round. Then Valerie and Hibbert went home for a celebratory two-step – I don't even want to think about that – after which he passed into a heavy sleep. She slept too, but she said when she woke at eight on Saturday morning, he hadn't even changed position, and he didn't surface until after ten.'

Slider sighed. He'd sighed so much lately he was going to have to replace his battery. 'I suppose she could be lying to cover him.'

'Two chances – fat, and slim. Now she knows about Melanie and thinks he killed her, she's desperate to be rid of him. She turned him in, remember.'

'She could just be trying to save her own skin.'

'But she doesn't know how the murder was done, or when, so she didn't even know she was giving him an alibi until I showed an interest in the detail. She seems to think 'e done 'er in on Saturday, when he left her ostensibly to go to the wedding. Now she knows Saturday night was important I think she'd like to take it back, but she can't.'

'Always the problem,' Slider said. 'You can't ask people questions without warning them about what you want to know.'

'Fine, fine, but can I come home now?' Atherton asked impatiently.

'You have to visit the restaurant first,' said Slider sternly. 'We've had enough of people giving us alibis they think we won't check up on. Go and be diligent. And quick, because if he didn't do it, I want to get rid of him. I don't like the bugger, not one little bit.'

'Valerie's a hero, really,' Atherton remarked.

'All women are heroes. There's not one man I know that I'd want to put up with on a domestic basis.'

'Except your dad.'

'Well, of course. Now stop stalling, and go.'

*   *   *

'So why did you run, you dipstick?' Slider asked Hibbert, who looked so unappealingly crusty a public health inspector would have closed him down.

The restaurant had amply confirmed the alibi – one of the waiters even knew the developer and was eager to tell them his name, address in a glamour-pad in Poole, mobile phone number and the identity of his mistress, a former beauty queen who had been Miss South Coast Resort two years earlier and was installed in a glass-and-chrome 'luxury' flat overlooking the sea on Overcliff Drive. And the ANPR had not found any movements of Valerie's car between Bournemouth and London, so even if everyone was mistaken about the time, he'd have had to go and murder Melanie by train. He was as clear as it was possible to be in this naughty world.

Hibbert was massively deflated. Out from under his latest trank, he had got a severe lungful of cold reality. He was not Cap'n Jack Sparrow, swooping up doubloons from under the noses of his fat corporate bosses. He was not Heathcliff, driven to noble madness and murder by overmastering love. He was a bloke with a job at an estate agent's (which he might well lose, if his scams came to light) and nothing to show for his life but a few flashy suits and a motor he still owed payments on. And no girlfriend. When he went home, Melanie was not going to be there. The house would be cold and smell funny and the washing wouldn't have been done. And he really had loved Mel. She had been part of his grand design, the top wife enhancing his status as he climbed to higher things. And she had adored him. Now she was dead. He stared at Slider in abject misery.

'I knew you lot were after me,' he said. His voice was hoarse from all his recent troubles. 'I thought you were going to frame me for Mel's murder.' His lower lip trembled. 'I didn't want to go to prison. I was scared. Terrible things happen in there. Ronnie told me once. About these big boss cons who run everything, all muscles and tattoos, and when someone like me comes in they—' He gulped and squeezed his eyes shut. 'I don't even want to think about it.'

Slider could imagine Fitton, who didn't like Hibbert and thought him a big soft ponce, indulging in a little light blood-curdling as they passed in the dustbin area of a Monday night.

'Then why did you say you killed her?'

Hibbert's frightened eyes were those of a small boy who had been egged on to something too serious for him by bigger boys. 'I – I s'pose I sort of got carried away,' he confessed abjectly.

Slider almost felt sorry for him. 'It happens a lot,' he said.

'And then there were none,' Porson said disgustedly. 'A week on, and we've got nothing. Unless Ronnie Fitton still comes up trumps.' He brightened slightly. '*He's* got no alibi, anyway, good or bad.'

'But we've no evidence against him.'

'*I* know that!' Porson snapped. 'Blimey, I wouldn't have thought you'd want to boast about your incomptitude at a time like this! Your job is to *get* the evidence. The press is going to be all over this by Monday.' He stamped about a bit, and Slider understood that his anger was not against him, but the perversity of fate and, most importantly, the pressure put on them all by their bosses' fealty to the press. He turned to Slider, steam now vented, and said quite kindly, 'You look all in. Go home. There's nothing more you can do today. They're going on with the fingertip search tomorrow, and maybe something'll come up. Take tomorrow off, do some thinking, come back fresh on Monday.'

'Yes, sir,' said Slider.

'Don't look so blue, laddie,' Porson said. 'We've come back from the brink before now. I had one case in Finchley where we didn't even have a single suspect until nearly three weeks in. Keep plugging away. Slow and steady wins the race.'

Likewise, Slider thought as he trudged away, if at first you don't succeed, don't try skydiving.

FIFTEEN

Tough On Crumbs, Tough On the Causes of Crumbs

'I'm so glad to see you,' Joanna said, meeting him in the hall. His heart rose for a fraction of a second before she went on, 'You did remember your dad's out tonight, then.'

'Tonight?' he said, bleary-minded.

'It's Saturday, honey. Scrabble club, Wednesday and Saturday.'

'And you've got a concert.'

'You know I have. Festival Hall tonight and repeat in Croydon tomorrow. Paris Symphony and Mendelssohn Italian. More dots between 'em than a Seurat mural. Oh my achin' fingers.' She eyed him warily. 'You *didn't* remember.'

'I'm sorry,' he said. 'But I'm here now. Dumb luck.'

'Just as well. I've got to get going.' She patted his arm. 'Don't look like that. I had a back-up plan. If you didn't arrive, I'd arranged with your dad that I'd ring him on his mobile and he'd come back.'

'He doesn't have a mobile.'

'Fat lot you know about your own household! He bought himself a pay-as-you-go last week for this very reason. He said with two of us on impossible schedules, he had to make sure he was reachable at all times.'

'That man's a marvel. A giant of conscience.'

'He's a lot like you,' Joanna said, leading him towards the kitchen. 'Or you're a lot like him.'

'And you're a giant of understanding,' he said. 'I don't deserve you.'

'Yes you do,' she said easily. 'Because I'm going to leave you to finish Georgie while I get ready.'

'We're not going to be calling him "Georgie" are we?' he asked anxiously. 'It sounds like the fat spoiled boy in a *William* story.'

'Oh, get on with you! He's just a little lad. He'll have a dozen names before he settles into one.'

George lifted a beaming face to his father, a smile that washed away all the day's miseries and the sins of the Hibberts and Wisemans of Slider's world. 'Daddy!' he said, as if it was the best thing that had happened to him all week.

'How's my boy?' Slider replied. He was sufficiently devoted to family life not to blench at the quantity of mashed food spread around George's face and the immediate vicinity. The only good thing you could say about it was it gave purpose to the sea of crumbs underneath it.

'Can you finish giving him his supper, and then he'll need a bath before bed. You needn't wash his hair, though. I've got to hustle now. There's roadworks in Earl's Court *and* on the Embankment, so it doesn't matter which way I go.'

'Fine, hurry along. I'll hold the fort.' He drew up a chair beside his son and peered into the plastic bowl. 'What is that you're eating?'

'Cabbot, Daddy,' George said, digging his spoon into the orange gloop. Mashed carrot, one of his favourite things. And the other stuff was avocado. 'Green!' George called it, digging in his rusk with the other hand. And chopped chicken, Slider recognized.

'Yum yum,' he said encouragingly.

'Yum,' George agreed. 'More now.' He was pretty efficient with the spoon, as long as he concentrated; though he had to be supervised or he often reverted to his hands; and if he grew bored he had learned a lot of interesting things you can do with purée, a spoon, and human bodily cavities – not necessarily his own.

'Let's see some action, then, son. Lock and load,' Slider urged.

George obliged, glad to show off his prowess before the other half of his parent, but he wasn't really eating. It was the mechanical process that interested him, and after watching for a bit Slider took the spoon from him and despatched the rest in a few swift scrapes.

Having wiped the slurry from his son's face and hands, he said, 'What's next? Is there pudding, boy?'

'Puddie! Yogog!' George said. And, as his father approached with it, 'New spoon.'

'You're getting very dainty in your old age,' Slider remarked. 'Speaking of which do you know how old you are?'

'Two o'clock,' George answered.

Slider was impressed that he knew a numerical answer was required. 'Not yet you're not,' he said, and spooned yoghurt into him. Usually George was determined to feed himself, but he was tired now, and allowed himself to relax and be serviced by the Big Stoker.

Joanna came back in, looking gorgeous, as always, in her Long Black. She didn't like changing at the Hall, and travelling in her black meant she could make a quicker getaway at the end. Slider gave her a wolf whistle and she smirked self-consciously. 'You watch it, or I'll make you put your money where your mouth is,' she threatened.

'Oh yeah?' Slider sneered back. 'My dad can beat your dad.'

'I haven't a doubt. I'm going to leave a bit early, if you're OK, because of those road works. Has he eaten everything? You are good! You and your dad are much better with him than I am.'

'But he only has one mother.'

She stooped to kiss him. 'Bless your heart, I'm not jealous. Listen, I can see you've had a hard day and I want to ask you about your case, but I just haven't got time now. If you can stay awake, shall we talk when I get home?'

It was only after he heard the front door slam behind her that he realized he hadn't asked what was for supper. Never mind, he'd find out sooner or later. He went through the pleasant, laundry-scented, life-affirming rituals of bathing his son, putting him to bed and reading his story with his mind idling in neutral; kissed the rose-petal cheek, and went downstairs to the kitchen to feed the inner beast. He was hungry now.

But for once the system had broken down: nothing had been prepared for him. Nothing in the slow oven, nothing in the fridge, no little billy-doo anywhere explaining what had been planned. Homer, i.e. his perfect wife, had nodded. Probably she had thought Dad was doing something and Dad had thought she was. Well, it just showed how lucky he was to be catered for every other evening, like someone out of a 1950's Electrolux advert. Anyway, the fridge wasn't bare. There were eggs, there was cheese, there were tomatoes and – treasure trove – some cold potatoes. With a few herbs and a dash of Tabasco he knocked up a handsome big omelette – well, big, anyway – and ate it at the kitchen table with the newspaper open and unread beside him. His eyes might focus on the Middle East or the latest MP sex scandal, but his mind wouldn't. It wanted the evening off.

Joanna rang during the interval. He could hear the thunderous murmur of voices and the clinking of glasses behind her. 'I forgot to get you any supper!' she wailed.

'I managed. I'm not helpless, you know.'

'That's my seven stone weakling! George go off all right?'

'Couldn't keep his eyes open. How's the concert?'

'I can't tell you here – far too public.'

'Oh, like that it is? Conductor woes? Or too much scrubbing?'

'Both. In spades. How well you know me.'

'I'm a fully paid-up orchestra husband. Good audience?'

'Is this you chatting to me on the phone, like you used to before we were married?'

'Romantic, isn't it? Reminds me of those heady days when—'

'Be careful how you end that sentence. If you were going to say "when we were in love" . . .'

'No, when we couldn't see each other whenever we wanted.'

'I wouldn't call them heady, then. Anyway, we still can't see each other whenever we want. Little thing called work, remember that? Listen, gotta go. The Leader wants to use the phone. *Jawohl, mein fuhrer. Zu befehl*,' she said aside, and then to Slider: 'He loves all that kind of thing. You should see him puff up . . . Ow! Ow! Not the hair!' And she was gone.

She got back tired, but not terribly late, and not yet 'down' from the performance, so he easily persuaded her into a large g-and-t on the sofa with him before the fire.

'Dad in?' she asked.

'About ten minutes ago, but he went straight to his own rooms.'

'Did he say anything about his Scrabble-fest?'

'Like what? I don't think winning is the primary reason for going.'

'Of course it's not. I think he's got a girlfriend.'

'What? No. Not Dad.'

'Why not?' she said with vicarious indignation. 'He's a very attractive man. You're not one of those people who think your parents can never love again once they're widowed?'

Despite himself, Slider thought of Melanie. He said mildly, 'He never has, all these years.'

'Well, he probably didn't have much chance,' Joanna said, 'stuck out there in carrot country, a hundred square miles of mud in every direction. Doesn't mean he's not a man all the same.'

'Well, what makes you think there is someone?'

'Woman's instinct,' she said mischievously.

'Don't give me that baloney.'

'You don't really think he's developed a craze for little plastic tiles in his old age? And what about the new trousers and jumper he bought? And the aftershave he wears when he goes to "Scrabble night"?' She did the inverted commas with her fingers, ludicrously exaggerated.

'All circumstantial,' Slider said. 'Give me one piece of firm evidence.'

'Well, oh mighty detective, it so happens I saw him outside that mini-mart on the High Road when I went past in the car on Thursday, talking to a very nice-looking lady of mature but well-preserved aspect.'

'I dare say he talks to a lot of people. He's a friendly person.'

'Believe me when I tell you, they weren't just discussing the weather. There was body language going on. Possibly hand-touching, couldn't swear to that, but definite, incontrovertible body-language.'

'And you saw all that while whizzing past in the car?'

'Who said anything about whizzing? The lights were red and I was slowing down for them.' She looked at him over her tumbler. 'You're not jealous, are you?'

He rearranged his face. 'No, of course not.'

'You sounded cross. And looked it.'

'Oh, not about Dad. I'd be delighted if he had a new—' He couldn't think of the word.

'Amour?' she supplied facetiously. Then, 'It's the case, is it?'

'Yes. All our suspects have turned out not to be, and after a week of grind we've got nothing at all.'

'Do you want to talk about it?'

He looked at her for a long moment, his brows furrowed in weariness and trouble. But he said at last, 'Not really. Not now. Or I'll never sleep. Tomorrow morning, if you're up to it, I'd love to dump all my problems on to your shoulders. You haven't got a rehearsal, have you? It's a repeat?'

'Just a seating rehearsal in the afternoon, so I'm all yours for the morning. We'll get your dad to take George out somewhere for an hour, and have a nice heart-to-heart.'

'That'll be nice.'

But he was still furrowing, so she said, 'Would you like to hear my troubles? Like a nice go of toothache to take your mind off your dicky tummy?'

He roused himself. 'Have you got troubles, my love?'

'Boy, howdy! This cold weather is terrible for us fiddle players. Makes it impossible to tune. You're up and down like the Assyrian empire. And I'm terrified the old girl will crack with it, and then what'll I do? Even if the insurance is enough to replace her, I'd have a whole new fiddle to get used to. And coming in from the cold and having to start playing right away is the worst thing for the old tendons. And my neck's been killing me for weeks now – I think it's partly because the boy's getting so heavy, but it's probably mostly from playing. It gets us all in the end, you know – the unnatural position, sitting for long hours, the tension of performance.'

'Have you—' he began, but she was off and running.

'Patsy's left and I've got a new desk partner. Kid called Ravi Shukla – nice lad, but still wet behind the ears, good technique but he hasn't learned yet to be a section player. And he comes in late *every single entry*. It's driving me mad. And he keeps forgetting to turn – seems to think that because I'm a woman, it's my job. I've told him the inside player turns, and he just smiles with those perfect bloody white teeth and says sorry and lets it drop clean out of his mind. Next time I'm going to kick him, hard, and he'll probably put in a formal complaint and get me sacked.'

'Couldn't you—'

'And to crown it all, we've got Daniel Kluger conducting us for a whole season. *Kluger*! With his curly bloody hair and his perky little bum and his teenage groupies hanging round him, and his press conferences, and the media think the sun shines out of every orifice, but he *can't conduct for toffee*, and we're the poor schmucks who have to pick up the pieces when he carves up – which he does with monotonous regularity. But he's got recording contracts so we have to have him, and we have to suck up to him, and say *sorry maestro* when he tries to bring us in a bar early and we ignore him for the sake of the bloody music.'

She stopped, drew a breath, smiled, and said, 'That's better.'

'Is that it?'

'That's it. Just about. For now.'

He leaned across and kissed her. 'Thank you,' he said humbly.

'For what?'

'For reminding me that I'm not the only person on this planet with problems. I tend to get immersed to a state of blinkeredness. I'm sorry if I've been selfish. As soon as I can get out of the other side of this case, I'll make it up to you.'

'That'll be nice.'

'Think about something I can do for you, to make you happy. When the case is closed.'

'Oh, there is something. And it doesn't have to wait until then.'

'What's that?'

'Finish your drink and I'll show you.'

Slider lay awake, the darkness pressing on him soft and unpleasant, like a fat person sitting on his face. The wind had gone round and the iron grip of the cold had loosened at last – the temperature must have gone up ten degrees since they went to bed. He had to slip his feet surreptitiously out from under the duvet to cool off.

Beside him Joanna was full fathom five, down deep where the busy and good go by night; but he had known as soon as they turned out the light that he would not sleep. Somewhere in the darkness, untouchable and near, Melanie Hunter waited, creeping towards him in encroaching tendrils like grave-damp. She was dead; nothing for her now but decay and oblivion; nothing of her but the faint whimperings of her ghost.

But what had she been? She had lost her father when she was hardly more than a child; had lost her own child soon afterwards. She had gone to the bad, then had tried to make good. Her child taken from her – she had always been more sinned against than sinning. She had done her best to be what she had been expected to be, worked hard, succeeded, got a career, helped others, tried to love Scott Hibbert – tried so hard, because you have to love someone, don't you? And good boyfriends are hard to come by. But she had not wanted to marry him, not dared risk a child. How far had she really consented to the abortion? How deep did the guilt run in her?

He heard her in the darkness, but could not hear her words. *Tell me who did it*, he begged her. He felt around restlessly in his mind for the end of a thread to catch on to. He had spent the evening, before Joanna came home, reading through his copy of the notes, which he had brought home; but they refused to fall into any pattern, just whirled about like leaves blown by a gusty wind.

She had tried to be good, make something of herself, had succeeded pretty much. But something was wrong somewhere. Ronnie Fitton had said there were things no one knew about her. She had a secret. Was it the secret that killed her?

Fitton said she wasn't a happy person; that everyone fed off her and no one cared how *she* felt. Life and soul of the party – the smiling clown, sad under the paint, that old cliché. But clichés became clichés because they were true. She was loved by many – but not enough. And then, perhaps, someone had loved her too much?

Wiseman and Hibbert, both so tempting, but both out of the frame. So unless it was Fitton after all . . . Say, for the sake of argument, it wasn't Fitton. We're back where we started; clean slate. Begin again, forgetting surmises. Begin again with what we know.

She went home, stopped off for a Chinese takeaway – but it wasn't for her. She'd just had a big meal; and she didn't, in fact, eat it. She must have bought it for someone else. But who would you buy a late-night takeaway for? A flatmate, your boyfriend, a housebound neighbour just possibly. Someone close.

She parked the car and went into the flat, but came out again with only her door keys. And, presumably, the takeaway. So it must have been almost immediately or the takeaway would have gone cold. Came out with only her keys, so she had expected to go back, and soon. Just pop out and back again. To deliver the food? Where? A neighbour? But then why hadn't they come forward?

She came out with just her keys but she didn't go back in. She wasn't killed in the flat or anywhere in the house. She left the area – but not in her car. So: someone else's car. She got into someone else's car and drove away with them, despite having only her keys with her. If she wasn't coerced, it must have been someone she knew and trusted – like Hibbert. But it wasn't Hibbert.

And the takeaway – she must have taken the takeaway out with her. So could it be that she had bought it *for* the person in the car? But why, then, drive off with them? And if they had a car, why couldn't they get their own takeaway?

Because they had no money? There was the missing two hundred quid. Hibbert could have taken it, of course. But maybe it was the takeaway person. But they had a car. Yes, but you can have a car and be strapped for cash on a short term basis. But who would she do such a thing for? And even if she gave them money and food, *why did she get into the car*?

Hibbert worked because he was the person closest to her; Wiseman worked because of his temper and because he had spoken to her on the phone just before she left the Vic and bought the takeaway. Why had he denied that, by the way? But it wasn't either of them.

Something happened in his mind, a click and thunk, of things shifting and falling into place. It was like the bit in an Indiana Jones film when a lever is pulled and massive blocks of stone rearrange themselves to reveal a secret door. It couldn't be, could it? He felt the blood running under his skin as the excitement of ideas increased his heart rate. It seemed unlikely; there were large problems in the way; and yet it answered many other questions.

At all events, they had nothing else to go on; it was worth a shot. And he knew that now he had thought of it, he would never rest until he had made the enquiries. He oozed carefully out of bed, gathered his clothes and took them to the bathroom to dress, went downstairs and put the kettle on. He couldn't go yet, not at this time of night. He would spend the rest of the time, until it was a civilized enough hour to leave, reading the file again.

If it were true, would she have told Fitton? No – and Fitton said he didn't know. But might he have guessed? Possibly. Possibly. He was a man who had had more to do with sudden death than your average punter. And he had loved Melanie.

Joanna came downstairs with George who – Slider realized belatedly – had been bouncing and chuntering up there in his cot for some time, possessed by the urgency of his usual early morning hunger.

'Couldn't sleep?' Joanna asked. She put George in his chair and located and delivered a rusk to his grasp almost without opening her eyes. She yawned mightily and George stared at her with huge eyes, David Attenborough encountering a new species.

'Sorry if I disturbed you,' Slider said.

'You didn't, this time. I was out to the wide.' She rubbed her eyes, and only then registered what he was wearing. 'You're going out? she said, and didn't manage to disguise her disappointment. Well, she was only human. And she'd planned a lovely leg of lamb.

'I'm sorry,' he said abjectly.

'It's because it was a girl, isn't it? You're never like this when the victim's a man.'

'Not true. I always feel responsible.'

'All right, but it's worse when it's a female. Especially a young one.'

'I can't help it,' he said unhappily. 'Men are supposed to protect women and children. That's what we're for.'

She softened. 'You're a dear old-fashioned thing.'

'Don't mock me. Not you.'

'No, I wasn't. You're right. So, can you tell me about it?'

He hesitated.

'OK, I know.' He never would articulate when his thoughts were only half formed, in case speaking drove essential links away. 'But you're going out,' she said.

'I'm sorry,' he said again.

She shrugged. It was only what she had come to expect. Unlike Irene, his first wife, she didn't resent him for it. But then she had a job that took her away at unreasonable hours, too. Perspective made all the difference to a marriage. 'Just tell me this – you're not going to do anything dangerous, are you? There won't be guns? Or knives?' she added. Knives were almost worse. For while a bullet might go anywhere, a knife was almost sure to go somewhere.

His face cleared and he smiled; like one of those April days when the clouds suddenly part and for an instant the sun belts down as if it had been doing summer up there all the time. 'I'm just going to look at some records,' he assured her.

It was definitely milder. The wind, he discovered as he stepped from the house, had backed westerly, bringing with it an unbroken grey cover of cloud, too high for real rain, but dispensing the sort of fine mizzle you don't even realize is there until you turn your face upwards and feel it prickling your skin like tiny insect feet. Haar, his mother had used to call it. She said it always came when you'd just put your washing out. The absolute disproof of the adage it never rains but it pours.

Greenford came under Ealing police, and he went first to their headquarters in the hope that they had kept copies of everything, because otherwise it was the Home Office or the Department of Transport, neither of which was likely to be welcoming, let alone accessible on a Sunday. The previous boss of the Ealing CID, Slider's old nemesis Gordon Arundel – a serial womanizer known behind his back as Gorgeous Gordon, who had also been notoriously unhelpful to coppers outside his own borough – was no longer there, having been promoted suddenly up and sideways like a lamb snatched by an eagle. Rumour had it that he had been doinking the borough commander's wife and daughter at the same time, unknown to any of the three of them, or his own wife, until one exquisitely embarrassing Christmas party when a social collision took place that would have seen the Hadron physicists drooling with envy.

On the other hand, DC Phil Hunt, the rhyming policeman, who had once been one of Slider's firm, was still there, and as luck would have it was on duty that day. Hunt was easy to manipulate: chit-chat a few minutes, reminisce a few minutes, hint that they could do with his unique qualities back at Shepherd's Bush (with fingers crossed behind his back that he didn't take him at his word and put in for a transfer) and Hunt was ready to move heaven and earth to prove to Slider that he *could* move heaven and earth. The crash records? Yes, no problem at all. Yes, they had everything, except the papers from the subsequent public enquiry – all the original records from the time of the crash and the immediate aftermath, certainly. He would take Slider down to the records room personally and make sure he had everything he wanted.

The records clerk was a young female uniform who looked at Hunt as though she had just found him on her shoe. Hunt, however, had always been as perceptive as a box of rocks when it came to women, and said in a proprietorial manner, 'This is Mo Kennet, the wizard of the records room. My old boss, DI Slider, Mo, all the way from Shepherd's Bush on an important mission. The lovely Mo will see you get everything you want, guv. Just leave it to her.'

Hunt loitered as though he intended to stay and officiate, and Kennet and Slider stood locked in a bubble of embarrassment, until she roused herself to say, 'Thanks, Phil. I'll take care of it. Hadn't you better get back and man the phones?'

He beamed nauseatingly. 'Always looking after my welfare,

is Mo. Famous for her kind heart – isn't that right, love? When are you going to come for a ride in my car? I know you like motors.' His voice changed from crass suggestiveness to pure love when he went on, 'I've just had this new exhaust kit put in – cost over a hundred quid just for the parts, but it was worth it. You should hear her now – purrs like a big kitty till you put your foot down, and then—'

Hunt always had been able to bore for England about his cars, which Slider had believed had taken the place of a sexual partner in his life. He intervened while he and Kennet still had the use of their faculties. 'Thanks a lot, Hunt. I appreciate it. I can manage from here.'

Kennet made an eloquent face at Hunt's departing back, but became completely sensible when she turned to Slider to ask him what he wanted. In ten minutes he was sitting at a reading desk with the first of the files, while she brought in more and dumped them on the neighbouring desk to leave him room.

'That's the lot, sir,' she said finally, brushing her hands off. She looked at him curiously. 'If there's anything I can do to help . . .? I mean, it was before my time, of course, and I only know what I remember from the news, but I'd be happy to trawl for you if there was anything in particular you were looking for?'

'Thanks, that's very kind. I'm on a bit of a fishing expedition, but I'll give you a yell if I need help.'

'Okey-doke. I'll just be through there.' She gave a rueful smile. 'Nothing much on today, so I'd be glad of something to do. Get you a coffee or anything?'

'No, thanks, I'm fine. Thanks a lot.' He smiled at her kindly and she obediently removed herself, though curiosity was sticking out all over her like boils. A good girl, that, he thought. She could go far.

He began to read.

SIXTEEN
Sleight of Hand

I t had been a terrible incident, with a hundred and eight killed and two hundred and twenty-four injured: the second worst rail accident ever in England, surpassed only by the Harrow crash of 1952 which involved three trains, two of them expresses. The Greenford incident was a head-on crash between a passenger express out of Paddington, diverted from the fast rail because of engineering works, and an eastbound local train that had just left Greenford Station. The subsequent long and costly public enquiry had finally blamed driver error, which was easy to do since both drivers had been killed; but badly placed signals and lack of sufficient training had also been cited, management of both the train and track companies had been obliged eventually to resign, and compensation claims had dragged through the courts for years.

Slider read the general reports from police and fire brigade to get the overall picture, and then went on to the medical records. Yes, here it was at last: Hunter, Graham Dennis Ormonde, aged forty-two. Dead at scene on arrival of medical personnel.

His head had been crushed by falling debris, which had also almost decapitated him, severing the neck almost to the cervical spine. Death would have been instantaneous. A very quick glance at the photographs were enough for Slider. Hunter had been identified on the scene by paramedics going through his pockets, who had discovered a wallet in his inside jacket pocket containing business cards and credit cards, and in another pocket a letter addressed to him from an individual in Bristol, and several bills.

His wife had also subsequently identified him at the temporary morgue from these documents and from his clothes, wrist watch and signet ring. She had had to be given medical treatment for shock and distress and had been referred to her own GP for ongoing sedative prescriptions.

There was no doubt about it.

He read through it again, the back of his mind imagining the scene, the smoke, the fires, the vast mangled engines flipped outrageously on to their sides like dying dinosaurs, the debris, the bodies, the wounded moaning, the trapped crying out for help, the stunned survivors wandering in shocked silence until they bumped into the helpers scrambling down the embankment from nearby houses, almost as shocked themselves. And then the emergency services arriving . . .

He had been at one or two major incidents in his time – what copper hadn't? None as bad as this, thank God. The newspapers always talked of screaming, chaos and panic – well, they had to sell copies. But in his experience there was never panic, just empathy and selflessness. The walking wounded always went immediately to the aid of the worse hurt, and the latter waited with a bitter patience and courage for the 'authorities' to arrive. As for screaming – the overall impression was always one of an eerie quiet, murmuring voices usually accompanied by background hissing and metallic ticking from whatever machines had been involved. The 'chaos' lay in the physical appearance of wrecked artefacts: the human element were always stunningly calm.

The official reports were equally lacking in hysteria. They didn't need any more drama – they had enough of their own to last a lifetime. He read on, through all the deaths, impelled by a terrible pity to absorb them all: each one a cataclysm for its own small universe. Then, in a groove, he went on through the injuries. Some were horrific, and subsequently added to the final death toll; others were lifelong crippling. And at the end were the minor injuries treated at the scene by medics. Not all such were, of course. Some people would have just tied a handkerchief round the cut and carried on, or were patched up with an Elastoplast by the locals coming down to help.

Near the end, a name caught his eye. Bad gash across the left palm. Paramedic had found him trying to bandage it with a handkerchief and had taken him to the aid station, where the doctor had put three stitches in it and given him a tetanus injection. William McGuire, age 55, hospital porter, Flat 2, Brunel House, Cleveland Estate, W2. He knew the Cleveland Estate – they were 1930s council flats, very like the White City ones on his own ground; a smallish estate within a short walk of Paddington Station. You could see them from the elevated section of the motorway as you headed westwards, facing the multiplicity of railway lines disgorged from the terminus.

So McGuire had been in the Greenford crash as well. Of course the medical reports did not say which train any of the victims had been travelling on, let alone why. And it could be nothing but a coincidence. But Hunter and McGuire were both injured in the same train wreck, one of them fatally, and ten years later Hunter's adored little girl was murdered and her body was discovered by McGuire. It made you uneasy, to say the least.

It made you think.

He went to Walpole Park and walked there for a long time, thinking things through. The haar had stopped and the park was quiet, nobody around but pigeons and squirrels, going about their daily business, bothering nobody. The humans were not up yet: enjoying the Sunday lie-in; the early dog-walkers would have come and gone already. There had not been enough water in the haar even to drip from the trees, but the grass was wet underfoot, and smelled green and damp and spring-like. That was the worst of prolonged cold spells that extended winter – no smells.

He had a new theory, now the old one had been dismissed, but there was one big problem with it, one thing that made it impossible in execution, so impossible that it would never get past the planning stage. The planner would look at the problem and say, 'Oh, forget that, then.' But the maddening thing was that it felt right to him.

Back at his car he rang Mrs Wiseman. The child answered, and when he identified himself, she volunteered the information that her dad was out, watching the Sunday league down at the Rec. He felt a surge of relief, and said it was her mother he wanted to talk to, and could he come round right away. He heard her shrug, even over the phone. 'If you ask me, she's going a bit dippy. But you can try.'

'I'll be there in five minutes,' Slider said.

Mrs Wiseman was sitting in the same armchair where Connolly had last interviewed her. In fact, she might not have moved since then, for she looked definitely *mal-soigné*, and there was a selection of untouched drinks and snacks on plates and in mugs on the various surfaces around her. The child, Bethany, greeted Slider with a mixture of aggression and relief that told him she had been left to cope more completely than she ought, or than she was capable of. And the dog, coming straight to Slider and putting its head into his hands, tail wagging pleadingly, told him most clearly of all that the ship had become rudderless.

'She's hardly eaten anything,' Bethany told him almost in the first breath. 'I keep bringing her stuff, but I can only do sandwiches and cornflakes really, and Dad keeps going out all the time so *he's* not cooking. I think Mum's going a bit la-la with all this stuff going on, but I don't know what to do for her. She slept in the chair last night. Wouldn't go up to bed. And when Dad tried to talk to her she just screamed at him to leave her alone.'

'Well, let me have a talk with her, and I'll see if I can help.'

She looked anxious. 'You won't hurt her, will you?'

'Of course not. I'm a police officer.'

'But I've heard some policemen are bad.'

'Well, I'm not one of those. Look, see how your dog likes me? They always know.'

She looked at the dog, which was leaning against Slider's legs with its eyes shut in bliss while he massaged its scalp, and said moodily, 'He's not my dog, he's Mel's. Wish he *was* mine.'

'It seems to me,' Slider said judiciously, 'that he is yours now. Your mum and dad won't want to be bothered doing things for him, will they?'

She brightened. 'No. They're too old. They don't even remember to feed him.'

'And dogs need a lot of attention. He'll need someone to

play with him and take him for walks. Dogs have to go for walks every day. Tell you what, why don't you take him out for a walk now, while I talk to your mum? He'll need about twenty minutes. Have you got a watch?'

Her eyes narrowed. 'You just want me out of the house so you can talk to her without me hearing.'

Slider didn't try to deny it. 'That too. Grown-ups sometimes have to talk privately. You know that. But the dog does need a walk.'

Suddenly she was close to tears. 'Marty. Don't call him "the dog" like he wasn't a person. His name's Marty.'

He hunkered, and she was in his arms, straining her rigid little body against him while he folded his arms round her, and the dog licked whatever portions of her bare arms it could reach. How long was it, Slider wondered, since anyone had held the poor child? He didn't imagine Wiseman was a huggy sort of dad at the best of times, and Mrs W had been out of it since Melanie died.

It only lasted a moment. She pulled herself free and dashed away with her sleeve the few tears that had managed to squeeze out. 'All right, I'll take him out. But don't upset my mum,' she said, roughly, to prove she was not a soft touch.

He saw her off, with the grateful dog on a lead, and then went in to Mrs Wiseman.

She was staring at nothing, her hands folded in her lap, still as death. He drew up a leather pouffe and sat so he would be as near as possible to her face-level, and said, 'Mrs Wiseman, it's Bill Slider from Shepherd's Bush police. You remember me. I came once before. I want to talk to you about your husband.'

'Ian's out, at the football,' she said automatically in a tone-less voice.

'No, not about Ian. About your first husband. About Graham Hunter.'

Now her eyes came round to him, examined his face for a long time. He looked back steadily, and saw a trembling begin in the rigid facade. 'He's dead,' she said at last, faintly.

'Is he?' he asked with the same steady look, though his heart was thumping with the urgency of the moment. If she didn't tell him, he had nothing.

And slowly her eyes widened and her mouth crumpled. 'You know,' she said. He saw how afraid she was.

He nodded, trying to project sympathy. 'Tell me about it. The train crash. That day, when you had to go to the morgue – no one should have to go through that, identifying a body. That was a terrible thing you had to do.'

She nodded, her eyes held by his as though fascinated. 'But there were lots of us, all together. That helped a bit. We sort of hung on to each other. Some of them were crying, but I couldn't.'

'Shock takes people different ways,' he said.

She nodded. 'Those of us who weren't crying sort of helped the ones who were. And they called us in, one by one, to look at the bodies.'

'They told you they had found your husband's wallet in the inside pocket, and other things with his name on – a letter, some bills?'

Her mouth turned down at the mention of the bills. 'It was always bills. Gas, electricity, telephone. Everything. He'd open them and take them away without showing me. I'll pay them, he'd say. You don't have to worry about things like that. But the first thing I'd know, a man would come to cut us off. It was humiliating. And right there in the morgue they showed me bills with Final Demand on them in red. And betting slips – must have been a dozen. Right in front of all those people, doctors and policemen and such. I was so ashamed.'

'But they were his things all right,' he said. 'His wallet – credit cards and so on.'

'Oh yes. Everything he had in his pockets – even his hanky. I ironed them often enough, I knew all his hankies.'

'But,' Slider said, inwardly holding his breath, 'it wasn't him.'

She looked away into history. 'They'd covered his head with this green cloth thing, like in an operating theatre, so only his body was showing,' she said tonelessly. 'They said his head was too crushed to recognize, but I'd have known him by something – his hair, his ears, something. I loved that man for a long time, more than I can tell you. The real reason they covered him up was because they thought I wouldn't be able to stand it. And they were sure who he was anyway, because of the things in his pocket. It was just a formality. But I knew right away it wasn't him. They weren't his clothes, to start with.'

'A person can change their clothes.'

'Yes, but why would he? And he'd never have worn horrible cheap things like that. He had fancy tastes. Pity he never had the money to go with them. Besides, I could just see it wasn't him. This man's body was a different shape, he was older. It wasn't Graham's hands. I'd know his hands anywhere.' She shivered.

'But you told them that it was him anyway.'

Her eyes returned to him, to the present. 'It came to me, all of a sudden, what had happened. He'd been there, he'd seen this poor man, whoever he was, swapped the contents of his pockets with him, and walked away. He'd walked out on me. I'd been afraid all along he'd do that one day – he wasn't the sort of man to stay put for ever. But doing it this way, it was obvious he wanted to get away completely, not just from me but from everything. Start a new life with a new identity. And my first thought was, what an idiot! He must know I'd know it wasn't him. So I thought I'd denounce him, tell them what he'd done, have him hunted down and punished for – whatever crime it is to do that. Interfering with a body, or something. It must be a crime, mustn't it?'

'Yes,' said Slider. 'What changed your mind?'

'It all happened in a second, you understand,' she said, looking at him anxiously. He saw that it was a relief to her to tell someone after all these years, but she wanted to be forgiven, too. 'As soon as I realized what he'd done, and I saw how stupid it was, how it couldn't work, I saw how, if it was a way for him to leave me, it was a way for me to be rid of him, too.'

'And you wanted to be rid of him?'

'Oh!' An indescribable sound of pain and longing. 'I loved him, I always loved him, but he was impossible to live with. You don't know what it was like. The lies, the bills, the stupid big ideas that were going to make him a millionaire, the let-downs. I'd save and save and scrape a little bit of money so

Melanie could have something she needed, or a little treat, or a birthday present, and then he'd find the money and blow it on some stupid "investment".' She said the word as though it were a sleazy night with two prostitutes and some furry handcuffs. 'The drinking – he wasn't a violent drunk, but he was a *silly* drunk. Oh, he made Melanie laugh with his clowning, but I hated the smell on him, and it made me mad that he was throwing away our money on drink when there was so much we needed. He humiliated us, week after week, time after time. I couldn't hold my head up around the neighbours. And Melanie was like an orphanage kid next to those rich girls at school. I half wish she'd never won the scholarship, then she could have gone to an ordinary school and not stuck out so much. But she was always bright – and Graham was so proud of her.' A bitter look came over her face. 'That was the thing, you see. She loved him. They loved each other. No matter what he did – and I tried to keep the worst of it from her – she adored him, much more than she ever did me. I was just the one who worked and slaved to keep food on our plates and clothes on our backs. He was the fun one. He was magic. She never saw what a lousy husband and dad he really was.'

Slider nodded sympathetically. 'So it's no wonder, when you saw a chance to be rid of him . . .'

'I thought, if he wants to go, why stop him?' she said bitterly. 'So I said it was my husband. I said I knew his wrist watch and his ring – though Graham would never have worn a ring. He hated jewellery on men.'

It was what Slider had picked up on in the records office. 'And they were satisfied with your identification.'

'Along with everything else – why not? And once I'd said it, I couldn't go back on it.'

'Did you want to?'

'Often and often. I still loved him. And whatever you think, when you're married, about being rid of him, it's different when you're all alone and you've got to face up to looking after yourself and your child with no help. But you see –' she met his eyes now with misery and a plea for forgiveness – 'there was a life insurance, and for a miracle he'd kept up the payments. It wasn't much but we desperately needed it, Melanie and me. And once I'd taken the insurance money, I could never tell. And so I never did.'

'You never told Melanie?'

Shake of head.

'Do you think she guessed?'

Another definite shake. 'Not then. She believed her daddy was dead. I can't tell you what that was like. I told myself she was better off without him, but to hear her crying, night after night . . .'

'And then you got married again.'

'Don't look at me like that!' she cried, though Slider was sure his expression hadn't changed. The blame was in her own mind. 'I was desperate by then. I couldn't cope on my own, and Melanie was having to do too much, and the insurance money was all gone and I didn't know which way to turn. Ian was my only chance. And I sort of convinced myself that Graham really was dead, that I'd been mistaken at the morgue that day. After all, I'd been upset. I was on tranquillizers for ages afterwards. So obviously I must have imagined the whole thing. That's how I fixed it in my mind. All his things were in the pockets, so it must have been him and he really was dead. So I married Ian and – that was that.'

'Except,' Slider said, and now he really was punting, 'Graham didn't stay dead, did he?'

She looked wary. 'Why d'you say that?'

'Oh, come on, you've told me the worst, no point in holding back now. Did he contact you?'

'No,' she said definitely. 'Never. I was always scared he would, but I suppose he had as much to lose as me. He'd have gone to jail. No, he never contacted me.'

'Melanie, then? He contacted Melanie.' She didn't want to answer, and he added, 'About two years ago.'

She shuddered and looked down. 'I don't know. She never said anything to me, but I guessed something was up. It was just after she and Scott got together. I was so glad she'd got a nice boy at last, one who wanted to marry her and everything. And she was so happy at first. Then they moved into that flat together, and soon afterwards she started acting strangely. She

wasn't happy any more – not the way she used to be. I think
she tried to tell me a couple of times, but she never managed
it. Then one day, when we were washing up after Sunday
lunch, she asked me about her dad dying, asked me about
identifying him at the morgue, and I just knew she knew. And
how could she, unless she'd seen him, unless he'd told her?'

'What did you say to her when she asked that?'

'I just told the lie again. What could I say? I couldn't tell
her he'd been alive all that time and I'd let her grieve for him
for nothing, could I? That I'd committed bigamy? Not to say
insurance fraud. She'd have hated me. So I let her think I
didn't know, that I really thought he was dead, and after that
she got sort of – strained with me. I suppose it was always
on her mind, wanting to tell me but not daring to.'

'For all the same reasons.'

'Yes.' She brooded a moment. 'He should never have done
it. But he loved her so much, I suppose he couldn't keep away.
Me he could leave and never see again, but his little Mel . . .
And he was always a selfish man. He wouldn't leave her alone
for her own good. It would be *his* wants he'd be thinking about.'

'But you never actually knew anything about his whereabouts? Or that he had definitely contacted Melanie? It was
just surmise on your part.'

'I didn't know anything. But I *knew*, if you understand me.'
She looked up at him sharply. 'How did *you* know?'

'I guessed. A couple of things. The ring, for instance. And
the fact that she bought a takeaway meal for someone that
night – it had to be someone close to her.'

She was struck by that. 'God, was he making her buy him
food? I suppose he was broke again. What was it, Chinese?
He loved Chinese. I can't stand the stuff.'

'And then there was the fact that Melanie had a call from
someone that evening, someone she called "Dad". But you'd
said she never called Ian "Dad".'

'No. She never did. Not once that I remember, ever.'

They had come to the place of dread.

'And then you said to my colleague, "A father wouldn't
hurt his own daughter, would he?" She thought you meant
Ian, but when I read it in her report, I wondered.'

'You don't think,' she began, and it was a plea rather than a question, 'that he had anything to do with it, do you?'

'I don't know. I have to find out. But to find out, I had to know the whole story.'

'But why would you even think – I mean, apart from Melanie, nobody knows where he is, even what name he's living by.'

'I think I do,' Slider said. 'I think he's the man who found her body.'

All the implications seemed to fall on her at once like a rock slide. She gave a terrible cry – not loud, but agonizing – the like of which Slider would be glad never to hear again.

'Did you ever hear her mention a man called William McGuire?'

'No,' she said. 'Never. Is that him?'

'I don't know. It's possible.'

She twisted her hands together and rocked in her agony. 'If he killed her, it's my fault, for not telling her, for lying to her all these years. If she could have told me he'd contacted her, I could have protected her.'

'I don't know—' Slider began, but she was beyond reaching.

'I've killed my own daughter,' she said. And she rocked, silent and dry-eyed, in a place of unimaginable nightmare.

It took some nifty telephoning and hard talking back at the office to get in touch with the head of the Parks Department, who was extremely miffed about having to go in on a Sunday to access the employment records of one of his very minor minions. Slider was preparing to go and meet the man himself, there being no one in the Sunday-slim department to send, when Atherton walked in.

'Why aren't you at home?' Slider asked him.

'Why aren't you?' he countered.

'I've been following up something that occurred to me—'

'In the stilly watches of the night,' Atherton finished for him. 'Whereas I have been reclining on the sofa all morning with two cats sitting on me, watching *Chitty Chitty Bang Bang* until I'm ready to kill myself.'

'Why watch it, then?'

'I wasn't watching it – I said the cats were. It's one of their favourite films. Vash's got a *thing* for James Robertson Justice. Emily's not back until Tuesday and my mind is racketing itself to pieces, so I thought I'd come in. And here you are. What's the panic?'

'I'll tell you in the car,' Slider said. 'You can come with me. I'll need you there for the last bit, anyway.'

'So,' said Atherton, some time later, as they trundled towards Uxbridge, 'you were going entirely on her calling someone "Dad" over the phone? You didn't think it could have been a misspeak?'

'Anything could be anything. But remember, less than a week before, he had slapped her face. I don't think the word "Dad" would have leapt to her lips for Ian Wiseman at that point. But there was also the takeaway. Who do you buy food for? It's either charity, or love. No one's come forward to say she brought them a lifeline of Chinese food that evening. I'd have bet on Hibbert—'

'But he's out of it.'

'So who else did she love? And there was another problem. If she bought Chinese for someone, and then got into their car and drove off with them, there must have been a reason. It wasn't exactly closing time, but—'

Atherton got it. 'He was drunk? Turned up drunk in his car to collect the grub, and she thought, oh bugger, I'll have to drive him home?'

'He was a drinker in his previous incarnation. And there was the matter of her savings going missing over the past two years, and the two hundred on the Friday. Who was she giving that to?'

Atherton thought he'd spotted a flaw. 'If she drove him home, how was she going to get home herself?'

'My guess is that she'd drive herself home in his car, and then either he'd come and collect it the next day, or she'd take it back to him and come home by bus or taxi. It would be a Saturday, remember, so no work. And Hibbert was away, so there'd be no complications from that direction. And if she was worried about Fitton seeing her drive in in a strange car, she could have always parked it round the corner. But as it happened, the need didn't arise.'

A silence fell between them on that thought, which lasted all the way to the council offices, where a very annoyed Trevor Parrott was waiting to give them his full and generous cooperation on this matter of importance.

'I can't see why it couldn't have waited until tomorrow,' he grumbled. 'Then you needn't have bothered me. One of the girls could have given you the information you wanted.'

'Operational reasons, I'm afraid,' Slider said smoothly. 'I can't tell you more.'

'Well, if this man is a dangerous criminal, you ought to arrest him, not leave him running around loose to endanger other people. And you should have warned us about him so we could dismiss him. What did he do, anyway?'

'He's a gardener, I believe,' Slider said.

Parrot mottled. 'You deliberately misunderstood me. I meant what *crime* has he committed, of course.'

'I don't know yet that he has done anything.'

'Then why on earth did you have to drag me out on a Sunday?' Parrot cried in frustration, back at the front of the loop.

'We won't keep you long,' Atherton said soothingly, seeing that all the soothe seemed to have leaked out of his boss for the moment. 'It's good of you to help us out. We wouldn't ask if it wasn't important.'

It didn't take long. William McGuire had joined the department two years ago as an under-gardener, after a short spell on benefits. Before that he had been self-employed, a minicab driver, for eight years, first for Remo's Taxis, Fulham, then Magic Cabs of Shepherd's Bush. Previous address in Fulham. And there was a note that, in view of the location of his work for the council, he had been offered a council-owned one-bedroom maisonette in Lakeside Close. No black marks against him since he took up employment. His wage, Slider observed, was minuscule, which accounted, he supposed, for his being taken on with no previous parks and gardens experience. Probably no one else had wanted the job. It was hardly worth coming off benefits for. And he had been absent from work for the past week without notice.

'So that closes the last gap,' Slider said as they walked back

to the car. 'The less fussy minicab firms – and I know Magic
Cabs – will take on anyone with a clean driving licence, no
questions asked. And a short spell on benefits gave him an
insurance number to take to an actual employer. All we don't
know is why he changed from being a driver to being a
gardener.'

'If you think that's all we don't know, you must be on something,' Atherton observed. 'Whether he came back into Melanie's
life; why he did; whether he killed her, if he did; why he "found"
the body – not to mention that we don't actually *know* he's
Graham Hunter at all. That's just a guess on your part. You'll
look a right wally when it turns out he isn't.'

'Thank you for that comforting thought. But McGuire's
record only goes back ten years, to the time of the Greenford
crash. Before that he was a hospital porter living in a council
flat in Paddington. Why the sudden break?'

'He might well have wanted a complete change after the
trauma of the crash. Why not?'

'And there's the fact that he and Hunter were both in the
crash, and he's the one who found Hunter's murdered daughter
ten years on. That's one hell of a coincidence.'

'Ah, well,' Atherton admitted lightly, 'there you have me.
I'll go for a coinkidink every time over hard fact. Makes life
so much more interesting.'

'You're supposed to be polite to me and flatter me. You seem
to forget I'm your boss,' Slider said, plipping open the car and
climbing in. 'I should hate to see you throwing everything away
when the world is at your feet.'

'Usual place for it,' Atherton observed, getting in the other
side. 'Where are we going now?' he asked, as Slider started
the engine.

'Where d'you think?' said Slider.

'Oh boy,' said Atherton. 'I feel a lawsuit coming on.'

'There's something else,' Slider admitted after a silence,
'and it's my fault.'

'What?'

'When Norma brought me the forensic report on the clothes,
I was busy. I told her to precis for me. I didn't read it until
last night.'

'And?'

'The dog hair on her clothes wasn't black, it was white. And Marty doesn't have a white hair on him.'

Atherton wrinkled his nose. 'McGuire had a white dog,' he admitted, 'but it was the dog that found her. The hair could have got on her clothes then.'

'She was found lying on her back. The hair was on the seat of her skirt. So unless the dog managed to turn her right over and sit on her—'

'Ah, I'm with you now.'

'Every dog owner has the dog in the car at some point, and dog hair is the devil to get off the upholstery. So if we can DNA match McGuire's dog's hair to the hair on her skirt—'

'We've got him. Hallelujah, some firm evidence at last.'

'But we won't tell him that to begin with. If I'm right, I think he may confess.'

SEVENTEEN

Dieu Que Le Son Du Cor Est Triste Au Fond Des Bois

There was no answer from McGuire's half of the maisonette. 'I hope he hasn't skedaddled,' Slider said.

'Or done himself in,' said Atherton.

'Thank you for that cheery thought.' He rang again. 'The dog's not barking,' he observed.

'So he probably has flitted,' Atherton said.

'Or he's taken it for a walk.' He tried one more ring.

A window upstairs opened and a woman stuck her head out. 'He's prob'ly down the pub. The Bells. Round the corner. Why don't you try there? I can't hear the telly for your ringing.'

They left the car and walked round. The Six Bells, like most pubs since the smoking ban came in, had to use food to entice the customers in, and most of it was laid out for restaurant purposes, though there was a small bar area in the back. They strolled round the whole premises but there was no sign of McGuire. The bar and waiting staff were all young, mostly East European and temporary, and even when you could get them to stand still for a minute, they had no knowledge of the customers. But there was one older woman, smartly dressed from the Valerie Proctor catalogue, who came out from the back just as they were admitting defeat. She clocked them at once for what they were (*what was it? The suits?* Slider wondered. *Or did they have 'policemen's eyes'? Horrible thought*), backed them into a quiet corner and said, 'Looking for someone? What's he done?'

'Why does everyone always ask that?' Atherton said plaintively. 'As soon as we want to talk to someone . . .'

'He's just a witness,' Slider said. 'Or we hope he might be.' He described McGuire.

'Oh, yeah, Old Bill we call him. His name's Bill,' she added helpfully. 'Got a little dog. We don't mind dogs if they're well behaved. Not in the restaurant area, of course.'

'Of course not,' Slider agreed kindly. 'Has he been in tonight?'

'Not been in – ooh – a while. Quite a regular usually. Weekends, mostly, though he does come in of a weekday night, but he doesn't drink then – has something soft. Very strict. Says he'll never put his job in jeopardy. Mind you, Friday nights and Saturday nights he tanks it a bit. But he's never any trouble. Have to stop him singing sometimes. Got quite a nice voice, but we can't have the punters singing. Gives the wrong impression.'

'Can you remember when you last saw him?'

'No, not offhand. It's been a while, though. Couple of weeks, maybe.'

'Can you remember Friday week past?' Slider asked. 'Was he in then?'

'Dunno. Maybe. Probably – Fridays are his big night. Wait a minute, was that the night he ran out of cash?' She screwed up her face with effort. 'I think it could've been. It was a Friday, anyway. He tried to get credit, the cheeky bastard. I told him to sling his hook.'

'Do you know what time that would have been?'

'Are you kidding? I can't remember stuff like that from weeks ago. It was before chucking out time, I can tell you that, though. I only remember it was a Friday because he was back in the next night – Saturday being his other drinking night – and I told him no credit before he could open his mouth, and he got out his wallet and showed me cash.' She frowned again. 'Now I think about it, he wasn't his usual self that night. Usually he's the life and soul of the party, laughing and joking and trying to sing, like I told you. But that night he just sat down at the end of the bar and threw 'em back, not a peep out of him. I think that might've been the last time I saw him, come to think of it. Has something happened to him?' There was an eagerness for disaster in her voice that Slider didn't want to feed.

'Not that I know of. I just want to talk to him about something he might have seen.'

'Well, if he comes in, I'll tell him you're looking for him,' she said.

They walked back to the car. 'Ran out of money on the Friday, got chucked out early,' Atherton said. 'That fits. A phone call to Melanie – "Can you lend me some money, pet?" And when she agrees to meet him outside her flat with the cash, "You wouldn't get me a Chinese on your way, would you?" And she says, with a degree of irritation, "All *right*, Dad." As per report.'

'And on Saturday night he's drinking to forget.'

'He'd got some balls going to the pub at all. If it was him.'

'If it was him, he might feel he had to stick to his usual pattern. But couldn't quite hack the bonhomie.'

'Well, I like him better for that, anyway,' Atherton said. 'If there's one thing I hate, it's a cheerful murderer.' They reached their car. 'What now?'

Slider was looking past him, towards the Lido. 'Here he comes,' he said quietly. 'He must have been taking the dog for a walk. Why didn't we think of that?'

McGuire was shuffling along, hunched into his clothes, the little dog trotting at his side, looking subdued, glancing up at his master from time to time in that anxious way dogs have when something doesn't feel right. He didn't seem to see the two men waiting for him until he actually reached them, and then he stopped and looked at them with an appalling resignation, and so much pain, if he had been an animal Slider would have wanted to put him down right there and then.

'Mr Hunter,' he said quietly, 'can we have a word with you?'

He showed no surprise. He just looked old – his face lined, his eyes bagged and raw, his skin slack and grey. It was as if all the lost years of William McGuire had been added to his own, a terrible reverse Dorian Gray of a punishment. The dog watched them warily, nose working hard, waiting for a cue from its master as to whether to wag or growl.

At last McGuire said, 'You'd better come in.' His voice was different from the way Slider remembered it, from their first interview: lighter, his accent posher, more suited to an educated man rather than a manual labourer. So he had been a bit of an actor as well, Slider thought as they followed him to his door. Well, that was no surprise. There was always a bit of an actor in the man who lived by his charm. But there was no sign of that charm now. This was a beaten man; the spark had gone out.

There was no smell of drink in the room, or from McGuire. He let the dog out into the back garden, and came back, caught Slider sniffing, and said, 'I'm not drunk. I haven't touched a drop for five days. I'm never going to drink again.' He sat down heavily in an armchair whose seat bore the impression.

'You didn't react when I called you Mr Hunter,' Slider said. 'For the record, you are Graham Hunter, aren't you?'

He seemed to think about it for a moment; or perhaps he was choosing his words. 'If you've got as far as asking me that question, I suppose there's no point in denying it. I've gone all these years wondering when it would come, but after a certain point, you think it's all been settled in your favour, and you stop worrying. Yes, I'm Graham Hunter – or at least, I was once. I feel as if he died a long time ago. I wish he had,' he concluded bitterly.

'Tell me about the train crash,' Slider said. 'What do you remember about it?'

'Not much about the actual crash. I was going down to Bristol to see a man about a business proposition.' He made a wry face. 'Importing edible insects from Latin America – cicadas, beetles and ants. Dried, and mixed in small bags. He said it would be the next snack food craze – eat them at the bar instead of peanuts or pork scratchings. Seen any lately in your local?' he enquired ironically. 'I remember there were engineering works and the train was quite slow to start with. Men in red safety jackets beside the line as we went slowly past. Then not long after we speeded up—'

He paused. The dog came in, flip-flap, from the garden, and looked at them, then sat on the invisible frontier between the sitting room and the kitchen.

'It's funny,' Hunter went on, 'I don't remember a noise. There was a terrific bang, but it was a feeling rather than a sound. The train was packed and I hadn't been able to get a seat, which probably saved me. I was standing in the space by the door between two carriages with a lot of other people. Then came this bang. I remember feeling as if all the breath was pressed out of my body. Then I hit the ground, or the ground hit me, and there were bits of debris falling all around me. A twisted piece of metal fell on my outstretched hand. Cut my palm. I was lucky it didn't sever it completely. I was bruised and breathless, but otherwise I wasn't hurt. I just lay there thinking, what happened? It seemed like ages, though I suppose it couldn't have been more than a minute, before the power of thought came back to me, and I said to myself, "The train crashed."'

Slider guessed this was the first time he had told this story – who would there have been to tell it to, after all? – which was why he had it all honed and ready. He must have gone over it in his mind a thousand times. All he and Atherton had to do was sit still and listen.

'I sat up,' Hunter went on, 'and looked around. There were the trains. The express had ridden over the top of the slow train, so there were three carriages sitting on top of it. Both engines had derailed and were on their sides and one of them had caught fire. Some of the carriages were catching, too. And there was debris everywhere. And bodies.' He stopped. 'Well, I suppose you've seen pictures of it.'

'Yes,' said Slider.

'I got up. I was a bit dazed, I think. I wandered around a bit, just looking, unable to take it in. Then I thought about seeing if there was anyone I could help. The first person I came to was obviously beyond help. A massive great metal thing – looked like a cast-iron water tank – had landed on his head. He was dead as a nail. I didn't even think about moving that thing – I didn't want to think what was underneath. But as I knelt there looking at him, I saw the blood dripping from my hand, and realized it was quite badly cut. I couldn't find my handkerchief for the moment, but I saw one poking out of the dead man's pocket, so I pulled it out, and it looked clean, so I thought, "He won't want it any more," and I tied my hand up with it. And that was when it came to me.'

He looked at Slider, as if to check that he really knew.

'The idea of swapping identities,' Slider supplied.

'It was the maddest thing. I think it was a symptom of shock that it even crossed my mind. But I thought, here was a way to start again, a clean slate, leave all my troubles behind. My life was a mess, my marriage was on the rocks, I had debts from here to Timbuktu. If I could just walk away from the lot, I could start a new life, all clean and clear. Like a snake shedding its old skin. I went through his pockets. He didn't have much, poor bugger. I found a driving licence with his name and address on it, a cheap wallet with a few quid and a Blockbuster card, and one of those plastic name badges on a lanyard – a hospital pass for Queen Mary's isolation annexe in Greenford – the old fever hospital. Given that, and the fact that his address was in Paddington, I think he must have been on the local train. Well, it was the work of a moment to switch what was in his pockets with what was in mine. And then I walked away. I had a bad moment when a paramedic grabbed me and insisted on looking at my hand – the handkerchief had soaked through and I was fiddling with it. He made me go to the first aid tent they'd set up, and a young doctor stitched it for me. I remembered to tell them my new name for the record, but I couldn't remember the address. I looked dumb and gave them the driving licence, and I suppose they decided I was in shock. Anyway, they took down the information from that, even worked out I was fifty-five. It was a funny thing – I felt a sort of pang about that. I thought I'd lost thirteen years of my life. But then I was free to go. They were giving out cups of tea and sandwiches in another tent nearby and I got something and sat down for a bit – I was starting to shake with the reaction. But I didn't want to hang around – I was afraid someone would find out about the switch, God knows how – everyone had too much to do. So I walked to the nearest bit of civilization, which turned out to be Greenford, and got myself a bed in a cheap hotel for the night, took the aspirin the doctor had given me, and slept like the dead.'

He sighed and looked down at his hand, flexing it absently in the manner of someone who has grown used to the ache and stiffness of age. Slider thought he saw, among the natural creases, the faint scar of an old wound across the palm. The dog thought the movement was for him, and trotted forward, and sat hopefully at Hunter's feet, but he didn't notice it.

'Of course,' he resumed, 'in the morning I realized what a stupid scheme it was. There was no possible way it could work. My wife would be called to identify the body, and she'd know right away it wasn't me. I haunted the papers for days, expecting some outcry. When I finally saw my own name on the list of casualties – well, it gave me a jolt, I can tell you. That's a strange thing to read. And then there was a notice of my death in the deaths column, and the date of my funeral.' He looked at Atherton as if anticipating the question, though Atherton had not made a sound. 'No, I didn't go. I wasn't quite that mad. By then I'd realized what had happened. Rachel had decided that if I wanted out, she was going to let me. She must have known the body wasn't mine, but she'd gone along with it anyway. And then I remembered the life insurance. I was more use to her dead than alive. So I stayed dead. I didn't blame her. Life with me wasn't a bed of roses for her, poor bitch. If she preferred the money to my company, who's to say she wasn't right?'

'What about William McGuire? How did you go about becoming him?' Slider asked.

Hunter sighed with a sort of weariness, settling back in the chair as if he needed help to get to the end. The dog, seeing the movement, and tired of waiting, jumped up on to his lap, and he moved his hands automatically to accommodate it. 'I went to his address the next day. It was a council flat.'

'Yes. I know the estate,' Slider said.

'I watched the place for hours to see if anyone would go in or out. Then I thought, this is stupid, bucked myself up and went and knocked. When there was no answer I used the key from his pocket. It was a grim sort of place. One bedroom, small and very dark, sitting room with a kitchen area and a tiny bathroom. Hardly any furniture or belongings. Hadn't been decorated in an age. Smelt funny, too. But right away I could see he'd lived alone. There was no woman stuff there, no women's clothes in the wardrobe, no make-up or anything in the bathroom. And the cooking arrangements were primitive. Sliced bread and a tub of Flora in the fridge. A few tins of baked beans in the cupboard. Dirty plates in the sink. I never saw such a bleak place in my life – well, I hadn't then. I have since. I know a lot about the William McGuires of this world now. But it was just my dumb luck that it was him. A fifty-five-year-old bachelor, works as a hospital porter, lives in a council flat: a person like him disappears, and no one will even notice for weeks. And when they notice, they won't care. I don't know if he had any relatives. There was nothing in the flat to suggest it. Maybe he had some, far away and out of touch. I still sometimes wonder if anyone ever asked themselves what had become of old Bill.'

'Did you stay there? At the flat?'

'God, no! That would have been too weird. And maybe dangerous. Once I'd had a look round, I just left, and never went back. I had to find a room to rent and a job. I had five hundred quid in cash with me – it was going to be a down payment to the man in Bristol, to get me in on the scheme – but that was all, and I couldn't use my credit cards. I needed some way to support myself with no questions asked. Poor old William didn't have much, but the one thing of value he left me was his driving licence. I went to the library and went online, found a ten-year-old Nissan saloon in decent condition, well looked after, with eleven months MOT, for three-fifty. I got myself a room, from an advert in a newsagent's, in Maida Vale, and went along and signed up with a minicab company. Within a week, I had my new life all set up. I moved around a good bit for the first year, to foil the scent, in case anyone was looking for me. But in the end, I concluded that old Bill hadn't had any friends in the world, and I settled down in Fulham.'

'Why Fulham?' Slider asked.

'Oh, it was as good a place as anywhere,' he said listlessly. 'A man I knew, one of the other drivers, said Remo's in Fulham paid more than where I was, so I drifted that way. It didn't matter to me where I lived by then.'

'You were unhappy,' Slider suggested.

'It's strange,' Hunter said reflectively. 'At first I found it exhilarating to be someone else. And being someone like

McGuire was such a relief – no one expected anything of him. He had no responsibilities, no standards to live up to, nothing in the world to do beyond turn up at work long enough to earn the cash and not piss off the bosses. I played to my new role. I was dumb but reliable. A loner. A very, very dull person. No hobbies, no habits, no friends. I drove my car, in the evenings I watched telly. At the weekends I got drunk. When I was flush, I went down the betting shop for a flutter on the ponies. When I was broke, I worked overtime. Once I went to the pictures, and bought fish and chips afterwards and ate them out of the paper.' He paused. 'I think that was what finished me, that night, going to the pictures on my own.'

'Finished you?'

'I ended that night lying on my bed staring at the ceiling and thinking, "What have I done?"' He lifted haunted eyes, tired to death. 'You can't imagine what a life like that is like. The utter pointlessness. The tedium. The loneliness. I'd done the best bit of acting of my life, I *was* William McGuire, but what was the use? I could never go home again. I could never see my daughter again.'

Now they had come to it, Slider thought. 'You missed Melanie?'

'So much,' he blurted. 'I can't tell you. It was like a gnawing in the guts, longing for her; day after day, and it got worse all the time. It was worse than if she'd died, because then I'd know she was beyond reach. But I knew she was there, some-where, and I could go and find her and see her and talk to her – only I mustn't, not ever. That's why I drank so much, to try and keep it at bay. In the end, I lost my job. I went in to work still under the influence and they told me to sling my hook. That was the one thing they couldn't allow – that and stealing.'

'So what did you do?'

'I saw an advertisement for an under gardener for the Parks Department in Ruislip, and I thought a change would be good – the outdoor life might soothe me. And the word "Ruislip" reminded me of the Lido. I used to bring Mel and her little friend here when she was a kid, on fine Sundays – cheaper than the seaside. She loved it. They were happy times. I never thought I'd end up living right next to the Lido, but when I said I lived in Fulham, they told me I could have this place, to be on hand. Sometimes there's emergency work, if a tree blows down or a bank collapses, and I have to turn out. So I moved here. I thought, this time I'll be happy. I even got myself a dog.' He looked down at the terrier, which had curled itself up on his lap, as if noticing it for the first time. He caressed its ears, and it waggled its stump tail without waking up.

'But you weren't happy,' Slider said.

He shook his head. 'Living here only made me think about her more. The longing for my old life was terrible. One day I went to the Natural History Museum, because it was another favourite place of hers when she was a kid. And I saw her.' He seemed to be staring at his memory now, as if at a movie. 'It was a long time – eight years – and she'd grown up a lot, but I knew her. I'd have known her in the dark. She was walking away down a corridor. I followed her, just in time to see her go in through a door marked "Private, Staff Only". She'd used the security keypad by the door, so I knew she must work there. It was a funny thing, just as she was pushing in through the door she paused and looked round, as if she felt me watching her. I jumped back behind a pillar. She didn't see me. She wouldn't have known me anyway – I'd grown this beard. But I think somehow she'd felt my presence.

'After that, I couldn't keep the feelings down. I was drinking more than ever – weekends only. I didn't want to lose this job. But it was no good. I had to see her. One evening I waited outside the museum and followed her home.'

'Did you speak to her?'

'Not then. It took a lot of nights, standing across the road from her house, watching her go in and out, before I could pluck up the courage. Then one night she came out alone and walked off along the street. She looked so happy and busy, living her life, I followed her, really just to see where she was going, maybe to suck in some of that happiness. I don't think I meant to speak to her. But when she stopped at the pedestrian lights, waiting to cross the road, I just walked up to her and before I could stop myself, I said, "Melanie?"'

'She looked round. She was scared for a second – there

was this bearded old man who knew her name – and then there was a sort of dawning in her face, and she said, "Dad?"'

At that point, he flagged so alarmingly with, Slider supposed, sheer emotional exhaustion that he looked for a moment as though he was having an attack of some sort. He slumped back in the chair, his face drawn and putty-coloured, breathing through his mouth.

'Take a breather,' Slider said. 'Do you want a drink? Is there anything in the house?'

'No,' he said, a protest, though a feeble one. 'I'm not drinking, never again.'

'Tea, then?'

'A cup of tea,' Hunter agreed weakly. He licked his lips. 'Mouth's dry.'

Slider got up before Atherton could move. 'I'll do it,' he said. The dog lifted its head sharply at the movement. Slider went into the kitchen part, took the kettle to the tap, and leaned against the sink for a moment, his eyes closed. He found his hands were shaking. Emotional draining didn't only happen to the narrator, he discovered, but to the interlocutor too.

It had been wonderful at first. Of course, she had been shocked at what he had done, and it had taken a lot of explaining before she could accept that he had done it for her and her mother's own good. Then she had had to tell him about her life, and there were some painful parts to that, too. And her mother's remarriage, to Ian, who she didn't like one bit. And Scott, whom she adored: Hunter had had to grit his teeth against the jealousy.

They couldn't meet very often, because no one could know about him, and the secrecy was wearing on them both. She would meet him somewhere, a café, or just a bench, in her lunchtime usually. Evenings and weekends were difficult. Mostly it was snatched meetings just to catch up, though they talked on the phone when they could. But of course, the problem for any addict is that having a little bit only makes you want more; and he was addicted to Melanie.

He hadn't meant to ask her for money. But she had been shocked at the way he lived, and how little he earned, and the shabbiness of his clothes. She had given him money, against his protests, the first time, so he could buy himself a new jacket. The next time, he asked her. The strain of the situation meant he was drinking and gambling more at the weekends, and that went through the money more than anything. She didn't like giving him money just to waste it, but she never refused him.

But then she started urging him to put things right. She wanted him to tell her mother he was alive. It was cruel, she said, to leave her in ignorance. He'd told her that revealing himself would make her a bigamist, and then she'd got angry. He had to do the right thing, she said. He must go to the police and make a clean breast of everything. They couldn't go on like this.

'I think in the back of her mind,' he said sadly, 'she had the idea that if only I would do that, everything could go back to the way it was. Ian would somehow disappear, I would come home and live with Rachel, and we would be a family again. She was a bright girl, but when it came to that, emotionally she was just five years old. I tried to explain to her how impossible it was, but she persisted with the idea that if only I would confess, everything would be forgiven, just like that.'

And so they came to the Friday night. The tea had been drunk, had revived him a little, but he still looked ghastly. Slider felt exhausted; Atherton looked apprehensive. Only the dog slumbered comfortably on his master's lap. Hunter stroked it slowly, over and over, as he told the last part of the story.

He had gone for his Friday night drink at the Six Bells. It had been a hard week, he'd had words with his immediate superior, and there had been hints that departmental cuts might lose him his job, despite the fact that there was too much work for the staff they had. He had gone to the pub determined to tie one on, only to discover, before he was drunk enough for oblivion, that he had run out of money. He'd asked for credit – he was in there often enough, for God's sake – and the barmaid, the snotty one with the voice like a bandsaw, had given him short shrift and long contempt. He was furious and humiliated and wanted nothing more than to get back at her

– turn up with enough cash to flash at her to make her sorry she'd been sharp with him.

Outside, he'd rung Melanie. She was out with friends – he could hear the sounds of people having a good time in the background. A wave of self-pity had come over him. He'd told her he was in a bad way for cash and spun her a story which he could hear she didn't believe, but she'd agreed to meet him at her house with funds as soon as he could get there. And he'd asked her to get him a takeaway as well – he hadn't eaten since breakfast – and she'd snapped at him. It hadn't boded well.

When he arrived at her house she'd come down with the carrier bag in her hand, and got in beside him to talk to him. But right away she'd peered at him and sniffed and said he was too drunk to drive home, and insisted on switching places with him and driving him back.

When they reached Reservoir Road she'd driven to the Lido car park and pulled up there 'so I can talk to you'. It was a long harangue, on much the same lines as before, about him 'doing the right thing'. She'd been doing some sums while she waited for the Chinese food, and realized how much of her money he had gone through in the last two years. It had to stop, she said.

He'd eaten the food while she talked but he hadn't enjoyed it, which annoyed him. He tried to tell her all over again how it was impossible for him to go back, and how it wouldn't help anyway. The harangue had turned into an argument. He'd got out of the car to escape it, but she followed him. He tried to get it through her thick skull that if he went to police it would end up with him and her mother in prison, but she persisted in assuring him that wouldn't happen.

She got angry with him, about having left her all those years thinking he was dead, about his drinking and his poor little bets on the ponies, called him a coward for not facing his responsibilities, told him if he didn't put things right she'd stop seeing him.

He got angry too, and accused her of emotional blackmail, and of being a silly, naive little prig.

And in the middle of all the anger, he had grabbed her by the neck and shaken her.

'Not hard. I didn't grab her hard. Even losing my temper, I was enough her father to check myself, not to hurt her. But she was shocked. I'd never laid a rough hand on her before. She jerked away from me, just as I let her go. She lost her balance, her foot skidded on the mud, and she went over backwards, hitting her head sharply on the edge of the car roof.

'I didn't mean to hurt her,' he said in a faded voice of horror. 'I would never hurt my little girl. I knelt beside her, slipped my hand under her head, felt the blood. I called her name, and I thought she looked at me, but then she was limp and her eyes weren't looking anywhere. Just staring. But I never meant to hurt her, I swear to you. If I could have died instead . . .'

'But you didn't,' Slider said.

EIGHTEEN
The Devil Wears Primark

'That's a terrible story,' Joanna said. 'That's the worst thing I've heard. The poor man.'

Slider had rung her on her mobile to say he didn't know what time he'd be home, and she had diverted after the concert and come to the station to hear about it first hand. She was sitting on his desk now, still in her long black, a breath of fresh air from the outside world – the real world, if you wanted to look at it that way, in which people lived their lives without ever murdering or being murdered.

Sitting as he was in his normal chair behind the desk, he was looking up at her. He admired her almost painfully. She had just been engaged in something of extraordinary, unimaginable skill – playing the violin before an audience of thousands, recreating great music from tiny, random-looking dots on a page – something so beyond his comprehension that it stood in his mind like a conjuring trick in a child's: genuine magic. She was a hummingbird, a kingfisher – airborne, delicate, a jewel of brightness and a quicksilver of movement. He was a humble duck, patiently drudging about in the weed.

She was also his wife, which was a pretty damn fine thing, whichever way you looked at it.

'But,' she said, 'if it was an accident, why didn't he just go straight to the police?'

Atherton, sitting on the cold radiator as usual, answered. 'Because of this whole identity swap thing. He was afraid it would all come out and he was terrified of going to prison. So he carried her into the woods and laid her half under a bush. He had to make it look as though she'd been concealed, but he wanted her to be found, so he chose a place not far off the path. Then he went home and waited.'

'It must have been hell,' Joanna observed.

'Yes,' said Atherton, 'particularly when she *wasn't* found. Saturday went past and Sunday went past, and all the usual visitors and dog walkers kept going in there and nothing happened. He didn't want to be caught, but he couldn't bear to leave her lying out there any longer. I mean, not just the agonizing suspense, but what with foxes and stoats and such—'

'Don't.' Joanna winced.

'So on Monday morning he finally broke, and "found" her himself. He was in a terrible state when we interviewed him, but then, finding a dead body is not a nice thing for the ordinary punter, so we didn't think anything of it. And then, when we didn't come back for him . . .'

'I suppose he was on tenterhooks, wondering if, and whether, and when,' Joanna said thoughtfully. 'A whole week of it.'

'Yes, I think he was just glad in the end, when we did come for him, that it was all over.'

'Hardly that,' Slider said. They looked at him. 'Not all over by any means.'

'Well, no, there's all the mess to clear up,' Atherton admitted. 'And *what* a mess he's made of everything! His daughter's dead. His wife's marriage is bigamous.'

'That's easily remedied, surely? Divorce and remarriage would fix that,' Joanna suggested.

'It was still knowing bigamy on her part, which is a crime. Not to mention the insurance fraud. She could do time. And the marriage is ruined anyway. Ian's not going to want her back. And his life will never be the same, either. He'll have to change his job – if he can get another one after being a suspect. Though it's hard to feel sympathy for him, given the Stephanie incident. There's the child, Bethany – she's bound to find out everything sooner or later, and it's not a pretty story. What will that do to her? And then there's Toby.'

'Who's Toby? Joanna asked.

'Hunter's dog. It was the one thing he asked as we arrested him – what's going to happen to Toby?'

'Well, what does?'

'A local dog charity took him. We have an arrangement with them for such eventualities. They'll keep him for a bit, and if Hunter ends up going inside they'll rehome him. That

was the one thing he talked about in the car on the way here.
He said, "Toby'll be dead by the time I get out." We could
have given him – the dog – to Mrs Wiseman-stroke-Hunter
– Marty could do with a brother – but with the chance she'll
be going away at Her Majesty's pleasure as well, we couldn't
risk it.'

Joanna contemplated for a bit. 'You're right. It is a mess.
What must he be feeling?'

'At the moment, he just wants to die,' Atherton said. 'He's
killed his darling and there's nothing left for him. He'll have
to be put on suicide watch, which is a great nuisance to everybody. Then, of course, there's William McGuire to consider.
We'll have to try and track down his relatives, if any, and tell
them. We haven't yet checked with MisPer whether he was
ever reported missing. If he was, that'll make it easier.' He
rolled his eyes. 'Just the paperwork of undeading Hunter and
redeading McGuire is a nightmare.'

'And then there's the case to prepare,' Slider said. Joanna
noticed that he had been curiously silent all through this.
Usually the relief of getting to the end of a case made him
talkative. But he was sitting with his head bent in a dejected
attitude, twirling a pencil round and round in his fingers.

'But if it was an accident, not murder, what case is there?'
she asked.

'Failure to notify a death. Interference with a human corpse.
Concealing a crime. Impeding a police investigation. Plus the
original identity swap fraud, and complicity in insurance fraud,'
Atherton enumerated.

'If it was an accident,' Slider said. They both looked at him.
'We have no evidence about the death. No evidence either for
him or against him. No evidence at all.'

'But – he confessed,' Joanna said.

'Confessions can be retracted. We get false confessions all
the time. He can go back to saying he only found the body,
that it had nothing to do with him. Claim he was upset and
didn't know what he was saying.'

'But there's Toby's hair on her clothes,' Atherton objected.

'A good counsel will get over that, given he and Toby
found the body.'

'The wound could be matched to the roof edge of his car.'

'It's a common make and model. Without any traces of her blood on it . . . And he was a minicab driver. One thing he knows how to do is wash a car. There were no witnesses. We've got nothing but the coincidence of her being his daughter.'

'But she was *there* – only yards from his home!' Joanna protested. 'Doesn't that mean something?'

He shook his head. 'He used to take her to the Lido when she was a kid. Who's to say she wasn't just having a nostalgia trip and got killed by a nutter walking in the woods? We can't prove he knew she was there. She didn't tell anyone he had come back into her life, and we don't know that they were ever seen together. The CPS would never go on a confession alone, particularly one like that, made under emotional strain, if it was retracted. No, if he thinks better of it, there's nothing we can do.'

'Well, perhaps losing his beloved daughter is punishment enough,' Joanna said, and then caught up with something he'd said. 'What do you mean, "if it was an accident"?'

'He said her foot skidded in the mud,' said Slider. 'But the ground had been frozen hard for weeks. There was no mud. I noticed myself when we arrived on the scene, because I was thinking about possible footmarks.'

'Maybe she skidded on something else,' Joanna said reasonably.

'Maybe,' Slider said. 'But someone falling backwards against a car like that – you wouldn't expect the blow to be hard enough to kill. But if, being drunk and furious *and* afraid, he dashed her backwards with all his considerable strength – he was a manual worker, so he was pretty sinewy . . .'

'But it would still be an accident,' Joanna said.

'The law wouldn't see it that way,' Slider said. 'Intent to hurt someone, if it ends in killing them – especially with the deliberate cover-up afterwards. He tied her scarf round her neck to make it look as if she'd been strangled. He must have been afraid his hands would have left a mark. That's quite calculated, you know. Not the action of a man in a blind panic. It would weight the evidence against him. If . . .'

'If?' she asked.

'If the CPS decided to go with it.' He gave a shrug, 'Not my problem, fortunately. Those of far higher counsel than me will go through it all and decide what to charge him with and why. And there's plenty to play with, so they'll get him for something. And as you say, maybe losing her will be punishment enough.' He thought of Ronnie Fitton and his crime and punishment speech. It was never enough, was it, for those who cared?

'Surely your opinion will be taken into account,' Joanna said, concerned for him now, rather than the unknown and now unknowable Melanie.

'Me? I don't have an opinion. I'm just the meek ass between two burdens. More than two, it generally feels like.'

'Issachar was a strong ass, not a meek one,' Atherton said, to lighten the mood. 'I don't usually get to correct you on the Bible, but if you're going to quote . . .'

'All asses are meek,' Slider said.

'Ah, well, there I have to disagree with you,' Atherton said. 'What about McLaren?'

'Oh, poor McLaren,' Joanna protested. 'You're always picking on him.'

A twitch of a smile moved Slider's mouth. 'One thing I will say about him: he may be weird, but at least you know he probably won't reproduce.'

Some time later, after Joanna had gone home to relieve his father, Connolly brought him a cup of tea. There was so much to do that several of the team had been invited to come in and do some overtime, and she was one of those who had accepted.

She found Slider surrounded by young skyscrapers of documents, but staring at the studio photograph of Melanie Hunter. He didn't look up as she placed the tea gently on his desk, but he said, 'Now it's just The Melanie Hunter Murder – a shorthand reference in books and papers, coupled in the minds of those who remember at all with this picture.'

She sought for something to say. 'But you got a result, boss. That's something.'

'Not to her,' he said. He put the picture down with an air

of squaring his shoulders. 'Thanks for the tea.' She gave a little *you're welcome* gesture, and as she didn't immediately turn away, he said, 'You're glad it didn't turn out to be Fitton, aren't you? I think you had a soft spot for him.'

'Not exactly soft. Just not desperate hard. I think he cared about Melanie.'

'Not to the extent of finding out what was going on in her life,' Slider said, thinking of that *Not my business*. 'I don't think anyone cared that much about her, poor girl.'

'Marty did,' said Connolly, and then wished she hadn't, because far from giving him any comfort, she'd clearly just given him someone else to worry about.

Eventually they had the firm's traditional celebration drink at the Boscombe Arms. So far, Hunter had not retracted his confession, and the mess of possible charges was under consideration. Slider's worry was that the CPS would end up thinking it was not worth the money it would cost to take it to trial, especially as the story was such a good one it would probably get the jury's sympathy. But Porson had said they would have to move on the 'tampering with a body' side of it, at least, *pour decourager les autres*. 'Can't have people faking murders to cover up accidents,' he had said, with no apparent sense of irony. And Paxman, meeting Slider in the canteen one day, brooding over mulligatawny soup, had said that if they went on the tampering bit, it would make no sense without the rest. 'He'll be jugged, good and hard, don't you worry,' he had concluded with unusual sympathy.

It was good that they had found out a little bit about William McGuire. According to MisPers, an elderly aunt from Colwyn Bay had reported him missing, but two months after the train crash, and only because he had missed sending her a birthday card, which he always did, and had not responded to a letter she had sent asking why. He had no other relatives. Nothing much was done about it at the time. As Hunter had said, when someone like McGuire goes missing, no one is very surprised. The old aunt, now 87 and in a home, but still with all her marbles, was contacted and told that he had died in the Greenford rail crash, and it was reported to Slider that she had been glad to know at last what had happened to him, having long made up her mind to it that he was dead.

The superintendent of the home sent Slider a photograph which the old lady had asked to have 'put in his grave with him'. It was of McGuire, in palmier days, standing with his elder brother Robert, whom he had hero-worshipped. Robert was in uniform – he had been an NCO in the Welsh Guards, one of forty killed in the Falklands. Their parents had died when they were in their teens and Robert had always looked out for William. William had wanted to follow Robert into the army, but wasn't bright enough – he could barely read and write. 'He was a little bit simple, poor lamb,' the Colwyn Bay auntie was reported as saying, 'but always ever such a good boy.'

Quite how you put a photograph 'in a grave' Slider wasn't sure; finding the grave at all would be an extra, time-consuming task he could well do without. He was glad, at least, that what with all the other wrongs done him, McGuire had not been murdered. And for the sake of closing files in his mind, he was glad to discover what he had been doing on the train that day – the auntie had said he was on night duty at the annexe, so he would have been on his way home. He wasn't just fulfilling his meeting with destiny.

And so to the celebration, and the astonishing fact that McLaren had sidled to Slider's door shortly after it had been announced and asked, with a casualness that would have fooled nobody, whether they were 'bringing people'.

Slider hadn't got as far as thinking about that – there was so much stuff in his in-tray by now, the bottom layer had turned to coal. Traditionally the celebration had been for the firm only, but Joanna had sometimes come, and though that was probably a special dispensation for him as the big boss, there was no stated rule against it. What was far more inter-esting was that McLaren wanted to bring 'somebody', which presumably meant a woman, and Slider knew he would lose his place in his team's heart if he denied them the chance to see what sort of woman would go out with McLaren.

So he said yes, and as soon as McLaren had gone, hastened to telephone Joanna to tell her to come.

*   *   *

He didn't say a word to anyone else, but perhaps McLaren himself had mentioned it. At any rate, tension grew through the day, and when they finally decamped for the pub, you could have sliced it, buttered it, whacked a slice of corned beef between and sold it on a sandwich stall. When they got to the Boscombe and secured their usual corner, there was no sign of any extraneous bodies, but McLaren had an air of nervousness, and the usual loud conversation was curiously muted as everyone watched the door while attempting to appear not to.

The publican, Andy Barrett, brought the pints and some grub. It had gone upmarket a bit of late, and instead of the lopsided doorsteps and pork pies of yore there were three sorts of sandwiches in neat triangles on a big salver, with salad garnish; nachos and salsa; and a selection of Indian snacks – samosas, bhajis and pakoras.

Joanna came in. Everyone hitched up a bit and she squeezed in beside Slider.

'What's all this?' she asked, indicating the snacks. 'Posh grub?'

'The clientele is getting younger,' Atherton said across the table, with a touch of moodiness. Emily was away again. 'An effort has to be made.'

'I miss the old days,' Joanna said. 'Those fluorescent-orange Scotch eggs. The Barbie-pink pork pies.'

'That's just colour prejudice,' said Atherton.

'So when's the main event coming off?' she asked.

Slider made a shushing face, but Connolly, who had heard, had no shame, and turned to McLaren and said, 'Yeah, right, Maurice, where's this bird of yours? Sure I'm starting to think you've imagined her.'

'She should be here any minute,' he said, with what Slider would have sworn was a blush. 'She's coming from work.'

Every ear was pricked. 'What's she do, then?' Connolly asked. 'Nurse, is she?'

Joanna exchanged a private smile with Slider. Male musicians often went out with nurses for the same reason – they understood impossible schedules.

'No, she's a beauty therapist,' McLaren said.

Everyone was too stunned to lay tongue to the obvious retorts, which was probably just as well.

'At the Jingles Sports and Beauty Club – you know, down Chiswick, by the river. That big white building.'

'Yes, I know it,' Joanna said, to rescue the poor mutt from the prevailing shock and awe. 'I've gone past it a few times going down to Barn Elms, to the recording studios. That must be an interesting job.'

'Yeah. She's the senior consultant,' he said with pride. He met Joanna's eyes and said, with an air of flinging himself off a cliff, 'She's been giving me a make-over.'

The explosion of suppressed derision from around the table was fortunately masked by the door opening again and McLaren saying with rather touching eagerness, 'There she is.'

Atherton, who had been fiddling with his mobile, wondering whether it would seem too needy to ring Emily again, looked up, and felt his jaw drop like rain in Wimbledon week. McLaren's girlfriend stood framed in the doorway, looking around for a friendly face. She was a good deal older than him, for a start, but seemed to have forgotten to take that into account when getting dressed. Her skirt was short and black, her shoes vertiginous and strappy, her top was clinging and fuchsia pink, and displayed a cleavage Carter and Caernarvon would have felt compelled to stick their heads down. 'I see wonderful things!' But more Tooting Common than Tutankhamen. Her make-up was blatantly professional, her hair brazenly highlighted, and her costume jewellery so bright it could have been used to signal aircraft. All she needs, Atherton thought in astonished awe, is a pimp and a lamp post.

McLaren had lurched to his feet, and Atherton, turning his gaze that way, saw Maurice's face so soft and marshmallowy and eager and proud, it would make you vomit if it didn't touch you to the quick.

'Everybody, this is Jackie. Jackie Griffiths,' he said in a voice of wonder. And suddenly Atherton could not bear to see him kicked, even in a friendly manner. He was getting to his feet, but Slider was ahead of him, and because they had both risen, oddly everyone else did, too, and a kindly formality came over the party, keeping those who might have mocked silent.

'Good to meet you, Jackie,' Slider said, reaching out a hand across the table.

'This is the boss, our guv, Mr Slider,' McLaren babbled.

'Pleased to meet you,' Jackie said, shaking the hand. Her nails were long, square cut and French varnished. She smiled a professional smile. 'Maurice has told me a lot about you. About all of you.'

Was there a hint of threat in that? Slider wondered vaguely. The introductions went round, a chair was brought, Jackie sat down, and the moment for ribaldry was safely past. McLaren went to the bar to get her a drink, and she looked round them all, beamed, and said, 'What d'you all think of Maurice's new look? I think it's an improvement, don't you? I said to him, you're a nice-looking chap, but you don't make the most of yourself.'

Slider had never considered McLaren as being nice-looking, or indeed anything-looking. He was just McLaren, the food disposal system, the man for whom the question had been coined, 'Are you a man or a mouth?'

'We all noticed the difference,' he said.

She turned to him happily. 'Well, I'm glad my hard work wasn't all for nothing! D'you like his new hairstyle? I'm not sure I've got it quite right yet, but I'll have to wait a few weeks before I can cut it again. Lucky it grows so fast. He's got lovely thick hair. I told him—' McLaren returned with a gin and tonic to place before her, and she looked up at him. 'I told you, didn't I, you've got lovely hair, but you don't do anything with it.'

'You live somewhere out Ruislip way, don't you?' Slider asked, to settle at least one question in his mind.

'Northolt,' she said. 'How did you know?' Luckily she didn't wait for the question to be answered. 'It's a bit of a trek out to Chiswick, where I work now. I was thinking of moving when I got the new job, and it'd be nice to be a bit nearer to Maurice, but you've got to think of house prices. Of course, they do say two can live as cheaply as one. Maybe I could get someone to share with,' she concluded with a gay laugh and a roguish glance at McLaren, who only gazed back at her, obviously entranced by her vivacity. Slider had never known him so silent.

Mind you, Jackie talked so much there was no need for anyone else to do a thing. It occurred to him sadly that there might now have to be a rule about bringing people in future. But he couldn't feel anything but kindness towards someone who was willing to go to so much trouble to bring happiness and an appearance of living in the twenty-first century to someone like McLaren, the man civilization forgot.

On the way home, Joanna said, 'It didn't feel much like a celebration.'

'I'm afraid she did talk a lot,' Slider said. 'But there's no harm in her.'

'I didn't mean that,' she said. 'It's just that there's usually a certain elation because you've got your man. The Mountie syndrome. But everyone seemed a bit subdued.'

'It's the uncertainty, I suppose. Not knowing what Hunter will be charged with or whether it will go to trial.'

'But you solved the problem. The mystery. You started off knowing nothing, and now you know it all. That must be a satisfaction. Intellectually, at least, if not emotionally.' She looked at him, at his face waxing and waning as they passed street lamps. 'And Auntie McGuire knows what happened to her Billy at last.'

He smiled. 'All right, I give in. It's a triumph of sorts, and I'll accept the bouquets and put it behind me. Now what shall we talk about?'

'We could talk about my troubles.'

'Have you still got troubles? Oh yes, you're stuck with Daniel Kluger for the rest of the season. Can't you just rise above him?'

'That's the trouble. It might just be possible. There's a job being advertised – co-principal in the LSO. More status, more money, a chance to get away from Kluger. And my laggard desk partner.'

Slider was alert. 'Are you thinking of going for it?' he asked carefully.

'Maybe,' she said. 'They don't mind women any more. Jack – our leader, I mean, Jack Willis – thinks I could get it. But.'

He waited a bit and then said, 'But what?'

'It would be more work – which is great, more money – but I'd be away a lot more. Concerts, recordings. Travelling. Not being there to put Georgie to bed. All the babysitting problems that come with it.'

'Luckily, we've got Dad,' he said.

'George needs his parents too.'

'I can be fairly regular when there isn't a big case on.'

'Hmph,' she said. And then, 'Not seeing so much of you. Is it worth it?'

'I can't answer that,' he said. 'It's your career. It would be a big step up for you, wouldn't it?'

'Yes. Different pieces, different artists, different style of playing. Exciting. Challenging. Living on my wits – even more than I do now.'

'But you love all that, don't you?' He glanced at her sideways. 'Or don't you? You don't have to do it, you know, if you don't want to.'

'I *do* want to! Of course I do! But it's the old dilemma, isn't it? I'm a married woman with a child. I can't give my all to my career without failing the other side.'

'And vice versa,' he said quietly.

'Oh, blast you, why must you always see both sides?' she said, with an exasperated sort of laugh. 'You men just don't know what it's like. You *can* have everything.'

'Well,' he began.

But she said, 'There's something else.'

'Yes?'

'If I do go for it, and I don't get it – I don't know how I'll cope with that.'

'Why shouldn't you get it? You're good enough, aren't you?'

'It isn't always a matter of that. There's style, too, and personality – getting on with people.'

'You get on with everyone.'

'And age.'

'Ah,' said Slider.

'Music's getting to be more and more a young person's

field. They don't value experience and knowing the repertoire
and all the rest of it. Not above youth and looks, anyway.
Suppose I went for the audition, and I didn't get it. You know
how I hate to fail.'

'You can't let that stop you trying things.'

'Yes, that's the point isn't it?' she said, giving him another
amused and rueful look. 'Would I feel more of a failure for
failing, or for not trying?'

He made a helpless gesture with his hands. 'I can't tell you
that. How can I tell you that? You really want Atherton for
these abstruse, philosophical discussions. I'm just an ordinary,
common-or-garden copper.'

Another silence. She resumed: 'I'll tell you one thing,
though.'

'What's that?'

'It made you forget Melanie Hunter for a while, didn't it?'

He looked indignant. 'Was that what it was all about? This
whole job thing was just a ruse?'

'Wouldn't you like to know?' She grinned.

What was it she had said – toothache to take your mind off
stomach ache? And yet . . .

While he was still thinking it out, she said, 'Those snacks
weren't very substantial, I must say. Fancy some fish and
chips? It's not too late, is it?'

'Never too late for fish and chips,' he said.